ur name?"

...ed as he continued undressing,
hard muscles rippling
like liquid beneath his skin.

It was distracting to watch him, keenly aware of her own partial nudity. To have both of them quietly undressed made her feel more vulnerable than standing up to his rage.

"My name is Hari," he said, his eyes so intense she wanted to look away. She could not, and he was the one who finally broke the connection. He lowered his leather armor and weapons to the floor. His pale linen undershirt, bloodstained and torn, followed. Warmth crept up Dela's neck. Warmth, then a chill.

Words had been burned into Hari's chest.

Dela found herself tracing the deep grooves with her fingertips, spreading her hands against his chest, touching everything, soaking in the impression of his pain.

Hari made a small sound. A faint flush stained his cheeks; the intensity of his eyes changed, darkened. Dela suddenly realized where her hands were—how freely she was touching him—and gasped softly, pulling away.

"I'm sorry," she apologized, embarrassed. Her emotions were running high. Anger, fear, confusion; she had felt all these things about the man standing before her, and now compassion could be added to the list. "Who did this to you?"

"What does it matter?" Hari backed away from her. "It is done and gone. There is nothing left to speak of except the present."

By Marjorie M. Liu

IN THE DARK OF DREAMS
THE FIRE KING
THE WILD ROAD
THE LAST TWILIGHT
SOUL SONG
EYE OF HEAVEN
DARK DREAMERS (anthology)
THE RED HEART OF JADE
SHADOW TOUCH
A TASTE OF CRIMSON (Crimson City Series)
TIGER EYE

Marjorie M. Liu

Tiger Eye

THE FIRST DIRK & STEELE NOVEL

A V O N

An Imprint of HarperCollinsPublishers

This is a work of fiction. Names, characters, places, and incidents are products of the author's imagination or are used fictitiously and are not to be construed as real. Any resemblance to actual events, locales, organizations, or persons, living or dead, is entirely coincidental.

AVON BOOKS
An Imprint of HarperCollins*Publishers*
10 East 53rd Street
New York, New York 10022-5299

Copyright © 2005 by Marjorie M. Liu
ISBN 978-0-06-202015-4
www.avonromance.com

First Avon Books paperback printing: January 2011

Avon Trademark Reg. U.S. Pat. Off. and in Other Countries, Marca Registrada, Hecho en U.S.A.
HarperCollins® is a registered trademark of HarperCollins Publishers.

Printed in the U.S.A.

10 9 8 7 6 5 4 3 2 1

To Elfin Mudder, Genghis, and Daisy.
Meow, with love.

ACKNOWLEDGMENTS

Without the love, support, and encouragement of my parents, none of this would have been possible. My gratitude is endless. Thanks also to Cord Buckner, detective and lawyer-extraordinaire, who let me use him in my (shameless) search for knowledge, and never once complained. To my grandparents, family, and friends—many thanks for your cheerful support and compassion. And to my editor, Chris Keeslar, and my agent, Lucienne Diver, thank you again and again for being so kind and so very supportive.

Finally, deep thanks to all of my wonderful friends and teachers from Clarion East 2004. What a group. You guys are the best. Here's to a bright future of making our word choices "more better."

Woof.

CHAPTER ONE

DELA had mysterious dreams the night before she bought the riddle box. A portent, maybe. She did not think much of it. She was used to strange dreams, only a few of which had ever come true.

Still, she was alert when she left the hotel the next morning, stepping into the dry furnace of a rare clear Beijing day. Winds had swept through the night, sloughing away the smog and scent of exhaust and decay. Blue sky everywhere. Sun glinted off the glass of skyscrapers, cars, diamonds, the aluminum spines of umbrellas shading dark-eyed women, casting sparks in Dela's unprotected eyes. The world trickled light.

The city had changed. Ten years of capitalist influence, spinning a web of glass and advertisements; a modern infrastructure sweeping over the land as surely as the fine Gobi dust imported by the northern winds. A new cultural revolution, here in the city, across China. It mattered to Dela, the form and result. She could hear Beijing's growing song, the soul of the city, the collective soul of its thirteen million inhabitants, etched into the steel.

Dangerous, alluring—she did not like to listen long.

There was too much hunger in that voice, overwhelming promise and hope, twisted with despair. A double-edged blade, forged from the dreams of the people living their lives around her.

Just like any other big city, she reminded herself, pouring strength into her mental shields. *Devils and angels, the lost and found.*

Cabs swarmed the hotel drive, like fire ants, fast and red, and Dela jumped into the first one that squealed to a stop. Directions, spoken in perfect Mandarin, slipped off her tongue. One week in China, and her old language lessons had returned with a fury. True, she sometimes practiced with her assistant, Adam, a former resident of Nanjing, but regular life had settled its wings on her shoulders, years without stretching herself, dredging up the studies that had once taken her around the world. Dela thought she might have forgotten all those parts that were not metal, of the forge, and was glad she had not.

The cab wrenched from one clogged lane to another, a hair-raising mish-mash of roaring engines and squealing tires, curving down a tree-lined street where colorful exercise bars lined a scrap of shaded park. Elderly men and women pushed and pulled their way through rotating stress exercises, children screaming on seesaws. Bicycles overburdened with cargo, both human and vegetable, trundled down the crowded street, cars swerving to avoid the monstrously wide loads, as well as the packs of ragged young men darting across the road.

Dela saw a familiar low wall, cracked with age, its carved flowers and barbed wire still unchanged. She tapped the plastic barrier and the driver let her out before the wide entrance, scratched blue doors flung open to admit both foreigners and locals who made their way through a treacherous maze of parked bicycles. Dela saw faces bright with curiosity and greed.

Entering Pan Jia-Yuan. The Dirt Market. Tourist trap, hive of antique rip-offs and bald-faced lies—a treasure hunter's paradise. And Dela was in the mood to hunt.

Dust swirled around her feet as she slipped past crooked old men and women hawking nylon shopping bags to beleaguered early birds, hands already full of purchases. Stepping onto the concrete platform shaded by a voluminous tin roof, she listened to cheap jade jingle: bracelets, statues, necklaces. Pretty enough, and quite popular, if the gathered crowds were any indication. Nothing caught her eye. Potential gifts, perhaps, for acquaintances who would appreciate the gesture. Not good enough for actual friends, few and far between, deserving of special care, something beyond trinkets.

But, later. Dela had something else to find.

She combed the shadowed interiors of the open-air stalls, searching until she heard a familiar call inside her mind. *Weapons.* She followed the whispers to their source.

Scimitars and short swords; Tibetan daggers, hilts engraved with piled grinning skulls. Mongol bows, rough with use and age, quivers flimsy with faded embroidery, metal trimmings. Everywhere, dusty tinted steel—but all of it disappointing. The metalwork was poor; these were cheap imitations for not-so-cheap prices.

Dela stared at the eager merchants, who smiled at her blond hair, pale skin, and electric eyes. Easy mark. She could see it written on their faces, and their judgment made her feel lonely; a foreign emotion, and unpleasant.

Bad enough they probably think I'm dumb, she thought sourly. Solitude was a gift, but only when paired with anonymity. The disinterested observer.

Dela frowned to herself. *You shouldn't have returned to China if you didn't want to stand out. Buck up, girl.*

She left the weapons stalls, ignoring protests—some of which bordered on desperate—with a polite shake of her head. Those weapons offered her nothing. She knew quality when she saw it, age and history when she felt it. A simple thing, when one worked with steel as much as she did. When it sang its secrets inside her head.

Still looking for treasures, Dela simply wandered for a time, soaking in the heat, the scents of incense and musty artifacts kept too long in shadow. She watched children sell boxed breakfasts of fried noodles and onion pancakes, crying out prices in high voices. She listened to an old man play a lilting melody on a stone flute, and bought one of his small instruments. He laughed when she tried stringing notes together, the hollow stone wheezing miserably. Dela grinned, shrugging.

After nearly an hour of browsing, Dela found something perfect for her mother. Generous rectangles of linen, dyed a vibrant navy, embroidered with delicate stylized flowers—a bouquet of colors, random and perfect. She bargained like a fiend, dredging up every scrap of charm and language she possessed, and by the end of the transaction, both she and the seller were grinning foolishly.

"Aiii yo," sighed the older woman, smoothing glossy silver hair away from an oval face that looked at least twenty years younger than her body. Gold-flecked eyes glittered, but not unkindly. "It has been a long time since I met a foreigner who made me work for a sale."

Dela laughed. "It's been a long time since I met anyone I enjoyed arguing with."

The woman quirked her lips, and for a moment her

gaze changed, becoming older, darker, wiser. "I have something else you might want."

"Ah, no. I think I have enough."

The old woman ignored her, already digging through the tapestries and knickknacks piled at her feet. Dela watched, helpless. She did not have the heart to simply walk away. A good haggle created a bond, a certain unspoken etiquette. The "last chance" possibility of a final transaction.

The late summer heat was growing oppressive; air moved sluggishly between the stalls thick with wares and milling bodies. The scents of dust and grease tickled Dela's nose. Sweat ran down her back. Slightly bored and uncomfortable, she turned full circle, gazing at the throng of shoppers.

A man at the end of the aisle caught her eye. He was of an indeterminate race, darkly handsome, wearing sandals and loose black slacks, as well as a white shirt with the sleeves rolled up. He was crisp, clean, and somehow out of place, although Dela could not determine exactly why.

At first she thought he was staring at her—and perhaps he had been—but now he studied the old woman digging through her wares, and Dela felt inexplicably uneasy. His eyes were cold, measuring, haunted by a simmering intensity that would have been overwhelming if not matched to such an attractive face and body.

When the old woman popped up with a triumphant sigh, Dela stepped close.

"Behind me," she whispered, not caring if the woman thought her strange, "there is a man watching you."

Her gold-flecked gaze flickered; something hard rippled through her face. "I am used to him. He seems to think I have something he wants."

"I don't like him," Dela said.

The old woman smiled. For a moment, her teeth looked sharp, predatory. "Which is why I am going to do you a favor. For one yuan, you may have this riddle box."

Dela stared. One yuan was an incredibly low price for the Dirt Market, where everything was inflated to exorbitant amounts, especially for foreigners. She gazed at the object in the old woman's hands. Loosely wrapped in linen, she saw soft lines, rounded edges. Wood, perhaps, although she imagined the hint of something harder beneath the cloth. No metal. Nothing called to her.

"What is the riddle?" Dela asked.

The old woman bared her teeth. "Choice."

Dela looked at her sharply and reached for the box. The woman pulled away, shaking her head.

"Bought and sold," she whispered, and Dela was struck by the intensity of her stare, more powerful than the gaze of the strange man still observing them. "It must be bought and sold. One yuan, please."

Dela could not bring herself to argue, to refuse. Despite the odd air surrounding the transaction, the vague uneasiness pricking her spine, she fished a bill from her purse and handed it to the old woman.

Another sigh, and the old woman looked deep into Dela's eyes. "A good choice," she said, and Dela sensed some deeper, inexplicable meaning. She carefully slid the wrapped box into Dela's purse—a swift act, as though to conceal. Dela felt uneasy.

You know better, she chided herself. *This "box" could be full of drugs, and you're the stupid American courier, traipsing around until you get pulled over by the cops, and thrown into a sweaty prison.*

Or not, she thought, staring into the old woman's mysterious face. *Dreams and portents,* she reminded herself, fighting down a shudder. The stifling air was suddenly not warm enough. Her bones felt cold.

The old woman stepped back, smiling, and suddenly was just like any other Dirt Market hawker. Eyes sharp, but somewhat glassy.

"Bye-bye," she said, and turned her back on Dela.

The sudden reversal in attitude, from intimate to dismissive, took Dela off guard. She almost protested, but from the corner of her eye felt the strange man's attention weigh upon her. An odd sensation; tangible, like sticky fingers on the back of her neck. Impossible to ignore.

Go, whispered her instincts.

Without another look at the old woman, Dela walked down the aisle, away from the strange man and his searching eyes. She did not look back; she moved gracefully through the thickening crowds, slipping between stalls and merchants, ragged men and women rising from their haunches to shove vases in front of her flushed face. Her chill vanished; the heat suddenly felt overwhelming, the press of bodies too much, the sensation of being hunted tightening her gut. Premonition haunted her.

When Dela finally broke free of her winding path, she found herself near the front gates. Heart pounding, she jogged to the street and hailed a cab. A breath of cool air brushed against her sweaty neck.

"My," drawled a smooth masculine voice. "You *are* in a hurry. What a shame."

Dela was used to unpleasant surprises, but it was still difficult not to flinch. The strange man stood beside her, intimately close. Perfectly coifed, breathtakingly handsome.

She disliked him even more. He was too perfect, fake and unreal. Even his voice sounded over-cultured, as though he was trying to affect an unfamiliar accent. There was nothing kind about his smile, which skirted the edge of hunger, conceit. He made Dela's skin crawl, and she stepped out of his shadow, frowning.

A cab stopped in front of her; Dela opened the door to slide in. The stranger caught her hand. His touch burned, and she barely kept from gasping at the strange sensation. His skin felt thin as parchment, ancient, but with such heat—actual fire, to her ice.

Shock turned to anger.

"Get your hand off me," she said, low and hard.

He smiled. "It has been a long time since I had a conversation with a beautiful woman. Perhaps I could share your cab? I know a lovely courtyard restaurant."

Conversation? Beautiful woman? Dela would have laughed, except he clearly expected her to say yes; he even nudged her toward the cab, maintaining his iron grip on her hand, his smile as white and plastic as a cheap doll.

"I don't think so," Dela snapped, surprised and pleased to see his dark eyes shutter, his smile falter. Did he really think she would be so easily cowed, so stupid and desperate? "And if you don't let go of me this instant, I am going to start screaming."

Perhaps it was the cold promise in Dela's voice; all charm fled the stranger's face. The transformation was stunning. He leaned close, his breath hot, smelling faintly of garlic, pepper. His gaze, dark and oppressive, lifted the hairs on the back of Dela's neck. Something fluttered against her mind, bitter and sharp.

Dela clenched her jaw so tight her teeth ached. The stranger smiled—a real smile, bright and blistering and sharp.

"How interesting," he said, squeezing her hand until

her bones creaked. The pain sparked rage, striking Dela's fear to dust. No one hurt her. Ever. Not while there was still breath in her body.

Loosening her jaw, she smiled—and screamed.

It was a marvelous scream, and Dela took an unholy amount of glee in the look of pain that crossed the stranger's face. Bikes crashed into cars; passersby stopped dead in their tracks to stare. Dela pulled against his hand.

"Help me!" she screeched in both Chinese and English. "Please! This man is trying to rob me! He's going to rape me! Please, please . . . *someone!*"

Dela did not think she had ever sounded so frightened or pathetic in her entire life, but the horrible part was that while she had started out acting, the growing fury in the man's face suddenly did scare her. He looked like he wanted to kill her with his bare hands—as though he would, right there with everyone watching. Her entire arm screamed with pain as his fingers crushed bone.

Soldiers, common enough on Beijing's streets, ran from the gathered crowd of onlookers. The strong young men latched on to Dela's assailant, wrenching him away from her. It was quite a struggle; he was very strong and refused to let go of her hand. When he did, a cry escaped his throat; a bark of frustration, anger.

Dela slipped backward into the cab, fumbling for the door, eyes wide upon the hate distorting that handsome face. The urge to run overwhelmed her, and she rapped her knuckles on the plastic barrier. The startled cab driver did not wait for her destination. He swerved into traffic, car brakes squealing all around, horns blaring. Within seconds, the Dirt Market—and the ongoing struggle outside its gate—was left behind.

Dela rubbed her arms, shuddering. Her face felt hot

to the touch, but the rest of her burned cold. She bowed her head between her knees, taking deep measured breaths. The breathing helped her sudden nausea, but her heart continued to thud painfully against her ribs. She managed to tell the driver the name of her hotel, and then held her aching hand, trying to forget the feel of the stranger's fingers squeezing flesh and bone. The hot ash of his skin. The cool tremble against her mind.

A great stillness stole over Dela as she rode the memory of that sensation. She could count on one hand the number of times a stranger had purposely pressed his mind to her own, and while her shields were strong—her brother had made sure of that—Dela was in no mood to test herself against anyone who really wished her harm.

But he didn't know I was different until the end. Which meant the stranger had followed her out of the Dirt Market for another reason, one that had nothing to do with her psi-abilities. Dela remembered his cold dark eyes, how he had watched the old woman long before paying attention to her. What was his need, his purpose?

Through her purse, Dela felt a hard lump. The riddle box. Clarity spilled over her, and she almost examined her tiny purchase then and there. She caught the driver watching her through his rearview mirror, and hesitated. If she really had just purchased something awful like drugs or God-knows-what, she did not want any witnesses when she began poking her nose into Trouble. If that was what the riddle box represented.

He can't find me, Dela reminded herself. *That creep has no idea who I am, and this is a big city.* It was a small comfort.

When Dela arrived at the hotel, she stumbled up to

her room, ignoring the strange looks people cast in her direction. She caught a glimpse of herself in the elevator's polished steel doors, and winced. Her blouse had popped open, her face was beet red, and her hair looked . . . well, just plain bad.

"Round one goes to the Evil Minion of Satan," she muttered, holding shut the front of her blouse. A nearby businessman gave her a strange look, and Dela laughed weakly—which didn't seem to comfort him at all.

Once inside her room, Dela turned all the locks on the door and threw her purse on the bed. The linen-wrapped box spilled out onto the burgundy cover, and she stared at it for one long minute. Stared, then retreated into the bathroom for a shower. Dela couldn't take any more bad news—not just then. She desperately wanted to scrub away the morning, the lingering miasma of the stranger's presence.

Dela remained under the hot water for an indecent amount of time, until at last she stopped shivering. Infinitely calmer, she wrapped thick towels around her body and hair, and returned to the main room. She flopped on the bed with a sigh and picked up the wrapped box. Such a small, innocuous object.

Sometimes a cigar is just a cigar. The box may have nothing to do with that guy crawling all over you. He could have just pegged you as a victim.

True, but what had the old woman said?

He seems to think I have something he wants.

Frowning, Dela carefully unwrapped the layers of fine linen—surprising, to find such quality on an object from the Dirt Market—and caught her breath as the riddle box was finally revealed.

It was exquisite, with the breathless quality of some

exotic myth. Round, no larger than the palm of her hand. Rosewood, polished to a deep red that was almost black, inlaid with silver and gold, onyx and lapis. The lid was etched with some foreign, incomprehensible script that looked more like musical notations than words, and the curved sides displayed an elaborate series of images, a story: a magnificent tiger inside a thick forest; the beast suddenly a man, fighting, raging—and then the tiger once again, prone, locked inside a cage.

The detail was incredible, impossibly precise and subtle. Dela had never seen such clarity of pinpoint and line—not even in her own art, and her methods were unorthodox, to say the least. Dela ran her fingers over the carvings, the bright inlays. She felt the tiger's gold-lined fur beneath her fingers, sensing his capture. The sensation of imprisonment made Dela inexplicably unhappy.

She pressed the riddle box against her cheek and closed her eyes. She could finally taste the trace of metal inside her head, but it was faint, faint, an ancient whisper like the brush of a brittle leaf.

Its age startled her, sent a rush of pressure into her gut. Dela rolled the metal inside her mind, listening to its sleepy secrets. Millennia old. Two millennia, maybe more. She felt breathless with awe.

What was that old woman thinking when she sold this to me? It's priceless.

But Dela thought of the strange man, the old woman's cryptic remarks, and his behavior suddenly made sense. She cradled the small treasure in her palms, turning it over in her fingers as surely as her thoughts were turning, twisting. Yes, someone might very well kill for this—or kidnap, assault. But why had the man waited until he thought Dela possessed the box? Why not go after the old woman if he suspected she had it? Surely she would be an easier target.

Dela sighed. She could understand the old woman wanting to rid herself of the box if she thought it would cost her life, but the black market would have offered her more money than one yuan! It didn't make sense.

Dela tried opening the lid, but it was stuck fast. She studied the box, and smiled. A true riddle. It took her fifteen minutes of careful fiddling, using her instincts more than her eyes, but she finally found the two releases, set in an onyx claw and a silver leaf. Pressing them simultaneously with one hand, she unscrewed the box lid—

—and the earth moved.

Violent vertigo sent Dela reeling into the pillows, clutching her head. Scents overwhelmed her: rich loam, sap, wood smoke. Some essence of a verdant forest, come alive inside her room. Darkness, everywhere, but her eyes were clenched shut—Dela was afraid to open them, scared she would no longer be in the hotel. Dorothy, transported to Oz. Her displacement felt that complete.

Dela slowly became aware of the bedspread beneath her bare legs. The pillows, soft against her face. *Silly imagination,* she chided herself, and turned to look at the box.

It was no longer on the bed beside her.

Something in her stomach lurched, another premonition. She felt a ghost of movement, behind her, and she twisted—

—only to watch, dumbfounded, as sheer golden light spiraled through her room, shimmering in steep waves, a sunset palette of colors stroking air.

The light slowly took form, a gathering pressure of intense pinpricks. Dela blinked and, in that moment, the light coalesced. She felt thunder without sound, an impact to the air that lifted everything in the room, including herself.

The light disappeared, and in its place: a man.

CHAPTER TWO

SHOCKING, worthy of multiple aneurysms, explosions in her shrieking brain. Dela skittered off the bed so quickly she almost lost her towel, but her own near-nudity felt less outrageous than the impossible figure towering over her, the top of his head a mere hand's length from brushing the ceiling.

The man was lean, long of muscle and bone, his skin tawny from the sun. Thick hair brushed broad shoulders, an astonishing mixture of colors—red, gold, sable—framing a chiseled face almost alien in its golden-eyed beauty. His presence engulfed the room with a power that raised goose pimples over Dela's entire body. A shiver raced down her spine.

Predator, she named him, meeting his eyes, unable to look away. It was the second time that day she found herself in the presence of the arcane, but this was infinitely stranger. Unexpected, bizarre, extraordinary; she had seen the gathering of flesh from light, and still she could not believe. Her mind was screaming *no*, again and again. Impossible. Unreal. She was so shocked, she did not think of escape. She did not even think of rape, murder—his appearance was that unbelievable.

But it was his eyes that finally stunned Dela into sensibility. They were filled with such disdain and revulsion, so profound a dislike, she felt slapped in the face by his ill will. The last time Dela had seen such an expression on a man's face had been in college, caught making out in a secluded library alcove with her then-boyfriend John. Their observer had looked at Dela like she was dirty, trash—and not because she was kissing in a public place.

John was black. Dela was not.

That same unreasoning disregard and disgust—an awful superficial judgment—closed like a fist inside the man's eyes, and Dela's splash of fear dissipated into anger, which snapped through her brain like a whip.

"Who are you?" she demanded. The fact that she was half-naked and vulnerable barely registered; she rode the edge of a terrible righteous fury. Her temper was in complete control of her body. If this man wanted to hurt her, he was going to get a fight.

In the part of Dela's brain that was still dispassionate and rational, it occurred to her she had not felt this brave earlier in the day outside the Dirt Market when she had been fully dressed and surrounded by a crowd.

Holy shit. The irony is going to kill me.

Not literally, she hoped.

The man blinked. He rested his large hand on the golden hilt of a sword strapped to his side. Numerous weapons were belted to the battered leather armor covering his chest.

Dela ignored the whispering steel, the taste of old blood and death. She wanted answers to his impossible arrival; she wanted to wipe that hateful expression off his face. In her head she calculated distances to the lamp, the chair—anything that could be used as a weapon. Although, from the look of him, she might need an Uzi.

"If you want my name, you will have to command it from me," said the man, and Dela shivered at the sound of his voice: deep, rough, and unbearably cold. Not the voice of an illusion.

He clamped his mouth shut, and it seemed to Dela that despite his challenge, he was actually waiting for her to command his name. There was a breathless quality to his posture; his size and strength would have hidden the slight tremor if Dela had not been standing so close. His barely perceptible shiver made her feel strange. The edge of her anger dulled slightly.

Very slightly.

"Don't be an asshole," she snapped, craning her neck to maintain eye contact. "I don't know how you got here, or who you are, but you're looking at me like I'm rat shit and I *know* I don't deserve that. Give me some courtesy. You know what that is, don't you?" She was testing him with her insults; if he was going to hurt her, now would be the time. Dela was a firm believer in getting things over with.

Something that might have been bewilderment passed through the man's face, quickly concealed behind a cool mask. Disgust slowly drained from his eyes, and in its place appeared something darker but far cleaner. A cousin to curiosity, dressed in anger.

Dela lifted her chin, demanding an answer with only her eyes and body. A part of her still shrieked, but she tuned out her fear. Weakness would only invite intimidation.

Honey, you are *intimidated. Do you really think this guy's holding back just because you're acting tough? Gimme a break. He could kill you with his pinky.*

"You will not command my name?" His voice rumbled, an echo of thunder. "What then will you command?"

Dela stared, caught between laughter and a scream. This was all too surreal. "Nothing. I won't command you to do anything." She took in his size, his weapons. "How could I?"

His eyes narrowed. "Are you saying there is no battle to fight, not one person you wish me to kill?"

His words were too matter-of-fact, completely chilling. Dela threw up her right hand, while the other clutched her towel. She stepped away. "Hey, now. I don't want anyone to die."

His mouth tightened into a hard white line. "I see." He gave her a slow once-over that, oddly, managed not to feel degrading. "If you did not bring me here to kill or fight, then I was summoned to pleasure your body." He looked like he would rather impale himself face-first on a bed of nails.

For a moment, Dela forgot how to speak, and he seemed to take her silence as a resounding "yes." He began unbuckling his armor, his movements sharp, efficient. Getting the job done. No more talk of commands.

He walked toward her, rolling on the balls of his feet with an unearthly grace that distracted Dela long enough for him to step within reaching distance. She slipped away from his outstretched hand, furiously shaking her head, and backed up until she hit the wall.

"No, no, no. Stop that. Stop that! I don't want you to . . . to . . . pleasure my body. Just stay away from me. *Stay. Away.*"

The man instantly stilled, his expression unreadable. For a moment, Dela felt something trapped between them—fragile, delicate—a breath of time in which they were just two confused people, marveling at the absurdity of the world.

The moment passed. He took one long step away from her, and then another, until the entire room separated their bodies. Dela let out a shaky breath; she wanted to rewind the day and start over, except this time she would stay in bed and watch government-edited airings of CNN.

Calm down. He didn't hurt you. He stopped when you said no.

A small comfort, but Dela kept her back pressed against the wall.

"Tell me why you're here," she said, desperate to know how a seven-foot-tall man, armed to the teeth, could appear out of thin air like magic.

Because it is *magic, you idiot.*

Impossible, right? Dela's own psychic gifts were strange, but at least they had some basis in science. This . . . this man . . . was completely inexplicable.

He just stared, and Dela sensed his confusion. It was odd, that crack of vulnerability in the stranger's golden eyes. It made him more human, more man than magic. No less threatening, though.

"Well?" she prompted, unwilling to be cowed into silence.

The man stooped and picked up the riddle box, so tiny in the wide planes of his hands. He carefully replaced the lid.

"You summoned me," he said very slowly, as though speaking to an idiot. He held up the box, and set it on the edge of the bed. "You removed the lid, did you not?"

Dela laughed, but not for long. Her amusement seemed to ignite the man. Three long strides and he loomed over

her, golden eyes ablaze. He did not touch her, but she felt
the heat of his body lap over her exposed skin; powerful,
shattering.

"You are lucky I am imprisoned by the terms of the
box," he growled. "There was a time when I did not
tolerate amusement at the suffering of others."

For just one moment Dela did feel afraid, but anger
was the stronger emotion and she fed her indignation.
She pressed her palms against his chest, and pushed
hard. He did not budge. She made a low sound, gritting
her teeth.

"I would never laugh at the suffering of others," she
said, with the very same scorn she had hated seeing in
his face. "I laughed because this is all completely, impossibly, insane. I saw the light and I saw you appear,
but men *don't* come out of boxes like genies from a
bottle. It's ridiculous, and I want to know what the hell
is going on. I can believe a lot of things, but this is too
much even for me."

The man grabbed her hand, pressed it to his chest.
His grip was warm, firm, but he seemed conscious of
his strength. He did not hurt her.

"I am *real*," he hissed. "I am not an illusion."

Stubborn, so stubborn—she was going to protest, but
she looked closer, deep into his eyes, and what she saw
gave her pause. Anger, shifting to confusion, bedding
down with desperation. It was like watching the seasons
pass in fast motion, winter blurring to spring—summer
dying against the fire of autumn. A full circle, playing in
his fierce face.

It was too much; she felt trapped in the center of that
circle, and she tore her gaze away, down, down to their
joined hands, lower to the brace of knives strapped to

his waist. Sharp hooks, the short blades snared her vision, the steel whispering her name.

"You do not believe me," he said, releasing her. A strange melancholy coated his words. Dela's gaze flickered back to his face. She had trouble finding her voice, her mind ringing with the call of the blades, secrets softly singing.

"These are real," she murmured, returning her attention to his weapons.

He snorted. "Of course they are real. All my weapons are *real*."

"No," Dela said. She plucked one of the knives from its sheath, so intent on studying the blade she missed the look of utter astonishment that filled the stranger's face. Her fingers caressed the perfect imperfections of the steel, drawing in the hum of its age. Stories slept inside the weapon, a collection of deaths, wrought again and again.

Dela opened herself to sensation, sinking into a quiet made heavy only by the most ancient and beloved of objects. Energies, accumulated over years through contact with flesh, gave an ambient life to the steel.

"This blade is over two thousand years old," she whispered. Just like the mysterious riddle box.

"How do you know its age?" There was caution in his voice.

Dela barely heard him. She could feel his presence in the steel, the taste of his rage, bitter discontent. Guilt, regret, longing. Loneliness.

She drowned in emotions not her own, lost to the story of the blade, the man. Rolling deep, deeper, into a forest of sharp teeth and steel, cutting her mind on desperation, an echo plunging through the flashing images and sensations of endless battle, violence. Every death had meant something to the man who held this weapon. Every drop of blood was a dark testimony to some terrible heartbreak.

Dela pushed, and she caught a glimpse of warmth, a pure clean flame. She tried to touch the light, but it was snatched away, swallowed down a rose-colored throat striped with growling shadows.

No! Dela screamed, struggling. She ran from the beast, the nightmares and dreams, and as though drugged, slowly rose through the gloom of imprinted memory, escaping from the tomb of the past to open her eyes into the present.

Her knees buckled, and the man caught her arms. He steadied her against the wall, leaning close, his hands strong and firm against her bare skin. Dela felt surrounded by his quiet, still heat. Her hand hurt; she found herself clenching his knife in a tight fist. Blood seeped from her palm.

"You cried out," he said, and his voice curled fingers inside her gut, thrumming the metaphysical fibers still linking her to the weapon in her hand. Dela took a deep breath. She had measured the soul of the blade, and had almost lost herself, engulfed by the soul of the man who wielded it.

That same man now watched her with eyes that were dark with curiosity, distrust. His gaze flickered down to the weapon she held, to the blood dripping down her wrist. Dela cleaned the knife on her towel, leaving bright red streaks. She returned it to its sheath, fingers lingering on the hilt. The voices were quiet, but she remembered. She remembered—and despite the violence, was no longer afraid.

Dela pressed her throbbing palm against her stomach; the wound felt shallow, but it hurt worse than a burn.

"I was taken by surprise," she said, unsure how much to tell him, wondering if it mattered anymore. Surely her secrets were less bewildering than this man.

His lips tightened. "I have seen reactions like yours. Though only one has ever worked his magic on me."

"It's not magic," Dela said, wishing she could lie down, pretend this was all a dream. She did not want to talk about her visions—not to this stranger, who was suddenly not so strange. She had danced through the echo of his soul and been drawn too deep into his heart. Now when she looked into his eyes, she saw more than she should. Some link remained; she could feel it humming inside her body, as though they were both made of steel, and the metal of their flesh was being bound close by fire.

Dela shook her head, rubbing her uninjured hand over her eyes.

"You really came out of that box," she said, more in statement than question. She knew the truth. His weapon merely confirmed what her eyes refused to believe. Steel never lied, not even about men with burning eyes who took flesh from light.

How do they do it in the books, when the frog turns into a prince and the genie comes out of the bottle? Everyone is always so calm.

Maybe because the characters already believed magic was possible. Because, unlike Dela, they lived in a world where impossible things regularly happened.

Well, there's impossible, and then there's impossible.

Dela thought the man might laugh, but not from amusement. He stepped away from her, and his face was a riot of emotion: confusion, exasperation, uncertainty, that ever-present anger. She wondered if he felt the connection she had accidentally forged, and decided it would be better if he did not. He disliked her enough as it was.

"There is more proof," he said roughly, as though the words pained him. He once again began removing his weapons and armor. Dela held up her hand. The man paused.

"I cannot hurt you," he promised quietly. "And even if I could, I would never harm a woman."

Odd wording, but Dela believed him. His sincerity was unquestionable, tangible and bare-boned. To doubt him in that moment would have felt like a grave insult. An uncanny thing, her temporary trust, but she had seen something bright and clean beneath the shadow wrapped around his spirit. She had tasted its light.

"What's your name?" Dela asked again as he continued undressing, hard muscles rippling like liquid beneath his skin. It was distracting to watch him, keenly aware of her own partial nudity. To have both of them quietly undressed made her feel more vulnerable than standing up to his rage.

She thought he might not answer, might begin again with his stubborn refusals. He surprised her.

"My name is Hari," he said, his eyes so intense she wanted to look away. She could not, and he was the one who finally broke the connection. He lowered his leather armor and weapons to the floor. His pale linen undershirt, bloodstained and torn, followed. Warmth crept up Dela's neck. Warmth, then a chill.

Words had been burned into Hari's chest.

Incomprehensible lines, forming a distinctly hideous pattern from the edge of one pectoral to another, dipping into his breastbone like grotesque canyons.

Dela found herself tracing the deep grooves with her fingertips, spreading her hands against his chest, touching everything, soaking in the impression of his pain. A brand had done this, or a red-hot knife. A blunt, wide tipped blade—meant to press and catch flesh, cruel and deliberate. Dela bit back words of pity, but her eyes felt far too hot. She tried not to blink, afraid she would betray herself with tears.

The words were achingly familiar, and a different kind of pressure bore down on her vision as she remembered where she had last seen such markings.

The lid of the riddle box.

Hari made a small sound. A faint flush stained his cheeks; the intensity of his eyes changed, darkened. Dela suddenly realized where her hands were—how freely she was touching him—and gasped softly, pulling away.

"I'm sorry," she apologized, embarrassed. Her emotions were still running high. Anger, fear, confusion; she had felt all these things about the man standing before her, and now compassion could be added to the list. Indignation, that anyone could do this to another human being.

Dela waved her hand at his scarred chest. "Who did this to you?"

"Why does it matter?" Hari backed away from her. "It is done and gone. There is nothing left to speak of except the present."

"Nothing left?" Dela stared at him, incredulous. "You call those scars on your chest 'nothing'? I may not know you—or even like you very much—but no one deserves to be hurt like that. No one."

"I almost believe you mean that," he said.

"Believe what you want," she said. "But you still haven't answered my question."

Some old pain moved through his face, fleeting, quickly swallowed by defiance. "My chest was branded by the same man who imprisoned me in the box."

Dela looked at the tiny box sitting on the edge of her bed. It was too much to take in—one more revelation to add to the madness—but she pushed on, stubbornly clinging to the dying hope that something about all this would eventually make sense.

"Why—and how—would someone imprison you?"

Hari's smile was infinitely bitter. "Because he could."

"That's a shitty answer."

"Then command a better one," he taunted.

"Screw that. What is it with you and these commands? Can't you do anything of your own free will?"

"No," he said, anger returning to his face. "And you know that, having read the inscription on my chest and the box."

Dela gaped at him, wondering who, exactly, was the insane one in this room. She looked at his scars, and nothing was intelligible.

"I have no idea what you're talking about," she said slowly. "I can't read those words. They look like gibberish to me."

Hari narrowed his eyes. "That is impossible. Even illiterate simpletons can read the script. That is part of the curse."

Dela clenched her jaw. "I am getting sick of arguing with you about things I don't understand. I won't deny that you're real, or that you came out of that box, but defying the laws of physics will only get you so far. You tell me something, Hari—something I can use. *Who the hell are you, and why are you here?*"

The last came out as a shout, and Hari raised his eyebrows.

"You truly cannot read the inscription?" he asked cautiously.

"I truly cannot," Dela snapped.

"But you summoned me."

"Trust me, it was an accident."

His confusion bordered on pathetic; Dela wondered if she looked that shell-shocked, and imagined after today it might take plastic surgery to return her face to its original expression.

Hari sat on the bed, the springs groaning perilously beneath him, and closed his eyes.

"You ask me who I am. I am a slave. Your slave, until the day you die." He opened his eyes, and his words, combined with his defiant glare, stole Dela's breath away. "The inscription states the terms of my enslavement, the words you must speak to command me—just as hundreds of men and women before you have so done."

Horror crowded with comprehension, and she shook her head. She did not want to know the words. She did not—but there was a look in Hari's eyes, a promise and a threat, and for the first time, she felt like begging.

"Don't tell me," Dela said, throat tight. "Please, don't tell me."

" 'Thou shalt,' " he spat, standing, fists curled tight against his thighs. " 'Thou shalt' are the words you must speak to own my actions. I cannot flee from you. I cannot harm you. My body and skills are yours, and yours alone." His voice rang like a deep bell, tolling anger, anguish.

Dela had never heard anything more hateful in her entire life.

"Why?" she cried. "Why did you tell me? You could have kept it a secret so you would be safe."

A bitter smile tugged on Hari's lips. "How do you know I have not lied?"

"Because you're not a liar," she said sadly, her mind still resonant with his spirit.

His smile died. "You wanted to know who I am and why I am here. I have told you. Use me as you will."

The idea was appalling, but beneath Dela's disgust, clarity filled her. She spoke before she could stop herself.

"This is why you hate me," she said. "Because I am supposed to be your master."

Hari tilted his head, and the old disdain crept back into his eyes. Dela gritted her teeth; she detested his scorn. She preferred clean cold rage.

"Don't look at me like that," she said. "You don't know me well enough."

"You will be like the others," Hari said. "You will use me like a plaything until the day you die, or until you tire and send me back into the box."

"So you can see the future now?" she asked. "Remarkable. A man of many talents."

A low growl emerged from Hari's throat. "Do not mock me."

"Why not?" Dela asked softly. "Isn't that what you expect, the reason you've given me the keys to your slavery? Hard to break a man of his habits, and you seem plenty used to pain."

Hari's mouth twisted. "Give me something to do. Issue a command."

"Like what?" Dela hugged her waist, partly to hold the towel more securely against her body, but also because she needed to touch something familiar and real. "You asked if I needed you to kill anyone. Is that what you do?"

"Yes," he whispered. "I kill. I fight."

"And the sex?"

A shadow passed over his face. "Yes. I have also been used for such purposes."

Dela's stomach clenched with disgust. "I don't know what you're trying to prove, but you're not my slave, Hari. I'm not your master. I won't ask you to do anything against your will."

Hari stared, and though his face was cool, she was reminded of his aching loneliness, the bitter edge of grief that had swallowed up her mind. So much pain imprinted on that steel—millennia worth. Had he been a slave for all that time?

And you want him to trust you. What a joke.

"You don't believe me," Dela said, an echo of his earlier words to her.

"Why should I?" Hari's voice was little more than a whisper, as though all the strength contained in his body was not enough to fuel his voice.

"I give you my word," Dela said. "If that means anything to you."

They watched each other, measuring, and Dela felt compelled to make some deeper statement. She no longer feared this man. Fear was impossible, after everything she had seen, and the profound pain she knew he was hiding made her desperate to prove her worth, the existence of compassion. That *she*—and the irony was not lost on her—would not hurt *him*.

Dela's palm throbbed; blood oozed from the shallow cut. She held out her hand and gestured at Hari's knives, still on the floor with the rest of his armor and clothing.

"I swear on my blood," she said, remembering long nights around a campfire in the Rockies, talking to her brother and their agency friends about loyalty and

promises. They had decided promises were as much
ritual as intent—like signing a contract. It was one
thing to make an oral promise, another to write it down
with a signature attached. That upped the seriousness of
the oath. In this case, blood would have to do.

Hari looked at Dela as though he were seeing her for
the first time. She met that conflicted gaze, and waited.

She did not wait long. Hari unsheathed one of his
knives and slashed open his palm. He reached for Dela
and they clasped hands, mixing their blood.

Dela's arm tingled, a sharp chill arcing through her
spine into her scalp. Hari's nostrils flared and something dark and wild roared through his golden eyes.

"Say the words," he said, managing to make it both a
threat and a plea.

"I swear I will never command you to do anything
against your will. You are not my slave, and I am not
your master. You are a free man, Hari."

"No, not truly free," he said hoarsely. "But it is a start."

Hari slowly released her. Dela unwrapped the towel
covering her wet hair and handed it to him. He tore the
towel into two strips as easily as if the thick cloth was
made of paper. He then bound Dela's bleeding hand,
movements swift and efficient. Dela, speechless, did the
same for him.

Hari's hand was much larger than her own, his ta-
pered fingers rough with calluses. Muscles corded his
long lean arms—a killing strength, Dela knew—and
the heat of his naked torso washed over her shoulders,
making her cheeks red.

"Why are you doing this?" Hari asked, and Dela
jumped slightly, startled by his voice, which was both
soft and hard, loud in its quiet. He looked at her like she
was a puzzle, and Dela felt like one.

"Hasn't anyone ever been nice to you for no good reason?"

Hari opened his mouth, then hesitated. "No," he finally said. "Not for a very long time."

"I'm sorry," she said. Then, very quietly: "Why were you imprisoned?"

Hari pulled his hand away. "I committed no crime."

Dela rolled her eyes. "Not everything I say is an insult, you know."

Hari looked down at his hands. He clenched them into fists, knuckles white with bone. "It is an old story," he said, "and I have seen it played again and again in different times, among dissimilar people. It begins with a woman. My sister. A powerful Magi wanted her to bear him a child, but she was already pregnant. When the Magi discovered this, he threatened to kill her. I arrived before he could take her life, and we made a bargain. I would be his servant if he spared her and the child. The Magi agreed, but he killed them anyway. When I tried to take revenge, he captured me—branded my chest with his curse—and cast me into the box. I have been a slave ever since."

The sorrow in Hari's eyes was immediate, raw; a shocking revelation of emotion. Dela could not find words to speak—his story was too horrible, too strange. Hari turned from her, his face grim as death. He put on his clothes, his weapons. He paced the length of the room, examining everything. Searching. Learning.

Hari looked completely out of place among the dark standard dressings of Dela's hotel room. He belonged inside a myth; the tragic hero of some epic tale, exotic and poignant. He was magic, and this was not a magical world.

And the grace of his movements—stunning, lethal.

Dela watched him, trying to reconcile the impossibilities of his existence, his story, with everything she knew to be true. The touch of his soul was still resonant within her.

Accept it, she told herself. *You don't have to believe. Just accept.*

Because true belief required a commitment of the heart, which at the moment, was more than Dela could give. Acceptance, on the other hand, was just that. Like a huge stain on a brand-new blouse—you don't believe it happened, but the proof is there, so you just accept it.

"Will you stop staring?" Hari suddenly snapped, whirling on her.

"I'm thinking," she replied mildly. "This is all very strange."

"You do not seem upset."

"Would you prefer hysterics?"

"I would prefer a clear purpose," he said, then faltered. "I do not frighten you?"

Dela smiled. "What do you want, Hari?"

He raised an eyebrow. "The last time I was asked that question and answered truthfully, my master peeled the skin off my back in strips."

Dela swayed, and quickly sank to the bed. "What was your answer?"

"That I wished to bury him in sand and watch his head be eaten by wild dogs."

It was not funny—not at all—but Dela still found herself laughing out loud. Better than being sick all over her covers. She remembered Hari's earlier reaction to her laughter, but this time he did not look angry. Only startled. The hint of a grim smile appeared on his lips.

"It was not an intelligent answer," he admitted. "But

I did not care." His smile disappeared. "My master died a year later. The intervening time was . . . unpleasant."

Dela sighed. "Did you ever try to escape?"

"If I am separated from my master—my summoner—for any length of time, I develop an overwhelming compulsion to return to his or her side. It is instinctual, maddening."

"So does that mean you and I . . . ?"

"Until the day you die or return me to the box." He reached past Dela to pick up the box, and his sudden closeness made her breath catch. She smelled moss, the musk of some forest cat, sharp and hard. Her face felt hot.

Hari did not seem to notice her sudden discomfort. He held the box out to her.

"To repudiate me, all you must do is open the box. I will begin to disappear. Close the lid and I will be gone for good."

Dela took the box from his hands. He watched her expectantly.

"What?" she asked, incredulous. "Do you *want* me to lock you up again?"

"I do not know what I want," he said, but she sensed that was not entirely the truth.

Dela stood and placed the box on the night stand. "Well, when you figure it out, let me know." Her neck hurt from staring up at him. "Is there any way to break the curse?"

A profound quiet stole over his body. "The Magi stole my skin when he killed my sister. He told me the curse would only be broken if it was returned to me."

"Your skin? I don't understand."

Frankly, Dela didn't understand anything, except that this whole situation was worse than a fairy tale. But if she had to deal with the fantastic, then she was going to be as brave as any character from a book or movie, or else die pretending.

"This is not my only body," Hari said gravely. "I am a shape-shifter. I run as a tiger. Or I did, before the Magi stole my skin and my abilities."

"Oh, boy," Dela said, and sat down again.

"You have never heard of my kind." His voice sounded hollow as death.

"I've heard of shape-shifters," Dela said weakly. "But they're only legend. They don't really exist." Which seemed like an absurd statement, if one accepted the idea that Hari was cursed to spend eternity as a slave—living out of a box, no less.

She suddenly remembered the story carved into the riddle box, and knew then that it was Hari's tale. Man and tiger, from the forest to the cage, captured. She felt lightheaded thinking of it.

If you can accept everything else, then why not a shape-shifter, too?

Because I will go insane, she answered herself.

Dela shook her head. "I need to get dressed. Make yourself comfortable."

"Your wish is my command," he replied, without the faintest hint of a smile. He sprawled gracefully on the bed, unaffected by her scowl. He watched as she dug through her suitcase.

Dela could not stop thinking of his gaze, hard against her body. Cheeks flushed, she grabbed clean clothes and darted into the bathroom, relieved to escape his presence.

IT WAS A STARTLING THING, SUDDENLY BEING treated like a man again. Looked at with eyes that did not see an animal or killer. Startling, and sad.

I thought I had forgotten.

But no—just one spark, a promise, and hope had come crawling back to sniff at his heart. Hari felt a moment of resentment as his mistress scurried into the adjoining room, her gaze averted, pale skin and long clean lines flashing in his vision. The thudding door clipped her bare heels.

How dare she make him remember hope!

Hari took a deep, shuddering breath, and rolled off the bed. The walls shackled his body—everywhere, a cage—and he forced himself to breathe deep of the stale air; dust-coated, with the hint of metal and mold. The room had not felt so small with the woman present, but in her absence he could find no respite.

He went to the window, desperate for some sight of the world beyond, some temporary escape from the illusory cage. During his argument with the woman, he had glimpsed something beyond the glass, a strange vision that was surely fancy—

No. Hari steadied himself against the wall, trembling. His legs felt weak.

It was like seeing Rome for the first time—gleaming white-hot, boiling with people. The city, rising on its haunches like some barbed, beautiful nightmare. Nothing in Hari's life had prepared him for Rome. Nothing since had prepared him for what he now saw.

An immense city sprawled before him, a conflagration of towering monoliths, sheathed in steel and glass, searing his vision. Far—Hari looked far—and the sight did not change. Everywhere, buildings of impossible height. Cold, hard, remote. Below, he saw colored objects move on choked paths; he saw people milling, the strange dance of foot travel, viewed from a God's height.

A tower in the clouds. A marvel. And then, *I am afraid.*

There was very little left that could frighten Hari. After two thousand years, his innocence was long dead. There was no cruelty, no word or sight, that could surprise him. Nothing.

So he had thought, until the woman.

So he had thought, until this city. This endless, steel-clad city.

The world always changed between summons—that was the way of it. Hari was a man outside time. Yet he realized all those differences had still been familiar, and now the familiar dead were truly gone. All to dust.

No, he corrected himself. *No. For two thousand years I have been summoned to a world of death, disease, and cruelty. I cannot believe it has changed so much. Perhaps the surface is different, but beneath, hearts will still be drunk on venom.*

It was an odd comfort, shallow and bitter.

Hari tore himself away from the window and padded across the room to the door opposite him. The odd cloth-covered floor swallowed the sound of his passage. He listened to the woman move behind the other closed door. Water splashed.

Hari's senses were acute; even without his skin, he retained the powers of the tiger. He smelled the woman everywhere, on his body. Jasmine, lavender; sweet, soothing scents, completely at odds with the fire in her eyes.

Hari permitted himself a small smile. It was a millennium since he had encountered a woman who possessed such an unflinching stare, so raw a tongue. Defiance, courage—she had stood up to his rage, matched it with her own; and she had done it all without realizing her power over him. She said she could not read the inscription on the box or his chest, and he believed her; she did not smell like lies.

Remarkable, a stunning revelation. Warlords and kings, knowledgeable in box lore, had never dared so much as this woman—not without a command on their lips, an immediate assertion of power. As though to do less would reveal some intolerable weakness Hari might exploit.

He wanted to laugh. Exploitation was the last thing on his mind. His only concern was to survive a summons with spirit intact, to live day by day as an unbroken man.

Hari listened at the woman's door for a moment longer, then glanced at the other door. The exit to this bedchamber? He fumbled with the latches, the knobs, and finally managed to open it. He thought there might be guards, some sign of life, but he found himself looking down an interminably long hallway lined with yet more doors, one after another. It was an empty, eerie sight, and it made him uncomfortable.

The woman emerged. Her hair was still damp, pulled into a thick braid framing one side of her moonstone face. She dressed in unfamiliar attire: dark blue pants that revealed everything of her lean form, as well as a tight white shirt that did the same.

She should have continued wearing that scrap of cloth, Hari thought ruefully. This was almost more distracting.

Her lips quirked. "You thinking of making a run for it?"

Hari frowned and closed the door. "That is impossible."

"Doesn't mean you don't want to try."

"And if I did? What would you do?"

The woman moved past him. "Probably cheer you on."

"I find that hard to believe."

She looked at him over her shoulder. "You think very highly of yourself, don't you?"

Something sharp fell on Hari's tongue, but he swallowed it when he saw the odd light in the woman's eyes. She was baiting him! How . . . astonishing.

"You are fearless," Hari said, that odd fleeting hope whispering against his heart. He shoved it down, ruthless, angry for feeling even a bit of respect for this woman.

But his respect was a stubborn thing. He had given her the keys to his slavery and she had repudiated them with blood. He had shown her his scars and instead of disgust . . .

She had touched them. So soft, her hands and eyes full of the very compassion for which he had long ago given up the search. Men and women feared him, coveted his strength, his legend. They did not *feel* for him. The woman's eyes had been as shocking as frozen steel in a desert, marvelous and terrible. For just one moment, Hari had felt the need of a man on fire searching for water. Need for compassion. For sweet respect.

No, he warned himself, afraid of his need. *She may have sworn a blood oath, but in time she will be like the others. The temptation to use me will be too great.*

To allow himself hope, only to be betrayed—such pain would be unbearable. A heart-death, with him trapped in his tiny coffin, reliving the nightmare in his dreams.

Never again, he thought, a prayer and a promise. *Never again.*

"What do I need to fear?" asked the woman, trailing

her fingers along the stiff wood back of a chair, the only one in the room. She no longer smiled, but her voice was easy, calm. He noticed she did not place the chair between them.

"Nothing," he said. "I cannot harm you."

She made a small sound, her eyes far too sharp. "Do you *want* to harm me?"

"Why do you ask me these questions?" Anger pulsed in his throat. He did not want to answer her. "Why do you push me with your words?"

The woman blinked. "I'm not trying to push you. I just want to know you. How am I supposed to do that if I don't ask questions?"

How, indeed? Hari turned away, suppressing a growl. "You do not need to know me," he said, fighting against hope, the compulsion to dream.

He looked for her reaction and found her mouth tight, her eyes flashing with a righteous fire that was almost becoming familiar. Hari steeled himself for her anger, dimly aware that a part of him looked forward to it.

"You don't have the right to tell me what I can or cannot do," she said. "You poof into this room, scaring the shit out of me, and then unload a bunch of crap about us being stuck together until the day I die—and you have the nerve to tell me I don't need to know you?" She took a step toward him, fists on her hips, cheeks flushed. Hari had to remind himself not to back up.

"Well, let me tell *you* something, mister. Don't you dare get pissed off at me. I'm not the one who enslaved you. I'm not the one who treated you like shit for the past two thousand years. I don't even want you. I've all but cut off my right hand and beat my head against the floor trying to convince you of that, but hey—what does my word mean to you? Apparently nothing."

It was the longest speech anyone had made to Hari in a thousand years, and he took a moment to savor, somewhat guiltily, the sensation of being talked to, rather than at.

I do not even know her name, Hari realized, surprised to find himself still capable of curiosity. He had stopped asking for names long ago. One master was like any other; some better, some worse, but the same in the end. Man or woman, they all wanted power. A prize. Someone to fight their battles, to do that which they had no stomach for. The things Hari had been forced to do over the long years did not bear remembering.

But he did remember. Nightmares plagued him, appalling reenactments of murders, soldiers shredded to bone—horrifying abuses. Such horrors were the reason Hari always arrived at a summons full of rage, defiance. A promise of resistance.

I am not broken. You will never break me.

This time had been no different. The long sleep, caught in obsidian amber, bursting from it with a fury—

"What is your name?" he asked quietly, swallowing his anger.

The woman stared, clearly suspicious. "Delilah. But everyone calls me Dela."

"Delilah." He rolled her name on his tongue, tasting the long lines of its sound.

She frowned. "You going to yell if I start talking again?"

Hari raised an eyebrow. "I do not believe I have been the one yelling. I also do not believe you would stop talking even if I did raise my voice."

Dela opened her mouth, stopped, and sighed. She stepped close, and Hari was acutely aware of her strong, feminine lines. Her heady scent was disconcerting. He did not move away.

"You don't trust me. That's fine. I don't really trust you. I have no idea how we're going to make this work, but you're here, and I'm here, and that's the way things are. We'll figure this out. Unless . . . unless you want to return to the box." Her mouth twisted with distaste.

Hari glanced at the box sitting so small on the bed. Darkness waited for him there, the long sleep. She had already asked him this question once, and he had been unable to answer her. Would this new life be worse than the nightmares?

"No," he said. "I do not wish to return to the box."

"Then we're stuck with each other." Dela looked unhappy. "You should know, I like my solitude."

"As do I," he said. The company of others had come to mean only pain.

But I am tired of being alone. A slip of a thought, unbidden, quickly suppressed.

"Fine. Good." Dela rubbed the back of her neck, as though she shared his astonishment at the words slipping from her mouth. But he sensed her determination, the power of a decision made. Dela turned the full force of her gaze upon him. Her eyes were the blue of sky, bright as dawn. "I don't trust people very easily," she said, blunt. "Please don't betray me."

Please don't betray me.

They were powerful, simple words, said with such dignity only a fool would have called it begging. Her words resonated through his bones, whispering a silent song in the shape of her voice. Her eyes left him speechless for one long moment.

"I also do not easily trust others," he said, when he

could rely on his voice not to expose his new weakness. "For good reason. Will you betray *me?*"

She flushed, but not from anger. "You are not a slave. You are a man. I will always treat you as a man, with as much respect and compassion as you show me."

"Then I will do the same for you," he said.

"That's all I want to hear," she said.

He nodded, unable to tell her that it was more than he had ever been offered—more than he himself had promised since the curse. He held out his hand, and for a second time they touched palms, wrapping fingers warm and tight around each other's smooth flesh. A strange tingling rippled up his arm, lifting the hairs on his neck. Her hand was small and warm, her grip firm. Hari found it difficult to let go.

They stared at each other and the silence was awkward. Silence had never before been uncomfortable. Of course, until now, no one had ever expected him to talk.

"Are you hungry?" Dela hooked her hands into the tiny pockets of her pants. "Do you need to sleep or bathe?"

With the edge of anger fading from her face, she looked smaller, more vulnerable. Shy, even. It made Hari feel strange—protective, perhaps, though the emotion was so foreign he could barely name it. Heat filled his chest. His former masters had never asked such questions. His needs had never occurred to them.

"Yes," he said. "I would like to eat and . . . wash." Despite Dela's assurances, the offer might not come again. He would be a fool to refuse. If nothing else, it set a standard. If she was as good as her oaths, she might not treat him as a slave, but with his inability to wander far from her side, he would be dependent on her goodwill to keep him fed and sheltered.

This unnatural reliance had always rankled, but now it seemed especially wrong. He did not know what he wanted from this woman, but it was not charity. He wanted her to see him as more than a liability. More than a slave.

Your pride has returned. Be careful it does not ruin you.

Dela walked to the nearby table where she picked up a slim book. She flipped open the pages, began to hand them to him, and hesitated. "You can speak my language," she said carefully. "Can you read it as well?"

Hari glanced at the book in her hands, the strange clubbed script. He shook his head. "Spoken language was part of the spell, so I might always understand my masters, no matter their tongue. Very few people read, so it was not a concern. Except . . ."

"Except?"

"You should have been able to read the inscription on the box," Hari insisted. "Even the illiterate have been able to discern its meaning, and you are clearly educated."

"It just looks like a series of lines to me. Incomprehensible lines."

"That is very strange."

Dela made a low sound. "All of this is very strange, Hari. At least to me. Let's worry about one thing at a time, okay? Food, first of all. I don't think I can handle anything more complicated."

Her consideration made him uncomfortable, but he told Dela what he desired: meat, fruit, wine. Hunger overwhelmed him, sent shackling pain through his gut. His mouth tasted dry and bitter.

Dela picked up a curious object made of some dark shell and spoke into it. He watched her with care, bitterly aware this new summons had released him into a much different world than he was accustomed. He had so much to learn.

Why should you bother? No matter this woman's oaths, you are still hers—bound and leashed. Knowledge is wasted on you. You will never be able to use what you learn, never be allowed to stray from her side.

"They said twenty or thirty minutes." Dela looked at him, and Hari wondered if she sensed the coiled wariness in his body, the sudden tension singing through his muscles. "That should be enough time for you to bathe."

The "bath room" was excruciatingly small, the fixtures unusual but not incomprehensible. Dela showed Hari how to use the strange latrine, as well as the basin with its remarkable hot running water.

He wondered if he could ask, and decided now was as good a time as any to test her true willingness to accept him as a sound mind, and not just a body.

"Will you tell me how this functions? I have never encountered such a thing." He adjusted the knobs, feeling the water instantly change temperature. A marvel.

She smiled. "I don't know much about plumbing, but I'll try." And she did; he was pleased. When she finished telling him about pipes and heaters and electricity, he began to remove his weapons and clothing. Dela stumbled from the room, blushing. "Enjoy," she said in a rush of breath, firmly closing the door behind her.

Hari stared, wondering at her reaction, the feel of her body so close to his own. He wondered, and when the emotions became too much, tried to focus on his first bath in ages.

DELA STUMBLED TO THE BED, INHALING DEEPLY. She smelled Hari in the air, on her covers, the same scents that had filled the room when she opened the box: a coalescence of leaves and wood. Wild and resonant, a reflection of the man.

God help her, she was actually beginning to like him.

She sank to the mattress and hugged her shoulders. A fine tremor ran through her body; her heart thudded dully, loud and coarse.

I just obligated myself to help this man for the rest of my life.

The enormity of that decision slammed into her brain, and she lay down, staring blindly at the ceiling.

What have I done? and then: *What was the alternative?*

The alternative was unthinkable. Dela had no intention of sending Hari back into the riddle box, could never live with herself for returning him to a prison where he didn't belong.

He could be lying. Maybe he was put there for a good reason.

Dela closed her eyes, recalling the sensations wrought from her connection to his weapons. After a moment, she shook herself free and rubbed her eyes. No, he was not lying.

Two thousand years as a slave, an unimaginable expanse of time. Dela turned on her side, fighting the choking sensation that crept into her throat. So much pain—and somehow, through some incredible strength of will, he had kept his sanity, an element of grace. Dela wondered if she would be as strong.

She heard water splash; an oddly cheerful sound, innocent and ordinary.

Don't go soft, she told herself. *You shouldn't trust him. Not completely. He'll eat you up if you do, and you're just another way to keep out of the box. Men use women for less.*

True enough, although Dela's friends—with one exception—were all men whom society considered unsafe, untrustworthy, and notoriously foul; and yet they were the complete opposites of such virulent labels. There was something about Hari that reminded her of them, a bright kindness beneath the razor shell. Dela had caught a glimpse of light beyond the shadows in his soul. She could not forget the comfort of its stunning warmth.

Dela blew out her breath. Something strange had come into her life, and as Grandma liked to say, "That's that." Of course, Grandma had always embraced the uncommon, even more so than Dela's brother, Max, who had a great deal more talent than his younger sister when it came to the "unnatural and strange."

She smiled, thinking of her brother. The last she had heard, he was in South America with the boys from Dirk & Steele—a name always good for laughs, as long as you weren't doing the laughing in front of the actual Dirk and Steele—trying to follow leads on some tourists who had been kidnapped by guerillas. She worried about him only a little; she was well aware that stalking evildoers was his idea of fun, and those other guys . . . sheesh. Boys with toys, indeed.

I should know. I made some of their "toys."

Someone knocked. Room service.

Dela felt safe; she was distracted and did not think. She opened the door without looking through the peephole and caught the flash of something long and sharp, cutting her mind with fury.

Dela cried out, slipping sideways as a long blade slashed through her shadow. Instinct took over and she grabbed the hand holding the knife. Dela glimpsed dark eyes set in a flat face, a line for a mouth, and then she was knocked backward as a sharp fist slammed into her shoulder.

Dela never hit the ground. Strong arms caught her; Hari's chest felt like a warm wall against her back. Her fingers brushed wet thigh as he helped her stand. She heard a growl, low and menacing, and realized it was rumbling from him.

Dela's assailant darted forward, knife poised for an underhand strike. His eyes were dead, cold as scales— and much to Dela's horror, they were completely focused on her.

Hari pushed her out of the way, rising to meet the attack. He moved incredibly fast, his hands a blur as he grabbed the wrist holding the knife, slamming it so hard against the wall that several wooden panels shook loose. Even as the knife fell to the ground, Dela caught the glint of new blades in her attacker's free hand.

"Hari!" she cried, as the knuckle blades shot toward his exposed chest. Hari turned in time to prevent a lethal stroke, but the blades still ran over his shoulder and arm like claws, blood welling, pouring down his skin. Hari showed no indication of pain. His face set in a deadly grimace, he grabbed the man by the throat and squeezed.

The blades rose for another strike. Dela did not hesitate. She leapt on that lethal hand, holding it with all her might so the blades would not touch Hari. Hari shouted at her, but she paid him no mind. She dug her fingernails into pressure points, mercilessly piercing thick flesh, grunting with the effort. When the man finally dropped the blades, she kicked them away, deep into the room.

Her assailant's face turned purple; he was choking, struggling with all his might. Hari held him with only one hand.

"Who sent you?" he snarled, shaking him for emphasis. There was a killing rage in his golden eyes, some beast swirling beneath the surface of his burning gaze.

Hari never received an answer. Dela's attacker freed his hand from her grip. Grabbing her by the back of the head, he sent her careening into Hari, who was surprised enough that his fingers loosened. The man squirmed free and took off.

Dela scrambled into the hall, watching the man disappear through a fire exit. Hari began to follow, but Dela pushed him back into the room and closed the door.

"Let me go," he ordered. "I can track him."

"No," she said firmly. "If he escapes, so be it. You're hurt." And she absolutely did not want to draw any attention to them. She hoped no one had heard the fight and called security. If the police got involved they would ask questions, want to see Hari's passport—a vital piece of information that simply did not exist. Yet.

Another reason for Hari not to race down the hall—he was completely naked. Oh boy, was he naked. The image of his well-endowed intimates eternally emblazoned on her mind, Dela darted into the bathroom to grab some towels. She shoved one into his hands and pressed the other against his shoulder and arm, trying to stanch the flow of blood.

Hari stared at the towel. Dela rolled her eyes. "Wrap it around your waist," she said.

Something that could have been humor glinted in his eyes, quickly disappearing beneath simmering rage. "He hit you," Hari growled. He touched the space above her heart. "He was trying to kill you."

His concern surprised her almost as much as the attack. Though his fingers were light, they seared her, cutting straight through her carefully wrought control, a lifetime of training to control fear. Images overwhelmed her: eyes cold as an arctic sea, a flashing knife arcing toward her bared flesh, cutting Hari . . .

She began to shake. Hari watched her, a mystery in his silence. He wrapped the towel around his waist, beads of water coating his skin.

Control, Dela. Swallow your fear. Now is not the time to lose it.

Dela took a deep breath and pulled away to look at Hari's shoulder and arm. Despite her efforts, there was too much blood; her heart, already pounding, deafened her ears with thunder. "We need to get you to a doctor."

"It is nothing," he said. "It will heal in minutes."

Dela stared at him. "Minutes? But that's . . . that's . . ."

"Impossible?" The barest of smiles touched his lips, and he showed her the hand he had sliced open for their blood oath. The rough bandage was gone, the blood washed away. His palm was smooth, unharmed. "I cannot die, Delilah."

The full import of what he said hit her, lifting the hairs on her arms. Although, when she thought about it for a moment, immortality made sense. What good was a curse if you could catch an arrow through the heart and be done with it?

And by your calculations alone, dumbass, he's probably two thousand years old. He hasn't hung around that long just because he feels like it.

"It was brave of you to fight for me," Hari said, "but unnecessary."

"He hurt you, didn't he?" she asked, suddenly finding it difficult to speak. He took a moment to answer, and only then with a slow nod. Dela tried to smile. "Well, then. I think that's reason enough to stop someone from stabbing you."

Hari looked astonished. Encouraged by some brazen impulse, Dela snaked her arms around his neck and tugged down his head. He did not resist her, and she brushed her lips against his rough cheek. She turned her mouth to his ear. "Thank you for saving my life, Hari."

"It is nothing," he said. But that was a lie, and they both knew it.

CHAPTER THREE

WHILE Hari was physically incapable of harming his masters, there had been times over the years when he "accidentally on purpose" allowed some of them to die. Like the sheik who commanded Hari to shield the royal body with his own during a particularly vicious volley of arrows. Hari had looked, and felt, like a pincushion. A simple step to the right, a slight movement to block certain arrows and not others, and the sheik . . . well, he'd ended up looking nearly the same.

And back into the box, again and again. Taking orders, following them to the letter and doing nothing more—sometimes earning punishments so severe even practiced torturers were unable to watch. It was a miracle no one had yet broken him.

And yet . . .

Hari had heard Dela open the door, heard her cry out, and had not thought—he'd leapt from his bath, emerging just in time to see Dela struck hard in the shoulder. He'd managed to catch her, and for one moment remembered she had spoken no commands. He did not have to protect her.

But I do, he thought, the words so strong in his head

he could not be sure he hadn't spoken them aloud. It was the first time in all his years of imprisonment he'd actually *wanted* to help his summoner, and the need burned through him, creating a clean, cold rage. This intruder had hurt Dela; her life was in danger. That could not be tolerated.

The rest was a blur until Dela grabbed the attacker's wrist, fighting like an angry cat, grunting and hissing. She'd had no reason to put herself in harm's way, her pale flesh lethally close to the flashing knuckle blades—which Hari had tried to tell her, shouting orders to stay away, to run. His words might have been made of air. They passed through her, insubstantial, and he'd realized in one blazing moment of insight that she was trying to help. Her struggle was to keep the assassin from stabbing him. *Him.*

She does not know. And then, *She is fighting for me. Defending* me.

Unexpected, stunning. Actions told stories unexpressed by mere words, and her selfless courage staggered him.

And after the fight . . .

He dared not believe she was real, that she could risk so much, could speak such damning words as those which spilled over his soul, his open bleeding wounds, his old assumptions simmering in a brew of hate and tearing him apart. An hour previous he could not have cared whether she lived or died, and now . . .

Now I know why I had to protect her. She is worthy of a little spilled blood, if it means her safety.

Dela sat on the bed, head bent over her assailant's blade, gaze intense upon something only she could see. She had only just stopped shaking—the attack had unnerved her more than she would admit, but she had not cried or lost her senses. Grown men had shown less fortitude, men who did not care about the sacrifices made to keep them safe. Selfish, arrogant men—wrapped in veils of godhood, power—collecting enemies like silver, boasting of how many feared and hated their shadows upon the world. Inviting assassination as a dare, a challenge.

Dela was nothing like that. Hers was a quiet strength, a fire tempered by compassion. Or so he thought. Perhaps time would reveal another story, some reason even she had enemies desiring her death.

The attack was not random; Hari knew it in his heart. Someone had prepared the assassin, who had clearly expected Dela to be alone—strange to Hari, who had thought only shape-shifter women had the freedom to journey in solitude. Worry taunted him; an unfamiliar emotion, one long forgotten. Simple worry had no place in his life, not for two thousand years. How could an immortal, a slave, worry? The worst to come was pain, and he had experienced enough that the sensation no longer frightened him.

Still, worry. Not for himself, he realized, but for Dela.

Every moment spent in her presence bound her tighter and tighter to his senses—a dangerous attachment, unfathomable and confusing. He had never felt so many strong—and, if he dared admit it, passionate—emotions for a master.

No, Hari corrected—he had never experienced such feelings for anyone.

A low sound escaped Dela's throat. Like by command, Hari suddenly found himself at her side, unaware of crossing the distance between them. He almost touched her, but held his hand tight against his thigh. Familiarity was dangerous; his trust was already coming too easily. The last summoner to whom he had bared himself had ruthlessly betrayed him.

Hari did not speak. He allowed his presence to ask the question, and Dela seemed to feel the press of his silent words.

"I know this knife," she said, disbelief coloring her words. "I *made* this knife."

Hari gingerly sat beside her, again surprised. "You are a metalsmith?"

"Of a kind," she said, looking into his eyes. "I am an artist, but I also craft weapons. Do you think that's strange?"

Hari could not help himself; he allowed her to see his smile, and it felt good. "I am a shape-shifter, cursed to spend eternity as a slave: I exist in a box when not in flesh, and I cannot be killed. In the face of all that, I would say your ability to work metal is unbearably ordinary."

She laughed; a delightful sound, cut too short. Her eyes went dark as she stared at the long blade, the steel emblazoned with the intricate rendering of a coiled dragon.

"The knife was a special order for a client. I don't usually take personal contracts, but this fellow promised to donate a lot of money to an arts program for children if I crafted the blade. I don't like having my arm twisted, but he was adamant. He wanted an original Dela Reese knife, and he made sure everyone knew his donation hinged on my decision." She shook her head. "The knife was stolen three months ago, straight from its shipment to the client."

"The person who stole the weapon had a specific purpose in mind," Hari said, taking the knife from her.

The blade was as long as her forearm, closer to a short sword than a dagger. The hilt was elegant in its simplicity, deceptively subtle, the workmanship revealing a brilliant, breathless quality that begged an admiring hand. Hari's burgeoning respect deepened.

"Someone planned this," Dela said, horror shading her voice. "Someone with enough money and connections to track me down in *China*."

"Do you have enemies?" Hari traced the engraving with his fingers.

Dela shook her head. "I keep to myself, spend most of my time alone. I have a close circle of friends, all of whom are above reproach."

"A smile on the face hides a dagger on the tongue."

Dela began to protest and Hari inclined his head. "I am sorry, Delilah, but as you said, someone planned this. Someone who knows you well."

"You can call me Dela," she grumbled.

Dela is not the name of a queen or a warrior, he thought, but said, "I prefer Delilah. It suits you."

"Maybe when you say it," she muttered, standing up. Her eyes were hard as she looked at the knife cradled in his hands. Hari returned the dagger, hilt first. Dela's grip was firm, easy. He noticed muscles flex in her arm, lean and strong—arms of a woman accustomed to hard work. Yet there was something else in her movements when she held the blade, some graceful instinct that called to him.

"You have some skill with the weapons you make," he said. Dela shrugged, cheeks slightly flushed. Embarrassed, he thought, though he did not understand why.

"I'm no expert," she said.

"But you know enough to respect what you make."

A pleased yet sad smile touched her lips. "No weapon is ever truly ornamental. It's just sleeping, waiting for its purpose."

"Which is to harm others."

"You understand," she said. After a moment, she added, "It's strange, being drawn to make things that can harm or kill. Sometimes I feel guilty, but I still craft the steel, forge the blades. It's almost a compulsion." Dela grimaced. "I am not a violent person," she said, almost pleading.

"I believe you," Hari said. "But the weapons still fulfill something inside your heart, some desire. If not to kill, then to express the darkness that is part of every great passion."

Dela looked at him. "And how do you express the darkness of *your* passion?"

Hari felt cold. "I have no passion. And if I did, my hands are covered in two thousand years of blood. Death would be my expression."

"That's . . . depressing."

Hari grunted, and pointed at the dagger. She made him talk too much about himself. He wanted to change the subject.

"I once knew a dragon," he said, again doing what he had planned not to do, and yet unable to stop the spill of words. "A very kind man, if you were his friend. Enemies did not last long."

He managed to shut his mouth, afraid he had said too much, as though even that admission would curse him, call down some act of duplicity to tear his trust. Until now, he had never talked about himself to his masters.

Dela's eyes opened wide with surprise, innocent disbelief. "An actual dragon?"

"A shape-shifter, to be exact. A man who could, at will, take the body of a dragon, just as I once wore the shape of a tiger."

"You could really change your shape? It's so difficult to believe."

He could taste her wonder, and pleasure stalked him, unbidden.

"Look into my eyes," Hari said. "Look into my eyes, and tell me you do not see something not entirely human. It is there, waiting. Waiting for me to find my skin."

She did stare into his eyes, deep and deeper, but despite his best efforts, he could not perceive her emotions. He saw himself reflected in the sweet sky-blue of her gaze, and thought he had never seen such lovely, thoughtful eyes.

"How many of you were there?"

"At one time, many. Now, I do not know. We can be found in the water, on land, in the air. Dragon is a little of everything, but that kind was rare even then." Hari paused. "During my last summons, I found a date. 1423. How long . . . ?"

"Six hundred years," she said, growing pale. She pressed her fingers against her lips. "You've been imprisoned in that box for almost six hundred years."

A very long sleep, indeed.

He would have said more, but someone knocked on the door. Amid slight protest, Hari hurriedly tucked Dela into the small corner between bed and wall, concealed from the narrow entrance. She stooped to gather the bloody towels, tossing them deep into the shadows beneath the bed.

"Stay there," he whispered. Dela glared at him.

Amusement—biting, quick—flared in his gut. He

struggled mightily to keep his face straight. So she did not like being left behind? Or was that worry in her eyes?

Again, someone rapped on the door, this time harder. Troubled, Hari slipped into the bathroom for his discarded weapons, grabbing a dagger to hold tight against his thigh. Adrenaline sang through his limbs. He pressed his ear to the door, and—

"I smell food."

Dela appeared. "Room service. I hope." She carefully peered through a tiny glass hole he had not noticed, and smiled. "Hide that knife," she said. Hari frowned, holding it behind his back as he gently shouldered Dela aside to answer the door. This could still be a trap.

But the tiny gentleman who smiled and pushed in a large, laden cart did not threaten them in any way beyond a somewhat heavy glance at Hari's scars. Hari had long ago rid himself of self-consciousness; everyone stared when they saw his chest. Dela, however, spoke several sharp words that made the old man jump and shuffle his feet. She passed small papers into his hand and walked him to the door.

Her unexpected protectiveness startled him. It was another strange reversal of that to which he was accustomed, and he fought the urge to speak of it, to point out the needlessness of her consideration.

Hari laid his dagger upon the table. Warm, rich scents assaulted his nose as Dela uncovered their meals, and he feared acting like a true animal. Thick cuts of meat filled his plate, accompanied by green vegetables. Fruit, exotic and varied, was piled high in a wide bowl. Dela poured tea.

"Come on," she said, when he hesitated. "You haven't eaten in six hundred years. Pig out."

Hari was not sure what the last two words meant, but her intent was clear. He used his hands to pick up a slab of steaming meat, and had his mouth set to tear when he noticed Dela, eating delicately with fine silver utensils.

Dela saw him watching, and something passed through her eyes. She set down her utensils, plucked a vegetable from her plate, and popped it into her mouth. She licked her fingers. Her invitation was clear.

"Eat, Hari. Nothing you do will offend me."

Warmth rushed down his spine, pooling in his stomach. So much time alone, suppressing dreams of simple kindness, and here—finally—a woman who showed him effortless compassion over something so small as a meal. It was almost too much to bear.

He did not mean to, but hunger of an entirely different sort suddenly flowed through his veins. He imagined Dela stretched amid the food, splayed upon the table, creamy skin exposed to his hands and mouth—a consumption of the senses, filling, being filled, her legs wrapped around his waist. . . .

A flush stained Dela's cheeks, and Hari wondered what she saw in his eyes, whether his desire was so transparent. He found he did not care if she knew how much he wanted her. Shame had left him long ago. Though he had lost his skin, the beast still lived—and both the tiger and the man suddenly wanted this woman with shocking, aching intensity.

She might betray you.

Hari pushed aside fear. He had to taste her—thought he might die if he did not. In one step he was by her side, dropping to his knees. She stared, wide-eyed.

"I am going to kiss you," he said, more for his benefit than hers. Before she could protest, he wrapped one large hand around the back of her neck and pressed his lips to hers. He tried to be gentle, to give her that much courtesy, but she surprised him by leaning into his body, opening her mouth for an even deeper kiss that sent ribbons of lightning through his flesh.

Her tongue darted past his lips and he took her invitation, stealing the breath from her lungs as he sank himself into her body, tugging her close, exploring the sweet, hot curves of her mouth. He had never tasted anything so wondrous, and the beast responded, turning circles in his chest as it, too, drank in the scent and flavor of the woman. Sunlight, piercing the dark heart of the forest: that was how she felt to him—and he wondered if he would ever let go, if he would be able to stop.

But he did stop, with great difficulty, and it was Dela who pulled away. Her eyes were glazed, lips swollen with his kisses, her breathing ragged as a spring storm. His heart pounded, blood rushing down, down, though there was enough left to heat his face.

"I don't even know you," she whispered, brushing her fingertips against her lips.

Those were not the words Hari had been expecting to hear, not with the musk of her desire scenting the air, the heat in her eyes. Truthfully, he had not been expecting anything, especially the still-vibrant rush of her presence sinking sweetly beneath his skin. His bones felt cushioned by velvet, his body much too warm.

All from a kiss.

He saw uncertainty seep into Dela's eyes, and the sharp edge of panic made him slide backward. He dropped his gaze, and suddenly his chest was tight for a reason other than arousal.

"My apologies," he said. "I was too forward with you."

"Yes," she said, but softly, without anger. "Why did you kiss me?"

It was the first time he had ever been asked such a question, and he blinked, wishing he was better with words. Loneliness roared deep inside his chest, striking him hollow, stripping away his new warmth with the force of a blunt mace. How could he share the terrible need that had arisen in him? There were no words to describe his desire that would not sound obscene against the air they breathed, and his compulsion was nothing so base or dark. It felt full of light, stunning and sweet.

"To do otherwise would have been difficult," he finally said.

"Oh," she breathed.

"I will not touch you again without your permission," he promised, regretting his words even though he knew they were necessary. The urge to touch her still threatened to overwhelm him, but his instincts urged caution. This was not a woman he could press too soon, nor did he want to. His own heart was still too fragile. He did not understand what Dela was doing to him.

I am vulnerable. Starved for kindness, and when I receive it, I lose my mind.

"Thank you." Dela rested her hands in her lap, quivering, some strange energy humming against her skin, flowing out to touch him. Hari quickly stood, trying to hide his conspicuous arousal. He suspected Dela noticed. He did not look at her, afraid of what he would see in her eyes.

"So," she said, after he took his seat, "I hope you're still hungry."

Relief, and some strange wistfulness, coursed through him.

"Yes," he said, although his low voice, the heat in his

face, most likely revealed his hunger had little to do
with the food set before him.

Dela, sipping water, coughed. Her cheeks grew even
redder. Hari took pity on her and lowered his gaze to his
meal.

*I have said and done too much. I will make her
afraid.*

His food had grown cold, but he did not care. He attacked it with single-minded intensity, trying to concentrate on something other than the woman seated across
from him. He ate and ate, and after a time began to taste
his food, the rich juices, flavors vibrant on his tongue.
Only when he was done scouring meat to bone, and
fruit to hard pit, did he stop to look at Dela.

She had barely touched her meal, and was watching
him thoughtfully. No one had ever studied him so openly,
without fear. It was a curious sensation—her eyes
searching his face—and he felt himself laid open as if
before a pure flame.

Even at their cruelest, his masters could never stare
long into Hari's face. He frightened them, even when on
his knees, guts strung out under the sun. He made them
uneasy. The razor edge of captivity—a slave in name
only, never in spirit. They could feel his power, and it
was threatening. No one ever forgot that.

But Dela was not intimidated. She looked deep into
his eyes, as though she could summon the secrets of his
heart. Hari could not fathom what lay revealed. He did
not want to know.

When she spoke, he thought she might address their
kiss, but she surprised him.

"I should have told you earlier," she said slowly. "This
morning, before I opened the box, someone else attacked me."

Dela explained the market, the old woman who had sold her the box, and the strange man who had watched the transaction and then tried to kidnap her.

"It is a simple thing," Hari said, feeling ill. "Someone knows you have me. If they kill you, I return to the box, ready for a new owner."

Dela frowned. "Surely the same person can't be responsible. That knife was stolen months ago. Who could foresee . . ." She paused, and then, "I mean, it just doesn't make sense that the two events are related. Killing me with my own creation is way more personal than just trying to knock me off so the box changes hands. Besides, I don't think this morning's bad guy knew who I was."

"Then you have two problems. My apologies, Delilah. I have added to your difficulties."

"Hari, you saved my life." Her voice was low, serious and earnest, a match to her stubborn frown. "Listen, we'll find a way out of this. Every problem has a solution. Even your curse."

He laughed, but it sounded cold, hollow. "I suppose you could destroy the box."

"Would that set you free?"

"I do not know. It might kill me, but I think I would prefer to die, rather than continue on in darkness, enslaved." It was a choice he had never dared voice before now.

Hari saw her consider it. He also saw her falter.

"Seems to me fighting is the better option." Dela's voice gained strength. "You can't give up, Hari."

"And what do you know of fighting?" he asked, deliberately harsh. "I have spent the past two thousand years as a *belonging*, enduring humiliation, torture, committing atrocities. You have no idea what that means."

"Maybe not." Dela narrowed her eyes. "But I know cowardice when I see it."

Hari stiffened. "Are you accusing me of dishonor?"

"If you ask me to kill you without even attempting to find an answer to your problem, then yes. I am."

Her words stung. Hari stood, but the room suddenly felt far too small. He ended up at the window, arms braced on either side of the thin glass. The city sprawled beneath him, unspeakably alien, strange objects moving at miraculous speeds. People, tiny at this great height, traveling in numbers greater than he had ever imagined. In that moment, he hated it all.

"What would you have me do?" he growled.

"Live," she said, rising to stand beside him. He glanced at her.

"Live for myself, you mean? Everyone I know is dead. I am alone."

He expected anger. Instead, Dela looked down at her hands, quiet and thoughtful. Which was almost worse.

"I once knew a girl," Dela finally said. "An orphan. She was completely alone, as much as you. A very bad man kidnapped her, and hid her in a hole beneath his home. She stayed there for a week, in the darkness, and he did terrible things to her. Just terrible." Dela swallowed heavily. "But do you know how she survived? She fought. She fought every time he came to her, and one day she got lucky and was able to escape."

"Delilah," he breathed, appalled. "Tell me you were not that child."

Her smile was infinitely sad. "No, but Amy was my best friend. She's dead now. After all she went through, she contracted some rare brain cancer. Didn't last six months. But she fought that, too."

Silence descended. The moral of her tale was painfully clear, and Hari could barely stand to look at her as his anger leaked away, down his belly through his toes.

"You shame me."

"I play dirty." Dela touched his arm, her fingers gliding down his skin. "And I'm not ashamed of it, especially if it keeps you going. You've lived for two thousand years, Hari. What's a couple more, especially now, when you've got a friend?"

"Friend?"

Dela pointed at herself. "If anyone needs one, it's you. Unless, of course, you prefer to go it alone."

"It is what I am used to," he said, finding it difficult to speak.

She smiled, and it was too much. Their kiss had been powerful, but Dela had a way of overwhelming him with her actions and words that was completely terrifying. Hari was twice her size, but he knew, even without the curse, that this woman could bring him to his knees with her voice alone. With a smile.

Hari made room for Dela at the window.

"I bet this looks strange to you, huh?" And then, when he did not immediately answer, she said, "You told me the spell can only be broken by finding your skin."

Hari sighed. "It has been two thousand years, Delilah."

"Well, what is it? Fur?"

Hari had to laugh. "No, not fur. When the Magi stole my skin, he stole a piece of my heart. A piece of my heart, in the shape of my sister. To find my skin, I have to find my heart, and I do not know how to do that with my family dead."

"Would it help if you found others of your kind?"

"I doubt it."

Dela quirked her lips. "At least we're not looking for some mangy piece of hide that's been buried for two thousand years in some godforsaken jungle."

"There is that," he said dryly.

She smiled. "Everything has an answer, Hari. Even your heart."

"And in the meantime?"

"In the meantime, I show you this world. I take you home."

"And if there are no answers?"

Dela touched his face. Her fingertips were cool, light as butterfly wings. He wanted to kiss her palm. "Then you live, Hari. You live, with all the time you've got, and the life you want."

Dela turned away from him, and it took all Hari's willpower not to wrap his large hands around her waist, to hold her against his body. He wanted to share something intimate, if only for a moment. He was so hungry for such things, for some soft touch. Before, when he kissed her, he'd thought one taste would be enough, but he now realized his mistake.

Be careful, whispered his mind, a litany not powerful enough to suppress the emotions and desires he thought long dead, shrugging free of the places he had buried them. Dela's presence was the key. She made him want more. She made him believe freedom was a possibility. She made him want to live again.

Stories and lies, he told himself, but he did not care.

How beautiful, he thought, his doubts and fears falling silent as he watched Dela rummage through her bags. *Perhaps I do have a friend.*

* * *

I AM LOSING MY MIND, DELA THOUGHT, WATCHING Hari disappear into the bathroom to finish the soak that had been interrupted by both assassin and meal. He seemed clean enough; she suspected he just wanted to put some distance between them, a bit of breathing room.

Fine by her. It gave Dela more time to contemplate her burgeoning insanity—a first-rate madness in which a kiss was suddenly more important than inexplicable assassins, magic boxes, and immortal shape-shifters.

I am losing my mind, she thought again.

But oh, her lips still burned, her entire body flushed with desire. Dela had never been kissed like that. Just the press of Hari's mouth, his taste and scent, and fire had roared through her body, shearing muscle and bone, convulsions twisting her lower stomach.

She had been so prepared to box his ears—if she ever recovered from the smoldering, devastatingly erotic way he looked at her—but once he touched her neck, her mouth, all coherent thought had fled screeching into the dark recesses of her mind.

Dela wanted him. Bad. And it shocked her, how wanton she felt. Priorities, priorities. The only thing that had kept her from falling from her chair into his lap like an overeager poodle had been the knowledge that Hari was still a stranger. A stranger who might push, interpreting her desire as an invitation to do more.

But Hari had not insisted. He had pulled away, apologizing. Hearing him speak, she wanted to hold him, lay her cheek against his throat. *Make no promises,* she wanted to say, and yet, she was glad for them—thankful for the vow of distance. Her control around men had always been perfect—distant, even cool—but Hari was a completely different force to be reckoned with.

She blamed the echo of his spirit still resonating inside her head; he was a part of her in a very intimate way, his presence as familiar as her own, as though she had known him her entire life.

Disturbing.

She shook herself, and opened the address book she had just retrieved from her luggage. Using her phone card, Dela placed a call to Roland Dirk in San Francisco.

Part bear, part lumberjack, and part GI Joe, Roland had been a member of Dela's inner circle and family for almost ten years. He was dirty, twisted—a criminal mastermind of the lowest order—and one of her favorite people in the entire world. He was also the perfect person to help her.

It was midnight there (or as her night-owl brother Max liked to say, "freakishly early"), but this counted as an emergency. The phone rang once, twice, and Dela fought panic.

Come on, you big pussy. Answer the damn—

"Yo," Roland groaned. "Whassup? Better be good, 'cause I was having the best wet dream."

Dela rolled her eyes, knowing he could see her and inviting his commentary.

"Stop that, Del."

"I hate you," she groused affectionately. "Cellulite has more personality."

"Especially yours. Now, what d'you want? Must be good, calling from China—unless you finally decided to give in to my demands for phone sex."

Ah, pleasantries. "Papers for a friend," she said, getting down to business. "I need a passport, social security number—the whole works. Plus, an airline ticket out of China. I need to be on the same flight as this individual, so I'll give you my confirmation number, let you work out the details."

A moment of silence. "For a minute there, you sounded like my mother."

"No wonder you're so screwed up."

"That's your brother's fault. He drives me nuts. You know what crazy shit he's into this week?"

"Does it have anything to do with South America?"

"Right on, babe. He's down there like some Rambo wannabe, stirring up rival guerilla groups, trying to get them at each other's throats so he can ferry some kidnapped tourists out of the Amazon. A *distraction,* he calls it. He's going to start World War III, just for a simple snatch and grab."

"Hmph," she grunted. "Max can take care of himself. What about those papers?"

"Jeez. Okay. You needed them yesterday, huh? Something about this friend I should know about?"

"Nope."

"Sure? You know I'm always looking to extend invitations."

"Oh, God, no." The thought of Hari working for Dirk & Steele horrified her. He was dangerous enough, without having the Kamikaze King on his back. "This guy is a friend. I promised to help him out."

This time it was Roland who grunted. "Just a friend?"

Dela blushed, and he instantly sighed. "Okay, babe, no problem. You know I got your back. What's his name?"

"Hari. H-a-r-i. No last name. Feel free to make one up. And thanks, Roland. You're a sweetheart. I'll take a picture of him with my digital camera and send it to you."

"Whatever. Anything else?"

She hesitated, but Roland had to be told. The attack might have been personal—but if not, then the target was much greater, more important than just herself. Everyone in the agency might be at risk.

"Someone's trying to kill me."

The result of that particular announcement required Dela to hold the phone away from her ear while semi-inarticulate gurgles emerged from the earpiece.

". . . AND DON'T YOU HOLD THAT PHONE AWAY FROM YOUR HEAD! I CAN SEE YOU, AND IT DRIVES ME CRAZY!"

Dela grimaced, and returned the receiver to her ear. "You're going to give yourself a heart attack if you don't calm down. You know what the doctor told you."

"Calm down? Jeeeezus, Del. Who the hell is trying to kill you?"

She told him about her attacker, giving him a full description. She also explained the knife and her fears regarding the agency.

"We haven't been compromised," Roland said. "I would know. What about you, though? Enemies?"

"None I can think of, and most of the people I meet are at fancy social gatherings. I'm perfectly charming at those things."

"Which means you've probably got a dozen people who want you dead, and who could afford to do it right."

"Only a dozen? I'm hurt, Roland."

"Sarcasm will get you everywhere, babe. Don't worry, Dirk & Steele is officially on the case."

"Lovely." She meant it, too. "When is the earliest you can get me those papers?"

"Tomorrow evening, or the morning after. I'll twist some fingers, pour in some cash. I'm worried about you, though. I can send some locals to watch your back."

"I'll be fine, Roland. No extra help needed. Or wanted.

And don't tell the family. Please. The last thing I need is them freaking out." Or getting involved.

"Give me Max, at least. I answer to your family if you croak, Del. Your grandmother alone will nail my hide to the wall."

"Not before she shaves off your balls with Grandpa's antique razor."

He sucked in his breath. "You're evil."

Dela smiled.

She asked Roland to send someone to check on her personal assistant, Adam—it stood to reason anyone close to her could be a potential target—and after sharing her contact information at the hotel, they ended their conversation with a simple 'bye.

Still grinning, Dela looked up to find Hari studying her. A simple thing, but she forgot how to breathe.

In the shadows of the hotel room, his tawny skin seemed to glow warm and golden. His deep scars did not mar the perfection of his body, covered only by a towel wrapped around his lean waist. Hair still wet, slicked away from his face, Hari's cheekbones appeared higher, more pronounced, and Dela could see the tiger in his face, in the flush of his sun-drenched eyes. Water beaded on his chest and shoulders, and for a moment, she felt the insane urge to press her mouth against the hollow of his throat, to taste his wet body with her lips and hands.

Down, girl.

Dela wanted to laugh. This was all too absurd. Still, she could not take her eyes off him. It occurred to her that Hari would be completely at ease walking in public with just that towel. Not because he was arrogant or vain, but because he was so comfortable in his own body. Hari might have been a slave, but it was in name only. He still owned himself where it counted. He owned his soul.

"You look like you're thinking of stalking me," she tried to joke. Her heart hammered.

A slow smile spread across Hari's face. "Who were you talking to?" His voice was light, deceptively so. Dela tilted her head, curious.

"An old friend of the family. His name is Roland. He's going to get you all the papers you'll need to leave this country and enter America. Borders are a lot more restrictive than what I'm sure you're used to. You can't just come and go as you please."

"I assure you," he said dryly, "I am quite used to restrictions on my movements."

Dela flushed, squirming. Before she could apologize, Hari said, "You are close to this man who is helping me?"

"Close enough," she said, surprised by his question. "He's practically family."

Hari grunted, eyes slightly narrowed. Dela almost laughed. Was Hari fishing for information about her private life? Could it be . . . did he wonder if she had a boyfriend?

Amused, wondering if her ego was running rings around her vanity, Dela hopped off the bed and grabbed her purse. The past few hours had been a nightmare of uncontrollable circumstances, demanding strict reactions. Now, it was time for equally rigorous action.

"I have a plan," she said. "But first, we need to find you some clothes."

"I have clothes," he said.

"Look at the way I'm dressed," Dela said. "Then think about what you arrived in."

Hari frowned. "I would rather think about your plan. Whatever it is."

Dela sighed. "If we're lucky, we'll be able to leave this country by tomorrow or the day after. If someone really wants me dead"—she fought down a shiver, swallowing fear—"he or she will find it more difficult to accomplish in America, where my home is. It'll still be dangerous, but there just aren't as many people. It's easier to keep track of who's around you." Not to mention, Dela had friends there to help watch her back. Dirk & Steele always took care of its own.

"Either way," Hari said, "you do not seem terribly concerned. I find that strange."

"I find *you* strange," Dela retorted. "And for your information, just because I'm not tearing out my hair or gnashing my teeth, doesn't mean I'm not afraid. I just handle it better than the people you're obviously used to dealing with."

"Obviously," he said.

Dela gritted her teeth. "Even if we're able to leave tomorrow, we still have time to ask some questions. I want to return to the Dirt Market and find the old lady who sold me your box. She knew what she was giving me, and I want to know why she did it. Maybe she even has information about your curse, or something that could help you."

It was already after three P.M., and the Dirt Market had closed at one. She and Hari would get there early tomorrow morning, hunker down, and wait for the old woman to show up. Simple.

Hari shrugged. "I, too, am curious, though it is likely to be a waste of time. The curse cannot be broken. My skin is gone."

"Negativity will get you nowhere." Dela rolled her

shoulders. "I'm going back to the Dirt Market, and I'm going to pick that woman's brains."

Hari blanched, and Dela shook her head, holding out her hands. "No, I don't mean that literally! It's a saying we use. I just meant that I want to find out everything she knows."

Hari still looked haunted. "There was a time when people truly did . . . pick each other's brains in order to divine information. The best way to do it was while the individual was still alive."

"Ew. That's just . . . *ew*." Dela shuddered. Disgusted, she nevertheless wanted to ask him more questions, but the pale white line of his mouth, the tight skin around his eyes, shriveled up her curiosity. Perhaps there were some words better left unsaid, some memories better left unremembered.

"Tell me something about the shape-shifters," she said instead, hoping to make him forget whatever horror her words had summoned. "You said they were numerous two thousand years ago?"

Hari took a deep breath, his face softening. "Some kinds were numerous. Creatures of the water and air lived in great numbers, but the land-dwellers were beginning to feel the press of humans. Tigers were still plentiful, although we rarely interacted with anyone outside our family clan."

"A lot has happened since you were put away. Normal tigers are . . . well, tigers in the wild are almost extinct."

"Extinct?"

"Gone forever. So few tigers are left that, if some of them are shape-shifters, I'm sure they've left the forest. It wouldn't be safe for them anymore."

Hari did not question her. He sank to the bed, staring

at the floor, his eyes cold and empty. It was a painful thing, seeing such a vibrant man reduced to such heart-breaking dismay.

"I cannot imagine it," he whispered. "We had no rivals in the forest. Humans believed us to be gods, though that was something we never encouraged. To kill a tiger was simply not done."

Dela sat beside him, fighting the urge to hold his hand. "Man grew bold. There must be others, though. Shape-shifters would be smarter than regular tigers; they wouldn't let themselves get killed off so easily." She hoped that was the case, anyway. It had been two thousand years since Hari had seen his people. A lot could have happened. "Would you recognize a shape-shifter if you saw one?"

"Yes," he said, straightening. "It is in our eyes, our blood."

"Well, then. We'll just take a walk. See what we can find."

Hari looked at her then, a measuring gaze full of power. His eyes were the color of burnished gold. Beautiful. Dela felt bathed in heat, awash in the intensity of his presence.

"Why are you helping me, Delilah? I have been alive a very long time, and no one has ever done for me what you have."

Her cheeks grew hot. "I haven't done all that much. Fed you, bathed you, yelled a little. Well, a lot—"

A long, strong finger touched her lips, instantly silencing her. Hari's gaze burned with both hunger and curiosity. Dela could not decide whether he wanted to kiss her, eat her, or just talk. Probably all three.

"You have made me feel like a man again. You have made me remember the beauty of compassion. I simply

want to know why you have done this. Why you are so
kind. You say my presence makes no sense, but to me
you are the mystery."

Dela pulled away from his touch. "I am not that kind.
I am not a mystery. I'm just . . . me." A woman who preferred solitude to a crowd, who kept her distance from
strangers—from anyone who would be afraid of her secrets. She was a woman who crafted art from weapons,
and weapons from art, who sometimes felt as cold as the
steel she listened to—but not empty. Never empty.

"I already answered this question," she said. "I'm
helping you because it's the right thing to do. Isn't that
enough?"

"For now," he said. Dela heard the promise in his
voice. *For now it is enough, but later . . . later we will
speak of this again.* She did not look forward to it. Self-
reflection was not her strong suit.

Dela swung her purse over her shoulder. "I'm going
out to get you something to wear. You still won't entirely
fit in—which isn't a bad thing—but at least I can get you
into the twenty-first century."

As long as there was a big and tall section in the
shopping mall below the hotel. Doubtful, but Dela was
a firm believer in miracles.

"You are *not* going anywhere alone," Hari said,
standing. Dela refused to back away. Her neck creaked
as she struggled to maintain eye contact.

"Excuse me? When did you become my boss?"

Hari's jaw tightened. "It is too dangerous for you, Delilah. Or have you forgotten the recent attempt on your
life?"

"No, I haven't forgotten, but I'll be in a public place.
Lots of people, witnesses. Besides, you can't go out

dressed in a towel. Women will have spontaneous pregnancies. Hairy men will go bald. Dogs will start wearing clothes and smoking cigarettes. Chaos everywhere."

Hari folded his impressive arms over his equally impressive chest. "If I do not go," he said, in a deadly quiet voice, "then you will not be permitted to leave this room."

Yes, the caveman cometh.

It occurred to Dela, in that particular instant, that she could just order him to let her go. The box supposedly gave her that power over his body. Dela also knew if she ever commanded Hari, he would hate her for the rest of his very long life, and that was something she could not tolerate. Ever.

Nor would she be able to stand herself for becoming the master to his slave. Some sins, once committed, could never be forgiven.

"You're very stubborn," she said, "but so am I. This is the twenty-first century, and women go where they please without the say-so of men. I am leaving this room, Hari—without you—and there isn't anything you can do to stop me."

Which resulted in a demonstration of Hari's ability to do just that.

When he finally lowered her to the floor and let go of her ankles, they worked out a compromise. Hari would wear his sandals, leather pants, and linen tunic, leaving his weapons and armor in the room, tucked under the bed.

He did not want to leave his weapons, but Dela was adamant. One simply did not run around in public armed with swords and knives—not without a certain amount of insanity involved.

Besides, with his size, strength, and speed, the man

was weapon enough. His every movement sang with dangerous grace, some ancient primal element of the predator. Rabbits would probably shed their skins for him on command—as might certain individuals of the human variety.

Hari quickly dressed and waited for her beside the door, smoothing down his sleeveless linen tunic. It looked rough, stained with blood (which Dela hoped would be mistaken for red dye), the edges frayed and torn. Still, it suited him, as did the leather pants. Everyone in the mall probably would think he was some über-cool, somewhat eccentric supermodel.

"Are there any particular customs I should be aware of before we leave?" Hari flexed his fingers.

"Don't kill anyone, and don't start a fight."

His lips twitched, and Dela held up her hand. "I'm serious."

"Of course you are."

She scowled at him, exasperated.

Dela, however, had little time to contemplate Hari's newly emergent sense of humor. As soon as they left the hotel room, questions began rolling off his tongue—questions about the lack of guards, the repetition in design, the great height at which he knew they stood. More, and more.

Technology fascinated him. Hari had already quizzed Dela about electricity and plumbing, but his reaction to the elevator reminded her of a marooned alcoholic finding a stash of whiskey on a deserted island: pure, unadulterated pleasure. Not that Hari was completely demonstrative; there was just something about his eyes, bright and quick-moving; the pitch of his deep voice, the coil of his fingers—all conspiring to tell a story of deep curiosity and excitement.

That, and more—until the elevator doors closed in front of him, and Hari's face shut down into a blank mask. The transformation was stunning; seven feet of man, standing absolutely still, breathless. Perhaps, even, unable to breathe. A light sheen of sweat broke out on his forehead.

Alarmed, Dela touched Hari's hand. *He's claustrophobic,* she realized, as a fine tremor raced through his arm. Dela lightly squeezed his hand; the doors slid open and he stepped through, dragging her with him. His chest expanded, a rush of air.

"Hari?" Dela asked tentatively.

He blinked, and surprise shimmered through his face as he glanced down at her. He looked at their joined hands. Silence, and then: "Thank you," he said quietly.

Dela nodded, releasing him.

The hotel lobby's walls cascaded marble and gilt engravings, enormous columns rising with dignified grace from floor to faraway ceiling. Leather chairs and sofas littered the yawning expanse, intimately arranged for the illusion of privacy, surrounded by potted trees with wide, shadow-casting leaves. Hotel attendants served tea and snacks, slipping from one area to another, clad in slender, high-slit chi-paos.

Dela and Hari swept through the lobby, heavy stares and stopped conversations dogging their heels. Dela lifted her chin, going for attitude. Not so difficult, with Hari at her side. He was like an instant shot of I'm-Too-Sexy, mixed with Mine-Mine-Mine.

You're ridiculous, she told herself sternly, but could not help herself. When had she ever been in the company of such a compelling man? And so what if Hari wasn't really hers? Though, if she wanted to get technical, she supposed he was, in an I'm-stuck-with-you-until-you-die sort of way. More permanent than most marriages, what with the magical voodoo linking them together.

Still, the intense scrutiny made her skin prickle. She rubbed her arms.

"Are you cold?"

It would have been easier to say yes, but instead she said, "I prefer anonymity. I always get a little nervous when I'm the center of attention."

A curious smile flitted over Hari's lips. "Does that happen often?"

Dela shrugged. "Sometimes. I'm a well-known artist in certain circles."

Hari glanced around the glistening marble lobby, taking in the curious, unabashed attention of the men and women watching them.

"I once felt as you did," he said. "It took me many years to grow accustomed to being a novelty, a prize to behold. Now I am used to scrutiny."

"Sounds as though you were treated like a piece of meat."

Hari made a low sound. "I have never heard it described in such a way, but yes. Walking, talking, fighting . . . *meat*."

Meat. That was all he had been to those people. It made Dela ill, but she swallowed down her disgust as they descended into the cavernous mall beneath the hotel. The mall itself was not as large as the one within the Oriental Plaza, located deeper in the city, but Dela had no time to be picky. She was just glad her credit limit was huge, and that she had enough money in the bank to pay off the damage. Bargain shopping was impossible—Bill Gates himself might have fainted at some of the prices.

Dela watched Hari's face as he took in the wide expanse of white tile winding a curling path before them. She led him to a glass balcony, and he gazed across the chasm at the floor beneath them, and then up at the high ceiling with its tear-drop lights. Glass was everywhere, sparkling. Storefronts full of mannequins, clad in shocking scraps of color, lined the broad, well-lit corridors. If the hotel lobby impressed Hari, he had not shown it. Here, he stared like a child, open-mouthed.

"So much has changed," he murmured, as Dela led him deeper into the mall. People, everywhere—the China World mall was the place to be seen, and Dela felt positively dowdy compared to some of the long-legged gazelles who sauntered past, trying their best to cast seductive, come-hither gazes at Hari.

It pleased Dela to no end that Hari did nothing more than glance at them, as though they were simply part of the environment he was beginning to explore.

Possessive, yes? Dela asked herself, wondering at her strange behavior.

As they walked, the first rush of amazed awe left Hari's face. Something more serious took its place.

"Delilah," he said. He did not touch her, but his voice left a print on her body. Her stomach tingled. "We should not stay long," he continued. "I did not imagine such crowds. It will be difficult to keep you safe."

Her heart did a little tango in her throat, her cheeks flushing. Embarrassed, she glanced up at Hari's face and found him wearing the focused expression of a dangerous man. Deliberate, deadly.

He is really serious about protecting me.

The revelation startled her, heightening her sense of awkwardness. When Dela recalled the way Hari first looked at her—his profound disdain and revulsion—it seemed a miracle that scant hours could change so much. Or had it? Was her safety just a way of staying out of the box?

The possibility stung, but Dela knew she would not blame him if self-preservation was a motivating factor in his new solicitude. Still, that would make Hari a big fat fake, and nothing of him—especially his quiet echo still lingering inside her head—smacked of shallow deception.

And his kiss . . .

This is all too confusing. One thing at a time.

Yes, one thing at a time. No matter how Hari felt toward her, Dela had offered her help, her friendship—a wildly rare act on her part—but the carrying on, in some way, of a family tradition. Only, the stakes had never felt so personal.

"Never you fear," she finally said, trying to sound upbeat. "We'll be quick."

Which was a complete and utter lie.

The problem was this: Men as tall as Hari were almost never built as he was—all thick muscle and sinew. It was easy for Dela to imagine Hari as he must have been before the curse: gliding through a forest of rippled shadows, one moment man, in the next, tiger. Formidable, uncanny.

Very dramatic, but not at all practical when buying clothes. Salespeople took one look at Hari, drooled and then ran. Dela was beginning to think that perhaps ratty linen and leather were good enough, when they finally found a men's store that had—and here the bells of heaven rang in her ears—clothes that actually fit.

They escaped more than an hour later. Hari looked faintly dazed, but firmly in the twenty-first century. He wore blue jeans, a white dress shirt with the sleeves rolled up, and had variations of the same in the bags he and Dela carried. Sleek muscles, long and fine, slid beneath the fabric of his new clothing. If anything, Hari looked even more handsome.

He was, however, very quiet as they walked through the mall to the hotel, and Dela—feeling rather secure— poked him in the ribs. Hari jumped, and stared at her with some heat.

"Do I *never* scare you?"

Dela raised her eyebrows. "I think we already had this discussion."

Hari grumbled something under his breath. Dela, still bold, tugged on his sleeve. "What's wrong?"

Dela's question was met with profound silence. Finally, Hari said, "I have been a slave for more than two thousand years, Delilah. Many of those years were spent asleep, but the time I spent awake was enough. I learned to ask for nothing, and I was given *nothing*." He paused, shaking his head. "Before, I thought you were being extravagant when you said I needed new clothing. Food, shelter—that is all I require. All I have ever wished from my masters."

"Besides a little kindness," Dela added.

The look he gave her was grave. "I stopped wishing for kindness a long time ago, Delilah. Looking for the impossible became too painful."

He tore his gaze from her face. "I was wrong," he said softly, and for a moment, Dela thought he meant something else. But then he said, "Out here, among these people, I can see I was wrong. You were right. I do not quite . . . fit in. But then, I never have. Still, this world has changed more drastically than I dreamed possible, and I do not know my place in it. I am completely dependent on you—more than I have ever been on any of my masters. It makes me uncomfortable. I do not know how to repay you."

Dela stopped walking and placed herself directly in front of Hari, so close her neck ached from looking at him. He was, quite simply, enormous—a mountain of muscle and bone. His new clothes did nothing to mute his breathtaking physique, the shine of his tawny skin, his eyes. Passersby stared, but Dela paid them no mind. Hari had her entire attention.

"I am not looking for payment, and it is not my intention to make you feel dependent on my good graces. Listen, Hari—I'm going to teach you everything you need to know to survive in this world. In the meantime, though, you'll just have to bear with me when I provide you with extravagant gifts such as clothes and food." Her voice sounded sharper than her intent, and Dela sighed, begging Hari to understand.

"Swallow your pride, Hari. I've got plenty for both of us. Worry about taking care of yourself *after* we break your curse."

It was almost funny, watching his awkward bewilderment. "How can you be so confident of our success?"

"Because the alternative is unthinkable," she said with simple honesty.

There was a response on his lips, in his eyes, but movement to Hari's left caught Dela's attention. She stared, stomach lurching, vision burning. Her hand ached, a sympathetic echo.

Perfect face, coifed hair, crisp clothes. But no smile, not this time.

Dela was dimly aware of Hari turning, following the direction of her gaze. Bags crashed to the floor. She

heard him make a sound—a terrible, strangled gasp—
and knew instinctively that Death had come.

Time slowed. Moments caught in glass, sheer and
solid.

"Magi," Hari snarled.

CHAPTER FOUR

No way. There is no way in hell that is the Magi.
It didn't make any sense. None whatsoever. But as Dela stared into the stranger's eyes, she felt the brush of cool fingers against her mind. Memories from morning washed over her, and she saw a shadow creep beneath the dusky skin of the stranger's handsome face.

Stomach clenching, Dela gritted her teeth and thought, *Yes, maybe he* is *the Magi.*

A low growl rumbled from Hari's chest, a sound that was more animal than man, and Dela's next thought was, *Oh, shoot.*

Dela prided herself on being the kind of girl who never ran from a fight. It was like SuperChick Deluxe, from the comic book—she looked like a pushover, but rub her the wrong way and she'd rip you a new one. Literally.

Still, there were times even in SuperChick's life when it was a Good Idea To Walk Away. Like now. It didn't take a genius to figure that Hari wanted to kill this man with his bare hands—and probably would, given the chance. If this was the Magi—impossible, *impossible,* but she was beginning to believe—then Dela wasn't too keen on stopping him.

Murder, however, in the middle of a crowded shopping mall was generally a bad idea. Especially in China.

Dela latched on to Hari's arm, holding him with all her strength. It was like embracing a volcano—all heat and certain violence. Hari trembled, face contorting with such fury that everyone who looked at him paled, instinctively back-pedaling in the opposite direction.

"Hari," she whispered urgently, shaking his arm. She glanced over her shoulder. The Magi smiled like a playboy—all sex and ugly charm—and began ambling toward them with a careless, arrogant grace that was both invitation and threat.

Hari shuddered, easily jolting free of Dela's grasp. She stumbled, caught her balance, and stubbornly threw herself in front of him, palms flat against his chest. Real fear pricked her skin—not for herself, but for Hari.

"Oh, no you don't," she said. "Hari! You have to listen to me. Hari!" He didn't seem to hear; his entire focus was on the man observing them. His eyes flickered from gold to blood-flecked copper, burning, burning.

You could order him.

The thought came unbidden, desperation momentarily clouding Dela's judgment. She discarded the idea with disgust. There had to be another way. What Hari needed was a good shock. Scenes from movies crowded her mind, absurd and awkward. Slapping, shaking, kicking—oh, but there was one she was willing to try.

Dela jumped up against Hari, scrambling to wrap her arms and legs around his hard body. It was like climbing a tree—solid, unmoving—except she had never clambered up an oak that had lips.

It was a clumsy kiss—desperate, hurried—but she managed to muster a little passion. Enough, anyway, to snap Hari out of his unthinking rage. For one moment she felt him kiss her back, his lips pressing hard as fire-warmed steel against her mouth. Dela savored his scent, his heat. Tears burned her eyes.

And then he stumbled, pulling away. Not far, only a breath, his eyes unveiling a story of pain, inhuman re-solve. Rage. Longing. Dela felt Hari's soul echo inside her heart, the bond that had gone quiet unexpectedly humming, electric and pure. She breathed in the memory of his golden light.

"I need to kill that man," Hari whispered, pleading.

"I know you do," Dela breathed, hating herself. "But if you kill him now, with so many witnesses, you will throw your life away."

His lips compressed into a hard white line. "Delilah, *please*. I have no life. Nothing but this. Let me go. I do not know how it is possible, but the Magi is here, *now*. I may not have another chance."

Dela shook her head, stubborn. She was not going to let him do this. Not now, no matter how much it hurt.

"Hari, no. He must have been waiting for you at the Dirt Market. Think about it. He wanted the box. He wanted *you*. This isn't over. This is just the beginning."

Dela knew she was right. This was not over. Not for Hari, and not for her.

Something passed through his face; a spasm, a trembling in his firm lips. For a moment, she was sure he would refuse, that she would find herself flung down, but then, slowly, carefully, he nodded.

Shaken, Dela pressed her forehead against his cheek and brushed her lips against the corner of his mouth. She could not guess what this was costing him.

"Thank you," she breathed, humbled. "Thank you for trusting me."

Dela heard clapping, and glanced over her shoulder. The Magi was smiling, applauding like a particularly smarmy wind-up monkey.

"A wonderful performance. Quite touching, considering the length of time you've been acquainted. And to think, I actually believed you did not like men."

"You're not a man," she said, thankful for her strong, sure voice. Her body felt like jelly. Hari helped untangle her limbs from his body, displaying gentleness completely at odds with the anger she felt sieving through his pores. His tenuous control, balanced on a razor's edge.

The Magi smirked. "That is not what Hari's sister said."

Dela almost forgot her own warnings, overcome with revulsion and the sudden desire to beat the Magi's brains to pulp. Instead, she clutched Hari's hand, eyeing the rapid pulse below the shape-shifter's locked jaw. If Hari committed any violence, there would be no hiding—not with so many witnesses, not with such a memorable face and form. Nor would the American government be any help—Hari simply did not exist yet. The Chinese legal system would never let him go.

Hari met her gaze, and she let him see her anger and grief, a sympathetic twin to his own apparent heartbreak. Emotion roared in his eyes and then was gone, drawn behind determination. He looked at the Magi.

"I thought you were dead," he said, unlocking his jaw. Dela heard it pop, crack. His voice was terrible to hear, low and visceral. "Dust to the ages. It was one of my few pleasures, but even that . . . even that you deny me. How many did you sacrifice in order to survive?"

Hari might have asked the time of day for all the reaction he received. The Magi tilted his head. "Would you believe me if I said none at all?"

"No."

The Magi smiled. "I am not here to fight you, Hari. Not yet, anyway."

Again, something slid against Dela's mental shields: thick, oily, persistent.

"Stop it," she snapped, unconcerned if she revealed herself. Hari suspected, and it was clear the Magi already knew and was testing her. She hated the feel of his mind, prying at the surface of her own like a thick crowbar. He made her feel dirty.

The Magi chuckled. "You are a very interesting young woman. A surprise, and I encounter few of those. Did you know, Hari, that your new mistress is herself a Magicker?"

The term was unfamiliar to Dela, but she could guess its meaning. Hari did not seem to care. "Leave her be, Magi. Do not even think of harming her."

"Or what?" His teeth were too white, sharp. They seemed to click when he spoke.

"Or I will kill you." It was a soft promise that made Dela shiver.

The Magi laughed, holding out elegant brown hands, fingers curled like claws. "You will do that anyway, Hari. But not today, in front of so many strangers. Not with so much left to do. No, no. Your mistress is right. Today, you and I will talk."

Dela glanced around; no one seemed to be paying attention to the substance of their conversation, though several elderly Chinese men grouped against the glass railing were watching avidly, whispering to each other.

Fine entertainment, as long as no one pokes out any eyes or plays tug-of-war with entrails.

"Talk." Hari's lip curled. "What could we possibly say to one another? You broke your oath, murdered my sister and her unborn child, and condemned me to spend eternity as a slave." He threw back his head, his throat working convulsively. A strangled gasp passed his lips. "You are a fool to show your face, but to expect more? Insanity."

The Magi glided close. It was disconcerting watching him, his shoulders relaxed, his smile lazy. His eyes betrayed him, though—they were cold glass, sharp and bright, completely unafraid. Even with Hari at her side, Dela felt isolated under that gaze, vulnerable. She had escaped this man once before, but looking into his face, she wondered if she had been lucky—if simple surprise had been her only savior.

Dela searched his body with her mind, seeking steel, any kind of metal. She found nothing. He was completely unarmed. No less dangerous, though—she remembered his strength, his inhuman rage. The hollow void of his eyes. He frightened her, and she did not trust him. Not one bit.

"I have been searching for you, Hari," said the Magi softly. "For nearly two thousand years I have walked the earth, hoping to tell you this: I am sorry. I was a different man then. Time has taught me the error of my ways."

To anyone else he might have sounded as sincere as the Dalai Lama, but Dela could taste his deceit like a squirming worm in her mouth.

"Bullshit," she said, angry. She felt Hari stir, but refused to look at him, instead staring deep into the Magi's frightening eyes. A deep calm descended over her mind. "Why are you really here?"

He did not try to pretend. His contrite mask evaporated like a noxious fume. A horrible, startling, trans-formation. "Can't you read me?" he asked, tapping his forehead, his smile sly.

"Do not speak to him," Hari warned. "Do not tell him your name, do not stare too long into his eyes. Any-thing you give him, he will use against you. He is a master manipulator."

The Magi lay a hand over his heart. "I am a survivor, Hari. Just like you. Perhaps our methods differ, but in the end, we are still both animals. Ruled by instinct, hunger—" He looked at Dela. "—lust."

Hari's muscles bunched, and again Dela squeezed his hand. The Magi's smile widened, and he said something in a musical language she did not understand. Hari stiff-ened, and a moment later spat out a tangle of incompre-hensible words.

"Oh, he likes you," said the Magi, once again turning his cool gaze on Dela. "How very interesting."

Hari tucked Dela behind him. She began to protest, but one look at his face and the words died on her tongue. This time, it was Hari who squeezed her hand, a gentle fleeting pressure, warm and solid.

"Say what you must," Hari said, his voice low, rough. "I am tired of these games. I can ignore you just as eas-ily as I can fight you."

"You were always a terrible liar." The Magi tilted his head. "There is too much history between us, Hari. Too much blood and pain. We are the tragedies myths are made of, bound together until some final end. You can no more ignore me than you can die."

"Very dramatic," Dela said, peeking around Hari's arm. "Do you have a point?"

The Magi's smile was fleeting, forced. "Indeed. I have a task for Hari. If he completes it, I will set him free."

"Only my skin can set me free." Hari narrowed his eyes. "Or so you told me, once upon a time."

"I have your skin. Help me, and I will return it."

Dela stifled a gasp as Hari threw back his head; his bark of laughter was sharp and cold, so cold. "I would rather remain a slave than help you. Oathbreaker. Murderer. I will have nothing to do with you, unless it is to cut your throat."

Something tightened in the Magi's eyes, a bright cruel hunger. "A life for a life, Hari. Was that so hard a bargain?"

"The kind a devil might make," Dela said.

The Magi's careful mask fractured. Real anger contorted the fine lines of his face, which suddenly appeared hollow, sunken: a breathing cadaver. Dela again smelled garlic, the spice of hot pepper. The Magi shook his head, backing away. Profound menace shadowed his eyes.

"I am done," he said softly. "Remember this day, Hari. You as well, mistress. I tried pleasantries. I should have stayed with pain." He looked at Dela. "I would have asked you for the box. I am sure you can guess how I will claim it now."

Hari growled, but Dela shook her head. "Bite me."

A cold smile, full of teeth. "I just might."

For a man who purportedly possessed the power to screw with reality, the Magi's departure was decidedly ordinary. Without a backward glance, he strolled down the corridor past a crowded Starbucks, and pushed open the great glass doors that led out to the taxi circle.

A strangled cry spilled from Hari's throat, and he began running after the Magi. The shape-shifter moved incredibly fast—a golden-eyed inferno—and Dela tried to follow, dodging startled shoppers left reeling in his wake.

The Magi, halfway through the doors, glanced over his shoulder and smiled. He raised his hand.

Dela screamed as something hard impacted her stomach. Crippling pain contorted her body. She crashed to the floor as claws raked the insides of her ribs, cutting bone.

Through blurred vision, she saw the Magi make his escape; it seemed to her that his shoulders were hunched, his arms wrapped over his own belly.

Strangers touched her. Dela wanted them gone, away, all those unfamiliar hands and voices, pressing against her useless body. And then Hari was there, pushing everyone aside, scooping her up into his strong warm arms. He said her name, but she could not make herself answer.

Darkness swallowed her.

DELA DREAMED, BUT HER DREAMS WERE ORDINARY, without secrets from the future. A tiger ate a chocolate bar, and she was dressed like Alice in Wonderland, perched cross-legged on a spotted mushroom, trying to outwit an evil, grinning caterpillar. Dela was just thinking of a witty comeback to the caterpillar's insulting remarks about her slug-shaped dancing shoes when she woke up.

Disoriented, eyelids gummy, it took her a moment to realize she was in bed.

In bed, tucked against a warm body, a heavy arm draped across her waist.

Dela inhaled the light, indefinable aroma of forest after heavy rain, which barely masked the scent of leather, man. Hari. Not that she had expected anyone else. His weight around her body was unexpectedly comfortable. Soothing. She was afraid to move; she did not want him to pull away. He made her feel safe, a precious gift after a most unsettling day.

She must have twitched—or perhaps her breathing changed. Hari stirred, carefully rolling from her. Dela caught his hand, but she did not look at him. Instead, she tugged Hari close, entwining his fingers in her own until he spooned against her back. His breath warmed her neck, and she sighed.

"Are you well?" he asked quietly, his voice low, rumbling from his chest.

"Better," she said. "I've never fainted before."

"The Magi sent his powers into your body. I think you made him angry. That, and you were a fine distraction."

Dela remembered her fleeting glimpse of Hari's anguish, and fought down a shudder of regret. "You could have gone after him."

"No," he said. "I could not leave you."

"The curse."

"No," he said again. "You."

Again she sighed, snuggling deeper into his warmth. "What happened after I passed out?"

"I brought you here. You were unconscious, but shivering. So cold. I could not seem to warm you, so I thought to use my own body in addition to the blankets. I hope you do not mind."

"I don't," she said. Boy, did she not mind. "And you're really sure that was the Magi, even after all these years?"

"Yes." Hari went very still with that one word. Dela tensed.

"I'm sorry," she said. "Sorry he's still alive, sorry you had to see him . . . sorry I stopped you. I must have seemed cruel."

Hari's chest rose and fell against her back. "Yes, Delilah. At first you did seem cruel. I wanted nothing more than to tear out his throat with my bare hands. I wanted to lap his blood. Taste his death. An old dream."

He sighed then, and it was a weary sound, ancient and sour. "But you were right. It was neither the time nor the place for my revenge." Dela felt him shake his head, heard soft laughter, full of bitter surprise. "You are . . . remarkable, Delilah. You made me listen to reason. Reason, in the middle of a true blood-rage. I do not know what you were thinking. No one comes between a tiger and his prey."

"Ignorance is bliss."

This time there was more warmth in his quiet laughter, and Dela felt it from the top of her head all the way down to her toes. She drank in the sound; with it, a memory, carried on the back of his voice.

"The Magi," she said slowly, trying to remember, to puzzle out the nagging inconsistencies. "Why didn't he use his powers on me at the Dirt Market? Why didn't he try to force the old woman to sell him the box? If he's really so powerful, why would he hold himself back, especially over something so important?"

"He still hurt you," Hari pointed out. "But you are right. Despite the harm he caused, his powers seem to have diminished. That, or he has learned caution."

Dela shuddered, recalling the feel of sharp fingers in her guts. "Caution, maybe—but if that's diminished, I don't think I want to know what he's like at full strength."

Hari's arms tightened. "You must understand, Delilah—when I first encountered the Magi, his might was such he could make the air burn with just his fists. If he did not concentrate on withholding his powers, he could not rest his hands on wood or cloth without setting it on fire. For that very reason, he lived in a cave and slept naked on a bed carved of stone."

"Nifty," she muttered, remembering heat, the touch of the Magi's skin. Comprehension made her gasp. "Wait. Is that how your chest was burned? Did he hurt you with just his hands?"

"Yes," Hari said. His arms tightened. "His fingers were the tools."

"Maybe I shouldn't have stopped you."

"No. A good hunter chooses the time and place. I will have another chance, now that I know he wants me back." Quiet revulsion tainted his voice, a low shudder of hate and bewilderment.

Now that I know he wants me back.

"But for what?" Dela asked. "It doesn't make sense, not after all these years. I'm sorry, Hari, but you'd think he would have forgotten you by now." *And just what do you know about psychotic sorcerers? Nothing, nada, zip. You're a babe in the woods.*

"I do not know, Delilah. Discovering he survived is terrible enough. That he wishes to become my master . . . intolerable."

Intolerable indeed. The idea of that cold-eyed awful man holding anyone's life in his hands made Dela want to run screaming for the hills. That, or go all Pompeii on his ass.

"How did he find us?" she asked. "I'm sure he didn't follow me to the hotel, and he doesn't know my name."

She felt Hari shrug, as though to say, "Magic." Dela, however, was not entirely comfortable chalking up the Magi's successes to simple power. Anyone who needed to use bad pickup lines to kidnap a woman was running low on *some* kind of cylinder.

"Be grateful he does not know your name," Hari said.

"I was careful not to use it in front of him. Your name might have given him power over you."

"How?"

"Familiarity. When you know a person's true name, it opens a crack into their life, into their mind. Your name is not what you are, but it is what you are called, and that is a profound knowledge to have over another."

"You gave me your name," Dela said.

"You were the first person to ask in a long while."

She sensed there was more to it than that, but she didn't feel like prying, not if she wasn't ready to hear the answers.

Her hand felt dwarfed in his loose grip. She freed her fingers and stroked the elegant bones of his wrist, watching the play of shadows against his skin. Surreal, being held by Hari, but she liked it too much to pull away. Perhaps it was the intensity of their shared experiences, her flight into his mind, but all her earlier hesitations were fleeing. She wanted to touch him. She wanted to be touched. His presence felt safe, familiar as home.

"He called you a Magicker," Hari said, after several minutes of comfortable silence. His lips grazed the tip of Dela's ear. She shivered. "I have also sensed your power."

Uneasiness replaced pleasure. *Guess it was too much to hope he would forget.*

"I suppose the Magi is also a Magicker?" she asked.

Hari nodded, solemn.

"It's complicated," she warned, still reluctant. Of course, Hari was a self-proclaimed shape-shifting warrior who had spent the past two thousand years imprisoned in a box. He could probably handle complicated. He could probably handle just about anything.

"If you do not wish to speak of it . . ."

But that was not an option. If she and Hari were truly stuck with each other, he had to know the truth.

"It's not that," she said. "What I do runs in my family, but it's not magic. Not magic like you, anyway."

"I suppose that is a matter of perspective," Hari said, and Dela wondered fleetingly if he wasn't right.

"The simple explanation is that I—we—can do things with our minds. My brother, for example, reads thoughts. If other people are weak or inclined to accept what Max is putting in their heads, he can manipulate, or encourage visions and beliefs."

"I can imagine the temptation for abuse."

Dela was not offended. "It's very serious. Even before our powers manifested, Mom and Dad raised us to adhere to strict rules of privacy and ethics. We couldn't get away with anything. My mother can read auras, while my grandmother is a pre-cog—sometimes she can see the future. Non-intrusive gifts, but because the power seems to change from generation to generation, my parents knew the possibility existed. They wanted to make sure we were raised responsibly."

"Can you also read minds?" Hari's voice was soft, unafraid. Dela slowly exhaled, tension draining from her limbs.

"No," she said. "I have good instincts for people, and sometimes I dream of the future, but my real talent is with metal. I don't know how or why, but it just . . . speaks to me. Besides being able to manipulate metal in subtle ways, I can always sense its components, its age. If a particular person has handled it long enough, I can hear that individual's echo—an imprint—and I can see the story of the metal. What it has been used for, where it has been. That doesn't happen often; it takes time for those energies to accumulate."

"My knives," Hari said thoughtfully. "They told you a story."

"Yes." Her palm still ached.

"What did you see?"

"Blood," she whispered. "Death. But that was the blade itself. I also felt you, and your echo was so angry, so lonely and sad. You carried such regret for all the lives you had taken."

"I have done terrible things in my life, Delilah. It is true I committed them against my will, but the stain is still there. I have killed and killed, for days without end. I have lived the nightmare."

"I know," she said softly.

"And still, after all you have seen, you do not turn away from me. Why?" There was such pain in his voice—pain, and a desperate longing. For what, she did not know. Forgiveness? Acceptance?

Dela rolled over in Hari's arms so she could see his eyes. She pressed her palm against his rough cheek. "At the core of you burns a pure bright flame, and it is made of kindness. That's why I can't turn away, why I'm not afraid."

"I do not feel kind," he said.

"But you are," she responded.

Hari kissed her palm. "I do not understand you, Delilah."

Dela smiled. "I'm not entirely sure I understand you, either, and I've been inside the shadow of your soul. Kooky, huh? Guess we're just stuck with mystery."

Hari did not look as though he minded. He traced her lips with the pad of his thumb, and Dela closed her eyes.

"I need your permission," he whispered.

"Tell me something first," she said, and it was difficult to speak. "Why your change of heart? Why don't you hate me anymore?"

He looked embarrassed. "I tried not to trust you. I did not want to like you. Hate has always been safe, Delilah. I have been hurt so much it is easier to assume the worst."

"But?"

He sighed. "But I am not a broken man, and everything you have done—your actions and words—has reminded me of that. I have not believed in anything for a very long time, Delilah, but I think I am beginning to believe in you."

It was the most profound compliment anyone had ever paid her, but there was something else in his voice that made her go very still.

"You're still waiting for me to slip up, aren't you?"

"Part of me expects it," he said. "An old habit, born of experience."

Hari's words hurt, but she was not surprised. His persistent doubts only made her more stubborn, more determined to prove him wrong and end the betrayal.

"It's a good thing you're used to disappointment," she said.

Hari smiled. "My lady. Your permission?"

"You have it," she said.

He kissed her. Gentle, tentative—a feather-soft brushing of lips. His tenderness was excruciating. Dela reached for him, pulling herself close until she lay flush against his hard body. Touching him felt so good.

"Delilah," he murmured, his breathing ragged. She was pleased he looked as dazed as she felt. "We cannot become distracted . . . there is too much danger now. The Magi will attempt to gain control of the box and kill you . . . and there are your other assassins. . . ."

"You sure know how to destroy the mood." Dela glowered, but his eyes were gentle, and she burrowed her face against his chest. Hari wrapped his arms around her, burying his fingers in her hair. He felt large and warm, safe. But the world itself was not safe, and she thought about the Magi, the man who had tortured Hari—who had tried to kidnap her, and then sunk his mental fingers into her flesh.

"How did the Magi stay alive all these years?" Dela wondered out loud. "If his powers have diminished, do you think he somehow drained himself in return for longevity?"

Strange, hearing such odd talk come out of her mouth, though in some ways, it didn't seem much worse than discussing telepathy and clairvoyance with her friends at the agency. She supposed it all depended on what a person was used to—and she was becoming used to quite a lot.

"I wish I knew, Delilah. I am embarrassed by my ignorance. All these years I should have tried to learn something, but I was so focused on the present, on each command, resisting my masters to keep from being broken . . ."

He stopped. Dela wanted to ask him more about his past, but held her tongue. There was too much emotion in Hari's voice. She felt uncomfortable pressing him.

"Hari," she asked instead, "why didn't the Magi summon you after he placed you in the box?"

The question seemed to take him off guard, and he thought carefully before answering.

"I do not know. He inscribed the curse on my chest, and then—darkness. Darkness, followed by light. My first summons, by a king who wanted nothing more than the deaths of his stepsons. I did not know why I was there, what had happened—only, I was compelled to follow the king's orders. I could not escape him, and I tried, Delilah. I tried so hard. Later, I found someone to read the words inscribed upon my body. Like you, I found them incomprehensible. It was a bewildering time, frightening because I had no control, and every summons was to a new place, new customs, living under the whim of unpredictable, often cruel individuals. I was never safe. No one around me was safe."

What would it be like, forced to murder, unable to control your actions, ever? Torture.

Dela chewed on her lip. "It doesn't make sense. You'd think the Magi would have retained control from the start, kept you as a trophy or his own personal whipping boy. On the other hand, I've also been wondering why you weren't just passed down from one master to another, constantly summoned within a particular family."

"*That* I can answer," Hari said, with a wry twist to his lips. "I am a slave, Delilah, and so I must be purchased by anyone who wishes to summon me. I, too, used to wonder why I was not simply summoned again and again. That part of the curse was not written down. Perhaps it was even unintended. It took me some time to understand. My masters, fortunately, never did. They must have believed my ability to serve was for one person only, and the box was either given away, stolen, or sold—upon which time the cycle began again. Assuming the new owner even bothered to open the box."

"Bought and sold," Dela murmured. Hari frowned, and she said, "That's what the old woman told me. She wouldn't even let me touch the box until I paid her money."

Hari made a soft sound. "She knew what she was selling."

"And the Magi was aware she had it. I wonder how long he waited there, trying to convince her to sell you to him."

"I am surprised she did not claim me for herself."

Dela snorted. "And here you thought *everyone* wanted your body."

"Most do," he said, and Dela laughed, lightly smacking him on the chest. Hari held her close and kissed her cheek.

Something tight unwound in Dela's stomach, a warm flush of comfort, but she still had one last question.

"Will you ever trust me?" she asked. Hari's smile faded.

"I trust you," he said gravely. "My heart has been broken one too many times, but I am willing to try again, to trust."

"Thank you," she whispered. "Because we're in this together."

"That is good," he said. "I am tired of being alone."

The phone rang, startling Dela. Hari, too, jerked with surprise. Dela rubbed his arm. "It's okay," she assured him, though really, it wasn't. She did not want to answer the phone. She wanted to pretend the world beyond did not exist—that no one could harm them, and they could press against each other and talk, talk and kiss, and express their newfound trust.

Dela answered the phone. It was her brother, Max.

"I hear someone's trying to kill you." Machine gun-fire punctuated his words.

"Back at you," she said, wincing as somewhere near, a man screamed. "Is this the best time to call?"

"Only time. After this, things get really hairy. I just wanted to let you know I'll be home in a week or so. Try to stay alive until then."

"Worry about yourself. I still can't believe you got talked into a team project."

"I'll be fine. Oh, uh, gotta go. Love—"

Click.

Dela stared at the phone. What a nice, normal family. She reset the receiver, and rolled back into Hari's arms. And what a day.

"My brother," Dela explained to Hari.

"Is he a soldier of some kind?" Hari asked. "I heard fighting."

"You've got good hearing. And no, he's not much of a soldier, though he is good in a fight."

The only light came from the bathroom, leaving Hari's angular face half-bathed in shadow. He closed his eyes, and Dela was reminded of a large cat, meditating on cat-like things. She watched him for a time, lost to awe and strange twists of fate, and managed—for a moment, just a moment—to forget things like danger and deception and magic.

Her stomach growled, and Hari opened one eye.

"Sorry," Dela said sheepishly. "I guess I'm hungry."

"We should eat. Do you feel well enough to sit up?"

"To be honest, I forgot I was hurt." Dela grinned, and Hari shared her smile with a heat that made her scalp shiver.

He helped her sit up, slinging one strong arm around her shoulders. She barely had to use her own strength; he carefully watched her face for any signs of discomfort. Dela breathed long and deep; her ribs and stomach did not ache. Still, memory: sharp fingers inside her body, digging against bone, clutching flesh. Her breath caught.

"Delilah."

"It's nothing," she said. "Just a bad memory."

Hari remained silent, but his eyes were dark and

knowing. With one long arm, he reached around her for the room service menu on the bed stand. Dela stared at it for a moment, caught between fear and longing.

"I still haven't taken you on that walk I promised," she said, deciding to jump into the void. "There's a lot of world outside this hotel you should see."

"It is too dangerous," Hari said, glancing across the room out the window. Night had fallen; the lights of the city twinkled silver, dashed with a rainbow of neon.

"Even this room is dangerous," Dela said, desperate for fresh air, for something more than four walls, caught like a mouse in a trap. "No place is safe. Not now."

"You are reckless," Hari told her, but without malice. He brushed the back of his hand against her cheek. Dela's smile felt tremulous, and he sighed. "All right. We will go for a walk, and our meal."

They stood from the bed, and while Hari used the bathroom, Dela turned on some lamps, and the television.

"I must apologize," he said, when he returned. "When I carried you back to the room, I left behind all the clothing you bought me."

"I figured that. I'm not sure how I would have felt if you'd had the presence of mind to remember your shopping bags at a time of crisis."

He began to reply, but noticed the images on the television. Dela explained the concept, and began flipping stations. *Gladiator* was playing on the hotel's movie channel, and Hari leaned close as Maximus appeared in the coliseum.

"Rome?" he asked, eyes intense upon the scene playing out before him.

Dela blinked, reminded once again of Hari's strange life. "A re-enactment of Rome; a play, a story."

"Except, very lifelike." Hari watched, troubled, as the gladiatorial games began. "I see some differences, but it is much the same. I was there, Delilah, early on in my captivity. I was quite popular in the arena, but my master made too many enemies with his gambling, and was gutted in his home."

He hesitated, still staring at the screen. "I do not know how much time passed, but by my next summons, the Goths and other barbarian tribes had begun to invade Rome. My master was the emperor himself, Valens. He was desperate for some good fortune. When he summoned me, I acted as his bodyguard, but most often fought with his army. We were finally defeated at Adrianople by the Goths, who attacked our flank while we were concentrating on some Visigoths. It was a terrible battle. So much blood. The ground was slippery with it. My master died. I returned to the box." He finally looked at Dela, the skin pulled tight around his mouth. "The irony is that my next master was a Goth. He did not live long, either."

Hari did not want to watch any more television. They went to dinner.

Night cast a cool breeze over the city. They ambled from the hotel down the wide sidewalk running parallel to Jianguomenwai, the main road leading to Tianamen Square and the Forbidden City. Under the giant towers of their hotel and the trade center, the neon glittering signs of Häagen-Dazs and KFC lit their faces in shades of imported red, white, and gold. Cars raced illegally down the wide bicycle lane beside them, honking and veering. The air smelled like grease and exhaust. Hari scrunched up his nose, clearly unimpressed by certain aspects of the modern age.

Bad smells, however, could not prevent Hari from

observing his new surroundings with acute, awe-stricken interest, and he asked careful questions about everything he saw. Skyscrapers, vehicles, roads, politics, culture—nothing was off limits. He was hungry for knowledge, and Dela felt an exhilarating rush as she talked to him, explaining her world.

But there were some things that remained unforgettable.

"I still do not feel comfortable with this walk," Hari said, for what felt to Dela like the hundredth time. He watched, through narrowed eyes, everyone near them. "It is not safe, Delilah. There are two different groups of people who want to hurt you."

"Thanks for reminding me," Dela groused, although since leaving the hotel room she had been scanning everyone near them for suspicious amounts of metal—anything that sang of gun or blade. It was tiring work, opening herself to so many. She felt a headache coming on as rings and watches gossiped in her mind, a golden wedding band revealing a particularly sordid story involving cucumbers and whipped cream.

Less than a mile from the hotel, Dela led Hari down a well-lit alley to a little restaurant she had found earlier in the week. The kitchen itself, a tiny space the size of a closet with glass for walls, sat beside the front entrance. Every diner had a perfect view of the frantic cook, a slender man surrounded by steaming pots and greasy pans, his delicate hands flashing like pale knives.

Almost every seat was occupied, but Dela and Hari found a table in the far corner under a rasping air conditioner. The shape-shifter managed to fold his body into a chair that was much too small, even by Dela's standards. He reminded her of an elephant—or rather, a tiger—perched on a bar stool.

Over the clamor of loud diners and slamming pots and dishes, Hari and Dela talked about food. Hari was, at first, tentative about his choices, and not simply because the food was unfamiliar. It seemed to Dela that the novelty of not being deliberately starved hadn't yet worn off.

They finally agreed on steamed dumplings: shrimp, tofu, and pork. As the pimply waitress shuffled away, Dela caught Hari sizing up everyone in the restaurant. He faced the entrance, his back to the grease-stained cracked wall, his wide shoulders blocking much of Dela's view. When she tried to move her chair to see the kitchen, he shifted, angling her closer to the wall. She realized, then, that he was shielding her.

"I don't want you to get hurt protecting me," she told him.

Hari raised an eyebrow. "If that were completely true, we would not be out in public."

"Ouch," she said. Hari held up his hand.

"I have insulted you, and that was not my intention. Simply put, Delilah, I cannot die. You can. It is logical you would assume I would protect you with my body."

Dela stared, open-mouthed with dismay. She wanted to protest, to get angry, but she thought very carefully about what he had said. Had she really been so thoughtless, so selfish? Had she truly taken Hari's new protectiveness for granted?

Yes, and yes.

"I'm so sorry," she breathed, profoundly ashamed. She could barely stand to look at him.

"*I* am not sorry," Hari said, and his voice was as soft and firm as his gaze. "You trust me to protect your life, and that trust is a gift. Do you understand, Delilah? You have faith in me. It never crossed your mind to ask if I was willing—you trusted me to take care of you."

"That doesn't make me feel better, Hari. I abused your trust. You suffer the same as everyone else and I don't want you hurt. I promised you that, and I've gone and broken my promise."

"You've broken nothing," he said, "Pain is a small thing, compared to the alternative." When she opened her mouth to protest, he stopped her with the gentle press of his finger against her lips. "No, Delilah. You have no idea what it means to me, what it is like to be allowed the freedom of choice—to be trusted enough to be given that freedom. My life was a series of commands until I met you. Commands to obey, to protect. Commands, because no one trusted my free will. And my masters were right not to trust me. I would have betrayed them—and I did, when I had the chance. But you do not think like that. You assume I will do the right thing. You assume I am good."

"You are a good man."

"You are the first to say so in two thousand years," he said. "You are the first to believe. That is an honor worth any pain. Worth even death."

"No," she said.

"Yes," he said. "If you trust me enough with your life, Delilah, then trust me to tell you my true feelings. I want to protect you, and the only way you will stop me is with a command."

Hari's golden eyes were fierce, and he cupped her face in his large hands, kissing her forehead. Chaste, and yet a warm tingle rushed down Dela's spine to her toes.

"You're going to make me cry," she said.

"Then cry," he said, and kissed her again, this time on the lips.

Their food arrived: three bamboo steamers full of dumplings. Hari surprised Dela by being quite proficient with chopsticks; apparently, it had been the utensil of choice in many of his summons. He seemed quite relieved, and Dela watched him polish off his dumplings with a single-minded intensity that made her grin. He looked up in time to catch her smile, and asked a question with his eyes.

"It's nothing," she said, and then, "I think I like watching you eat."

It was a strange thing to say; she knew it the moment the words passed her lips, but it was too late. Embarrassed, she waited for his response.

Hari gestured toward her plate, still half full. His meaning was clear, and Dela looked away, shaking her head and smiling. Hari leaned close, large and fierce, but with a strangely tender light in his eyes that was utterly mesmerizing. Dela forgot how to speak as he picked up a dumpling and lifted it to her mouth. He brushed the pearly dough against her lips.

"Eat, Delilah. Let *me* watch *you*." His voice was low, sensual; she felt his breath warm her face, wrapping her in delicious folds of air and power. Dela loved hearing her full name roll off Hari's tongue. He made it sound exotic, sexy. The kind of name that belonged to a woman who poured herself into silk loincloths and bejeweled bras. Not sweats and old flannel shirts.

Dela opened her mouth and took a bite of dumpling. Meaty juices from the filling ran down her chin. Mortified, she began to wipe away the grease. Hari caught her wrist. He leaned forward and licked her chin. His tongue was firm, careful, and utterly erotic. Dela had no idea having her face licked by a man could be such a turn-on, although she suspected the low-level inferno blazing through her belly had more to do with the man himself than the technique.

She stifled a moan as Hari pressed his lips against the corner of her mouth, and she opened herself to him, searching for the sweet comfort of his kiss, burying herself in the delicious, heady sensation of her mouth joined with his, making love with nothing but the lips and tongue.

When he pulled away, she caught glimpses of people staring, their expressions a mixture of outrage, embarrassment, and interest. The restaurant was very quiet.

They paid the bill and left. It was late, but neither of them felt tired. When they entered the mall below the hotel, Dela pulled Hari into Starbucks—the same one they had gone careening past earlier that day. She forced herself to look at the patch of floor where she remembered collapsing, facing down the fear her memories resurrected. If going for a walk and dinner had been one act of defiance, then this was another: Dela was not going to let the Magi—or anyone else—rule her life with terror.

The coffee shop was filled with young foreigners and locals, all trying to act super cool while sipping their lattes. Classical music played softly over the speakers. Dela ordered a mango frappuccino. Hari, understandably, had no preference, so she got him hot chocolate. Cats, milk, and all that.

Her drink was in a clear plastic cup, sweetly perspiring. Golden, chunky with ice. Tasty. She smacked her lips around the straw as the two of them found a small table in the corner where they could sit with their backs to the wall. Dela sent out a trail of thought, scanning for weapons. She found nothing, but kept her mind open for the hint of anything that could be knife or gun.

Go back to your room, she told herself. *Take the drinks and go. It will be safer.*

But no. Stupid, selfish—maybe Dela was all of those things for wanting to stay out—but if she began running now, hiding, then what good would she be? Just another victim, cowering.

Hari sipped his hot chocolate with reserve.

"Well?" she asked. He shook his head, a faint smile on his lips.

"It is very good." He drank some more, watching the flow of the murmuring crowd. Dela idly tapped her cup on the smooth tabletop, and Hari glanced at her with a question in his eyes.

"The Magi, I understand," she said, by way of explaining her thoughts, "but why anyone else would want to hurt me . . . or how they even managed to track me down . . ." She frowned, thinking carefully. "They must have gotten hold of my travel plans . . . but no, that doesn't make sense. I didn't write anything down, and the only people who knew where I would be staying were Adam, my parents, and my brother."

"Adam?"

"He's my assistant. He runs my gallery, contacts my suppliers—everything I don't have time for. He's actually from China. Adam immigrated to the United States around five years ago. I was one of his first employers."

"You trust him?"

"Absolutely. The crazy knife guy didn't find me through him or my family. Which means they either tracked my credit card or have a contact in the Chinese government, someone who could trace my passport number when I checked into the hotel." Dela dug into her purse and pulled out her little blue passport. She showed it to Hari. "I'm getting you one of these. It's the only way you can move freely between countries. In China, it's especially important. If you want to stay at hotels like the one we're at, you have to register, give them your identity number."

"In my time, when a man wanted to travel, all he needed to concern himself with were bandits, hunger, and disease."

"Thrilling. I prefer shuffling paper, if it's all right by you."

Hari inclined his head. "It was not such a hardship for shape-shifters. As a tiger, I could cover great distances. Food was plentiful. No one ever tried to harm me."

"Gee, I wonder why." Dela frowned. "How did you carry your weapons and clothes when you shape-shifted?"

Hari smiled. "Clothes are so very human, Delilah. Shape-shifters have very little use for them. As for my weapons, I did not acquire those—or my clothing—until after my first summons. By that time, shape-shifting was no longer a possibility. I had to learn how to live as a full human."

Ah. Hari's comfort with his nudity suddenly made sense.

"Okay," she said, after a moment spent contemplating a naked Hari running through the jungle, "so when you were still a full shape-shifter, where did you travel?"

"Everywhere." His eyes grew distant with memory. "Sometimes I visited neighboring clans—I did so more frequently as I grew older, looking for a mate—but often I traveled by myself, simply exploring. Going places where men had not yet trod."

Dela imagined Hari as a tiger, sleek and wild, traversing hidden worlds beneath the canopy of his forest home, traveling for no reason but simple curiosity. That and perhaps joy in his ability to do so.

"It sounds wonderful." She sighed, and then steeled herself for the question she had to ask, that had been nagging her for hours. "Did you . . . did you leave behind anyone special? Like a . . . a mate?"

Hari shook his head. "I never found anyone who suited me. Just before my sister was taken, I considered traveling farther south into the great jungles, to see what other clans I could find."

"I suppose if you had found someone, it would make your predicament much worse."

"Yes," he agreed, pinning her with his heavy gaze, as surely as if he had used his hands. "Shape-shifters mate for life."

"Oh," she said weakly, unable to understand why that particular revelation made her stomach flutter wildly. She wanted to ask him if his preferences were species-specific, but that was too much. Crazy, insane. Besides, weren't his kisses answer enough? And why did it suddenly matter so much? Idiot. One make-out session and she was losing her mind! But, no, she'd begun losing her mind the minute Hari appeared in her hotel room. The next time she told herself to embrace possibility, she was going to have to remember not to embrace *all* possibilities.

Hari swallowed, opened his mouth to say more, and abruptly froze. Lifting his chin, he cast his gaze around the scattered tables, sniffing carefully. He tilted his head, and muscles moved in his shoulders and neck, liquid smooth and graceful. She could see the tiger in his eyes, his exotic face, and could not bear to look away.

"What is it?"

"I thought I sensed another like me. A shape-shifter." His voice was hushed, strained.

"A shape-shifter?" Dela rose from her chair. "We should go look."

And they did, but only for a short time. Hari caught scent of something wild and familiar, but the trail—which led in a short circle around the hotel—petered out at the end of a service alley.

Hari stared at the wall in front of him, the end of the concrete path. There was no way out but up.

"Wings?" Dela asked. Hari nodded, his expression bereft.

They returned to their room.

The phone was ringing when Dela opened the door, and she dashed to answer it, hoping she wasn't going to hear some ominous voice whispering, *"I'm gonna kill you!"* on the other end.

But it was Adam, and he sounded almost as uneasy as she felt. Dela checked the clock. It was early morning on the U.S. west coast.

"I am so sorry to call you, Dela, but there is a man here in my home. He says he is supposed to watch out for me. He will not explain why, and he will not leave. When I threatened to call the police, he said to call you."

Dela sighed. Hari watched her face as he tried unsuccessfully to unbutton his shirt. Scowling, he finally pulled it over his head, popping several buttons in the process.

Oh, well. I have to buy him new clothes anyway.

Dela found herself staring at Hari's body, and shook her head to clear the libidinous cobwebs. "Adam, I did ask someone to check on you. I've been receiving some . . . threats, and I wanted to make sure you were okay."

"Threats?" He sounded appalled. "What kinds of threats?"

"Don't worry about it. Is that man nearby? Let me talk to him."

There was a moment of silence, and then someone who had an even sweeter voice than Adam coughed lightly into the phone. "This is Eddie, ma'am. Roland sent me."

Must be new. She hadn't met Eddie yet.

"I guessed that. Why, however, are you scaring Adam? I was hoping for something more discreet."

"Ma'am, Roland told me this is a high-priority job, and that the safety of you, your friends, and your establishment create a non-negotiable situation in which I, and my colleagues, are allowed full authority over certain aspects of your personal security."

It was a long sentence, spoken very quickly, and so obviously rehearsed that Dela had to smile. "Tell me what Roland really said. Word for word."

A moment of silence. "Ma'am, I don't think that would be appropriate."

"Humor me."

"Ma'am."

"Eddie."

Eddie took a deep breath, clearly torn between following the implicit order in her voice, and a very good upbringing involving Words You Never Say in Front of Women.

"Ma'am, Roland said, and I quote: 'I don't care what you beeping have to do to keep her and her peeps beeping safe, but if it means acting like the Good Lord Jesus parting the beeping Red Sea, then you will part that beeping sea, or else a certain region of your lower anatomy will be mine on a beeping stick.'"

"Delilah?" Hari appeared from the bathroom, a towel flung over his shoulder. He was clearly concerned by the strange choking sounds she was making, as well as the deep crimson of her scrunched-up face. "Delilah, are you all right?"

She nodded weakly, but that one small movement made her dissolve into a helpless fit of giggles. Hari began to smile—clueless, but taken in by her mirth.

"Ma'am?" Eddie said. He sounded like he was grinning.

"Thank you," she finally gasped. "I think I understand your situation a little better now."

"Actually," he said, "I would never have approached Adam, except we found evidence that someone has been tampering with the locks of your home. There was no sign of actual entry—probably because your security system was designed by Blue—but we thought it might be safer if one of us stayed on the inside at all times."

Dela ground her teeth. "Eddie, can you do me a favor? After this conversation, I want you to purchase a plane ticket to Hawaii in Adam's name. Book the hotels, all that. Roland's expense account, of course. Tell Adam that if he refuses to go on vacation, he's fired."

"Yes, ma'am."

Dela liked the fact that Eddie didn't argue with her. "Does Roland have any idea who's doing this?"

"Ma'am, if he does, he hasn't informed us."

Typical. She gave Eddie a few more instructions, mostly along the lines of "don't kill anyone unless you have to," and hung up the phone with a sigh.

Hari watched her with a somewhat bemused expression on his face.

"What?" She stretched out on the bed. Her head hurt.

"You are very fierce," he said, approaching gracefully, some mysterious intent in his eyes. He tugged off her shoes and socks, fingers tracing the fine bones of her ankles. Dela's breath caught. Hari clasped her hand and pulled her from the bed, guiding her toward the bathroom. "You remind me of my people."

Hari sat her down on the toilet, and then bent over the tub, fussing with the water until it rose, steaming, into the quiet air. Dela felt very small. It was like seeing the *GQ* version of a human King Kong crammed inside a teeny gift box. He filled the entire bathroom, not just with muscle and bone, but with the ever-expanding vibrancy of his presence. Hari was so much bigger than his body, but his energy was profoundly comforting—not intimidating in the slightest.

Right now, she didn't quite understand what was going through his mind, but she trusted him enough not to question it.

And you aren't a girl who trusts many people.

"This was not the day you expected," said Hari gently, perched on the edge of the tub. He looked deep into her eyes, his gaze slightly hypnotic, and ran an elegant finger along her chin. Her body thrilled at his touch. "You need to rest, Delilah. Forget everything but yourself. Do not think of today or tomorrow. Think only of the water, warming your body."

The sound of his voice was soothing; her eyelids drooped. She felt safe in the glow of his presence, utterly at ease. The day's events slipped from her mind, and all she cared about was that Hari was with her. She was not alone, and for the first time in a long while, that was a good thing.

Maybe she had not known him long—maybe there was a lifetime of stories left untold, tempers fit to fire—but she knew enough. In her heart, in her head. Hari was the best man she had ever met. Frightening, wonderful. She did not want to contemplate heartbreak, or danger to life and limb. In that moment, the future did not matter. Stupid, maybe—but she did not care.

Hari pressed his lips against her forehead, brushed her mouth in a kiss. "Bathe," he whispered. "Rest. Think of nothing but that. I will check on you in a while."

He left her, and after a moment of quiet contemplation, Dela stripped and sank into the hot water. She did rest, Hari heavy in her thoughts, and when she eventually slept, she dreamed of Hari, too.

And the dream became a nightmare.

WHILE DELA BATHED, HARI MADE HIMSELF A BED on the floor in front of the room's main door. He arranged his sword beside the spare blanket, his knives near the pillow (a pillow, a blanket! luxury!). Everything within easy reach.

She might let you sleep in her bed.

The memory of Dela's body pressed flush against his own was enough to drive him wild, but he knew if he lay beside her, more than kisses would follow, and it would be too much too soon. For both of them.

Besides, her bed was far from the door. Anyone who wished Dela harm would have only this entrance to come through, and Hari would be waiting.

He was not quite sure when taking care of Dela had become more important to him than staying out of the box, but the day had been strange, and events—both inside and outside his heart—were moving too quickly to follow. It was enough he wanted to keep her safe—desperately so. Dela stirred him to feelings of tenderness he had not known he was capable of expressing. All those years of brutal torment . . . and still, he cared. The idea stunned him.

He remembered her slender body pressed against him; her voice, soft—her lips, silken and sweet. The overwhelming emotion stirred by her compassion, her words. Everything Hari knew of pleasuring women had been learned through degradation and slavery. He had never wanted to be with his summoners or their friends, but he had learned to please them in all the varied ways they wished. Learned because he had been ordered.

His embarrassment was still piercing—jeers echoing hollowly in his ears as he knelt between a woman's thighs, sliding into a dismal, sickening heat that was empty pleasure, a worthless effort requiring nothing but endurance. Endurance against degradation.

Not so with Dela. For the first time in his life, he desired. He wanted her, and it did not matter how or why. Her pleasure was paramount, her comfort and safety of supreme importance. And it was his heart, not just his body, wanting these things.

I am frightened. I do not know what to do. It is too much too soon.

Too much too soon. Just like the Magi.

The warmth Dela stirred in his mind disappeared. Hari recalled turning, turning, and suddenly the old nightmare was upon him, made flesh—*I promise you anything if you will not harm her or the child*—again and again—*a life for a life*—and his skull, so full of memory and rage, felt pushed through the head of a needle.

A vision—golden eyes set in a smiling face, long strong limbs dappled with sunlight. An elegant hand, curved around a swelling belly.

I am with child, Hari. The father is a traveler from the mountains. I will be his mate.

And where is he now, Suri? I have not seen this man.

Laughter. *He will steal me away, and you will see him after the child is born. You know that is the way of it. But I will tell you a secret—he has returned to the mountain to prepare us a home.*

Oh, if only. If only his sister's dreams had unfolded as she thought they would. If only the Magi had not captured her mate. If only Suri had not been lured in blood-rage by the sight of his skinned hide. If only . . .

But the Magi was alive. Here. Now. Impossible, inexplicable—but no illusion. Hari would never forget that scent: hot coals, iron, spice. He would never forget that sly voice, the wide white smile. No other man could imitate that knowing sneer.

Hari's belly clenched with a rage so profound he found himself digging his nails into his palms to keep from growling. All the blood he had spilled, millennia worth, and none would taste as sweet as the Magi's.

So he'd thought, in that first moment of seeing. So he'd intended.

Until Dela wrapped herself around his body. Until she kissed him—so ferocious, her heat and scent enveloping his blood-rage, soothing the killer. Insanity to come between a tiger and the kill, and Dela had done so without hesitation, trusting he would not harm her, that somehow he would hear her voice and listen.

And I did. Not because she commanded it, but because I wanted to listen. Two thousand years spent dreaming of revenge, and I stopped because she asked me to. Because she trusted me to trust her.

But the Magi still lived, the how of it inexplicable, and wanted Hari to help him. Hari had no illusions of freedom, release. The Magi wanted a slave. The slave he had created.

But for what purpose? Dela was right: The Magi had already worked his worst revenge. Why search out Hari after all this time? Two thousand years ago, the Magi had asked for a child—with Hari's sister as the chosen mother. What he could possibly want now did not bear contemplating.

Oh, but it had been strange for Hari, hearing his mother tongue flow from the Magi's lips. From anyone else, with any other words, he would have taken a moment to savor the sound of the ancient language. But no, the Magi had stolen even that.

A fine breeder, the Magi had said, referring to Dela, her slender body pressed against Hari's side. *If you do not take her, then perhaps I will. Make her skin shine with my seed, like I did your sister.*

I will kill you first, Hari had snapped. *I will feed you your balls.*

Hari squeezed his eyes shut with the memory. He had no talent for subtlety. The Magi had read him too well, divining the depths of his feelings for Dela, and had manipulated him into confirming the emotions. If he had been more careful—pretended disdain, perhaps—the Magi might not have turned his powers on her. He would not have counted on Hari choosing Dela over revenge.

If the Magi takes hold of Dela, he will not just kill her. He will make her suffer first. The horror of that possibility staggered him. He would rather die than see Dela endure the same fate as his sister. The Magi might not want a child this time, but he was a man of deep, violent lusts. Hari could still see his sister's eyes, broken with sorrow, her bleeding hands clutching her naked belly. The young woman, trying to protect her unborn child—and unable to, at the very last.

Delilah would make an excellent mother. The thought

was unbidden, powerful. Hari buried the notion before his heart could burst from his chest. His life was too uncertain to think such things, his pain too great. His few words to Dela about his search for a mate had come far too close to some truth he was not yet willing to face. A dream long denied.

Hari felt Dela's scream before he heard it, some instinct tuning his ears to the bathroom as water splashed under the sounds of her terrified cries. He did not feel himself move, but suddenly he was in the bathroom, watching helplessly as Dela rocked back and forth, arms clasped around her knees. He knelt, resting his large hand on her head, soothing back damp hair and drawing her into the dry warmth of his chest.

"Hari," she whispered. "Something terrible is going to happen."

"Tell me," he said, the world listing sideways beneath him.

Dela shook her head, staring at the tiled wall. "I had a dream. A vision. The future comes to me that way sometimes, but this—this wasn't specific. Just that you and I will be put into a very bad situation." Dela looked at him then, and Hari suddenly became aware of her nudity. She hugged her legs closer to her chest.

"I am sorry," he murmured, standing, his eyes averted.

"Hari," she said, stopping him. "Thank you."

He nodded and closed the door behind him. Creating a little distance from Dela's presence helped clear his mind. He leaned against the wall, hands curled tight against his thighs.

Something terrible is going to happen. You and I will be put into a very bad situation.

Hari heard Dela step out of the tub, his ears picking

up her careful, measured breathing. Her control re-asserted. He had seen her fear, though—naked horror etched on her face—and he felt himself sink deep into a place he had not been for almost two thousand years. Without his skin, he could not become tiger in flesh, but the tiger was still within, restlessly dreaming.

Hari surrounded his beast, stroking and whispering. Too much time had been spent on dreams.

It was time to wake.

CHAPTER FIVE

VISIONS of death haunted Dela for the rest of the night, a fatal caress upon her mind. Resting in the darkness, she had trouble closing her eyes. Hari's anguished face filled her thoughts, and all she could hear was someone's sigh of death. Soft, lethal.

But the future never turns out the way you think it will. What you see is a glimpse, the shadow of a possibility.

A truth Dela knew all too well. When she was twelve, she had dreamed a car would hit BoBo, the family dog. The following week, BoBo was struck while chasing a ball into the street. A glancing blow only—he suffered a broken leg, and went on to live another five years before succumbing to old age.

Still, BoBo had been a ripple point in Dela's emotional life, which seemed to guide the frequency of her visions. Her grandmother was a card-carrying member of Oracles-R-Us, but Dela's visions always had been limited to events that would bear deeply personal emotional consequences. And at the moment, deeply personal emotional consequences were what she was all about.

She listened to Hari's quiet breathing, half the room away in front of the door. He had bade her good night with a deep kiss, then settled down in his makeshift bed on the floor. Seven feet of gorgeous magical man, guarding her. And a gentleman, no less.

The transformation in them both astounded her. Dela could not reflect on it long without feeling overwhelmed. So much had changed in this short day, not just in her life, but also—she suspected—in Hari's.

Magic really exists. Curses, immortals, shape-shifters—she remembered the Magi, then—*and cruelty. True disregard. Evil.*

Evil and its opposite. Dela felt her cheeks warm as she thought about Hari, and their first meeting. And yet, between them, a subtle shifting of roles. Strangers to friends—and now, deeper waters, sweet and mysterious.

Dela missed Hari's touch. She even contemplated bedding down beside him just to feel his body pressed against her own. Her need was outrageous and confusing, inexplicable, her feelings so far beyond the realm of anything she had previously experienced that she felt faintly ridiculous.

But thinking of Hari was far more pleasant than contemplating the person—or people—who apparently wanted her dead.

Dela stared at the ceiling, running through the past ten years of her life—every major argument or strange encounter—and came up with nothing important enough to kill over. Nothing worth her life. Nothing except the agency.

It was a risk they all lived with, that the government or military would discover their powers, that the media might catch wind of the agency's true purpose and light the fire of scrutiny under their collective psychic asses.

No one wanted to end up in a lab or on the cover of *National Enquirer*.

But Roland had been emphatic; Dirk & Steele was safe, its cover still intact. Which meant this was somehow *her* fault.

Dela blew out her breath, exasperated. True, she knew she had a talent for irritating people. She was too blunt, completely undiplomatic, with dislikes that were painfully obvious. But to hire an assassin?

"You cannot sleep." Hari's voice floated from the darkness.

"Did I wake you? I'm sorry."

"I was not sleeping, either. You are still thinking of who might want you dead?"

"Yes. I'm not coming up with anything."

"You know the answer, even if you are not aware of it. Give yourself time."

"Ha. You're implying I've actually done something deserving of murder."

"That is unfair," he said.

"Maybe," she conceded. "But true."

He was silent for a moment. "I find it difficult to believe you have enemies, Delilah. I have seen nothing in you to warrant such hate. But perhaps it is jealousy you are encountering. Men and women have been killed for less. Is there a . . . a lover in your past—or present—who would wish you harm?"

"No," Dela said. "There have been some men, but not for a long time. They wouldn't have any reason to hurt me, either. Our separations were amicable." Amicable because Dela and her few boyfriends had always known the relationship was temporary. Dela never allowed herself more.

She thought Hari sighed, but it could have been her imagination.

"Rest," he said. "I will take care of you."

Dela smiled. "And I'll take care of you."

"I do not dare dream of such a gift," he murmured, and they talked no more for the rest of the night.

Dela finally did manage to sleep, and when they both rose early the next morning to go to the Dirt Market, she felt more cheerful. Hari's fake papers were coming, and with those in hand they would get the hell out of China. Maybe this mess would follow them, but back in Dela's own territory, with friends to help her and Hari, the illusion of safety would feel fine indeed.

But when they exited the hotel, morning sun glowing silver through the light haze of Beijing's smog, Dela glanced up at Hari and realized they had another slight problem. A problem fully appreciated when a cab pulled up and Hari could not fit inside.

It was almost funny, watching his unsuccessful attempts to bend like a pretzel into the backseat of the small red vehicle. Foreigners and locals alike stared with open-mouthed fascination as Hari struggled to cram all seven feet of bone and muscle into an interior even Dela found tiny. A young bellboy finally darted into the hotel, reemerging with the desk manager.

The graying, bespectacled man looked at the massive leg hanging out the side of the cab and shook his head. He gestured at Dela.

"I can arrange a larger car for you, courtesy of the hotel," he said, his expression pained.

So Dela and Hari got a van, with a driver. The driver didn't seem to care that Hari was almost seven feet tall, or that he might have to drive them all over the city for the entire day. An unlit cigarette hung from the corner of his mouth, and his narrow dark eyes, set in a sweaty face, stared only at the winding road.

Even with the larger vehicle, the ride to the Dirt Market was uncomfortable. Hari's knees were pressed to his broad chest and his shoulders hunched so his head would not bump the ceiling. Dela worried about his claustrophobia, but the van's large windows seemed to ease whatever pain he felt from confinement.

Dela sat up front next to the driver, and whenever she glanced over her shoulder to see how Hari was faring, she found him watching the passing city, his eyes wide with wonder. Sunlight poured through the van windows, bathing his body. His variegated hair looked streaked by fire, his tawny skin glowing warm. He was unearthly, beautiful—a man outside time with another world in his searching eyes.

The blue gate had already been flung open by the time they reached the Dirt Market. The taciturn driver parked across the street, saying nothing when Dela reiterated their need for him to wait. When she handed him a twenty, he finally smiled, revealing a remarkable set of yellow teeth.

The merchants were still setting up. Dela and Hari stood in the shade of an old brick wall, watching men and women trudge through the gate with bicycles laden with wares. Wrapped vases stacked in carts; mountains of boxes holding jade, paper fans, statues of Buddha or Gu Gong; stone bowls, ceramic lions and crouching women; antique weapons, scroll paintings, charms, and musty books.

If Dela thought Hari attracted attention in the hotel and mall, it was nothing compared to the feast of eyes that followed his presence on the city street in broad day-light. Not that she blamed everyone for staring. In a place where blond hair or very dark skin might merit a specu-lative glance, Hari was seven feet of exotic temptation.

Children, accompanying their merchant parents to as-signed stalls, ogled Hari with speechless awe. So struck by him that they could not even muster the strength to point, the children stood in a loose circle, like an audi-ence to some silent show where Hari was the only star. A smile shadowed Hari's face, and Dela watched as he slowly knelt to tighten the straps of his sandals, the last remnant of his ancient clothing.

The children whispered. A little girl, her eyes huge in her heart-shaped face, shuffled close with an orange popsicle melting down her delicate wrist. Hari contin-ued to fuss with his sandals. Dela watched the little girl touch his multi-hued hair.

Hari's eyes snapped up and the girl smiled—so sweet, so pure, it made Dela's throat ache. Hari returned the smile, and it was everywhere: his lips, his eyes, in the hand that reached out to flick the child's nose.

The little girl squealed with laughter and tugged harder on Hari's hair, sticky fingers tangled in auburn, honey, and sable. He let her play with him, and there was nothing hard in his face; his eyes were completely unguarded. His gentleness profound. Emotion swelled in Dela's throat; her eyes felt hot.

"Where are you from?" the girl asked in Chinese. "The others don't think you're real."

Hari glanced at Dela with a mischievous slant to his mouth, and it took her a moment to remember the curse allowed him to understand different languages.

"I am from the forest and the mountain," he said in

perfect Mandarin, "and if your friends do not believe I am real, they are welcome to match your courage and see for themselves."

The child's nose scrunched with delight, and all Hari's young admirers were soon tangling his hair, trying to climb his arms and back. He got into the game with easy grace, standing to his full height while children clutched his shoulders and outstretched hands, shrieking with delight. He swung them in wide circles, a human merry-go-round. Dela had trouble keeping her eyes off him, and he shot her heated, playful glances that made her heart shake inside her chest.

Finally, almost painfully, she managed to look away and scan the growing throng. Quite a few people were watching Hari and the children, but beyond them, in the market, the stalls were almost ready for the mid-morning onslaught of tourists and local shoppers. The old woman would surely be there by now.

She glanced at Hari, hesitating. He was having such a good time playing mountain to the monkeys; it seemed a crime to interrupt. Surely there were enough people here that the Magi or her mysterious assassin would not try anything. Nothing had happened the night before, and this was much more public.

Keep telling yourself that, and maybe you'll eventually believe it. Preferably before you get shot, stabbed, or mentally mutilated.

But it seemed so mean to make Hari stop. Such a small thing, playing with children, but she could feel him basking in their laughter, in the freedom of being allowed a moment of innocent play. No blood, no war, no pain.

She almost left him then. A little danger seemed a cheap price for joy.

Perhaps Hari read her mind. He glanced at her, and something stern touched his gaze, though his smile never faltered. He said something to the children, and within moments they slid down his back and dropped from his arms like dark-eyed cherubs tumbling from a tree. When the last was safely standing, Hari waved good-bye and made his way to Dela. His smile faded.

"You were thinking of leaving without me," he said, a hint of disappointment in his grave eyes.

"Well," she said, suddenly feeling very small and somewhat rattled, "you were having such a good time with the children. I didn't want to take that from you."

Hari's frown deepened. "Your safety is all that matters to me, Delilah. If anything happens to you, I—"

"I know, I know." She held up her hands, lowering her gaze. Her heart hurt with shame, and something deeper yet. "If I die, you go straight back into that box. I'm sorry, Hari."

"Delilah." His voice was sharp. "I do not care about the box."

His voice resonated through her, and Dela stared in wonder, unable to speak, unable to find the right words for such an incredible statement. And just when she thought words might never be enough, Hari took her hand and pulled her toward the first gauntlet of stalls.

"Come," he said gently, "we have an old woman to find."

They walked quickly; it was early enough in the day that the two of them could move easily down the open corridors. Dela ignored pleas to stop, eager sales pitches becoming nothing more than a buzz in her ears. She opened her mind, seeking the presence of weapons on the people surrounding her, but there was too much metal—from the wares to the girders to the tin roof—

and she could not filter the whispers into anything comprehensible. Dela threw up her shields. Silence returned, blessed and sweet.

Dela retraced her steps, walking a circuitous route through ceramic jugs and cheap paintings—so new the oils and inks were still wet—until suddenly, vibrant Tibetan tapestries winked through a crack in the crowd. Relief coursed through her. Finally, some answers.

Hari stiffened as they approached. He stopped in the middle of the aisle, nostrils flaring.

"What is it?" Dela looked around. Everything seemed normal: dirty, crowded, loud.

Hari took a deep, shuddering breath. "Shape-shifter," he exhaled, rolling his shoulders. "A fresh scent. The same as last night."

"What are you waiting for?" Dela gave him a small push. "Go chase after it!"

"I cannot leave you," he protested, and there was a wild look in his eyes—torn, yet determined. He began tugging Dela behind him—in a direction leading away from the tapestries—and Dela growled, digging in her heels.

"No." She fought his grip. "You go without me. I need to find that old woman."

"Delilah," he warned. Dela shook her head, stubborn.

"You can't be with me all the time, and I can take care of myself. Please. Both of us have something important to do. It'll be better if we split up. Besides"—and here she smiled, pretending to be braver than she felt—"the curse won't let you leave me for long, right?"

Hari hesitated, and then leaned close. He wrapped a gentle hand around the back of her neck, and whispered, "I meant what I said, Delilah. I do not care about the box."

Dela smiled, this time for real. "Go find your shape-shifter, Hari."

Hari's lips compressed into a hard line; his thumb brushed lightly against her cheek, the corner of her mouth. He nodded once, then tore his gaze away, turning, slipping gracefully down the crowded aisle. Dela watched him for a moment, then went to find the old woman.

Except, the old woman was nowhere to be found. Dela padded up and down the entire aisle looking at each face, hunting for that youthful countenance with its wise ancient eyes.

"Excuse me," Dela said, sidling close to a young woman sorting embroidered cloth. Small and bony, her dark cheeks bore acne scars; as she turned to face Dela, a strand of black hair fell loose from a red butterfly clip and covered her glittering eyes.

Dela gestured to the stall beside them—which, minus its owner, looked ready for a good day's sale. "I was here yesterday and bought some things from your neighbor, an old woman. She wore dark red pants, a black t-shirt. I need to find her. Will she be back soon?"

The young woman's gaze went flat, cold, and Dela got the once-over from hell—the kind that was supposed to make a person feel like a dog caught eating its own shit. Because Dela was not a dog, nor inclined to dump a load in public, she simply raised her eyebrows and waited.

When the young Chinese woman finally spoke, her words were staggeringly unexpected. "She's dead." Simple, without a trace of emotion.

A sound escaped Dela's throat—blood roared in her ears. "That's impossible," she stammered. "She can't be dead."

The young woman shrugged and went back to sorting cloth. Dela grabbed her sleeve. "Her stall is set up for business. You're lying to me."

"Am I?" The woman glared at Dela's hand. "She's dead. I own her business now."

"I don't believe you."

The woman yanked her arm away, mumbling something about stupid foreigners. Dela gritted her teeth. "Where is she? *Tell me.*"

The young woman shook her head, lips pressed into a stubborn line. Like a mule; Dela wasn't sure dynamite would loosen those lips.

Face flushed with anger, Dela straightened, noticing at once that she held the badly concealed interest of every merchant in the aisle.

"I'll pay," she said loudly, lifting her chin when the young woman in front of her snarled something incomprehensible. "For anything. A name, a location, the *truth.* It's very important I find that old woman."

There was a moment when Dela thought for sure she had made a mistake; the looks people gave her were closed, damning, and it occurred to her that even if someone did talk, she might hear nothing but lies. But then she heard a shifting of cloth, and a low voice sighed, "Aiii-yo."

A titter from the other merchants, quickly hushed. Dela faced the man who rose from his haunches, a cigarette hanging between his elegant brown fingers. He was in his forties, black hair stuffed into a faded blue cloth hat. He did not look Dela in the eyes, but took the fifty dollars she stuffed into his hand.

"Long Nü." He ducked his head as several people hissed. "That is her name."

Long Nü. Dragon Woman.

Dela angled close. "Long Nü is still alive, isn't she? Why is she hiding? Why are all of you protecting her?"

The young woman Dela had spoken to spat something ugly, and the man flinched. Flinched, and then froze as he looked over Dela's shoulder. The look on his face made her skin crawl.

"Delilah!" Hari's voice, full of warning.

Dela turned just in time to feel something sharp caress her neck, so close to skin she felt its kiss of steel. The knife flew past the startled man in front her and thudded into a wooden post.

Dela dropped into a crouch. At the end of the aisle, surrounded by startled shoppers, stood her would-be assassin. His hands glittered with small knives. How had she not sensed the metal?

As he raised his hand for another throw, Dela glimpsed Hari vault over a merchant-constructed wares wall, his massive body flying through the air to land with perfect grace beside her. He came up hard against her body, engulfing her completely, hugging her so close she felt the ridges of his scars press against her forehead through his shirt.

She heard the impact of steel against flesh—once, twice—but Hari made no sound. He reached behind his back and Dela heard his body tear—wet sucking sounds. A bloody knife appeared in Hari's hand and then was gone, flying through the air.

The knife thudded into the assassin's throat, blade sunk to the hilt. The man gurgled, eyes bulging. He collapsed with his fingers still scrabbling at his neck.

People began pushing and shoving, swarming down the aisle, trying to escape the violence. Screams filled the air, loud and strident. The rough gasp of weeping. Chaos. Hari remained unaffected by the riot. He picked

Dela up in his arms and ran down the aisle, carving a path through the crowd with his size and sheer bullying strength.

Dela could barely see any of it, tucked as she was into Hari's body. She was only conscious of the blur in her vision, the thunder of his heart beneath her ear. When he finally put her down they were on the farthest fringe of the market, in a small empty lot behind a bulky group of stone lions, tacky Romanesque columns, and giant Buddhas. Nearby, a gap in the aluminum fence revealed the road and thick morning traffic.

"Are you hurt?" Hari asked roughly, the rumble from his chest sinking through her skin, into bone. He glanced behind them, and then lightly ran his hands over her body, her face, searching. He tilted her head so he could see her neck, and hissed. Dela touched the burning skin, but her fingers came away dry. It was just a welt.

"I'm not hurt," she insisted, pressing her cheek against his callused palm. "You?"

Dela saw the answer in his eyes and she squeezed out from under his arms to check his back. Blood stained his shirt; a small knife jutted out from under his shoulder blade. She sucked in her breath.

"Pull it out," Hari ordered. "Quickly, before anyone notices."

Dela glanced around; the area he had brought them to was secluded, but that would not last. In the distance, beyond the farthest edge of this stone garden, she could see the bustle of the market—and hear a rising chorus of distressed shouts.

Gritting her teeth, Dela took firm hold of the dagger and yanked it from Hari's back. He grunted, but that was all. Dela pulled off her lightweight cotton cardigan and stuffed it against the sluggishly bleeding wound.

There was another hole in his back, the flesh ragged and torn, but it had already stopped bleeding.

She glanced at the knife, feeling ill. It was not one of her weapons. The hilt was very slender, naked steel punctuated by five small holes. A commercial brand, ordinary and untraceable; something like a Lightning Bolt.

Death by blade. The steel whispered, but it was a new knife. Nothing of its owner had left an imprint.

"The trail disappeared," Dela heard Hari whisper, and when he turned, the fear in his eyes made her sway. "So I came back to find you. But I was too late. I saw that man, and I could not move fast enough. I thought you would be taken, right before my eyes."

It was difficult to speak. She managed a tremulous smile and said, "So I guess you'd miss me, huh?"

Hari drew in a shaky breath and pressed his lips against her forehead. He held her face, his hands large and warm. "I think it would be difficult to find another friend like you, Delilah."

Dela covered his hand, kissing his palm. "I'd miss you, too, Hari."

She still held the bloody knife; she wrapped the blade in her ruined cardigan, and dropped them both into her shoulder bag to dispose of later. She glanced once again at Hari's back. Both wounds had stopped bleeding, but his shirt was mangled, bloodstained.

"We need to get out of here." She looked through the statues at the main drag of market space. Several locals glanced in their direction, and Dela could hear sirens. No one in the city ever took the police very seriously—it was the soldiers who made people jump—but where there was one, there would be the other.

"Take off your shirt," she ordered. "And stay here. Please, Hari. I'll be right back, I promise."

"I already made that mistake, Delilah. We go together."

"No. You're covered in blood, and too many people saw you throw that knife." She touched his shoulder, taking strength from his warmth. "Last night you said you'd take care of me, and you have. Let me do the same, Hari. Let me take care of you."

"I will be the death of you," he said.

"Not today," she said, backing away, leaving him behind with his hands drawn tight against his thighs.

You're too cocky, Dela told herself. But what choice did she have? She knew the danger—there could still be another assassin out there, in the crowd—but if she let fear rule her, the game would be over for good.

And a girl's gotta do what a girl's gotta do, she thought, forcing herself to weave a path around the statues at a pace she hoped would not draw notice. The soldiers and police had arrived, milling near the entrance to the Dirt Market: bored young men with sub-machine guns and note pads. Several of them were listening to the excited chatter of apparent witnesses to the attack.

Dela scanned the crowd before she left the cover of the stone garden. She quickly found what she was looking for: a slender middle-aged woman with numerous black t-shirts slung over one arm, standing on the fringe of gathered gawkers. Dela reached her just as a team of medics emerged from beneath the market awning, a covered stretcher between them. Dela swallowed hard and looked away.

As Dela hoped would happen, her blond hair caught the attention of the t-shirt hawker, who immediately abandoned the growing fracas for the possibility of a sale. Dela bought the largest shirt she had for the first price quoted—which seemed to both disappoint and please the woman. From a black garbage bag at her feet, she whipped out several large baseball caps with the 2008 Olympic logo on them. Dela bought those, too.

She made her way back to Hari, sighing with relief when she found him in the same spot, his shirt already off and balled in his fist. He did not smile when he saw her, but he touched her cheek and it was enough.

The shirt barely fit and the artist's rendition of the Great Wall was embarrassingly tacky, but the black fabric covered the drying blood on Hari's back, and was less jaw-dropping than his half-naked body. They put on the baseball caps, Hari tucking away his distinctive hair.

Dela stuffed his ruined shirt into her bag with the knife and cardigan, and then she and Hari pushed themselves through the gap in the aluminum fence. Hari suffered some scratches on his arms as he shouldered past the metal siding. The gap opened out onto a busy sidewalk, and they caught some curious glances from passing locals. She smiled, hoping she looked more goofy than insane, and took Hari's hand.

They walked around the block, following the outer wall of the Dirt Market, looking for the hotel van. It was still parked across the street from the market entrance, which was now filled with military and police cars. Dela hesitated, and glanced at Hari.

"We must," he said.

They crossed the busy street, insinuating themselves among the locals who pushed themselves, inch by brave inch, into the ever-flowing river of vehicular traffic, until finally, one car stopped—and then another—and everyone made it safely across.

They reached the van without mishap; no one screamed or pointed fingers; no young men with guns began shouting orders. In fact, no one paid them any attention at all, except to stare at the very large foreign man in the awful shirt and touristy hat.

The driver looked at them curiously when they climbed into the van, but said nothing. Dela told him to head back to the hotel. Fast.

She sat in the backseat. There wasn't nearly enough room, but Hari dragged Dela in after him, refusing to let go of her hand. She did not mind being pressed against him. Her body was finally beginning to react to the attack, her limbs quaking, heart pounding a rough tattoo against her ribs. She felt sick.

"I really, *really* didn't think he would try anything in a crowded place, in broad daylight," Dela mumbled. "I should have known better."

"He was desperate. He already failed once, and could not afford to do so again." Hari spoke so quietly Dela could barely hear him. He covered her shoulders with a strong arm, his large hand resting lightly in her hair. His touch shot warmth through Dela's trembling body, and she closed her eyes, savoring the sensation of being comforted.

"You saved my life again," she whispered. "Thank you, Hari."

Dela felt him look at her, and was drawn to meet that serious, golden gaze.

"I killed a man in front of your eyes," he said, in a voice meant for her ears only. "Does that not bother you?"

Dela thought he was really asking if he had frightened her. She shook her head.

"I'm sorry you had to be the one to do it. I know you've had enough of violence. But I'm not sorry that man is dead. He tried to kill me twice, and men like that don't stop until they're called off or paid in full."

Bloodthirsty, cold, cynical—all those words passed through Dela's mind to describe herself, but she could not help telling Hari her own personal truth. She held her breath, awaiting his response.

"You continue to surprise me," he said quietly. Dela sighed as he tucked her even closer to his side. "Has this happened to you before?"

"No, but I know the rules, the way the game is played." She had to, as a member of the agency.

"I will not ask how you know these things," Hari said. "Not yet, anyway. But knowing these . . . rules, would you have killed him yourself, given the chance?"

Dela felt herself go very still. "I'm as good a mark with a knife as you are, Hari. And yes, I would have killed him in self-defense."

"Good," he breathed, pressing his lips to her temple.

"Good?"

"It would bother me more if you allowed conviction or a weak stomach to make you a victim."

"But stupidity is okay, right?"

"You are not stupid, Delilah. Merely . . . naïve. Or perhaps simply brave."

"I'm not sure I see the difference. And I'm not brave. I'm terrified."

"Terrified?" Laughter escaped him, sharp. "I have seen kings and warlords react with more emotion."

"Yeah? Well, I bet they weren't trained from birth to control their fears. Not like I was." Hari blinked, startled. Dela touched his hand. "You say I don't show fear? It doesn't mean I don't feel it. But control—control is essential for people like me, especially control over fear. It would be so easy to fear myself, Hari. The things I do aren't normal, not by society's standards, and if I let fear rule me, it will block my abilities. The same is true now. If I panic I'll be useless, and that's something I can't tolerate."

"Spoken like a warrior," he murmured. "Ah, Delilah. We are not so different. What you describe is very similar to the training I underwent as a child. Shape-shifters are born human, but the ability to transform comes at an early age. The first time is terrifying. You are told what to expect, but the mind is still too young to comprehend what it means to become something else, something alien. We must continuously learn to manage our fear of the change, at least until we grow old enough to control when and where it happens."

"And if you don't learn?"

Hari's jaw tightened. "Life becomes difficult."

Dela almost asked, but the look on his face said volumes. This was a story for another time.

Another time. She smiled at herself, amused she had already come to terms with the idea she and Hari would have time. Time shared, a future with stories to look forward to.

Insanity, she thought, with more happiness than fear.

"What are you thinking?" Hari asked.

"That you must've been an adorable cub," she lied, embarrassed to share the truth.

Hari's lips quirked into a wry smile. "I had very sharp claws."

"Some things never change."

Hari looked at his hands: long, lean, and strong. Dela covered them with her own—slender, winter-pale—and they spent a moment in silence, taking in the differences.

"Did you find the old woman?" Hari finally asked, breaking the quiet. "I forgot about her."

Dela grimaced. "What I found was a stone wall. According to the people who work near her, she's dead."

Hari froze. "Murder?"

"They're lying. Protecting her for some reason. The only thing I found out was her name. Long Nü."

"Dragon Woman," he mused quietly.

"Does that mean anything to you?"

Hari shook his head. "I do not know."

"Yeah, well, I don't believe in coincidence. She sells me your box, and the next day she's dead? Too weird for my tastes."

"The Magi could have killed Long Nü in retaliation for selling you the box."

"Or she's gone into hiding because of him. I prefer that possibility. I kind of liked her."

When they arrived at the hotel, Dela stopped at the front desk to check for messages. Several businessmen who thought they were the height of cool cast surreptitious glances at Hari. The extremely young women dangling from their arms did the same, except they were far less discreet.

"They want you bad," Dela teased, gesturing at the girls smiling coyly in Hari's direction.

Hari barely glanced at them. "They are shallow imitations of what women should be. You, however, are the real thing."

Whoa.

The desk clerk coughed, and Dela struggled to focus on his amused face.

"You have a package," he said, handing her a nondescript brown box with her name printed neatly on the label. No return address or postage stamps. Hand-delivered.

Dela smiled as she turned the box over. Scrawled on the bottom was a crude drawing of a skull and cross-bones, nestled in the middle of a giant heart. Roland's signature method of expressing affection. Dela wouldn't have been surprised to learn he had the same image tattooed on his ass, with the word "mutha" inscribed at the bottom.

"What is it?" Hari asked, as they made their way back to the room. His gaze did not rest long on Dela. He scanned the lobby, scrutinizing everyone, his body coiled tight. He seemed determined not to let her move more than a pinky's length away from his side. Which suited Dela just fine.

When they reached the elevators, Hari's jaw clenched so tight Dela imagined it might snap off his face. She squeezed his hand as they waited. He stared at the closed doors, looking ill.

"Your papers." Dela watched him worriedly. "Everything you need to function in society. Social security number, birth certificate, that sort of thing."

"I will take your word on it," he said a minute later when he ran off the elevator with her in tow, his ability to speak in coherent sentences restored. "This . . . family friend of yours was able to acquire all that for me?"

"Yes, but don't *ever* tell anyone. For all intents and purposes, you were born and bred in America, and got your papers the good old-fashioned way."

"Ah," he said, as they arrived at the room. "You deal with criminals."

"Nooo," she said, sliding the card key into the lock. "They're just extremely good at getting difficult things done."

"So am I, but my methods usually involve killing people."

Dela had a pithy reply on the tip of her tongue, but Hari pushed her aside as she opened the door, stalking into the room with an I-am-Going-to-Hurt-Someone attitude.

A moment later, Dela understood why.

The room had been torn apart, rock-star style. She was surprised the curtains weren't on fire. All their clothes lay scattered and cut to shreds, the bed covers were torn, the pillows cruelly de-stuffed. Every piece of furniture not nailed to the floor now pointed at the ceiling in weird angles, modern art at its worst.

Dela checked the closet. Hari's sword and knives were still there, although it was clear they had been the instruments of destruction. Bits of cloth clung raggedly to the blades. Guilt by association. Dela touched the weapons, but whoever had used them had not left an imprint. She was getting a lot of that lately. Very frustrating.

"Well, I'm officially irritated," Dela said. "Magi or mystery man?"

Hari's nostrils flared. "Magi. I am sure he was looking for the box."

Dela patted her purse, comforted by its slight bulge. "Bully for him."

Dela called the front desk and explained that someone had broken into her room. By the time the hotel manager arrived—the same gentleman who had so nicely provided the van and driver—Dela and Hari had packed his weapons and armor into her suitcase. Which, thankfully, still remained unscathed.

The bright side of the situation was that they were promptly given a luxurious three-room suite with two featherbeds, a whirlpool the size of a swimming pool, and views of the city that almost made Dela weep—but only because she didn't think they were going to be staying long enough to enjoy any of it.

At least she wasn't paying for the room—or any other expense accrued during her stay at the hotel.

You just saved me more than a thousand dollars, you son of a bitch. And Hari and I get to buy new clothes, all on the hotel tab.

Yes, the silver lining was all hers.

"How did the Magi find us?" Dela asked, when they were finally alone.

"Perhaps he is tracking *me*," Hari said moodily, arms folded over his chest. He leaned against the window, staring at the city. "The Magi invested much of his own magic in creating my prison. It could have produced a link, of sorts. A scent he can follow."

"Hmph. But why look for you now, and not before?" There seemed no good answer.

Dela used one of Hari's daggers to cut open Roland's box. Inside, she found a thick envelope and a typed letter.

Yo, babe–

    My sources finished this faster than I thought (money really can buy anything), and since the work was done on your side of the world, the package should get to you before the afternoon. Hope the proxy got my signature all purty.

    I've got you and "Hari" seats together on an evening flight back home. First class, of course. Try not to abuse the privilege by dropkicking any bitchy flight attendants or drunk CEOs.

Call if you need anything.

Ro

That guy looks scary. Are you sure I can't have him?

Dela grinned, setting aside the letter. She tore open the envelope and gestured for Hari to join her. She showed him his passport, but scowled when she saw the last name Roland has chosen.

"Why am I called Hari Dasypygal?"

Dela growled. "That's the last name Roland gave you. It's an obscure Greek word that means . . . having hairy buttocks."

There was a long moment of silence. "Well," Hari said, very carefully. "When I am in tiger form, I actually *do* have—"

She swatted him, laughing.

CHAPTER SIX

Four hours later they checked out of the hotel. It was not the way Dela had envisioned the end of her vacation—though nothing about this trip had turned out the way she expected—but she was taking home a new best friend, and perhaps more, which almost made up for the last two days of murder and mayhem.

Plus, Dela had new clothes. Always a good thing.

Dela currently wore designer jeans, a trippy little blue t-shirt with daisies scattered on the bodice, and soft leather boots that added a sexy inch to her height. Hari was back in jeans and white shirt, this time dressed up with a simple navy jacket. He also wore a new hat. Dela did not like covering Hari's beautiful hair, but she was afraid to advertise its rather unique hues in case the police had posted a description of the morning fiasco at the Dirt Market.

Not that he wouldn't attract attention anyway. He looked devastating.

No one tried to kill them on the way to the airport, nor were any knives thrown in their direction during check-in. Hari's armor and weapons were packed snugly in Dela's suitcase. His displeasure at the arrangement was eloquent and severe, but Dela didn't care. One *bing* from the metal detector, and airport security would be on them like fleas to fresh meat.

Thankfully weaponless (Dela mentally "searched" Hari, just to be sure), they crept through security and customs without mishap, Hari's passport holding up to strict scrutiny. Dela felt something hard in her stomach dissolve the moment they passed the last of the security personnel; if any of them had pulled Hari or herself aside for questioning about the morning's events at the Dirt Market, she had no good plan to save them. It seemed to her, though, that Chinese bureaucracy had won out— that, or the witnesses to the attack had lousy memories.

With time to kill before their flight, they relaxed in the first-class lounge, sipping tea and snacking on dim sum. Dela watched Hari fuss with his teacup and chopsticks, his large hands engulfing both with graceful aplomb.

Hari had perfect manners; Dela could not remember a moment when he had demonstrated anything but class and elegance, even when eating with just his hands. She wondered where he had learned such things, or whether it was just innate.

"How much time did you usually spend out of the box after you were summoned?" The lounge was not crowded; she and Hari were sitting in the furthest corner. Still, she whispered.

Hari's gaze turned inward. "The longest I ever remained free of the box was a period of ten years. That particular master was a minor warlord of the steppe who used me against enemy clans. He eventually managed to unite enough of them to create an army against China. He did not live long after the initial invasion."

He spoke casually, but Dela tried to imagine all that

Hari had experienced, the events he had witnessed with
his own eyes—places and people modern historians
could only dream about—and she felt the lure of the unknown, of mysteries solved. It was difficult not to pepper
Hari with questions. His memories were unpleasant—
she knew this, could see it in his unhappy face—but still,
that hunger.

"Ten years is a long time," Dela finally said. "Was it
always awful?"

"Not always, but I spent much of that time in battle.
My master was no different from others in that he believed I did not need food or rest. I was a spirit to him,
the essence of power. If I ate or slept, that would indicate
vulnerability, weakness. So I learned to do without for
as long as possible, eating when I could, sleeping when I
was unneeded. For ten years I did that, and it hardened
my body and mind. A good thing, I suppose. After him,
life became more difficult."

"And that's all it's been?" Dela asked, appalled. "Fighting, being used as a weapon? In all the time you've been
summoned, haven't you ever known joy?"

"They could not break me," Hari whispered. "And so
I remembered joy, and took it where I could. In a bite of
food, in blue sky, the wind. I found joy in protecting my
masters' children, who were innocent. I lived, moment
to moment, and that is how I survived. Me," he said,
touching his chest. "Not just my body. *Me.*"

Dela grasped Hari's hand. She felt power coil in his
grip, immense strength, but his fingers were achingly
gentle as they wrapped around her wrist, stroking skin.

"And now?" she asked softly.

"I still live moment to moment," he said, "but now I
live in joy."

Dela's breath caught, warmth engulfing her, desire

making her slick with hunger for Hari's body, his heart. She had never wanted anyone so much, so fast. Electricity filled the air; stunning and hot. For now they were just holding hands, but Dela's mouth went dry as she imagined their hands holding other parts of their bodies.

The sounds of screeching metal cut through her ears, her head—so close both she and Hari bolted from their chairs. Hari squeezed Dela's hand as she struggled for breath, dazed, trying to understand how the decorative railing beside their table could have come off the wall, warped and crushed like an iron ribbon.

A lounge attendant hurried over. Dela felt the stares of everyone in the room. She met Hari's eyes, heard his unspoken thoughts.

You did this.

She wanted to protest, to tell him it was impossible, that she was not so strong, but the words died in her throat. There was no other explanation. Her affinity was tied to metal. She had destroyed the railing without thinking of it. Her mind had expelled an excess of energy without focus or intent.

Fear shivered down Dela's spine. She had dealt with the effects of uncontrolled telekinesis during her adolescence, but even then she never had been able to break or lift things. Bend spoons, maybe—dent her dad's car or scratch up all her jewelry.

As an adult, she had to concentrate to make things move, and even then she was limited to metal—her art, her weapons. Which was good. Very good. Dela did not want to think about the trouble spontaneous telekinesis could get her in.

There was no good explanation to give the lounge attendant. Dela pretended stunned amazement—not very difficult, given the circumstances. She and Hari quickly left.

"I suppose that was unintentional," he said, as they walked to their gate.

"Uh-huh." She glanced over her shoulder to see if anyone had left the lounge to watch them. All clear. "I've never been able to break things like that. Even if I could, it shouldn't have happened without actually focusing on the railing."

"There was power between us. I felt it surround me."

"Oh," Dela said weakly. "I'm sorry."

Hari stopped walking and drew her close.

"Do not ever be sorry for who you are," he told her, the coarse tone of his voice softened by the genuine concern in his eyes. "This power is part of you, just as the tiger is part of me. You would not expect me to be sorry for the things I can do, would you?"

"No," she said immediately.

"Then look at this as a gift." Hari's affectionate smile turned devilish. He leaned close, breath hot against her ear. "Just imagine, Delilah, what you might do if we kissed like mates."

Dela didn't know how "kissing like mates" would be any different from regular kissing, but she couldn't wait to find out, erratic powers be damned. Let the entire airport come down!

Hari was still bent over her. Dela tried to kiss him. He smiled and pulled away, a finger against her mouth.

"We should wait," he said, and Dela—feeling very, very bad—took his finger in her mouth, sucking hard, swirling her tongue over his hot skin. Hari's eyes widened, a deep flush staining his neck. For a moment she thought she heard him growl.

Dela abruptly released him, smacking her lips. Completely oblivious to all the men who suddenly watched her with intense interest, she flounced off toward their gate. "You're right," she called over her shoulder, grinning. "We should wait."

When Hari finally caught up with her, he had taken off his jacket and was holding it in front of him. Dela wisely refrained from making any teasing remarks. It was going to be a long enough flight without creating more sparks. The way things were going, she might just depressurize the plane.

Lovely. Just don't think about having sex with Hari.

Dela would have laughed hysterically, but there were already too many people staring at her—well, at Hari really, although she received her own speculative glances. Probably wondering how a chick like her ended up with Mr. I'm Too Sexy for this Millennium.

The flight attendants were worse. When Hari stepped on the plane, bending over to get through the door, she thought bras and panties would spontaneously explode, or at least magically appear from beneath hastily discarded clothing. She saw one older woman fiddling with the buttons on her blouse, "accidentally" undoing several of them.

Roland had reserved them seats at the very front of the plane. First class was almost empty, peacefully quiet except for the clink of glasses and the occasional sounds of flight attendants talking in the galley. Dela would not have been surprised if Roland had bought out most of the empty seats surrounding them.

"This is a very small space," Hari commented mildly, gazing around the cabin through narrowed eyes. He sat straight, rigid like there was a metal bar up his ass. Very uncomfortable. Dela remembered the elevator.

"Just close your eyes," she soothed. "Would you like a drink? Wine? Something stronger?"

"No." He wrapped his fingers around her hand and took a deep breath. "I will be fine."

Dela kissed his cheek. "This won't be so bad. You can relax and sleep. Security is so tight, no one will be able to bring a weapon on board. No knives, no assassins, and I doubt the Magi thought we would leave China so quickly. Even if he can track you, we've at least given ourselves a head start. Anyone who has to get around town in a cab won't be following us immediately."

"Perhaps," Hari said, voice tight, eyes focused on the wall directly in front of them. His palm felt sweaty, and Dela gulped. He wasn't going to freak out, was he? This flight was thirteen hours long.

"Hari?" She stroked his hand as the doors closed and the plane began to move. The pre-flight informational session commenced, a deep-throated woman speaking over the intercom system, detailing safety measures and FAA regulations. Several flight attendants swished by, ostensibly to make sure everything was upright, in the locked position.

When one overly eager woman with itchy fingers began helping Hari with his seatbelt, he came out of his claustrophobic trance, catching her hands in just one of his.

"I will do it," he said firmly. The flight attendant gave a little moue, cast Dela a dirty look, and returned to the back of the cabin.

"Good call." Dela grinned, as Hari began fumbling with his seatbelt. "Um," she said, when he had no luck buckling it, "do you want me to help with that?"

"Please," he whispered. "I have not felt this incompetent since the first time I picked up a sword."

Dela giggled, reaching over to work on the seatbelt. It really wasn't so easy getting the thing put together, and her face grew hot with the image of her hands fumbling so close to the noticeable bulge in Hari's jeans.

Holy hot rocks, Batman. Catwoman has come to town, and she means to play.

"Why are you taking so long?" Hari growled. Dela glanced at his strained face; his mouth was set, something hard pulsing in his throat. His golden eyes were glowing. Literally, glowing.

"Um," she said, momentarily frozen. The buckle snapped into place and she snatched her hands away from his lap.

"How many hours did you say we will be in here?" The glow diminished only slightly.

"Thirteen," she said in a tiny voice.

Something ragged escaped his throat. "Delilah?"

"Yes?"

"Do you remember our discussion about control?"

"Uh, yes."

"Good. Please do not come near me again, or else I might just forget I have any."

Dela shivered, her nipples growing hard against her t-shirt. Hari quickly shut his suddenly radiant eyes.

Oh, yes. It was going to be a very long flight.

HE DID NOT DARE TOUCH HER UNTIL SHE SLEPT, and even then, his fingers were careful, light. Hours into the flight, the lights had been turned down until only his enhanced sight allowed him to see with any clarity the soft lines of her face, the invitation of her lips.

Dela was the only thing keeping him sane. The darkness, the confined space—it was too much. Hari did not recall what time spent in the box felt like—he was, thankfully, asleep—but he was still part tiger, and the beast inside him hated confinement.

Hari shifted quietly. He needed to stand, walk and stretch, but he did not want to leave Dela's side. He did not trust her assurances of security on this strange vessel. Dela, despite her courage and intelligence, seemed rather naïve when it came to her safety. She was obviously used to a secure, comfortable world where paranoia was unnecessary to survival. Not that Hari could truly count himself an expert, either. He had never tried to keep his masters alive beyond the strictest interpretation of their commands, and because he was immortal, personal safety had never been a concern.

So taking care of *anyone* was fairly new to him. His only advantage was that he had been witness to much more violence than Dela, exposed to darkness, the insidious creeping of small, cold hearts. Hari expected cruelty, betrayal. Dela did not.

But I am the fool, he thought, reliving the terror of that morning. So stupid—he never should have let her go off alone—but the call of the mysterious shape-shifter's scent had been too strong, a compulsion he could not shrug off. He had to follow—had been too weak to stop himself.

And that had almost cost Dela her life.

Too close. His heart still wanted to stop, stuttering with agony every time he recalled the sight of her assassin lifting his hand. The shout, torn from his throat, had made Dela turn—just in time, *just in time*.

Hari watched her sleep, wishing he could pull her into his arms. He needed the reassurance of her cool scent, the slide of her soft skin against his own. He needed to know she was real—that this was not some strange dream. But if he kissed her now, if he touched more than her hand, he would forget himself. The beast was calling for her, hungry for her taste, her scent.

She is human, but if I had met her in my day, before

the curse, I would still have taken her as my mate. Wooed her in the shadows of the forest, away from prying eyes, under the green canopy and blue sky.

And now? Now what would he do? He had grown used to simplicity—albeit, induced by slavery—but now he had choices. The choice, according to Dela, to do anything he wished.

Anything, except leave her side. And for that, he was grateful.

THEY DID NOT CRASH, THEY DID NOT BURN, AND thirteen hours later when the plane landed, Dela remained in a completely "ravage-free" zone. She did not know whether to be happy or disappointed. Public sexual acts had never sounded all that appealing to her, but when she thought of Hari in the seat beside her, stewing in his own juices so to speak, fornication à la first class looked better and better.

It's just as well, she thought, watching relief settle on Hari's face as he stepped off the plane. *The flight attendants probably would have demanded an orgy.*

She shuddered.

Apparently, though, skin contact was okay off the plane, because Hari immediately caught Dela's hand and brushed his lips over her knuckles. "Thank you for being so patient with me."

"Patient?" Once again, hysterical laughter would have been inappropriate, so Dela settled for a grin. "Maybe I should be thanking *you*. I've never made anyone's eyes glow before."

The memory of his golden eyes, radiant like a sunrise, had consumed her thoughts for much of the flight. Inhuman and beautiful—she wondered what other surprises he had in store for her.

Like now. Hari blinked, an expression of utter astonishment dancing across his features. "My eyes were glowing?"

"Yeah," she said, puzzled by his reaction. He acted almost as flummoxed as she had felt, seeing his eyes change. "You know, after the whole . . . seatbelt thing."

A profound quiet settled over Hari's body. His silence made Dela uneasy. "What's wrong?" she asked.

Hari shook his head, his gaze still distant. "Nothing that cannot wait. I will tell you some other day."

Dela pursed her lips, and Hari sighed.

"Please," he said. "I must think more on what this means."

"All right," she agreed, and then smiled. "For now."

He looked relieved, and Dela chastised herself as her curiosity burned bright. Hari would not pry into her secrets; the least she could do was show him the same courtesy.

But still, his eyes had *glowed*.

They passed through customs without mishap, though Dela's nerves barely survived their brief encounter with the craggy agent, who gazed up at Hari with a mixture of disbelief and aloof scorn.

"Basketball player?" he asked, just when Dela couldn't take any more of his silent staring.

Hari frowned, and Dela jumped in. "Martial arts," she said.

The agent grunted. "Even scarier."

He handed back their passports and waved them through.

Dela's suitcase was waiting for them at baggage claim, lazily swirling around the carousel. Hari hefted the giant duffel over his shoulder, and Dela decided not to remind him the bag had wheels. He acted as though its heft were nothing, though she knew for a fact it weighed in at seventy pounds.

Besides, he looks sexy when he's being macho. Of course, Hari managed to look devastatingly masculine even when learning the finer points of flossing—a novelty he had become quite taken with after watching Dela perform her nighttime teeth-cleaning ritual. Apparently, even immortal shape-shifting warriors disliked having meat stuck in their teeth.

Baggage claim was separated from the airport terminal by a set of large sliding doors. As Dela and Hari handed over the last of their customs paperwork and entered the main terminal, she noticed a young man in scuffed denim holding a sign with her name on it. He seemed to recognize Dela's face, the sign dancing in his hands as he took a couple quick steps toward her—only to be blocked by Hari's outstretched hand splayed against his slim chest.

"Uh," he gurgled, looking up at the golden-eyed tower of muscle and menace looming over him. It was a full-on "I will crush you like a bug, little man" moment. The startled youth tried to peer around Hari's body for another glimpse of Dela.

"Ma'am?" he called weakly. "It's me, Eddie."

The voice was the same, and it matched the face. Eddie was in his early twenties, with scruffy brown hair, dark eyes, and pale skin. He was the spitting image, in fact, of one of Dela's favorite actors—that cute elf-boy from *Lord of the Rings*.

Well, no elves were going to die today. Dela tugged on Hari's sleeve. "Stand down, Hari. This guy's on our side. He's one of the people guarding my home."

Hari immediately removed his palm from Eddie's chest. The young man's answering grin was faintly lopsided, and he shook Hari's hand before it completely withdrew.

"You're Hari, right? Roland said to expect you with Dela."

Hari frowned. "Roland is Delilah's family friend?"

"Uh, yeah." Eddie grinned. "I suppose you could say that." He glanced at Dela and gestured toward the exit. "My car is parked across the street."

It was still early in the afternoon, and the sun burned bright and clear in an empty blue sky. The temperature felt cooler than the late summer heat of Beijing, a nice change. Dela took a deep breath, trying to clear her lungs of recycled air. It was good to be home, on her own soil, with the tang of familiar steel inside her head.

She dropped her shields for just a moment—a taste was all she needed—and the airport hummed to her a tale of impermanency, unrelenting purpose and movement. Journeys and crossings.

Dela shut out the voices, thankful for the strength of her mental shields. Metal everywhere—buildings, cars, bodies, furniture, electronics—intrinsic and necessary, all with voice, some imprint of the human spirit. Stories, deep vibrations.

Without her ability to block those vibrations, the whispers left from human contact, Dela long ago would have gone insane. It had almost happened to her brother. Max, who was so talented at helping others learn to shield, but who could not manage it so easily for himself. It was the one reason Dela had been surprised to learn he was on a team mission in South America. Max almost always worked alone. It was easier on his mind.

"Did Roland get my message about the information search I need done in Beijing?"

Eddie nodded, guiding them across the exit terminal's access road to the covered parking lot. "He'll call you as soon as he finds anything."

Dela and Hari glanced at each other. Before leaving Beijing, Dela had called Roland, asking if any of his China sources could dig up information on Long Nü. What Dela already knew was next to nothing, but there might be whispers, told more readily to locals. It was worth a try, at any rate. She and Hari had left behind a lot of unanswered questions—questions Dela would normally have tried to answer on her own if the situation had not been so dangerous.

No less danger here. But home always felt safer, even if it was just an illusion.

Eddie's car was a black Land Cruiser, so new the license plates still hadn't been attached. The metal surface gleamed like obsidian, and the windows were completely tinted. "Nice wheels," Dela commented, sliding into the front seat. She ran her hands over the flawless leather interior.

"Thanks. This job pays better than my last one."

Dela peered at Eddie. "And what, exactly, did you do for a living before you began working for Roland?"

"I worked for myself. In the car business. Acquisitions, you might say."

"And what kinds of cars did you . . . acquire?"

"The good kind, ma'am." He was grinning now, and there was a dark mischief in his eyes that fit his face, but made him seem far older. Dela laughed, low in her throat. Leave it to Roland to recruit a former car thief into the agency.

Hari climbed into the back of the Land Cruiser, stretching out across the entire seat. He lounged like some exotic king in a fairy tale, his golden eyes missing nothing—inside and outside the car. Dela heard a low rumble that might have been a plane, but which emanated squarely from Hari's chest.

"There is a man watching us," he said, as Eddie started the engine. Dela turned. Hari stared out the back window toward the airport exit area, and indeed, there stood a man in a navy windbreaker, t-shirt, and jeans, looking in their direction. More than just looking; Dela could feel the intensity of his scrutiny like a pinprick against her eye.

Amateur, she thought.

He appeared Asian—black hair, high cheekbones. His body looked fit, but unremarkable. Dela couldn't tell if he was armed; there was too much steel surrounding her to pick out the whisper of something small, like a knife or gun. He talked into a cell phone, seemingly unaware he had been spotted.

"You have good eyes," Eddie commented, staring hard at the man.

Dela frowned. "He could be completely innocent."

"No," Hari said. "There is too much intent in his posture."

"Roland hasn't mentioned anything about hiring extra help, stateside," Eddie said. His gaze flickered sideways to Dela. A strange suspicion began percolating in her gut.

"Eddie," she said slowly. "Has someone been tailing me?"

His cheeks reddened, and Dela closed her eyes. Counted to ten.

"Eddie . . . did Roland hire the man watching us?"

"I don't know," he said, cringing. "I really don't, but

we'll find out. I do know Roland had someone in China—a local—watching your back. Though it sounds like he failed miserably."

"Well, he was certainly discreet," Dela said dryly. "And if he's smart, he's already started running."

"Roland *does* have a bad temper," Eddie said, so mildly Dela had to grin. She leaned back against her seat; the car windows were tinted, but she still wanted to sit out of the strange man's line of sight. "So he could be friend or foe. Too bad there are so many people around. We could have ourselves a nice little chat."

"The crowds could work in our favor," Eddie said. "It means he can't hurt us without witnesses."

"Witnesses did not stop the other assassin," Hari pointed out. "Besides, this man will not talk without persuasion. His kind never do."

Eddie blinked. "You sound as though you have experience with that sort of thing."

Hari just stared at him.

"Well, darn," Dela said, snapping her fingers. Eddie jumped. "I guess we'll just have to forget public torture and kidnapping. So where does that leave us?"

Eddie frowned, and Dela felt a burst of heat radiate from his body. Their observer jumped into the air, dropping his cell phone. Smoke curled from its plastic casing.

Eddie immediately pulled out of the parking space, his foot heavy on the gas. He took the sharp turns like a professional roadster, dodging cars and people with cool aplomb. They were out of the airport and on the freeway in a matter of minutes.

Hari raised his eyebrows in a silent question. Dela looked at Eddie.

"So," she said, a little too casually, "how long have you been with the agency?"

Eddie hesitated, still watching the road. "Three months as a full member, but my internship lasted more than a year."

A little longer than average, but Eddie was young and probably had a criminal record. Roland was extremely careful about the people he approached for the agency; no doubt Eddie had been run through the full gauntlet.

"What is this . . . agency?" Hari leaned forward. His scent filled Dela's nose, sweet as springtime in a deep wood, with the hint of new growth. She twisted under her seatbelt so she could look at him more easily.

"You remember how I said mental gifts run in my family? Well, a long time ago my ancestors founded an organization dedicated to finding people like themselves. People who aren't . . . normal."

A smile touched Hari's lips. "What is normal?" he asked, and Dela had to laugh.

"You tell me," she said. "But let's just say my ancestors were lucky. They weren't alone. They found others. None of them did much together, except pat each other on the back and occasionally get married, but when my grandparents took over, all that changed. The organization became an agency. A detective agency of sorts, going by the name of Dirk & Steele."

No one was quite sure what had come over Dela's grandparents—or how they managed to convince most of the standing members to change the focus of the organization and their lives. Nancy Dirk and William Steele still refused to speak of it, saying only "it had to be done." And so it had. No one argued with them, ever. It was the one reason Dela stayed as far away as she could. She loved them fiercely, but it was hard to live in the shadow of legend. Especially when that legend wasn't shy with an opinion.

"The agency is dedicated to using psi-talent to help others, to do the jobs the police and military can't, or won't, handle. For example, my brother is currently in South America trying to rescue some kidnapped tourists. The family can't pay the ransom, the local police are useless, and there just isn't a single organization willing or able to help them. Except us."

"The detective stuff is really just a cover for the public." Eddie jumped in, blushing slightly when Dela nodded at him to continue. "It allows us to operate on as many levels as we want, from solving murders and kidnappings, to bigger jobs like what Max is doing. Our success rate is almost perfect. Although, that's a hard thing to say when you find a kid who's been put through hell. Or worse," he finished soberly.

Dela thought of Amy, and how even the adult gifts at that time had not been enough to prevent her terrible abuse.

She saved herself, in the end. That's the thing about psi-powers—you can't really rely on them in a crisis, even if you want to. Sometimes courage is the only thing you've got.

Hari looked at Dela, thoughtful and serious. "And you? Where do you fit in?"

She shrugged, her smile lopsided. "I don't, not really. I'm a full member, but only because I'm family. If I'm occasionally brought in on missions, it's only because the agency is running short on hands and eyes. I'm not very important in the scheme of things."

Hari frowned, and Dela quickly pushed on. "Remember, Dirk & Steele recruits men and women who express psi-talent. Mental gifts. But it's not easy to do because there aren't many of us around, and those who are keep quiet."

"It's all very secret," Eddie said. "It has to be."

Dela quirked her lips. "We're always making fun of our cover. A detective agency? Dirk & Steele? It's way tacky, but it does serve a purpose."

"It diverts attention," Hari said, nodding. "It keeps you safe from other humans, from those who would fear your gifts, and covet them."

"Yes." Dela knew Hari would understand. "We don't approach anyone unless we've got a good idea of character and personality, and even then a recruit has a trial period before free access is permitted. We have to be sure they won't betray the agency or anyone connected with it. So far, we've never had a problem."

"How many of you are there?"

"Twenty-five, with several in retirement. Half of us are based with the San Francisco office, which is run by Roland, while the others are in New York with Yancy."

"It might sound like a small number," Eddie said, "but it's not. There are lots of people with natural ability—maybe they have the occasional dream that comes true, or can tell when a relative will call—but lifting things with their minds, or reading thoughts? In all the world, Roland and Yancy have only been able to find a handful . . . and just some of those people were right for the agency, or even willing to join."

"Are Roland and Yancy your parents?"

"No." Dela smiled. "My dad's not psi-gifted, and Mom didn't want to handle the business. Roland really is a family friend, distantly related through my grandmother, although Yancy is my aunt. She and I aren't very close."

Hari turned his gaze on Eddie. The young man seemed to feel the heat of those eyes, and turned his head slightly, watching the road, but focused on the man behind him.

"And what is your mental gift?" Hari asked, when he had Eddie's attention.

"I can start fires," he answered tentatively, glancing over his shoulder to gauge Hari's response. Hari raised an eyebrow. Eddie looked at Dela as though for support. "Nothing big, just small focused blazes. It's really an offshoot of telekinesis. All I do is move the molecules around, shake them up so fast they start generating heat."

Fire-starter. She had never met one of those before, and trying to imagine polite sweet-faced Eddie at the center of a fiery maelstrom was difficult. It explained the cell phone, though.

"When did you manifest?"

"Thirteen," he said, but there was a sudden tightness in his jaw that warned Dela not to ask any more questions.

A thought occurred to her. "Hari, you think that's what the Magi was doing all those years ago? Maybe he was such a strong telekinetic, the excess energy turned into fire."

"That still would not explain my situation," Hari said, although she could tell the idea interested him.

"You found another one of us?" Eddie stared at her with undisguised curiosity.

"Kind of," she hedged. "Although this guy is definitely using the dark side of the Force, if you get my drift."

"Easy enough to happen," Eddie said, something gloomy filling his eyes. "Some people can't handle power."

"Then human nature is the one thing that hasn't changed in two thousand years," Hari said, rolling down his window. His multi-hued hair glinted in the sun, his eyes half-lidded as he watched the city skyline and passing traffic. Like a lazy, languid, dangerous cat.

Eddie glanced at Hari, then Dela. She shrugged. "Hari's been around," she explained, rather lamely.

It hit her, then—a burst of startling emotion that stole the breath from her lungs. She had brought Hari home with her. A near stranger, who was going to live in her home. With her. Until they broke the curse or she died.

Intellectually, she had already known this—accepted it—but the emotion of her decision had not yet wormed its way into her heart. And now, now she felt a little scared. Not of Hari, but of how his presence was going to change her life.

Dela was a born loner, set in her ways. Was she going to become a grouchy curmudgeon when her routine was upset? Was she going to be waspish, disagreeable, and downright ugly when she did not have her home to herself after weeks and months of enforced co-habitation? Did Hari have bad habits? Did *she* have bad habits? Were they going to drive each other crazy?

Maybe Hari would beg Dela to return him to the box, if only to get away from her. Maybe she would be happy to oblige.

What an awful thought.

Dela studied Hari, the broad planes of his body, the clean lines of his face. He was gorgeous, exotic—but that was the surface, and she didn't like him only because he was handsome. The Magi was handsome, too. Good looks could hide hideous hearts.

But Hari's heart was not hideous. The echo of his soul still smoldered inside her mind, as did the memory of golden light burning beyond dark horror. Hari's light, warm and strong, unbroken by shadow. It was the reason she had fallen so easily into their friendship, why he had her absolute trust.

Hari noticed her watching him, and again, he stole

Dela's breath away. Except this time there was no fear. Just simple determination. A promise.

I will help you. I will make this work. I will not run from difficulty.

When Dela reached out her hand, he grasped it gently and brushed his lips against her palm.

"I am glad to be with you," he said softly.

"I'm glad you're here, too," she said, equally soft.

Eddie blushed.

They left the freeway and drove down a pleasant tree-lined road that contained forest and upscale suburbia— tame "country" escapes for the men and women who worked in the city but wanted to raise their families some-place quieter.

The air smelled good and cool, like leaf and cut grass, sunlight sparkling golden through the towering boughs covering the road. After five minutes the trees thinned out, until by the time they reached the town of Rose Apple, the only ones left stood like fine weathered soldiers on the sidewalk.

Rose Apple was by no means rural, but it was not entirely touristy, either. Restaurants, large and small, elegant and comfortable, lined the street; interspersed among them were small cafes and bookstores, a mom-and-pop pharmacy, several art galleries, and the required slew of novelty shops, dispensing knickknacks and antiques.

At the very end of Main Street stood a two-story brick building that took up half the block. A common response was to call it a warehouse; there was a cavernous quality about its rectangular shape, aided by the stream of large windows running the entire length of the second floor, on all four sides.

A warehouse, however, it was not.

A garden surrounded the building, thick and untamed, ranging far into a section of land that had once been a parking lot, and now sported small stone paths, comfortable wooden benches, and a simple fountain. An elderly couple was enjoying the flowers as Eddie drove past, and Dela caught the scent of roses and lavender—the summer fragrance of home.

Dela owned the building and the garden, which she had planted herself, with some minor input from the neighboring business owners. If anyone ever wondered how she, a young woman still in her twenties, managed to afford the former warehouse and all the renovations that had gone into making it habitable, they never voiced their questions to her face. Dela thought it likely they assumed she was wealthy from her art sales. Which was partly true. At this point in her career, she could have lived quite comfortably off the profits she made on her sculptures. But not this comfortably.

Oh, being a member of a family full of psychics had its advantages, especially when all the pre-cogs played the stock market. Sort of took insider trading to a whole new level when you could foresee the importance of certain medical or technological advances. Both Dela and Max had trust funds that would make Donald Trump's eyes roll up inside his head.

Not that anyone in the family abused the money they accrued. Much of it was given away—anonymously, always—while some was kept in reserve for . . . special projects.

Dela's heart warmed when she saw the familiar brick façade and gleaming windows. She opened herself to the imprint of girders, frameworks, and wiring, feeling the echo of her spirit, and something else, welcome her home.

"You've all been staying here?" she asked.

"Yes, ma'am. We've been taking turns using your guest rooms. There's someone inside and outside your home at all times."

"How many did Roland send?"

"There's four of us. Artur, Blue, Dean, and myself."

She grinned. "All the bad boys."

"They've been looking forward to seeing you," Eddie said, still blushing.

"I bet." Dela stifled a laugh. *Let the games begin.*

"More family friends?" Hari asked mildly. His hand snaked around the seat to caress her shoulder. Dela beamed, reaching back to touch him.

When they pulled into the small private lot behind the building, three of Roland's best were waiting: Artur Loginov, Dean Campbell, and Blue—who had yet to share his last name with anyone but Roland. The three men wore identical grins as Dela got out of the car, and Dean opened his arms for a hug that would make a bear squirm. His short hair was the color of honey shot with sun, and while he was not a tall man, he was lean and well-built.

"Hey, now," he said, blue eyes twinkling. "We heard you had some trouble and came a-runnin." Dean was from Philadelphia, but had lived in the South for a time. The accent had rubbed off. Dela thought it suited his personality.

"Oh." She grinned. "So it wasn't just Roland chewing out your asses that suddenly made my home so appealing."

"That, too," Blue said, running fingers through his long black hair, for once unbound. He looked slightly rumpled, as though he had just gotten up from a nap. His deeply tanned skin glowed in the afternoon light. The skin around his hazel eyes crinkled. "You should have heard the things he said to us. If anything happens to you, we might as well arrange for Artur's old buddies to come pack us under concrete."

"We never used concrete," Artur told him, his words thick with a Russian accent. "Who was doing any building? We just dumped bodies in the river."

Chances were good that Artur wasn't kidding; for years he had worked as muscle for the Russian mafia. Tall, broad, and lean, his brown hair framed spare, handsome features, pale skin that refused to tan. His eyes were dark, almost black, and keen with intelligence. There was something about Artur that always drew the eye: partly his face, but more often the air of reserved mystery that many women—including, once upon a time, Dela—found attractive. He had an aura of quiet danger, which Dela knew for a fact was no act.

"Sheesh." She shook her head and held out her hand to Hari, who was finally able to untangle himself from the backseat of the Land Cruiser. "I want you guys to meet a close friend of mine. This is Hari. Hari, this is Dean, Blue, and Artur."

Roland's boys backed up as Hari straightened to his full height. Eddie grinned.

"Holy . . ." Dean coughed. "Are you some kind of mutant? I swear to God, Roland's going to flip out when he meets you."

"No one is recruiting Hari," Dela warned. "He's much too nice for the likes of you scoundrels."

"I used to be nice," Artur said to no one in particular, stripping off a leather glove. He held out his hand to Hari. Dela opened her mouth to warn them both, but it was too late: An actual spark of electricity jolted the air as Hari shook Artur's hand. The Russian stumbled, his eyes rolling white.

Hari bowed his head, swaying. He passed a large hand over his eyes and looked to Dela for an explanation.

"Artur is a psychometrist," she explained, throwing the recovering Russian a mild glare. "He has the ability to learn about the history of a person, or object, simply by touching it."

"Yeah," Blue said warily, as Artur finally managed to stand on his own. "But he usually doesn't have *this* strong a reaction."

"Where are you from again?" Dean asked, his eyes dark with suspicion. He fingered a scar on his arm—one of many, the result of knife and gunshot wounds, inflicted during his teens while he had lived on the streets.

"Not where," said Artur, holding a hand to his head. He looked nauseated. *"When."*

Blue, Dean, and Eddie stared at him with the same skepticism that would have met a man claiming to be the reincarnated soul of a chipmunk.

"We're not talking about this outside," Dela said, as Hari took her suitcase from Eddie and slung it over his shoulder. "Someone might sneak by and stab me while you boys are wrapping your heads around Artur's visions."

Everyone instantly shut their mouths, although Dela did not miss the glares they sent in Hari's direction. Everyone but Artur, that is. He simply observed Hari with a great deal of puzzlement and a quiet wariness that reminded Dela of when she had first met him, adjusting to life outside the mob, where smiles never had been just smiles, and a bullet in the head might very well accompany every after-dinner smoke.

Dela had spent a lot of time with Artur, helping him adjust to his new life. And oh, the crush she'd had! Artur knew—she had told him, after several weeks in his company. Dela still remembered his kind, sad smile, his gentle letdown. She had walked away, not saddened or embarrassed, but somehow warm. The two of them had been friends ever since.

She wondered what Artur saw when he touched Hari's hand—and thought, for a moment, she did not want to know. The Russian carefully replaced his glove and threw Dela a curious, somewhat sympathetic smile.

The first floor of Dela's home was devoted entirely to her studio, although the front of the building facing the street had been converted into a gallery for her art. Without Adam to run the shop, Dela thought she would keep it closed. She had better things to worry about, and there was no shortage of cash.

Dela kept a working forge just inside the back of the building, with two giant doors that swung open to the outside world when she needed fresh air. A long worktable took up the right wall. Blowtorches, boxes of metal scrap, and half-finished works of art covered the gleaming surface; sketches were pinned to an equally long bulletin board.

Against the opposite wall sat an identical table with a similar bulletin board. Except there, no art of a typical nature. Only weapons.

Half-finished swords she kept near the forge, but several completed blades rested on the table, variations of the ancient and medieval, the exotic. Such as a Flamberg, with its thirty-inch kriss-style blade, steel guard, and pommel, the grip covered in fine black leather. Creatures of European legend were engraved into the blade itself. Unicorns and dragons; intricate and wild, with minute detail made possible only through Dela's telekinetic affinity for metal. She could "impress" the art upon the blade.

There were Kangshi-style swords, swords of ancient Greece and Mongolia, shining scimitars begging for sand and sun, Celtic double-edged blades with blood grooves and wood handles—and then the daggers, ancient styles with contemporary twists, as well as the opposite: Marine Corps knives with the blades curved and jagged to resemble flames, military Kukris bent like razor-sharp wings, engraved with delicate feathers. Everywhere the lethal was made beautiful.

The studio looked the same as she had left it, although some of the weapons seemed out of place.

"You guys have been playing, haven't you." She cast a significant glance at Dean.

He grinned. "It's better than porn."

Blue grunted. "You know Dean. He only feels manly when he's surrounded by phallic symbols."

Hari was the only who didn't laugh. He focused entirely on the weapons, running his fingers over the polished steel.

"Your talent is staggering," he said quietly. Dela flushed with pleasure. Compliments didn't mean much to her anymore, but Hari was a born warrior—had lived on the battlefield for two thousand years. If he said her work was good, then it really was. He should know, after all.

"If you see one you want, it's yours," she said. "Or I'll make you a new one, custom-fit to your strength and hand."

The look he shot her was pure delight, almost boyish. "That would be a gift beyond imagining."

"Sweet-talker," Dean muttered under his breath.

"And what is it you say when Dela gives *you* a new blade?" Artur asked, with a knowing smile.

Dean scowled.

They left the studio, walking up the stairs set against the farthest wall. Dela had converted the second floor into a cozy living space with four bedrooms, two baths, and a giant living room doubling as a library and entertainment center. Brightly colored rag rugs covered the dark hardwood floors. A gourmet kitchen, tiled in cherry red and navy, was nestled in the corner beside the front door, the curved counter embracing a pleasant dining area.

There was more window than wall; sunlight bathed the entire interior with a bright, cheerful glow. It was like standing outside with only the illusion of shelter.

Someone—probably Adam, before his forced vacation—had been thoughtful enough to place vases of fresh daisies on all the tables. The air smelled like baking cookies, warm and sweet. Dela's mail lay stacked inside a small wicker basket on the kitchen counter. She quickly flipped through the envelopes and magazines, knowing Adam would have taken care of everything important before his departure.

"I took the liberty of appropriating your Victoria's Secret catalogs." Dean grabbed a bottle of water from her refrigerator. "You can have them back if you want."

"Yuck, no. I don't even want to think about the awful ways those pages have been violated."

"Darlin', what I do ain't a violation."

"Tell that to page twenty-two and what's left of Tyra Banks and her rhinestone bra," Blue said, winking.

"Hey." Dean frowned.

A familiar hand pressed against Dela's shoulder, and she leaned into Hari's body, aware of the sharp glances the other men threw in her direction.

"Delilah," he said, and there was something tense in his face. Sympathy, tinged with guilt, assailed her. All of this had to be so very strange to Hari, and she had done little to prepare him for her houseguests. She covered his hand with her own, and gently squeezed. Hari's lips softened, and he said, "If these men are here to protect you, then I think it would be best if we informed them of our other . . . problem."

"What other problem?" Blue asked, sounding somewhat unfriendly.

Dela frowned at him, but Blue's eyes remained unapologetic. He had tied back his hair, revealing the high, stark cheekbones of his face, the strong lines of his throat. She looked from him to the other three men, and found she had their complete attention. Artur looked unhappy.

"There's someone else who wants me dead. Completely unrelated, but the goal seems the same."

Only Artur seemed unsurprised by her news, but everyone else went pale. "I need to sit down," said Dean, collapsing on the couch. Eddie joined him on the other end, while Artur remained standing, looking steadily into Hari's eyes. A strange understanding seemed to pass between the two men.

"I think the story would be better coming from you," Artur said. Hari nodded.

"Will someone please tell me what is going on?" Blue called out, throwing himself between Dean and Eddie with graceful abandon. "Or I swear to God I'm going to blow the fuse on every piece of equipment in this place."

"You do that and I'll show you just how hot a forge can get," Dela snapped, smoothing back her hair as all the men stared, startled. "I'm going to take a shower now. All of you, be nice to Hari. Everything he tells you is the truth. Pray to God none of you gets on his bad side."

Then she went to Hari, stood on her tiptoes to grab

handfuls of his hair, and dragged his head down for a deeply satisfying kiss that left them both breathless and shaken.

His expression was equal parts surprised and pleased, and having marked her man off-limits to extreme abuse, Dela cheerfully saluted all of her open-mouthed observers, and went away to wash off thirteen hours worth of dirt, sexual frustration, and confusion.

"WELL," SAID EDDIE, AFTER A MOMENT OF AWKWARD silence. "Does anyone want cookies? I'll go get some cookies."

"Dela kissed you." Dean looked confused. Hari, still feeling the burn of her lips, the press of her body against his own, could only nod and smile.

Uncertainty had plagued him from the moment he arrived at Dela's home to find these men waiting for her. Men she obviously knew well. It made him feel jealous and lonely, and while he was determined not to make a fool of himself, all he wanted to do was put Dela over his shoulder and drag her off to some dark place where he could wrap himself around her body and pretend they were the only two people in the world.

And that would only be the beginning.

But Dela had kissed him in front of these men, and now it was difficult to remember he had ever felt insecure about his place in her life. Her passion had been voice and thunder, an explosion felt in the depths of his soul. It was more than he had expected, but perfect. Perfect.

"She kissed you," Dean said again, somewhat plaintively. Blue rolled his eyes, throwing Hari a surprisingly apologetic look.

"Dean has always lived under the illusion that Dela

might one day fall head over heels in love with one of us. Doesn't matter we treat her like some kid sister, or that we act like a bunch of morons in front of her."

Hari noticed a strange look pass over Artur's face, quickly swallowed.

"You think she loves me?" Hari could not help but ask.

Dean grunted. "She kissed you. In front of us. Dela doesn't kiss anyone in front of us. She loves you. Or at least, likes you *a lot*." The strained look on his face seemed to say quite plainly that Dean did not understand the attraction.

Eddie returned with a tray of chocolate chip cookies. "Eat," he said, shoving them toward Dean. "Sugar will make the pain go away."

"Who raised you? Martha Stewart?" Dean grabbed several cookies, shoving them into his mouth. He gestured for Hari to join them, and the shape-shifter did, slowly lowering himself onto the soft green cushions of the couch. He tried a cookie, and thought his masters might have raised armies for food such as this.

Artur seized several, juggling them in his gloved hands as he moved to the door. "I have seen this story. I will go keep watch outside. The enemy must know Dela is back by now." He hesitated. "Eddie told me of your strange observer at the airport. Roland has not mentioned any new tails, but I will call him and see what he says."

"All right," said Dean, as the door closed softly behind Artur. "What's your story?"

Hari was not quite sure where to start—these men reminded him of past acquaintances—men of war with too much memory in their eyes and not a shred of innocence left in their bones. Without having seen him emerge from the box, Hari was unsure they would believe anything he had to say. Indeed, their disbelief might be bound so tightly with their obvious protectiveness toward Dela that no man—even a saint—would be readily accepted.

He could live with that. He had faced worse than mere skepticism.

"I have been cursed," Hari said, and then proceeded to tell his story, slowly and sparingly, leaving out some of the more intimate details he had shared with Dela.

There was a long moment of silence at the end, until Dean turned to look at Eddie. "Sure you just put sugar in those cookies?"

"Uh-huh." Eddie stared wide-eyed at Hari.

Blue rubbed his face. "You still have your armor and weapons?"

Hari rose and found the suitcase. Moments later he revealed his sword, knives, and leather armor. Eddie removed the cookie tray to make room for Hari's belongings, and the men crowded around the table, silently examining the weapons. Eddie seemed quite taken with the well-worn steel, ready to believe; the other two were more difficult to read.

Blue glanced at Dean. "You up for it?"

"Like a horny bunny," Dean said, resting his hand on the sword. A moment—and then something strange passed through his blue eyes, like the afterglow of lightning; the skin on Dean's face suddenly seemed too tight, his cheeks hollow. A low sound, almost a groan, emerged from deep within his throat.

"Dean?" Eddie said hesitantly.

"You say you've been a warrior all this time?" Dean croaked, still touching the sword. His voice sounded like it was being cut with a fine wire.

"Yes," Hari said, noting the odd look on Blue's face as he watched his friend.

"Got anything?" Blue asked, though there was something in his voice that suggested he already knew the answer.

Dean broke contact with the sword. He huddled in on himself, hugging his arms and shivering. He quickly recovered, but when he met Hari's gaze, the naked horror in his eyes was startling.

"The guy's legit," he told the others, still staring.

"You are like Artur," Hari said.

Dean shook his head. "No. I'm clairvoyant. I see events or objects that aren't here, that can be miles away. But I'm also a retro-cog. Sometimes I view past events."

"And what did you see?" Hari asked softly.

Dean took a long swallow of water. His hand shook. "I saw a battle. Horsemen, blood, screams. You in the middle of it all. I saw you . . . tortured." He shivered again. "God, man. I don't know what you're made of to survive what I saw."

Hari said nothing. What *could* he say? That he had danced on the edge of sanity for years at a time, enduring moment by moment the most patient of agonies? Or that sometimes the humiliations had not involved pain at all, but pleasure?

Blue stirred. "Can he be trusted?"

Hari thought it was a very brave—and very stupid—question, considering that he was sitting there with all his weapons, and clearly had at least a foot or more of height on anyone else present. Not to mention, many more years experience killing people.

Dean took a deep breath and slowly nodded. "The man is a walking death trap, but he won't hurt Dela. Doesn't have it in him."

"You sure of that?" Blue asked.

"Delilah is my only priority," Hari protested, feeling the first stirrings of anger.

"You need her or else you go back into the box," Blue said, and Hari heard his fear as clearly as if it had been spoken out loud. Blue was afraid Hari was using Dela, that he cared nothing for her. An intolerable offense.

The beast rolled through Hari's chest and he leaned forward, capturing Blue's gaze with his own. He had to make this man understand—had to make them *all* understand.

"It is true my life depends on Delilah, but I tell you now, my life means nothing without her. My desire to keep her safe has nothing to do with the box, and everything to do with taking care of the only friend I've had in two thousand years. I would never betray Delilah. Never."

Long silence greeted his words, broken with a sigh. Dean, shaking his head. "That's good enough for me," he said. "Especially after what I've seen."

Eddie, his face slightly red, nodded in agreement. "Me, too."

Everyone looked at Blue.

"All right then." He stared hard at Hari. "You understand, Dela's like family. In some cases, closer than the family we've already got."

"I respect your desire to protect her," Hari said. "I would not trust you otherwise."

Blue held out his hand and Hari clasped it. In that grip, a welcome—and a promise. If Hari ever hurt Dela, these men would make his life miserable. They would try to kill him, without remorse.

Good. I think I will like these men—as long as Delilah does not begin sharing her kisses with them.

They heard the squeak of hinges. Dela's soft hum echoed from the back bedroom.

"Is everyone still alive in there?" she called.

"Yes," they chorused, staring at each other.

"I know everyone's gifts, save yours," Hari said to Blue. "What is it you do?"

A brief smile. "I'm an electrokinetic. You know about electricity, right?"

The question was not patronizing. Hari nodded. "Delilah is teaching me."

"Well then, I can control electricity. Disrupt it, quicken it, make it more powerful. It's a handy talent, especially when I'm going places I don't want to be seen."

"Which is almost everywhere," Dela said, entering the room. Her hair was still wet, her face scrubbed clean and glowing. Dark loose pants and a form-fitting long-sleeved shirt accented all her curves. She collapsed in a boneless heap beside Hari, snuggling deep into his side. She smelled like jasmine, a cool breeze, some sliver of icy moon. Ethereal.

Hari handed her a cookie.

"Have they been treating you all right?" Dela asked, some subtle shading to her voice that made him wonder how much she had heard. Crumbs dotted her lips. He wanted to kiss her.

"I think we have an understanding." He glanced at the others.

Dela smiled, and Dean coughed uneasily. "Okay, so according to you, this Magi will be coming after Dela. What the hell do we do to keep her safe?"

Hari had thought of nothing else since learning the Magi still lived. "Killing Delilah accomplishes nothing if the Magi does not already possess the box. One of you could just as easily purchase me from the other, cast a summons, and renew the cycle."

"Where's the box now?"

"In my purse," Dela said. "But I don't feel like getting up."

Blue scowled, and walked over to the kitchen counter where Dela had dumped her bag. As Eddie and Dean trailed after him, Dela pressed her lips to Hari's ear and whispered, "You're my best friend, too, Hari."

His face grew hot, and for the first time in an age, he felt shy. Awkward.

"I did not know you heard," he murmured.

"I'm glad I did." Her smile faded into something serious. Hari's stomach tightened and he wrapped his fingers around her small pale hand.

Blue grimaced as he searched Dela's bag, but he finally found the linen-wrapped metal container. Dela waved him off.

"Don't bring that thing near me. I've been scared to death I'll accidentally do something to re-imprison Hari. If you want to look at the box, do it over there."

The three men crowded close, bowing their heads. Hari had no desire to join them. He contented himself with holding Dela close, sharing her warmth, her quiet words.

Blue finally rewrapped the box. "After we finish talking, I'm taking this to the bank and sticking it in a safety deposit box. Short-notice solution. Your Magi can't get to it there, right?"

"I am unfamiliar with this . . . safety deposit box . . . but if the location is secure, then perhaps not. Although, the Magi's gifts were always a mystery."

"What exactly can he do?" Eddie asked.

Hari saw the Magi's hands, burning scythes of flame through the air, tracking heat across his skin. Screaming, more screaming. Suri's broken body on the ground.

"In my day," he said, voice rough, "the Magi had the power to create fire, to move objects without the aid of a hand. He could see across great distances, and bind people with a word."

Dean, Blue, Dela, and Eddie glanced at each other.

"I know," Hari said. "His powers sound very much like your own, but your mental gifts alone could not have cursed me, nor kept him alive for more than two thousand years."

"That's some trick," Dean admitted. "Wish we knew some actual voodoo."

"The Magi's strength has diminished. Delilah and I do not know why, but it should work to our advantage."

"I hope so," Dela muttered, staring at Hari's displayed weapons. Something in her eyes changed, grew sharp.

"I am so stupid! Where's Artur? I still have my knife, the stolen one my assassin used the first time he tried to kill me. Maybe Artur can read some clues."

Eddie got on his cell phone as Dean clucked his tongue at her. "You're too used to living the mundane life, Dela. You forget all the magical things we can do."

Dela pointed at Hari. "See this guy? *He's* magic. The rest of us are just science experiments."

"What of Dean?" Hari asked. "He shares a similar gift to Artur."

Dean shook his head. "I'm an amateur compared to Artur. If you want an in-depth scan, he's your man. It's the difference between reading the middle chapter of a book, and reading the whole damn thing."

"Artur's on his way," Eddie said. "I'm going to take his place out front."

"Thank you, Eddie—all of you. I really appreciate you helping me like this."

"Ah, gratitude." Dean clutched his heart. "How rare it is."

"Shut up," Dela said, smiling.

When Artur arrived, he didn't waste any time with small talk or questions. He sat down on the couch in front of Dela's creation, the long-handled dagger emblazoned with a dragon. He stripped off his gloves and placed his palms against the blade.

A long moment passed, and then he made a small sound: a gasp, a sigh. Sweat beaded on his forehead. A fine tremor raced through his hands.

"No," he breathed, shaking.

"Artur?" Dela reached out to him.

Artur stumbled to his feet and ran to the kitchen. When he reached the sink he began gagging, spitting. Dela rushed to his side, smoothing back his hair, pressing a wet rag to the back of his neck.

Artur finally collected himself enough to splash water on his face. He flushed the contents of the sink down the garbage disposal. He looked at Dela, and then the others, something dark and sad in his eyes.

"I know why someone wants you dead, Dela. That knife you made—the one stolen—it was used to kill a child."

CHAPTER SEVEN

A FTER that particular announcement, Dela did her own share of vomiting, but in the privacy of her bathroom. She could hear the men talking in the other room, but their voices were muffled. Dela did not want to hear what they were saying. The horror was too great. Her throat felt thick with grief, but she could not cry. She wanted to, desperately, but tears refused to come. She stared at herself in the bathroom mirror, and hated what she saw.

I made that knife with my own hands. I gave it life, and it killed a child.

Her desire to craft weapons, knives—her knowledge of their dark purpose—had finally slammed together to form an awful, incomprehensible result.

But why was she surprised? Every time she made a weapon, it begged for blood. Not literally, but what else was a blade for, except cutting, spilling, encouraging pain and death? What else? Not just decoration. Not just art. Even she was not so naïve as to believe a knife was ever truly safe. Dela had reconciled herself to that.

But a child?

Dela felt reminded of scientists working in their labs

to build a better bomb or high-tech weapon, concentrating on the science, forgetting the human cost, the results of such experimental tinkering. All Dela ever thought about was the steel, giving it a useful shape. Death was a part of her considerations, but distant, a shadow. Unreal.

And yet, despite her disgust, her horror, she could still taste the need for steel at the back of her throat, the dark desire to forge and craft things other than "safe art." No soft rounded curves, but sharp, sharp, sharp.

Am I a monster? Dela asked herself. *If not, then what am I?*

Someone knocked softly on the bathroom door.

"Go away," she ordered. The door opened anyway, and Hari peered in. Their eyes met, and then distance blurred and he pulled her away from the sink into his arms. He held her tight, stroking her hair, and suddenly the tears no longer hid; they ran rivers down her cheeks onto Hari's shirt. Dela sobbed, and it was fierce, choking, and ugly.

Hari said nothing. He stood with her, warm and comforting, and she knew instinctively that no matter how bad things were, Hari would understand. He would understand because he had lived through worse than she could imagine. He would understand because he was her friend.

He would understand because . . . because he loved her?

Dela knew he desired her—that he lusted—but lust was not the same as love, and she had never been free with her heart or her body. And yet, she knew what Hari felt had to have some spark of the genuine. Even in her despair she could feel their connection, burning like a live wire in her heart, new and frightening and wonderful. Something deeper than simple friendship.

Love is a leap of faith. You must leap, and believe Hari will catch you as you fall. And if he does not, that is the way of things. You will not be the only girl to have ever suffered a broken heart.

Except losing Hari might hurt worse than death.

"Delilah," he whispered, hugging her even tighter. "Delilah. This was not your fault. You made the weapon, yes—but never with the intent to kill that child. Nor was it your hand that committed the act. You must forgive yourself."

"I don't know if I can," she murmured, pulling away just far enough to rub at her eyes and nose. Hari's arms hung loose around her ribs, his fingers trailing down her spine, curving into the hollow of her back. Dela gazed up into his eyes, searching for someplace to fall.

She found it.

THE SUNLIGHT IN HER HOME HAD NEVER FELT SO bright—almost painful—and Dela wanted to shield her tender eyes as she left the bathroom to face the four men ranged across her living room. Apparently, this group discussion took precedence over surveillance.

Dela did not want their pity, but she saw some in their faces. She looked for more than pity, some horror or disgust, but found nothing. Just quiet patience.

"I'll understand if you guys want to leave," she said, thankful for Hari's calm presence against her back. Mindful, too, of her hypocrisy. "Circumstances have changed, and none of you deserves to be in the line of fire for something so personal. I couldn't take it if any of you got hurt for something I've done. This is all my fault."

"You are so insane," Dean said, drinking directly from a bottle of vodka that had appeared on the coffee table. Dela didn't know she owned anything stronger than beer or wine. Artur frowned at his chugging friend, but it was the look of a man who wanted to gulp down his own shot of hard liquor.

"Even I can't defend you on this one." Blue threw up his hands. "You *are* nuts."

Dela looked to Hari for support.

"You remember the towel, do you not?" When Dela nodded, Hari smiled. "Then I suppose you know what I will do if you insist on this."

"You're evil."

"So it has been said, by people far more frightening than you."

"Dela." Artur slowly stood, a strange pleading in his eyes and hands. Strange because Artur was a man who rarely showed emotion, and here—here he was hiding nothing, the gentle mask gone. "You must let us help you. Roland did not just send us. We asked to come because you are our friend. You are more than a friend. You are family. Do you understand?"

Dean snorted. "Hell, Dela. We risk our lives and use our powers to help everyone else, and you're going to tell us to back off? I don't think so."

"Like white on rice," Blue said. "You're not getting rid of us that easily."

"What about you, Eddie?" Dela managed to ask, close to tears. The young man had remained noticeably silent. "You're new here and you haven't known me as long as the others. You don't have to stay."

To his credit, Eddie did not look at the three men ranged around him for permission, or help. His answer was instantaneous and confident.

"I'm staying, ma'am. Even if the others wanted to leave, I would still stay."

"Suck-up," Dean said pleasantly.

Eddie blushed, but his gaze remained firm. "Ever since I got here, all I've heard about is how no one had a place to belong until Dirk & Steele found them—and how after they were recruited they realized it wasn't the place, it was the *people* that made it home. And you're one of those people, ma'am. If not for me quite yet, then for everyone else. That's all that matters."

"Well," Blue said, after a long moment of silence. He rested his hand on Eddie's shoulder. "I think you're going to fit in just fine around here."

Dela tried to smile through the tears stinging her eyes. "I give up. I don't deserve any of you, but I guess that's my luck."

Hari held up the tray of cookies. "Here," he said. "Sugar makes the pain go away."

"I think I'm beginning to like him," Dean said, to no one in particular.

Dela took a cookie. "You should try kissing him sometime."

That raised a few uncomfortable smiles. Dela sighed, sinking into the couch. Hari gazed out the window.

"All right," she said. "How do we find the bastard who killed this kid?"

The men all looked at each other. Blue said, "We're going to find the killer, but I don't think he's the one you have to worry about right now. It's the parents who want you dead."

Dela closed her eyes. Took a deep breath. "I don't blame them."

Artur made a low sound. "The murder weapon changed several hands. The first pair was your own; the next belonged to the killer. I cannot tell you much, except the murderer was a man driven by revenge. He wanted to make an example of someone. I do not know who or

why, but the little girl was the chosen target. After . . .
completion," and Dela felt sympathy for Artur, who was
sparing her details he himself had been forced to ob-
serve, "the knife was left at the scene, where it was found
by the child's family. You have a signature mark on all
your blades, yes?"

Dela nodded. Her mark was always the same stylized
D engraved on the steel near the hilt.

"That is how they found and tracked you," Artur said.
"That is why they want you dead. I am not convinced
the family believes you had any personal involvement in
their daughter's death. They just want revenge on everyone whose hand touched the event, no matter how remote the connection."

"I made the weapon that killed their child. That isn't
remote. Not in the slightest."

"Jesus, Dela." Dean hung his head. "You think gun
manufacturers lose any sleep at night?"

Dela opened her mouth to argue, but Blue beat her to
it. "Shut the hell up, Dean. Dela's got every right to feel
the way she does, and she shouldn't have to defend herself from us. I'm just glad she's got the guts to face the
issue."

A lie. Dela had nothing left within her heart but
grief. Grief and determination.

Hari walked up behind the couch and gently squeezed
Dela's shoulder. His touch stirred memory; she heard
the words he had spoken just before guiding her from
the bathroom.

*You are miserable because you made the weapon, but
remember this: I was a weapon. I still am, save for the
grace of your heart. Listen to me. I can recall every face,
every injustice. I will never forget how much blood I
have on my hands, but I have learned to live with it. You*

will do the same, Delilah. You will do the same because this act was done against your will, and if you had known—if you had been able—you would have fought this with your last breath. Just as I did. You are an honorable woman, Delilah.

Dela took his words and wrapped them close to her heart, taking strength from his conviction. She did not believe she still had honor—it felt broken, bleeding—but she would find it again. Somehow.

"Can the family be reasoned with?" Hari asked. Artur shrugged.

"If they are anything like my old bosses, then no. They will keep coming until Dela is dead. Our only option is to find the murderer, if he still lives, and bring him to the family. But that is no guarantee."

"Are you saying they're mafia?" Dela asked, incredulous.

"That is what I sense. And they would certainly have the resources to track you, even overseas. There was another knife, yes? The one used in the second attack? Hari showed it to me. The man hired to murder you was paid a significant amount of money to see you dead, killed by a knife attack. He was a local, chosen because he would blend in more easily. His orders came from an overseas contact."

"This sounds like a frame-up. But why use me as the scapegoat?"

"We don't know," Dean said, "and, um, that trail Roland assigned to you in China wasn't able to provide us with any good intel, either."

Dela narrowed her eyes. "What about the guy at the airport?"

"An unknown," Blue said. "Probably working for the other side. Roland didn't hire him."

"Well, this is just great."

"Listen," Dean said, "it may be witness protection time. Nice little lodge in the Swiss Alps, you can blend in with the other snow bunnies—"

Dela shook her head. "Going into hiding is my last option. Besides, if these people really want to cut me up, they'll just go after Mom and Dad to draw me out. Better me than them."

"Then we must be proactive." Artur stared thoughtfully at his gloved hands. "I have already asked Roland to call Yancy. Some of the larger mafia families are located on the east coast, and there might be word of recent family losses."

Tension filled the room at the mention of Yancy. Hari stirred, frowning.

"This Yancy is your aunt?"

"Correct." Dela did not trust herself to say more.

"The two of them don't get along," Dean explained. "I mean, they can't even be together in the same room without one of them losing it. Scariest chick fights I've ever seen, and they don't even land blows."

"Girls don't have rules when they fight," Blue said with a straight face. "They're not as civilized as men."

"I could take her," Dela muttered.

"Of course," Artur soothed, as Eddie and Hari looked on, somewhat bewildered.

"Why are you on poor terms with your aunt? Has she hurt you?" Hari asked.

Dela sighed. "It's a long story. Yancy is excellent at her job and I respect her for that, but she's also got a superiority complex a mile wide."

"She's a racist," Blue said. "She doesn't like people who are different. In this case, folks without powers. Which is almost everyone."

Dela nodded. "She threw a fit when Mom married my dad, just because he doesn't have psi-gifts, and then she made life hell for my brother and me when we were growing up. Always testing us, finding fault, blaming my dad for all our problems. I bet she's getting a huge kick out of this."

"I doubt that," Artur said. "You are still her niece."

"And by God, no one has a right to bully you but her!" Dean thumped his chest.

Hari said nothing. He gently squeezed Dela's shoulder, and she wondered if he thought her childish. After all, his entire family was gone to dust and wind, and here she was, complaining about her own.

But in his eyes, she found only warmth. That and a quiet sympathy.

Blue left, taking the riddle box with him. He was gone for an hour, during which time very little was decided, except that Dela had to be carefully guarded at all times. When Blue walked through the door, he nodded at them, silent. No one asked where the box was. As far as Dela was concerned, the fewer people who knew, the better.

A warm glow filled the living room as early evening light shaded the distant trees and buildings of Rose Apple. Blue turned on the lamps with just a thought, while Artur closed the shades. Dela and Eddie began fixing dinner, an assortment of sandwiches and chips.

She sensed some lingering tension between Hari and the others, but a quick glance assured her that rough trust, and a little camaraderie, was beginning to form. Dean and Hari bent over his weapons. The shapeshifter seemed to be telling a story. Blue sat nearby, listening.

Artur came up behind Dela and she smiled at him

as she showed Eddie where all the paper plates were stored. She didn't think anyone—least of all her—felt like doing dishes tonight.

"I'm glad you're here," she said to the tall Russian. Artur's smile was sad, his eyes shadowed, weary.

"When I heard what happened, I could not stay away. None of us could." Artur hesitated. "How are you, Dela?"

"Tired," she confessed softly. "And scared. So much has happened in such a short time, Artur. I feel like my head will explode trying to make sense of it all."

"It is not just the threats on your life. It is also Hari."

Dela felt Eddie go very still, and a moment later he sidled away to the farthest corner of the kitchen, ostensibly to slather mayonnaise on the bread.

"Yes," she whispered, thankful for the illusion of privacy. "But he's also the reason I'm holding up so well. He's the reason I'm still alive."

"I know." Artur raised a gloved hand to his dark head. "I have felt him. These past few days have been very powerful for Hari. Life-altering."

"For me, too," she said, looking away.

"You love him."

There was a strange wistfulness in Artur's voice, in his pale face. She had no answer, save one, and slowly nodded.

Artur's face relaxed into a tender smile. "I am glad. Truly, Dela."

"Thank you," she murmured. "That means a lot, coming from you."

"We had our chance and I was not ready. That is the way of it."

Dela touched his arm. "You'll find someone, Artur, and it will be when you least expect it."

"Like you?"

There were two ways to understand those words, both radically different from the other, and Dela hesitated. "It will happen. Just give it time."

Again, his soft smile. He gently pulled away and joined the other men around Hari's weapons. Hari glanced up at Dela, and there was a quiet understanding in his golden eyes. She wondered just how good his ears really were.

The dining table was large enough for all her friends to find a seat, and dinner was a loud, boisterous affair. Dela sensed that everyone was trying to keep her spirits high, away from thoughts of murdered children, weapons, and parents trying to take revenge. Amazingly, there were moments when she did forget.

But not for long.

After dessert, which degenerated into a contest between Dean and Eddie to see who could eat the most ice cream, Dela professed exhaustion and retreated to her bedroom. She collapsed on top of the covers, curled into a tiny ball, and closed her eyes.

She did not know how long she slept, only that when she opened her eyes, the full moon cast a sheet of silver across her bed and the walls. A breath of movement caught her attention; in the corner, by the closed door, stood Hari.

He wore only a towel, and Dela thought she smelled shampoo. He did not approach, and when she slipped from the bed and went to him, he still did not move or make a sound. She touched his warm, damp skin. Her fingers tingled, her hands, arms—everywhere was tingling. Hari's eyes began to glow, and she welcomed the light, bathed in it as though she could wrap her body in a cocoon made of Hari's power. When Dela stood like this before him, all other men seemed like shadows, fleeting and shallow. So much without substance she doubted they existed.

"You are so beautiful," she heard herself whisper. Her words sent something hungry spinning through Hari's glowing eyes, and she felt his palms whisper against her waist. A moment of hesitation, and Dela leaned into him. Just one touch, a kiss.

Hari's hands were very large, his fingers long and elegant. His palms tightened around her waist, gentle and firm, lifting her closer. Gulping, she feathered his scarred chest with her fingers, her lips. Some breath of air escaped Hari's mouth; his eyes were closed, and he was still, so very still.

Dela traced the hollow of his throat with her fingernail, following the line of his collarbone. He was so tall she could not reach him with her mouth. Hari bent down. She thought, for a moment, he would kiss her. Instead, he pressed his lips against her ear. She shuddered.

"May I carry you to the bed?" His voice was so deep, luxurious as velvet against her skin. She nodded, uncertain of her own voice, and Hari gently lifted her into his arms. He did it easily, as though she weighed nothing.

He set her on the bed, stretching out beside her. He bent his knee, inserting a leg between her thighs. Dela gasped as he pressed close. He was hard, everywhere.

"Not all things must happen now," he said gently, touching her face, reassuring her with the softness in his eyes that was at such odds with the fierce cast of his body. "I just want to hold you. I have been alone for so long, Delilah, that just being able to put my hands on your body is a gift."

Something old and tired gave way in Dela's heart, and she stroked Hari's face, running her fingers through his fine hair. His gaze felt warm upon her skin, exquisite with tenderness, and she slowly, carefully, brushed her lips against his own. Fire filled her, spreading from her cheeks down her throat, through her breasts and deeper.

Just one touch, a kiss.

Hari enfolded Dela in his arms, his body swelling rock-hard, exquisitely painful. Every brush of Dela's soft curves sent waves of pleasure and torment through his body. He had never wanted a woman so badly, not even in his youth, before the curse; his heart shuddered with desire.

So strange: Only one night before, Hari had wondered if he was falling in love with Dela, but now he thought he had already fallen, and this wonderful feeling inside his chest, warming him, was the culmination. He did not know. He had never been in love. He had spent the past two thousand years as a slave to men and women whose requests of him had been violent and brutal.

Would Dela still accept him if she knew of his trespasses, the things he had done? Would he ever have the strength to tell her?

And what was love, anyway? What did he know of love, which was nothing but a distant, heartsick memory?

I want to make her mine, he thought, pressing his lips against her throat. *I want to make her free. I want to wrap my heart around her soul and keep her safe.*

"Hari?" she murmured, breathless. "What does it mean to kiss like mates?"

His laugh was low, sensual. "I would have to show you, but when I do, it will not be in a home full of other men."

Dela smiled, her hands drifting down his waist; lower, and still lower, until Hari growled. "Your eyes are glowing," she whispered. "Like the sun."

He shivered, but Dela would not let him pull away. She wrapped her arms and legs around him, and Hari was once again reminded that Dela was stronger than she looked. Steel in her arms, for the steel she smithed.

"What is it? Tell me." Hari closed his eyes. Dela growled, frustrated. "Don't hide from me!"

Hari opened his eyes, and he could finally see the glow reflected in her face, bathing her flawless skin in sheer liquid gold.

"My eyes should not be glowing. Without my skin, it is impossible."

"Why?" She was so earnest, so sincere. His heart lurched.

"Because it is an element of the change. Shapeshifters' eyes glow for a variety of reasons, arousal being one of them, but it always precedes a shift from one body to another. My skin is gone, Delilah. I cannot become the tiger, and therefore, my eyes should not glow gold."

Dela chewed her bottom lip. "Maybe you're wrong. Perhaps it just seems that way. Did anyone else ever mention your glowing eyes?" Hari shook his head, and she hesitated before adding, "And lovers? Have you had any at all over the years?"

Hari sighed, pushing his face into Dela's throat, drinking in her scent, his hands stroking her ribs, her breasts. She pushed against him, arching her back, but the question still loomed and he knew he had to answer.

"Some of my masters were women," he breathed, collapsing the painful memories into a pinprick he could partition. "Sometimes they used me for battle, but often they preferred to keep me in their bedrooms. I am not sure which was worse—fighting, or being used by them. Eventually, there was one whom I thought cared for me, and I felt some affection for her in return—but she betrayed my trust. Her husband was a king, and he had no knowledge of the box. When he found me in her chambers, instead of telling him the truth, his wife lied and said I raped her, that I had threatened to take her husband's life if she did not cooperate."

Hari shuddered, and Dela drew him as close as flesh allowed. "The punishment was quite painful," he said. "And I could not die, no matter what was done to me. When the king discovered this . . . this *gift* . . . he called me a devil, and proceeded to punish me even more. I was finally spared when he killed his wife for being tainted by a demon."

"No more," Dela promised, her voice shaking. "You will never have to go through that again, Hari. Not ever."

He pressed his hand to her cheek, savoring the smooth silk of her skin, the silver of moonlight on her hair and body. Even clothed, she inspired him.

"How can you be so sure?" he whispered, looking deep into her eyes.

"Because," and here she smiled, and he remembered the echo of her words from days past, "the alternative is unthinkable."

He kissed her then, tangling his fingers in her hair, gently parting her lips with his tongue, filling himself with the taste of her mouth, her scent. He could not imagine a more exquisite woman, a more extraordinary heart than the one fluttering so wildly beneath his hand.

Perhaps two thousand years was worth it, just to be here in this moment, with her.

He could feel energy building between them. Dela's

hands slid beneath his towel to cup his buttocks, fingers
stroking the sensitive crease. He gasped, and she used
the opportunity to deepen their kiss, her teeth scraping
his tongue. His fingers pushed up her shirt, his palms
rubbing lightly over her taut breasts. She moaned in his
mouth, and he stole her breath, fingers closing over her
nipples to lightly twist, pull. Dela trembled, breaking their
kiss to pant wildly against his ear. Her desire aroused
him even more, made him bold. One hand still behind
her head, the other crept down, past the waistband of her
loose pants, sliding soft against skin, down until his fingers met curls and a slick, hot heat.

Just one touch.

Dela buried her mouth against Hari's throat, trying
not to cry out. She did not know where the others were,
but they had to be close, and she did not want them to
hear her making love to Hari. The moment seemed too
intimate, too sacred, to share with anyone but the man
pressed to her.

She was unprepared for her body's response to his
kisses, his caresses. No one had ever given her this
much pleasure, and it both thrilled and frightened her.
*We'll never be able to do this standing up. I'd collapse
the first time he touched me.*

His fingers burrowed deep. Her thighs clasped tight
around his hand, increasing the pleasure as he stroked
harder, faster, guiding her mouth back to his. He swallowed her whimpers with his kisses, striking a rhythm
with his tongue that made her dizzy with pleasure.
When she came, it was thunder—lightning in her head,
arcing down her spine. Somewhere, she was distantly
aware of the steel girders groaning, the mattress springs
trembling.

Hari did not remove his hand, nor slow the fine quick

stroke of his fingers. Within seconds she came again, and a minute later, one more time.

A kiss.

"Hari," she gasped weakly, held tight against his chest.

"Shhh," he murmured, smoothing her hair. "Just rest. I have been wanting to do that for a very long time."

"How long? We've only known each other a couple of days."

"You were very fetching in that towel," he said, nipping her ear. She laughed, lightly punching his chest. And then, before he could prepare himself, her hands slipped beneath his towel, stroking him. He almost shouted, but bit his tongue before more than a low croak emerged.

"My turn," she whispered, her voice rough with desire.

Her fingers danced, a random patter of movement that made Hari strain against her, wild. Dela bared her teeth in a fierce smile; he felt her wrap forefinger and thumb around the base of his erection, gliding the twisting ring of her fingers upwards, alternating between quick and achingly slow. Her other hand caressed the area behind his balls, and he felt himself grow harder, each stroke of her hands more intense than the last. He saw stars—thought he saw the own glow of his eyes, reflecting inward—and his breathing sounded loud in his ears, painful.

Oh, but if this was pain, then he would take it all, always. With much effort, he pressed his mouth to her ear. "Delilah," he managed raggedly, even as she continued her magic. Her fingernails lightly scraped his balls, and something inhuman emerged from his throat. "Delilah," he tried again, "I would like to . . . to move inside you, but now . . . now is not the time, with all these people here, and I . . . oh . . . I want you to understand it is not because I do not want you."

"I know," she said, tongue darting in his ear. "I feel the same way. Consider this an appetizer."

And then she did something else. He did not know what, only that he exploded with an orgasm so powerful his back arched, his muscles swelling, contracting, a roped ripple that made him go blind with pleasure.

This time it was he who collapsed in her arms, and they both lay together, limbs tangled, curled around each other's bodies, occasionally laughing with some inexplicably giddy happiness.

"You've ruined me for anyone else," Dela told him, and Hari's heart swelled.

"Good," he said fiercely. "I do not want to share."

"Neither do I," she said.

Hari's answering smile was gentle, sweet. "Never have that fear, Delilah. Even without the curse, I am yours forever."

CHAPTER EIGHT

DELA woke to the sounds of muffled shouts. Her room was dark and Hari was beside her, naked, spooned against her back. He stirred, and was out of bed in an instant, padding silently to the windows.

"What do you see?" she whispered. Hari shook his head. She strained to listen for sounds from the rest of the apartment and heard nothing. Throwing back the covers, Dela crept to her bedroom door and opened it just a crack. All the lights were off.

She whistled, and a moment later her call was returned, soft as a bird's cry. Hari pressed against her shoulder, drawing her away from the door. "Stay here," he said. "I will go check on the others."

"Towel," she ordered. Hari's teeth flashed, and he grabbed his towel from the floor, wrapping it around his waist. A sliver of moonlight still haunted her room, and Hari's long muscles gleamed, his back rippling as he silently glided into shadow. Dela remained by the door, listening.

What the—this is my *home, too. I should be out there with them.*

Another shout, startlingly close, and Dela slipped

from her bedroom, staying close to the walls. The quiet within the apartment was preternatural—a dead silence, made starker by the intermittent sounds of fighting outside the warehouse—and suddenly, beneath her. She wished she knew who was out there; wished she could just talk with them, spill her heart.

And would anyone be able to reason with you if it had been your child?

No. Dela would die with grief—and be reborn in rage. Terrifying, twisted. No mercy.

But her guilt was not strong enough for suicide, or even despair. There would be no laying down of arms, especially if the other side remained hostile. If Dela was going to fight tonight, she would fight to win.

Just as her friends were doing, if the sounds rattling beneath her floorboards were any indication. Worry assailed her, thick and choking.

Artur and the others can take care of themselves, she told herself firmly, but it was weak comfort, especially when they were risking their lives for her.

Dela crept along the wall, looking for some sign of Hari and the other occupants of the apartment. She thought she heard breathing, the rub of clothing, and she peered around the corner wall to find Hari and Eddie crouched on each side of the front door. Hari held his sword in front of him—a warrior from a fairy tale, magical and powerful and strange. Eddie crouched in his shadow, and Dela caught the glint of something dark and metallic in his white grip. It whispered *gun.*

She cringed for the young man, drew a breath to speak. Hari heard her, and glared. *Silence,* he seemed to say. And then, *Go.*

Dela shook her head, stubborn, and Hari's lips pressed into a hard white line. He made a move toward her, but just at that moment, someone rammed the door, hard enough to make the hinges creak. Hari grabbed Eddie by the scruff of his neck, hauling him up and backward as the door was hit again. A single gunshot, then, the dull thud of a silencer. The lock blew out.

Hari shoved Eddie toward Dela as three men poured through the door. Dressed in black, with tight ski masks pulled over their faces, they carried guns in their hands. Knives whispered from sheaths tied to their thighs.

Her intruders were clearly not expecting to see a seven-foot tall, half-naked man with a sword. They hesitated, and Hari fell upon them, silent as a ghost, his sword flashing, the blade darting like quicksilver, piercing skin, plunging past ribs.

Screams shattered the living room; as the first intruder died, the others regained their wits, unloading their silenced weapons into Hari. Eddie moved to help, but Dela grabbed him before he could step into their line of sight. He stared at her with wild eyes, but stopped struggling when she silently pleaded with him to be still. Grim, he peered around the wall with his gun pointed.

One shot, close range, and an intruder fell to the floor.

Hari had collapsed to one knee and was struggling to rise. Dela wanted to weep for him, scream, but she swallowed her fear. *Hari is immortal,* she reassured herself, desperately hoping the bullets had not done more damage than magic could repair.

The last man shot at Eddie. His aim was off, but the bullet grazed Eddie's arm with enough force that he dropped his gun. Eddie staggered to the floor, scrabbling for the weapon.

Time slowed. Dela saw the intruder aim at Eddie, his

finger tightening on the trigger; behind him was Hari, now on his feet, lifting his sword. She knew, deep in her gut, that he would never make it in time.

Something immense surged through Dela's mind, and she threw herself between Eddie and the intruder, hands outstretched.

The gun fired.

She felt the bullet leave the barrel, an instant recognition of steel, leaving a trail of mercury fire through her brain as she clutched and grappled—*faster than the eye, fast—stay ahead of it now, stay—*

Stay.

Stay.

Her vision cleared; the room was deathly quiet, but she was still alive. She saw it then: the bullet, hanging in the air, just in front of her hand. She blinked, the connection broke, and she caught the bullet in her palm before it could hit the floor.

"Fuck," whispered the intruder.

"Yeah," said a familiar voice, tinged with awe. "That about sums it up."

Dean stepped clear of the doorway, followed closely by Artur and Blue. Hari reached the masked intruder first, easily tackling him to the floor—slippery with blood, the air thick with its scent. Hari pulled off the ski mask, revealing a pale face framed with black hair. The same face of the man who had been watching her at the airport.

Hari looked like a piece of raw meat—everywhere, blood. Bullet holes riddled his body. Even Eddie, pale with pain, gawked at him. Dela and Blue helped the boy to his feet. While Blue guided Eddie to the couch, she ran to the bathroom for towels to press against his shallow wound. Bodies filled her peripheral vision; she shut them out, swallowing hard.

Dela switched on lamps as she came back, flooding the room with yet more light to see the carnage. She brought towels for Hari, but when she got up close, all she could do was stare, helpless. She did not know where to touch him, how to begin.

"Why are you still alive?" Dean looked like he was going to be sick. Hari said nothing, his jaw clenched so tight Dela thought it would take a miracle to pry his mouth open again.

"Magic," Dela answered for him.

Hari's blood had begun to soak through the intruder's clothing; the man whimpered. Dean and Artur quickly stripped him of all his weapons and flipped him on his back, guns pointed at his face.

"Think anyone called the police?" Dela asked.

Blue shook his head. "It's three in the morning, and you're the only one who lives in this part of downtown. 'Sides, these guys were using silencers and we were careful not to fire our own guns outside."

"How many?" Eddie pressed a towel to his arm.

"Six. They weren't taking any chances this time. Trying to crack the security system when we caught them." He looked down at the prone man. "They won't be bothering anyone again."

Dela closed her eyes, feeling sick. "Blue, you better take Eddie to a hospital. Tell them he got mugged or something."

"Ma'am—" Eddie began to protest, but Blue shook his head.

"No problem. If they need an address . . . ?"

"Give them mine. They'll probably know who I am. Tell them you're my guests."

"Sure thing." He helped Eddie to his feet, the young man biting back his groans with a stoicism that made

Dela think he had been shot before. They stepped around the bodies by the front door and disappeared down the hall.

"Hari," Dela pleaded, as blood continued to pour from his wounds. "You need to rest."

The shape-shifter shook his head. The man on the floor stared at the enraged warrior with an expression almost pitiful in its fear and confusion.

Resigned, Dela knelt beside her intruder. "Who are you working for? Come on, now. I don't want to force you."

"*I* do," Hari said, finally breaking his silence. His voice revealed no pain; it sounded smooth, like dark honey with a hint of acid. He reached for his sword and blood spattered everywhere.

The man made a low croaking squeal as Hari pressed the tip of the blade against his trembling throat. He sounded like a dying pig.

"Answer her questions," Hari commanded, "or I will saw your head from the rest of your body. You will feel every cut. You will choke on your own blood. I promise you this, because I have seen it done. Now *talk*."

His menace was stunning; not with malevolence or cruelty, but with the heavy certainty of experience, commitment. No one, not even Dela, doubted him. Dean looked very impressed.

The man wet his lips. Dela could see his calculation: Who was more frightening? The bloody maniac standing above him with a sword pressed to his throat, or his bosses?

Apparently, Hari won hands down.

"I work for Wen Zhang," he confessed, hoarse. "He's based out of New York. Chinatown."

"And why does he want to murder me?" Dela knew

the answer, but had to hear it again, to make it real for herself.

"You made the knife that killed his niece. The entire family wants you dead. I just follow orders." The last sounded like a plea.

"What does your boss do?" Artur asked.

When the man did not immediately answer, Hari pressed down on the blade until he gasped and squirmed. "Okay, everything! There are two enterprises running Chinatown. Zhang heads one of them. Prostitution, illegals—all the body traffic goes through him. He controls the snakeheads, safe houses, all the new blood."

"What's he babbling about?" Dean asked.

"Human smuggling," Dela replied, grim. "Bring in illegal aliens from China, men and women who are willing to work under any circumstances. Indebt them for thirty grand or more so they can't ever escape, and then keep them in Chinatown, working for employers who get cheap labor for three dollars an hour, at conditions a rat wouldn't crawl through. If anyone objects, kill or torture them."

"Shit," Dean said. "And just when I thought my night couldn't get any worse."

Dela took a deep breath; the scent of fresh blood threatened to overwhelm her. She struggled not to vomit.

Control, she reminded herself, swallowing hard. *Keep your control.*

But it was difficult; she had never been witness to so much violence. Men dead, injured—and all because of her.

Dela staggered to her feet and went to the kitchen for paper and a pen.

"Dela?" Artur called softly.

"I'm going to write a letter. I don't trust this guy to remember everything I have to say."

The letter was short; there was nothing she could write that would adequately express her remorse. She kept it simple.

Words and actions will never be enough to make up for what happened. The knife was meant to be an ornament, never deadly, and when it was stolen from me, I had no idea what it was used for. I am so sorry.

"Add this," Artur said, when she showed it to him. "'We will find the murderer as a sign of good faith, but any more attacks will not be tolerated.'" He pulled off his glove and pressed his hand to the intruder's forehead. Artur closed his eyes. His jaw tightened, distaste etching shadows in his face. "'We know where you are,'" he spat, "'and what you look like. Be warned.'"

He wiped his hand on his jeans. "Did you get that, Dela?"

She nodded, and tucked the carefully folded letter into the front pocket of her would-be murderer's pants. Hari stood back and the man climbed unsteadily to his feet. With his shoulders hunched, his eyes big, he looked like a mouse caught under the gaze of hungry cats. Dean made a shooing motion with his gun.

"Get the fuck out of here, stupid. This is your lucky night."

"But if you try to hurt Delilah again . . ." Hari rumbled.

"Yes," Artur said. "We will not be so pleasant. Now go."

Her intruder did not need to be told a third time. Silent, quick, he stumbled through the doorway, hobbling past the fallen bodies of his compatriots without a second glance. Loyalty at its best. No one followed to make sure he left; they could smell his fear, his desperation. This man was not planning to hang around.

As soon as the intruder disappeared, Hari swayed. Dela called out his name, wrapping her arms around his waist, unmindful of blood. His sword slipped from his hand; Dean caught the hilt, swearing as he staggered under its weight.

"Bedroom," Dean ordered, laying Hari's sword on the floor. He propped the shape-shifter on his shoulder and grimaced. "This man's beginning to remind me of a vegetable strainer, except it ain't water that's pouring out." He looked at Dela. "I guess Hari full of bullets and still breathing would be a pain in the ass to explain, huh?"

"Try impossible," Artur murmured, holstering his gun. He slung Hari's other arm over his shoulder and the two men dragged him off to Dela's bedroom.

Hari coughed up blood as they walked, his lungs gurgling like an old air conditioner. He tried to say something to Dela, but the moment they lay him flat on the bed, his head slipped sideways into unconsciousness.

Everyone felt for a pulse. It was there—slow, but steady.

"Twisted," Dean muttered. "You sure know to pick 'em, honey."

Dela did not say anything. She sank down on the edge of the bed, wrapping her arms around her stomach, and sucked down the beginnings of a sob.

"Hey now." Dean pressed his lips into her hair. "It'll be all right, Dela."

Warm hands touched her cheeks, lifting up her face.

Artur, with his gloves off. He had never touched her before, skin to skin. He shivered, his eyes going dark with compassion.

"Nothing lasts forever," he whispered. "But this . . . all of us, and Hari . . . we will be with you for some time yet. We are not over. You are not alone."

The tight fist around her heart loosened. Dela took a deep, shuddering breath. "Thank you," she said, her gratitude encompassing everything: his kindness, his friendship, his presence.

He nodded, pulling on his gloves. Dean gently patted her shoulder.

The two men returned to the living room to take care of the bodies. Dela stayed with Hari, her fingers tangled in his hair—the only part of him not covered in blood. Events replayed in her mind, again and again, an incessant picture show.

She saw Hari lift his sword and kill the intruder; she watched him get shot, bullets filling his chest and stomach, blood jetting from the wounds. She watched Eddie fall, and felt herself leap between him and a gun. A bullet, racing toward her chest.

Dela shook herself and closely examined Hari's slack face. His silence during the attack had been complete, without a single gasp of pain. He had stood tall, eyes set, determined and angry. As though the bullets in his body were nothing.

She wondered, horrified, what Hari could have suffered during his enslavement that was worse than a body full of gunshot wounds. Something more terrible, suffered enough times that his current injuries were, in some way, manageable.

She heard a squelching sound, meaty. A flicker in her vision, and she looked down as one of Hari's entry wounds trembled, the edges around the hole rippling like a grotesque mouth. She saw metal, the glimmer of soft, round, edges. The bullet popped out of Hari's body, rolling down his stomach onto the bed. The wound sealed over, the skin knitting together before her eyes. A bloody hole . . . and then, none at all. Smooth flesh.

It was like watching a horror movie; Dela almost expected the slug to grow arms and legs, and do a little dance on the bloody sheets.

The cycle repeated itself, a slow process of rejection. Dela tuned herself to the bullets, listening as Hari's body edged them out. They had no stories to tell, and after a time, she raised her shields. It was bad enough watching; she did not want to feel it as well.

Dela was unaware of the passage of time, lost in watching Hari heal himself, but Dean eventually opened the door. He gestured for her to follow him. Sighing, Dela pressed a gentle kiss on Hari's forehead, keenly aware of a bullet wiggling out of his shoulder, scant inches away.

"How's sleeping beauty?" Dean asked, as Dela joined him and Artur in the kitchen. They looked tired, and it was clear why. Where blood and gore had covered the wooden floors and walls, now there was no sign of death or the gunfight. Everything glistened; she smelled bleach, vinegar, an army of cleaning fluids. Vanilla-scented candles burned on the kitchen counter. Dela wanted to hug and kiss them both.

But still . . . still, she could see the bodies, the blood. Violence, sprayed against her walls. Her home would never feel the same.

"He's sweating bullets," she said, holding one up for them to see. They stared at her, and then the bullet, until Dean suddenly blanched and scrunched up his face.

"Oh," he said. "That's gross."

Dela nodded. There really was no way to disagree. It *was* gross.

"Dean and I are going to take the bodies away," Artur said mildly, still looking at the bullet in her hand. "We will be gone for most of the night, but this is something we must do before light. I do not think you have anything to worry about."

"Um, sure." Dela took a deep breath. Dean patted her arm.

"Nothing to feel bad about, Dela. It was us or them, and the first law of survival: Always choose yourself."

She nodded, not entirely comforted, but willing to believe her friends harbored no regrets or resentment.

"Blue called me," Dean said, as she walked the men to the remains of her door. "Eddie is going to be fine. They had to file a police report, but everyone believed their story, especially when they dropped your name and their connections to Dirk & Steele."

"It's amazing what a good reputation can buy," Dela mused.

"A good reputation is priceless," Artur observed, pulling his gun from its holster. He handed it to Dela, safety off.

"You remember our lessons?"

"Yes," she said.

"Good," he said wistfully.

And then they were gone.

IT WAS IMPOSSIBLE TO STAY AWAY FROM HARI, BUT there was that big broken door to consider, and no matter what Artur said, men had entered Dela's home to kill her and her friends. Indeed, Artur passing over his gun did not inspire copious amounts of confidence in her own safety.

So, Dela darted from the bedroom to the living room, and back again, over and over, barely resting in one place before feeling the incessant urge to head to the other. She vomited several times, thinking of the dead men. She was not terribly sorry they were dead, and that made her feel guilty.

It was exhausting, and when she finally heard Blue call her name as he stomped up the stairs, she almost cried with relief.

"How's Eddie?" she asked, meeting him at the door and handing over Artur's gun. Blue frowned, clicking on the safety.

"Eddie's fine. Just needed some stitches. He wanted to come back with me, but the nurses wouldn't let him. You, apparently, are now his hero. He thinks you're the best thing since Buffy the Vampire Slayer."

Dela blushed. "Eddie's pretty nifty, too. You should have seen him, Blue. He acted like a pro."

"So did you." He gave her a speculative glance. "You've gotten more powerful, Dela. I know only one person who can stop a bullet with his mind, but that was after years of meditation and practice."

"You're talking about Michael, right? He's getting ready to retire, last I heard."

"Don't change the subject."

"I'm not. It's just . . . desperation can do wonders." Dela grabbed a can of ginger ale from the refrigerator. Her mouth tasted bad. She did not want to think about this.

"It can't do *that* much," he muttered, gesturing for a beer. She handed him one, and he leaned against the counter. There were circles under his eyes; he looked rumpled and tired, his long black hair coming loose from its tie. Dela had a feeling she looked a whole lot worse. She hadn't had time yet to change her clothes, which were covered in Hari's blood.

"I wasn't really thinking clearly when I did it," Dela confessed. "I felt the bullet leave the gun, recognized the metal casing inside my head, and just told it to . . . stay."

"Stay?"

"Stay."

Blue frowned. "We should run some experiments. You've always been sensitive to metal, more familiar with it. Maybe that familiarity made it easier for your mind to hold on to the bullet."

"Cool," she said, although she felt anything but. She had enough on her plate without her psi-powers doing unexpected things—even if they were *good* unexpected things. She held the cold can of ginger ale against her neck. "Let me ask you something, Blue. Did you ever imagine your life could get so weird?"

Blue smiled. "This is sane, Dela." When her eyebrows shot up, he laughed. "No, it really is. I've got friends I don't have to hide from, I'm helping people, saving lives, getting the bad guys. As far as I'm concerned, this is it. The Dream. So what if things get dicey every now and then. I wouldn't change a thing."

Dela opened her mouth, but the words that sprang to mind didn't seem adequate. Instead, she kissed Blue on the cheek. "Thanks," she said, as he blinked back surprise. "I needed to hear that."

"Sure," he said, smiling. "Now go and check on your Hercules. Dean called as I was leaving the hospital. Said your man was spitting out bullets."

"That's one way of putting it," Dela said. "Thanks for being such a good friend, Blue."

"Back at you," he said, saluting her with his beer.

Dela padded back to her room, carefully opening her bedroom door. Hari still lay on the bed, covered in blood. Bullets rested on the surface of his chest and stomach.

He opened his eyes.

"Delilah," he whispered, his naked relief a mirror of her own. He closed his eyes as Dela sat beside him. They did not speak.

"I had no idea," he finally said, very softly. "Such weapons make men like me unnecessary."

Dela shook her head, though Hari's eyes were still closed and he could not see her. Cupping his face in her hands, she ignored the scent of blood and kissed his lips. "You are not a weapon. You are a man. A good man. You could never be unnecessary."

Hari smiled. He ran his fingers through Dela's loose hair, and then hesitated, as though realizing the gruesome quality of his skin. He tried sitting up, and bullets rolled off his body, clanking, ringing dully against the floor. Dela pressed her hands against his shoulders.

"I need to bathe," he said, and then stopped, choking. "Delilah. You are covered in blood."

"Your blood," she quickly said. "Remember?"

Hari nodded, but his eyes were haunted.

"That man used his weapon against you. I thought I would be the one to die when I saw that. I could not move quickly enough to stop him." Hari wrapped one mighty hand around Dela's wrist, drawing her palm to his cheek. "I believed myself strong, so fine a warrior those men would fall to me before they could hurt you or Eddie. Arrogant, Delilah. I was too arrogant. I never realized how lax my skills have become."

"It's been a long time since you cared who lived or died."

"True," he breathed. "We are both fortunate you were able to save yourself, and Eddie."

"I stopped the bullet." The words were whispered. *I stopped a bullet.*

Hari's gaze traced the lines of her face, searching. "If that is what it is called, then yes, you did. A remarkable act, Delilah."

"It wasn't enough to help you." She choked on the words. "All my promises . . . I've broken them all. You've suffered so much pain since you met me."

Hari touched her mouth, gentle. "No. Every day I would do this, if it kept you safe. There is joy in these sorrows, Delilah. So much joy, because we are together, because you are my true friend. It is as I have said: A little pain is a small price to pay, compared to the alternative."

"A little pain?" A sob burst from Dela's throat and she buried her face against his filthy shoulder. Hari raised her up so he could look into her eyes; he kissed her lips, her cheeks. He tasted her tears.

"I am with you," he whispered.

So much in those four words. So much to live for, to take joy in. Dela tried to smile through her tears, and found it not so difficult. Hari laughed, and gently pushed her away from him. He rolled off the bed, bullets scattering like beads.

"I belong in a charnel house, not a beautiful woman's bed. I need to bathe."

"Well," Dela said, still sniffling, following him as he staggered into her bathroom, "you *are* on the smelly side, but at least you're not leaking anymore."

"A very good thing," Hari agreed. He seemed to have some difficulty bending over, and Dela squeezed past him, working the knobs until the showerhead began blasting out hot water. Hari dropped his towel.

Dela blushed. She had seen him naked before, but the lights were bright, and his comfort with her felt all the more intimate for its casualness. Hari caught her staring, and the heat of his gaze aroused her even more. He stepped close, partially erect, thick and heavy. Dela met his eyes with some difficulty.

"Do you know," he said, advancing on her with graceful menace, "that I have not yet seen your body? You are obsessed with concealing yourself—and me."

Dela found it difficult to breathe. The sink pressed against her back.

"You're not concealed now," she managed.

Hari's answering smile was predatory, sensual. His large, elegant hands, which she knew had killed countless men in battle—and one for her tonight—tenderly traced her collarbone. He ran his knuckles against the swell of her breasts—lower still, against her stomach, until his fingers found the hem of her shirt. He tugged upward, slowly, revealing inch by inch her creamy flesh until her arms were stretched high, breasts firm and taut beneath his golden gaze.

"Ah." Hari sighed, pulling the shirt over her head. Before she could drop her arms, he caught her wrists with one giant hand. He cupped a breast with the other, and Dela trembled against him, her vision going dark with desire. Everything inside her felt open to Hari—her vulnerability, her passion, her love.

"I will never hurt you," Hari murmured, dipping his head to taste her mouth. "I will be with you always, Delilah. You own me, heart and soul, regardless of any curse."

Just words, but from Hari they sang with truth. He released her wrists and she immediately pressed herself to his naked body, ignoring the blood, the stench of death. She clutched his back and lifted her face, words spilling hoarse and full from her lips.

"I love you, Hari. I don't know how or when it happened, but I can't help it. I'm yours. All of me, yours."

Hari froze, and then let out a long sigh that seemed to take years from his face. "I think," he said, very carefully, "that if we can move past murder and magic, and the crowd of men still in your home, we will be very happy together."

Dela laughed, scrunching up her nose. "Go on, get in that shower."

"Not without you," he said, working on her pants. She squealed, for a moment unmindful of anyone who might hear. Hari stripped off her pants with a sultry charm that left her grinning and breathless.

He sighed appreciatively, gold sparking in his eyes. Pressing his lips to her stomach, he lightly trailed his fingers from her delicate ankles up to her thighs. And then, in one blindingly fast movement, he straightened and lifted her in his arms. He stepped into the tub and hot water coursed down their bodies.

They kissed for a time, dazzling each other with the flames their lips and tongues could conjure, bodies licked with heat and soul-deep hunger. And then, slowly, hands gentle upon each other, they spread soap on skin, and washed away sweat and blood, the taint of loneliness.

"I suppose we're still waiting until the guests leave," Dela said, fingers tracing the air around Hari's erection.

"Do not tempt me," he growled. "I want the moment to be perfect, without . . . witnesses."

Dela grinned, lifting her hands. "Fine. I guess I'll just be getting out now—"

Hari grabbed her hands, leaning down to kiss her so deeply she saw stars. "Go," he ordered when he released her, his voice low and rough. His eyes glowed. "Go, before I do something we will both enjoy."

She left, but not before teasingly trailing her fingers down the length of his erection. He was still growling when she exited the bathroom.

THE PHONE RANG AND DELA RAN INTO THE LIVING room, buttoning a pink blouse, wet hair trailing down her back. The curtains had been raised, and the sky blushed lavender, with a hint of morning rose.

Blue winked at her and answered the phone.

"It's for you," he said after a moment. "Someone named Kit."

Dela smiled. Kitala Bell was one of Dela's few girl-friends, a young woman who was beginning to make a name for herself through her prodigious fiddling. They had met at a gallery opening two years past, and hadn't stopped talking since.

"Hey," said Dela, taking the phone.

"Who was that?" Kit asked. "New boyfriend? He sounds hot."

Dela laughed, and Kit began shushing her. Too late. "His name is Blue, he's not my boyfriend, and he is quite hot."

Blue gave her a thumbs-up sign from the couch.

"I'm going to get you for that," Kit said. "But before my revenge descends upon you and your heirs, maybe you would like to explain what you're doing back from China? I was just going to leave a message on your ma-chine. In fact, why are you up so early? It's not even six in the morning."

Dela was a notoriously late riser, while Kit always rolled out of bed before sunrise. Of course, Kit was also the type of person who poured a gallon of hot coffee down her throat ten minutes after opening her eyes. Which probably explained why she sounded so damn cheerful.

She also didn't have two men killed in her living room last night.

"I cut the China trip short because I . . . well, I sort of met someone. Which is the other reason I'm up so early."

Dela winced as a high-pitched squeal emerged from the earpiece. Blue was silently laughing, and Dela gave him the finger.

"Girl, you found a man? It's about time. What's he like?"

Dela looked up just as Hari walked out of the bedroom. He was wearing jeans, and little else. His muscles rippled with liquid grace, his tanned skin flawless despite the scars burned deep into his chest. His eyes were haunting.

"Dela? You're awfully quiet. Is he standing right there or something?"

"Or something," she breathed, and then snapped back to attention when she heard a badly concealed giggle.

"All right," Kit said, and Dela could hear her smile through the phone. "You don't have to describe him to me while he's in the same room. But I *am* putting on a show tonight in the city, and you're welcome to bring your new man, and that *other* cute guy. Bluuue."

Dela was insane to even consider it. "I don't think I can, Kit."

"Oh, come on. I'll save you a table up front. Besides, what could be better than me?"

Nothing, considering that Dela and her friends would probably be holed up in her home, armed to the teeth.

"Count me as a maybe," Dela finally said, figuring it couldn't hurt to entertain the possibility of going out. "But you better make it a big table. If I come, I'll be bringing more guests than just Blue and Hari."

"What aren't you telling me?"

Dela laughed weakly. "Just save us the table. Where and when?"

"Eight P.M. at the Kosmo Klub. And don't you try anything, Dela. I've got a black-belt in crazy, and I know where you live."

"Amen. I'll see you then, barring some emergency."

"We have a date?" Blue asked, as Dela hung up the phone.

"Who has a date?" Dean asked, coming through the door with Artur. The two men wore completely different clothes than the ones they had left in, and their hair was damp, as though they had taken showers.

"Clean-up go all right?" Blue asked.

"Well enough," Dean said. Dela did not have the guts to ask what that meant. Dean leaned against the back of the couch. "So what's this about a date?"

That was Dean. One-track mind.

Dela told them about Kit's concert in the city. "It's stupid, I know. It's not safe, and none of you are probably in the mood. I can call Kit back and cancel."

Blue shrugged, scratching his chin. "We've all been on ludicrous speed for the past few days. A little music and dinner might be a nice break, and I know I could use some down time."

"I'll drink to that," said Dean. He briefly stared at Hari's scars, but made no comment beyond a slight frown. "Glad you're in one piece, Hari. You had Dela scared out of her wits."

"We were all worried about you," added Artur, going

to the kitchen to wash his hands. Each movement was strangely deliberate—from soap to water to the rub, methodical and familiar—and Dela wondered if it was not part of some ritual, a coping mechanism. Washing his hands clean of the night.

As Artur dried his hands and replaced his gloves, he carefully looked at everyone in the room. "We now know the source of the threat—who these people are and what they do—which is far more than what they know about us."

"Hari and I gave their man an eyeful," Dela reminded him.

"Who's going to believe any of that?" Dean said. "I mean, come on. You guys were acting like comic book superheroes or something. That Wen Zhang will just think his guy was high on crack. That, or a really bad liar."

Dela was not entirely convinced, but she was in no mood to argue. "So what's next? Find the murderer?"

Artur nodded. "Someone with a vendetta against Wen Zhang."

Blue snorted. "After all I've heard, even I have a vendetta against that guy."

"I will make some calls," Artur said, his face curiously blank, "but I think some sleep is in order. I do not know if Zhang will take our message seriously, but we should be prepared for anything. We will not get far without rest."

"All of you sleep," Hari said. "I can stand watch. I am used to going without."

"You were hurt," Dela protested, but Hari shook his head.

"I have had worse," he said, and no one wished to

argue with the sudden darkness in his eyes. It was a simple statement burdened by two thousand years of story—and they all knew it.

Blue and Dean moved off to the guest rooms, while Artur began making his calls. Hari followed Dela into her bedroom and shut the door behind them. He watched as she stripped off the blood-soaked sheets and dumped them into a pile on the floor, bullets clanking. She pulled more sheets out of the linen closet, and as she began fitting them to the bed, he moved to help her.

Surprised, Dela smiled as they pulled and straightened the covers. It was curiously intimate, making the bed together, and she thought she might enjoy doing this every day—finding some excuse to mess up the sheets, so she could strip everything off and put it together again with Hari's help.

They worked silently until the bed was fixed, ready for a warm body. Hari unbuttoned Dela's jeans and slid them over her hips. He pulled her blouse over her head.

She stood before him in just her underwear, and Hari pressed his lips to her forehead, her cheeks, her mouth. She smelled the forest in his skin.

"Sleep," he whispered, making her stretch out under the covers. He tugged them to her chin, tucking her in. "I will watch over you."

"I love you," she said, catching his hand. She had to say the words out loud—she had to tell him again, every day for the rest of her life. Such a strange thing, their relationship. New and rich and wild. She was afraid of letting him out of her sight. He was magic; he might turn into a dream.

Hari smiled, his eyes glowing for one brief second. "I love you, too, Delilah. Now rest."

And she did.

ARTUR WAS STANDING IN THE LIVING ROOM WHEN Hari closed Dela's bedroom door. The two men silently studied each other, one predator to another.

"You are a dangerous man," Artur said quietly.

"Yes," Hari agreed. "But so are you."

Artur smiled, though his dark eyes remained cool, assessing. "Perhaps, although in a much different way. Our lives have not been easy, Hari, although I think I had the better bargain."

Hari leaned against the wall. "What did you see when you touched me?"

"Enough. I always see more than I wish." Artur held up his gloved hands. "It is why I protect myself."

"Must you protect yourself from everything?"

"From enough so that it feels like everything. But I am used to it, and my gift has saved me more times than I can count." Artur raised an eyebrow. "I was testing you when I shook your hand. It is something I do, to keep my friends and myself safe. Dela has good instincts for people, but I am always careful."

"When I saw so many of Delilah's friends gathered together, I suspected some sort of trial. I would have done the same."

"Good." Artur stretched, and Hari was reminded of a wolf, lean and quiet. "I do not pretend to understand your life, Hari. There is too much, and it is too painful. I have my own shadows to keep without attempting to grasp yours."

"I would not wish my life on anyone."

"So you say, but the past has a way of circling us in our sleep."

"Spoken like a man who knows."

"And as a man who knows, I will tell you this: Do not allow your past to hurt Dela. Women like her, they are the ones who pay for our misdeeds."

"Who paid for yours?" Hari asked, seeing the slip in Artur's mask.

For a moment, Hari thought he had pushed too far. He could smell Artur's pain, an old agony. When the Russian remained silent, Hari nodded.

"It is your private story. Forgive me for asking."

"You had a right," Artur said grudgingly. "I put the words into your mind. It is an old pain, Hari. You have your own. It is something we learn to live with. The alternative is a broken life."

"And the broken heart?"

Artur threw back his head, laughing quietly. "Look at us! Discussing life and love. Too ridiculous. I have nothing more to say on the matter, Hari. I need to rest."

"Of course," said Hari. "Rest."

Artur threw him a strange look, but slowly nodded. He disappeared into the last guest room, and closed the door behind him.

Hari shook his head. Artur reminded him of a distant cousin; a quiet, reserved man, who always managed to surprise his friends and family with outbursts of keen wisdom and fiery temper. Strong passions, running under a cool façade. Such men made good fighters and better friends, but they always kept a piece of themselves locked away. For protection, Hari thought.

Do not allow your past to hurt Dela.

Never, Hari swore, curling his fists. Never.

CHAPTER NINE

THE Kosmo Klub was a homey, smoke-filled bar built completely underground and accessible via a narrow stairwell so nondescript and unadorned, only the long line of people waiting to get in drew attention to the diminutive, old-fashioned sign nailed above the entrance.

Kosmo Klub: for a kosmic good time.

Cheesy, but no one cared. The Kosmo Club attracted the best musicians, provided truly delectable drinks and finger food, and had the most comfortable seating arrangements in the entire city. It also had one of the most endearingly eccentric owners to ever walk the planet, an elderly woman who called herself Dame Rose.

A self-proclaimed nymphomaniac ("The only reason I've slowed down is because I don't wanna replace any more o' my hips"), Rose liked to prowl the evening lines into her club, drawing out the men who pleased her, and showing them to the prime seats in her bar. The price might be some judicious butt-slapping and racy innuendo, but it was all in good fun, and everyone loved Rose.

It was a beautiful night—balmy, the sky full of

stars—and all six friends were rested, clean, and coiffed. They stood in line outside the club, joking among themselves while watching the streets for trouble. The only reason Artur believed it was safe to come out was that he thought it would take several days for the Zhang family to regroup from their failed attack.

Still, everyone was careful. Though none of the men had said a word, Dela could taste the hot tang of weapons discreetly arranged beneath their jackets. Hari had a knife sheathed between his shoulders, rigged in a harness; he was a skilled craftsman in his own right, Dela had found, watching him work a leather scrap from her studio into something usable.

The men still wore jeans, but Dela had opted for a tight red tank top and a playful white skirt that flared above her knees, the hem embroidered with roses and green vines.

"At least you'll look good when the goon squad comes after you," Dean drawled when she came out of the bedroom. Dela smiled, raising her skirt until everyone could see the slender throwing knives strapped to her upper thighs.

"That's a kick-ass piece of lingerie," Blue said, as Eddie's eyes widened.

"My cod-piece is full of love," Dean added.

Artur simply sighed, while Hari's eyes flashed gold.

They waited for almost fifteen minutes outside the club before Dela saw Rose hobbling down the sidewalk, examining her choices of "fine fresh meat." Her face lit up when she saw Dela, and she waved a dark mocha, fine-boned hand in her direction.

And then Rose looked past Dela.

For one moment, it was anyone's guess whether an ambulance would have to be called. Rose clutched her glittering silver-sequined chest, eyes rolling white in her head.

"Oh, Lordy. Dela, girl, I have fallen into the throes of a mighty fleshly lust. Carnal desire is giving me a hot flash." And she fanned her face with both hands.

"Rose." Dela grinned, glancing from the stunned expressions of her companions to the bar's owner, who was finally beginning to recover from her initial shock, a look of sultry determination filling her eyes. "I would like to introduce you to my very good friends."

Artur set the tone by politely bending over Rose's hand and placing a gentle kiss upon her knuckles. Rose pretended to swoon, and after that, it was kisses and fluttered eyelashes and enough choice words to make even a porn star blush.

Dela saved Hari for last.

"My lady," he said, and Dela's heart swelled with pride at the gentle respect in his voice. "It is my deepest honor to meet a woman who radiates such obvious passion for others."

Rose sighed, looking at his hair, his eyes, her gaze slowly inching over the rest of his fine long lines. "If I were only two hips younger," she mused, laughing when she saw Hari's confusion. She slapped his arm, still chortling, and gestured for them all to follow her. Artur and Dean held out their arms, and Rose, still beaming, slipped her hands into the back pockets of their jeans, squeezing. The men jumped, biting back gasps.

"Off we go!" she giggled, fondling their backsides. Artur and Dean, flushed red as beets, simply swallowed and allowed Rose to guide them down the sidewalk—two dangerous individuals, man-handled by a little old woman in front of an entire street of grinning observers. Eddie, buzzed with painkillers, laughed so hard Dela was afraid he would burst his stitches. Blue doubled over, and even Hari began chuckling.

"I like her," he said. Dela grinned, sticking her own hand into his back pocket.

They found Rose and her captured prey waiting for them at the main entrance of the bar, and as a group, they sidled into the smoky interior. Slow jazz filled the air, a soothing background to the clink of glasses and laughter. The walls were paneled in dark wood, covered with old photographs of famous musicians, including Rose herself—a jazz singer in her youth, standing on a stage with her eyes closed, arms outstretched to the audience.

"Kit told me you folks were coming. Saved you a table," Rose said, still holding Artur and Dean in her curious grip. The two men glanced at each other over her head, and suddenly, inexplicably, grinned. When they finally reached their table, set near the edge of the stage, Rose reluctantly released them. Dean instantly gathered the elderly woman into his arms, and pressed his lips to her cheek.

"You have excellent technique," he told her. "My ass is still tingling."

Artur was next, except he hugged her from behind, his lips hovering beside her ear. Rose's hands fluttered over his muscular arms. "Rose," he whispered, in a seductive voice that had everyone staring in astonishment. "Rose," he said again. That was it. Just her name. But it was enough.

"Oh my," she tittered, as his arms slowly slid away from her body. She pressed her palms to her flushed cheeks. "All of you, devils. Dela, honey, you can come 'round often as you like, but bring these boys with you. Drinks will always be on me." And she ambled away, still fanning herself.

The waitress came to take their orders. Just as she left, Dela heard a familiar voice call her name. It was Kit, looking like a million dollars in a long silky skirt dyed in variegated shades of gold and umber, and a matching wrap-around blouse trailing long silken ties. Her caramel skin gleamed, her hair loose and wild, bound away from her face by a brown velvet ribbon.

Kit whistled. "Holy Toledo. What is this, Dela? Studs-R-Us?"

Dela stood and hugged her friend. "Careful. Rose already stroked their egos."

"I bet that's not all she stroked."

Again, Dela went through introductions, and Kit was thoroughly charmed. She even went so far as to ruffle Blue's hair, which made him grin. To Hari, though, she gave a speculative once-over that was pure Kit.

"So you're Dela's new man, huh?"

"I am," he said gravely.

Kit leaned close. "You look tough, but break her heart and I'll turn you into a permanent bed wetter."

"I'm in love," Blue said.

Hari kept his solemn eyes trained on Kit's face. "I agree to your terms."

Kit stared, but whatever she saw in Hari's gaze seemed to satisfy her. She backed away and winked at Dela.

"I'll see you guys after the show," she promised. "I've got to go set up."

Blue watched her walk away. "She *is* single, right?"

Dean puckered his lips and made kissing sounds. Good-natured bickering followed, along with hot buffalo wings, cheesy nachos, and some very excellent beer. Dela contentedly munched on her chips, Hari's arm draped over her shoulders, and listened to the sounds of their

voices mingling. It was a wonderful feeling to be surrounded by so many friends.

Dela could almost forget her other problems. Almost.
She felt the knives strapped to her thighs, heard
them singing against her skin. Dela was an excellent
marksman—uncanny, Roland had once said, back before he took over the agency and had time to train her
in self-defense. After her escapade with the bullet,
Dela was beginning to wonder how much of her skill
was dependent on some unconscious use of telekinetic
ability with steel.

Kit began her set promptly at eight, striding out on
stage with her head high, a challenging glint in her eyes.
She was dazzling to look at, energy pouring from her
lithe body. Kit did not introduce herself. She simply
grinned at the audience, lifted her fiddle, and began to
play.

No one accompanied her, but additional musicians
would have been superfluous. Kit's fiddling had its own
body, mind, filling the room with a wild breathless heat,
invading muscles, sparking colors in eyes already en-
chanted by her writhing body, coiled around her instru-
ment. Fibers snapped in her bow.

Dela watched, unable to stop smiling, feeling a great
upswell of pride for her genius friend. Cries and shouts
of approval began to emerge from the crowd, and by
the end of Kit's first song, Dela could barely hear the
music through the applause. The men of Dirk & Steele
whistled and cheered, and Hari put his hands together
in naked appreciation.

Kit laughed. "Thanks, folks. This next song is a special request from Dame Rose, and it's dedicated to her
'Prisoners of Lust,' Artur and Dean."

The two men groaned as the audience roared. Eddie

held up his glass in silent salute, the entire table laughing over their drinks. Hari's smile was free and relaxed, his chest rumbling with amusement. He pulled Dela close against his shoulder.

And froze.

Hari's sudden stillness was preternatural, his muscles coiled, tense. Dela felt some primal instinct rise within her, skin prickling as she looked up into the face of a predator. Hari turned, and his slow movement attracted the attention of the others at the table, who felt the change in him, the inherent threat within his aura.

Hari stared at the entrance of the club. At first Dela didn't see anyone out of the ordinary; men and women, single and in pairs, mingling near the door, the bar.

Then she sensed something odd and stared harder, found someone watching them. Long wild hair framed a lean masculine face, dark with stubble. A whip-thin body, bare forearms riddled by tattoos. The man leaned against the doorway with casual grace, cigarette in hand, and when he finally walked toward them, Dela imagined she heard the heels of his cowboy boots striking the floor.

Hari stood as the man approached, unfolding from his chair with lethal grace. He towered a good foot over the stranger, who did not seem in the least bit impressed. Dela stared hard at his face, sensing something familiar, and almost gasped. His eyes were golden.

She remembered China, Hari's similar reaction.

I thought I sensed another like me. A shape-shifter.

"Hello," said the man, his gaze firmly on Hari. It was as though the rest of them did not exist. Hari said nothing. He slowly extended his hand.

Some smile quirked the man's lips, but when he

clasped Hari's much larger hand, something odd rippled through his face, which lost its cocky charm. His reaction lasted only a moment. Hari released him, and the man stepped away, his mask slipping back into place. Yet, when he raised his cigarette, Dela thought his hand trembled.

"Would you like to sit?" Hari indicated the free chair beside him.

It seemed to Dela that the man suddenly realized all the people at the table were staring at him. She could not imagine anyone—especially this lean, sharp individual—being so completely oblivious, but there was a puzzled look on his face that made her think he had been lost in some private moment, where the only two people who mattered were Hari and himself.

He looked like he would bolt; there was something wild in his eyes, as though sitting at the table might be the same as entering a cage. He rolled the cigarette around his fingers, considering, and they all waited, curious but uncaring. If he sat, fine—if he did not, Hari would explain the mystery. Perhaps he sensed their indifference; he perched on the edge of his chair. Hari turned toward the others.

"He is like me," Hari said, as though that explained everything. The stranger swore, and began to stand.

"Whoa there," Dean said. "You stay right where you are. What kind of explanation is that, Hari? You know this guy?"

"I assure you," said the man, still poised to leave, his voice smooth as old whiskey. "We are complete strangers."

"You do not act like strangers," Artur said.

"Hari," Dela whispered. "Is he a shape-shifter?"

The man heard her, and looked sharply at Hari. "She knows?"

"They all know," Hari said. "And they can all be trusted. I would not be here with them otherwise." And then, almost eagerly: "What do you call yourself? What do you run as?"

The man hesitated, clearly unnerved by Hari's blunt questions in the presence of so many strangers. And yet, he did not leave. He slowly, carefully, sat down, eyeing them, measuring.

"My name is Koni," he said, watching their reactions. "I fly as raven. And you?"

"I am Hari. I run as tiger."

"Tiger." Koni seemed taken aback and, for a moment, appeared once again to forget his observers. "Tigers are legend. You must be the last of your kind."

"And you?" Dela asked sharply, sensing Koni's words somehow hurt Hari. "How many of your kind?"

He raised an eyebrow. "Too few."

Behind him, Kit still played her heart out, music dazzling the air. For an instant, though, she caught Dela's eye, and the message was clear: Questions would be asked, and by God, questions would be answered. No one ignored Kit when she played, especially when the song was dedicated to the two men with their backs turned to her. Kit missed nothing when she was on stage. Absolutely nothing.

"Ooookay," said Dean, laying his hands flat on the table. "It's obvious I'm once again caught in the middle of the Twilight Zone. But let me get this straight, because hearing it from Hari is one thing—from you, entirely different." He took a deep breath. "You can shift your shape from human to animal, and when you

don't look like a man, it's because you're going all
Tweety on someone's ass."

"I'm not sure I appreciate the imagery associated
with that statement, but yes, that's about it."

Dean pinched the bridge of his nose. Eddie patted his
back.

"Look," said Koni. "It's great that you all are okay
with what I am, but this isn't comfortable for me, so if
you don't mind, I'm out of here. Hari, pleasure to meet
you. Hope you don't go extinct."

"Wait." Blue waved a waitress over. "Have a drink.
I'm curious to know why you approached us in the first
place. This is a very public setting, and Hari is at a table
full of humans. You must have known how strange it
would seem, a complete stranger hopping over, shaking
hands with our man and then running off. Why didn't
you just stay away, curb your curiosity?"

Koni stared at him. It was a good question, a fair
question, and even the shape-shifter seemed to realize it.
"Whiskey," he said, glancing up as the waitress finally
arrived. "Bring the bottle."

"Bring two," said Dean.

Koni glanced at Hari. "Are you sure they can be
trusted?"

"Hey," Eddie protested.

"Absolutely," Hari assured him. "They are like clan."

Koni grunted. "They're not *my* clan, but I'll take
your word for it, one shifter to another." He looked each
of them in the eye, a stare that was dispassionate and
cold. A *don't screw me you motherfuckers* look. "As I
said, there aren't many of us. Hari is the first shifter
outside my family I've seen in over three years, and I
get around."

"Rarity doesn't explain obsession," Blue pointed out.

Koni grimaced. "I am—was—not obsessed. What you don't and can't understand is that when our kind catches each other's scents, we get tunnel vision, start running on instinct. It's worse, now there are so few of us. We have to find the other shifter, look 'em in the eye. Comes out of the old days, when territory was more important, when the animal was free to emerge."

He glanced at Hari, his eyes troubled. "You have issues, man. Your beast—"

"Is not the topic of this conversation," Hari warned. "I already know the problem."

"If you say so." Koni inclined his head. The waitress brought the whiskey and glasses. When she was gone, and Kit's music could once again cover their voices, he leaned forward. "Now I have a question. Who are all of you, and why the calm acceptance? And don't tell me it's just Hari. You people smell strange."

Five sets of eyes stared at him, and then Hari.

"Do I smell different from other people?" Dela asked. Hari hesitated.

"It is not so much your scent, but the energy I feel inside you. I can sense your power rubbing against my skin. I would have mentioned it earlier, but could not think of the right words."

"Yeah," Dean said. "It's never easy telling a girl about all the ways she 'rubs' you."

Koni snorted. "I'm still waiting."

"You're a real barrel of laughs, you know?"

Artur poured himself a drink. "We are like you, Koni, in that we are blessed with certain . . . gifts. Telepathy, clairvoyance . . . take your pick."

"Spoon bending?"

"That would be me," Dela quipped, raising her hand.

Someone's cell phone rang. Artur answered quickly, rising from the table. He wandered away from the stage, toward the bar. Uncomfortable silence descended, with everyone trying desperately to listen to Kit, and not hearing a note.

Artur returned less than five minutes later, his jaw clenched, eyes dark with profound determination and something . . . else. Something painful.

"We have a hit," he said, voice pitched so only their table would hear. "We have to go now if we want to intercept our target."

The child's murderer.

"That was fast," Eddie commented, puzzled, as he rose from his seat.

"I had quite a few details to pass on to Roland and Yancy's contacts," Artur said. "More than I really wanted to discuss, considering the nature of the crime."

"What's going on?" Koni asked, bewildered, as everyone stood.

"It's work-related," Blue said, handing him a business card. "If you ever want a job where you don't have to hide, call this number. Ask for Roland."

"Shit. You're not the mob, are you?"

Dean grinned. "My man, we are the good guys. Just put that name in the Internet and do some research. You'll find out all you need to know, except"—and here he leaned close, his eyes suddenly dangerous—"that we got secrets like you. Tell anyone what you heard at this table, and you're fair game. And I ain't no little Red Riding Hood."

"Yes, good woodsman with the ax. I get the hint. Although for future reference, your threat would work better if I were a wolf."

Dela waved at Kit, mouthing "call me" when the musician turned in her direction. Kit rolled her eyes, but Dela knew she wasn't angry. They liked each other too much to ever walk out on any personal event without a good reason. And Dela had a good reason—just not one she would ever be able to share with Kit.

"Good-bye, Koni." Hari smiled. "Perhaps we will meet again."

"Sure," he said, with a marked lack of sincerity.

They met Rose on the way out, and everyone thanked her for a wonderful time, rattling off some excuse about a family emergency. She abandoned the young man she was escorting into the club and grabbed Artur's hand, which she pressed to her breast.

"Come again, my darling Artuuur."

"Rose," he said, managing to smile. "Sweet Rose."

"How come she didn't ask *me* back?" Dean grumbled, as they jogged down the street to the parked Land Cruiser. Everyone stared at him, and he raised his eyebrows. "What? I've got an ego, too."

"You said we can intercept this guy," Blue reminded Artur. "But I thought the murder took place in New York. What's he doing here, on the other side of the country?"

"Seems like too much of a coincidence," Dela said. "Me here, the murderer who used my knife in the same town." They piled into the car, Hari sitting up front for the extra leg room. Dela perched on the seat behind him, holding on to his shoulders and leaning forward to get a better look at Artur. "If I didn't know better, I'd say this guy is out to get me, too."

She was the only who laughed. The men glanced at each other.

"No," she said. "*No.* I am not the Anti-Christ. Not that many people could possibly want me dead."

"It makes sense," Hari said. "The weapon was not chosen at random. Someone knew you were making a blade, knew when you would send it, and intercepted the shipment."

"The killer was setting you up, Dela." Dean frowned, staring out the window. "But why you, specifically?"

"Who did you tell about the knife?" This from Blue, who removed his gun from a hidden compartment beneath the car seat.

"The customer, Adam, my suppliers—people I deal with all the time. They wouldn't have had any reason to betray me."

"The man who commissioned the knife is dead," Artur announced. "He was found on his yacht several hours ago."

Silence greeted his announcement. Dela felt like she was going to be sick.

"He was a businessman," she finally said, voice breaking. "Didn't they even stop to think? How could they—"

"He was not just a businessman," Artur interrupted gently. "He worked for the rival crime syndicate in Chinatown. Zhang may have peddled flesh, but this man handled drugs, racketeering."

More stunned silence, and then: "How the hell do you know all this?" Dean asked. "If you already had this information . . ."

Artur shook his head. "I knew the murder was in retaliation for something Zhang had done against the killer, but I did not know for what. I had our contacts pore over everything, everyone, including the customer who ordered the knife. All I just told you, I learned during the call I took at the bar."

"Does this killer have a name?" Hari asked.

His silence made Dela's toes curl, her stomach hurt.

"Artur?" she asked, some horrible dread spilling into her throat.

"Adam," Artur said softly. "The murderer's name is Adam Yao."

CHAPTER TEN

INCONCEIVABLE—he had to be wrong. Adam would never betray her. Never.

"Artur," she breathed, pleading. There was no space in her heart to be angry at Artur for making such an accusation; not when there was so much sorrow in his eyes, a quiet appeal for forgiveness. Artur was her friend; he could be trusted—just as Adam . . . *Adam* . . .

"It can't be true," she murmured. "Adam—he and I are friends. I've known him for years. I gave him his first job in America."

"Not his first, Dela. He was in America for two years before he ever found you. There is no record of him entering the country, but he did open a bank account in New York, and that was seven years ago."

"How did you discover his name?" Hari asked.

"It was part of the same background investigation I performed on Dela's customer. Inconsistencies arose, and when my contacts dug deeper, they found that Adam registered with a New York hotel around the same time I sensed the child's murder had occurred."

"Do you remember him going to New York?" Blue asked.

Dela shook her head. "He took a vacation about two months ago, but that was to Toronto to see a family member who had recently immigrated." She stopped, looked at them frantically. "No, no, *no*. Even if . . . even if he lied about how long he was in America, about his trip, he would never murder a child. Adam wouldn't do that! You know I have instincts about people. He doesn't have it in him! Artur, when you touched the weapon, did you feel anything like Adam on it?"

"Punishment and retribution, Dela. That is all I picked up. The only way to be sure is to find Adam—tap into him—and right now, our sources say he used a credit card to check into the Four Seasons, right here in downtown."

"He's supposed to be in Hawaii for another week," said Eddie solemnly. "I drove him to the airport myself, made all the reservations."

His words hung in the air like broken crystal, sharp and biting.

"Delilah." Hari twisted in his seat, reaching back to cup her chin in his hand. They stared at each other, and Dela saw a story in his eyes: compassion, understanding, memory. "You must accept the possibility."

"I don't make mistakes like this, Hari. Ever. If I accept that Adam might betray me, where does that leave all of you?" Her voice was rough, her tongue full of burrs.

"It leaves us praying for your faith," Hari said, caressing her cheek. "Faith that if you fall, I will catch you."

"We'll all catch you," Dean added, gruff. "But don't go jumping off any buildings—metaphorical or otherwise—until we get this guy's story and Artur lays his hands on him. We may be leaping to conclusions, getting worked up over nothing."

It was a dream to hope for, but the worm of doubt had found a crack in her heart, and it was wiggling deep, straight to the core. So few people knew about the knife and her client, and if Adam had lied, if he *had* been in New York . . .

Oh, God.

When they arrived at the Four Seasons, Artur parked down the street, away from the main entrance. Only three of them were going in: Dela, Artur, and Hari. Hari, because he refused to entertain the possibility of Dela going into a potentially dangerous situation without him. She worried he would attract too much attention, but did not argue when he insisted. Hari made her feel safe, and she needed that now, more than ever.

They strode into the hotel, blinking as bright lights blinded their night-sensitive eyes. Marble gleamed, trimmed in gold; the air hummed with refined voices, veiled by the classical strains of a violin and piano, played softly over invisible speakers.

It was not the kind of place one might think to find a murderer.

Forgive me, Dela silently begged Adam. *If you are innocent, forgive me for doubting, for approaching you with this.*

And if he was guilty . . .

Artur already had Adam's room number. They waited by the elevators, uncomfortable and quiet. Just as the doors slid open, Dela glanced across the lobby.

"Delilah?"

She couldn't talk, and the two men followed her stricken gaze as Adam walked from the shadowed depths of the hotel lounge. His face looked pale, his mouth set in a firm line. Silver stained his hair. He wore dark slacks and a crewneck, a black knapsack slung over his

shoulder. His face was devoid of emotion, his pace un-
hurried. Instead of walking toward the elevators, he
headed for the front doors.

"Shit," she whispered painfully. "Oh, shit. Adam,
you better have a good explanation."

They inched closer until they glimpsed Adam jump
into a cab, then ran for the exit, heedless of all the
people staring at them. The Land Cruiser was already
there, waiting with the doors open, Blue at the wheel.
He began chasing the cab before all their legs and arms
were in the car, and Hari leaned over the blurred road to
swing shut the doors.

They barely managed to follow the cab, and eventually lost it—but Adam's destination was clear as they
drove down familiar streets and neighborhoods. Dread
gathered in the pit of Dela's stomach.

"He's heading for my place," she said, and all of them
shared identical grimaces. Hari's hands were clenched
tightly in his lap. He stared blindly out the window and
Dela wanted to touch him—to be alone with him so he
could shut out the world and hold her, to tell her friends
never wore two faces, never went to homes in the night
to do harm.

But Dela knew Hari would never tell her such things;
he was too honest, had seen too much darkness. She
wondered what he made of all this—her life. He said he
loved her, and she believed him, but he was not from her
world, and she had promised him something better, safer.
Yet from the moment they had met, violence had surrounded them, dogging her steps.

*The good and the bad. It always happens together,
and all you can do is press on. Press on.*

But if Hari was ever disappointed, if he wished—

He turned, as though sensing her thoughts, and held

out his hand for her to take. She did, marveling at how the simple press of his palm against hers could be so intimate, as though their souls were in their fingertips, rubbing against each other through skin, flesh, and bone, down to some essential essence of spirit.

As she held his hand and looked into his eyes, she felt his strength, his love, pour through her, and it dulled the ache, made her feel safe again.

Safe, until they reached the warehouse, and saw a light burning through the upstairs window.

A DIFFICULT NIGHT—A LIFETIME—AND WHILE HARI wished he could say he'd had worse, such a declaration would have been impossible. Yes, in his former life there had been agony, excruciating pain—days and nights of torture so horrific he had almost lost his sanity. Battles, too—blood and bone and unending screams. But he was immortal, a slave; and pain, death, never broke his heart.

With Dela, everything was different.

Her pain, her fear and suffering took knives to his spirit, sharp incisions into the very fabric of his being. When she hurt, he hurt. Her misery made him feel small and helpless, and for the first time in over two thousand years, his strength meant nothing; his skill with a sword worth less than spit. Dela was suffering from heartbreak, and that was something no one—not even he—could protect her from.

But if Hari could not protect her with his body, then he would shelter her with his heart and spirit. It was all he had to give—and more than anyone ever had offered.

When they arrived home and saw the light in her window, Hari shook his head.

"Let me go first. It could be an ambush, and he cannot kill me."

"Hari," Dela protested.

"No, Delilah. I insist. Stay here with the others. Give me time."

He left before she could begin arguing with him, trusting the others to keep her safe. In truth, he did not trust anyone but himself to that task, but these men were Dela's friends—almost, he thought, like brothers-in-arms—and he did not want to do anything to alienate her from them. He planned on staying in her life a long time, and a good man allowed his mate her freedom in all things.

Mate. It was impossible not to think of her as such, even though he had known her so short a time. From the first, Dela had seen the man—not the warrior, slave, or plaything. The man. And because of that, he had fallen into friendship—a rare, beautiful thing that still hurt his heart with pleasure. Pleasure and love.

She loves me, he thought, still marveling at the enormity of that blessing. But to be her mate; for them to be joined as one, when he still lived within a curse . . .

I will outlive Delilah, even if that life is measured in sleep. I will outlive our children.

The idea almost paralyzed him. He could not imagine a more horrific fate, and it was one he had already suffered by living while all his people lost their shadows to the earth. Could he once again do such a thing to himself—and to her?

Do not think of this now. You have a murderer to catch.

The tiger shifted within him, closer now to the surface than it had been in over two thousand years. He could almost feel his claws, the spread of fur upon flesh, and his muscles rippled loose and smooth as water. His eyesight sharpened as he crept up the warehouse stairs, a wraith in the gloom, pursuing the unfamiliar scent filling his nose. He tasted man—nervous, hesitant—the tang of sweat and spice.

Dela's door, which Blue had fixed earlier that day, now stood ajar. Lamplight curled into the hall, and Hari crept close until he could peer through the crack in the entranceway. He saw nothing of value, but heard the rise and fall of unsteady breath, felt the presence of the man beyond the door.

Hari placed his finger on the door, and pushed.

His instincts had told him what to expect, and he was not far wrong. Adam Yao sat cross-legged in the middle of the floor, facing the entry. He held a very long knife in his hands.

Adam's eyes widened when he saw Hari crouched on the other side of the slowly opening door, but before he could speak or move, Hari held up his hand. A hypnotic gesture, full of power.

"You do not know me," Hari said quietly, "but I have reason to hate you. I desire your death, but I am a man of control. Tell me why you are here. Is it to kill Delilah?"

"No," said Adam, blinking rapidly. Sweat broke out on his forehead, and still he did not move. "I have come to make amends."

"Ah," Hari sighed, terrible fury sweeping through him. "So you did betray her."

Adam shook his head. "No! Where is Dela? I must say this to her face."

"I'm here, Adam." Dela stepped from the shadows with Artur and the others close on her heels. Hari had heard her coming; he did not want her here, not now. It was too soon. He predicted there would be blood, and it was a memory he did not want her to carry, not with all the other violence still running in shadows through her eyes. And yet, he knew Dela too well. Her sense of honor compelled her to face this traitor. For him to convince her to do otherwise would be committing another act of betrayal.

She has a gentle heart, and yet she is a warrior.

Still, Hari would not let her stand too close. He made her stop just beyond the doorway, keeping a shoulder interposed between her body and Adam. The man did not smell like murder, but Hari was taking no chances.

"Did you kill that child in New York?" Dela wasted no time voicing the question she dreaded most. Her face was pale but determined. Hari felt pride for her.

Adam nearly choked on his breath. Clearly it was a question he had not been expecting, and right then, Hari knew the answer. To Adam's credit, he did not pretend ignorance.

"Dela, that family . . . they are *murderers*. They commit unimaginable crimes against the men and women they transport to this country. They used us as slaves, made us work in their businesses and homes for *nothing*." He stopped, breathing hard. "They killed my family."

Hari closed his eyes.

"Oh, Adam." Dela whispered. "Why didn't you tell me? I . . ." She stopped, shaking her head. "I'm so sorry for your loss, but I have to know. Did you kill that child with my knife?"

"Yes," he breathed, and with that admission, Hari felt death sigh through the room. "Yes, I did. I wanted the

Zhangs to live the same nightmare I went through when they gutted *my* daughter. I wanted them to pay."

"And so you took the life of a child." Artur's voice was cold, flat. Adam shook his head, a convulsive motion, desperate.

"You don't understand," he whispered brokenly. "I wanted something better for my family. I knew English. I began looking for opportunities outside Chinatown. Opened a bank account so they couldn't touch our money. But someone told, and the Zhangs sent their men. They raped my wife, beat my children, and when I resisted, they killed them all. They would have killed me, but I escaped. I don't know how. I kept running, and didn't stop until I found this town, and Dela."

He bowed his head. "I thought I had moved on, but when I learned you were making a knife for Lo Dai, their rival, I knew it was time. I could take care of two problems at once. I could make them suffer."

Hari felt Dela's rage and disappointment curl around her body like smoke, acrid and bitter in his nose. A thundercloud, hovering in her head, and he felt the power coil like a snake.

The blade in Adam's lap darted into the air, the razor tip coming to rest against the hollow of his throat.

"Dela," Blue warned, but she ignored him.

"You could have told me, Adam. We would have found another way." Her voice was gentler than her eyes, than the furious ticking in her cheek. It was frightening to see, and even Hari felt thankful he was not the target of her anger.

It took Adam a moment to piece together his voice. Hari was not sure what most unnerved the cringing man: the levitating blade, or Dela's eyes.

"What way?" he finally gasped. "The law? The government knows about the abuses. The police know. Everyone knows. Nothing is done. Ever. The criminals are too powerful, the community too afraid. No one will talk."

"You could have talked. Instead, you gave up on everyone you left behind. You gave up on me."

Adam shook his head, shiny with sweat. "I didn't think you would ever find out, Dela. I never imagined they would trace the knife, or hold you responsible. I thought the killing would remain in New York, within the two families. I didn't want you hurt."

"That doesn't make it right! *You used me to kill a child.* Was it worth it? Was revenge so sweet, Adam? I can't imagine how you suffered, but now what do you remember? When you think of your family, what do you see? Them, or that child you murdered? How do her screams sound in your head?"

Her screams sounded horrible, if the expression on Adam's face meant anything. Hari had seen such a look in men's eyes before—men who had given in to demands Hari himself had fought with every fiber of his being. It was the face of empty despair, loathing.

Adam moaned, rocking forward against the blade, tears racing down his cheeks. "I thought it would be worth it . . . but it wasn't. It wasn't. When I discovered the Zhangs had set their people after you, I didn't know what to do. I left town, like you wanted, but I couldn't stand the guilt. I came here to confess everything. I've sent a letter to the Zhangs, explaining the truth, that you had no part in the murder."

Dela began to weep, but the blade remained steady at Adam's neck. Hari noticed the other men's uneasiness.

They seemed alarmed by her sudden increase in power—or perhaps, it was her control they feared.

Hari did not fear.

"I thought you were my friend," Dela whispered. "A good person. No matter what was done to you, how could you murder a child? How could you?"

"They broke him," Hari told Dela, knowing Adam would never be able to explain his actions, not to anyone's satisfaction, not even to himself. Hari crouched, and gazed at the crying man without pity or disdain. "I will tell you something, Adam Yao. I have been a slave also, and though I was forbidden to disobey orders, there were things I would not do—that I could not do, no matter the compulsion or punishment. What these Zhangs took from you, what you forgot, is that there are some things worse than mere pain and death. Some acts that cannot be forgiven."

Hari rose to his feet and stepped in front of Dela, blocking her view of Adam. He placed his hands on her shoulders, and looked deep into her stricken eyes.

"He is already a dead man, Delilah, and you are not a killer. Do not walk down his path. Let it go."

Her eyes were huge, a drowning gaze full of sorrow, but his words caused ripples and he saw the answer. Hari did not look to see if the blade descended to the ground. He trusted Dela. He gathered her into his arms and she nodded blindly against his shoulder, crying.

"Dela." Adam held the blade in his hands. "Do you forgive me?"

Dela stepped away from Hari, although she held his hand in an iron grip. "I forgive you for betraying me. But I can't forgive you for killing that child. Never."

Adam nodded, looking at the blade. "I'm sorry," he

mumbled, and before anyone could stop him, he plunged the knife into his chest, hilt deep.

Dela screamed, racing to Adam's side. He had done the job well; he took his last stuttering breath as Dela knelt beside him. Her face was the last thing he saw before his eyes glazed over.

CHAPTER ELEVEN

"THIS place is going to have some major death cooties," Dean muttered, minutes after he and Artur returned from "stashing Adam." They had already called New York, leaving a message with a restaurant manager who, according to Artur's contacts, was familiar with Wen Zhang. If Zhang wanted Adam's remains as proof of his death, they would give him the dead man's location.

If not, fine. Adam would be cremated, his ashes scattered. None of the men were particularly concerned that anyone, including the police, would come looking for Adam. Artur had been careful to check with his sources: Adam was an undocumented alien, without a single living family member in North America. His story about relatives in Toronto was a lie. There was no one left who knew him, no one left who cared.

Hari was unfamiliar with the term "death cooties," but he had a good idea of what it meant. He agreed with Dean, and wondered if Dela should find another home. Besides the bad memories, places where violent deaths occurred sometimes carried destructive energy.

He did not want such forces imprinting themselves upon Dela's life.

"I can't believe how selfish Adam was," Eddie remarked, staring into a glass of lemonade. "I mean, besides the murder, he killed himself in front of Dela! Didn't he realize how much that would hurt her?"

"I don't think taking care of Dela's feelings was high on his list of priorities," Blue said, stretched out on the couch. He had a pillow pressed to his face, muffling his voice. "All of us judged that man wrong. He was a self-centered SOB."

"Not like it happened overnight, though," Dean pointed out. "The man went through hell."

Artur said nothing. He was the only one who had seen the murder, and they all knew the child's death had affected him deeply. It was anyone's guess what the Russian thought Adam's punishment should be, but odds were that death was part of the equation. Suicide, however, had probably not been the imagined method of execution.

Hari stared at the bedroom door. Dela had gone into her room after the men took the body away, and she had not yet come out. He respected her need to be alone, but everything inside him was screaming to go to her.

He finally gave in; she could always tell him to stay away.

Hari rapped lightly on the door and opened it just enough to see Dela curled on the bed. Her eyes glittered with tears, but she did not ask him to leave. He quietly entered and shut the door behind him. Dela hiccupped, swallowing new sobs. Balled-up tissues were scattered everywhere like snowdrifts.

"Tell me about Adam," he said, lying down behind

her. He pulled Dela into his arms, spooning her deep against his body. "Share with me your memories."

And she did; reluctantly at first, but with increasing enthusiasm, regaling Hari with stories of five years together: first as employer to employee, and later, as friend to friend. Dela talked for a long time, and Hari listened, silent except for the occasional prodding question.

"I miss him," she said, when her stories were done and she had gone silent for a time. "I can't believe he's dead, Hari. I just . . . I keep seeing him lift the knife, and I feel like it's my fault. That I drove him to it. But I just couldn't forgive him for killing that child, not even after hearing what horrible things were done to his family. I still can't forgive him."

"He made his choice," Hari said quietly. "And he could not live with it. Your forgiveness would not have changed this night's outcome, Delilah. Adam wanted to die."

Dela shuddered. "I can't stop remembering the good times. We were even talking about opening a new gallery downtown. He was going to be co-owner."

Hari's arms tightened. "You *should* remember the good times. There is nothing wrong with that. He was your friend, but his past intruded and he could not control himself. I have seen it happen before, Delilah. Good men broken by their enemies, set adrift—and then a moment comes to test their spirits. Is the soul stronger than the opportunity, the anger? When a man has been truly broken, the answer is no, because nothing matters. Not life, not honor. He can pretend such things are important, maybe he even believes it. But it is an illusion, cast away with the perfect temptation."

Dela was silent for a time, digesting his words. "What

did your masters want you to do that would have broken you?"

Ah, she remembered. At first he did not know what to say; the words were painful, the memories worse. Eyes so terrified, watching his every move. He had been the embodiment of a nightmare.

"My masters commanded me to rape and kill women and children," he said, unable to soften the horror of those words. "The enemy's or their own. For some, it was just a vicious sport. See a child on the street, order me to take my bare hands and break its neck. Or violate the daughter of a visiting warlord, to make a point. I refused, always, but it was a tremendous struggle. The spell requires me to obey every command my master gives, but to do those things? My body would move, while my mind fought—and always, I won. I had no choice. As you say, 'the alternative was unthinkable.'"

"Were those the only commands you could fight?"

"Yes," he breathed. "And I believe the only reason I was able to resist was because hurting women and children was so alien to my nature. My mind could not accept such orders as real. We tigers are the protectors and caregivers of our families. Harming them is inconceivable."

He paused. "Do you understand what that means, Delilah? That all the other violent acts I committed were somehow acceptable to me. Not abhorrent."

Dela turned in his arms, and he saw he had made her forget Adam, if only temporarily. Her entire focus was on him, and to be the center of such fiercely tender compassion made his breath catch, his eyes grow hot with unshed tears. Dela stroked his cheek with her fingertips, her thumb brushing his lips with loving care.

"You didn't *want* to kill those people, Hari."

"Not consciously, but if murder had truly been against my nature, I would have been able to resist."

Dela sighed. "There is a tiger inside you. A predator. Have you ever heard of a tiger who does not kill?"

"I am also a man, Delilah."

"A man who would kill in self-defense, correct? If you could kill to save yourself, then the capacity is there. It isn't shameful, but it's there. There, to be used against you."

Hari went very still. Could she be right? Was the logic of that horror so simple?

It does not matter. The past is past, and no logic can change the death on my hands. I have killed in battle, in cold blood—I have murdered men whose crimes were nothing more than an opinion or straying eye. There is no forgiveness for that.

And yet, to have some new understanding of *why*; to be allowed the possibility that inside him, there was not a monster secretly hungering for the suffering of others . . .

Hari closed his eyes. "How did I survive before I met you?"

Dela gently kissed his cheek. "You're very resilient."

He choked, a gasp of laughter and heartache. So much memory in that one quiet sound, and Dela somehow heard it.

"You were punished for disobeying."

"Yes," Hari whispered, "and they were very creative. The worst ever imagined has probably been tried at least once on me."

"And you were alone. You never had a friend."

"Never," he said. "Until you."

Dela tucked her head under his chin, wrapping herself around him like a warm cocoon. Hari breathed in the scent of her hair, her skin, glorying in the miracle tangled against his body. He could no longer conceive of his life without Dela, and he realized there was another way to break him: losing her.

Hari felt a little more sympathy for Adam, though he knew there were still lines he would never cross. Lines that would become homage to Dela's integrity and compassion, her memory.

She is not dead yet, he thought, raw desperation clawing his throat. *She will live to be an old woman.*

But not Hari. Hari would never age.

He could not talk to her about it—not now, with her heart broken. But if not now, then when? He could easily put this conversation off forever, and it was necessary. Before they grew any closer.

"Delilah," he said hoarsely. "Forgive me for being selfish. This is not the time, but there is something you should consider about us, something important we have not discussed. I should have, but I could not bring myself to say the words."

Dela looked wary. "Hari—"

"You know I am immortal," he said in a rush, hating himself for adding to her burden. "I love you and would gladly stay by your side for all time, but you will grow old, as will our children . . . should we have them. Everyone but me will age and die."

"Hari," she said, lacing her fingers through his own. "Why are you talking about this? I believe we can break the curse, although the 'how' of it is still a mystery. But even if we can't, I would rather spend every minute of my life with you, than just give up because one day you're going to look younger than me."

"I don't want to lose you," he breathed, trying to make her understand..

"What do you want me to do? Order you *not* to love me? Return you to the box and bury you in the desert?"

"Perhaps. I sleep. I would remember you as a dream."

Hari instantly wished he could take back his words. The hurt in her eyes, the anger—

"You selfish son of a bitch." Dela pushed away from him and rolled off the bed. "A dream, huh? I guess you'd rather have the dream than the real thing. And what about me, Hari? I'd be living out the rest of my life alone, except I wouldn't have the luxury of hiding in the dark, pretending. I'd have to face my pain, every day."

"Delilah." He got off the bed, but she backed away, shaking her head, tears running down her face.

"Your timing is lousy *and* you're a coward," she spat. "Or maybe you don't really love me and this is just your way of letting me down easy, getting out before things get too tight."

Hari crossed the distance between them in an instant, pinning her against the wall with a snarl. "Do not dare say such things, Delilah. I want your happiness more than anything else in this world, and if giving you a normal life with a normal man would do it, then I am prepared for the long sleep."

Dela tried shoving him. "Bullshit. Sounds like you're worried about your own happiness."

"Maybe," he confessed, "but I am more terrified of losing your love than your life."

"My love? But why—Hari, do you think I would stop loving you because you can't die? That I would . . . would resent you for your youth?"

"You might. Not just for yourself, but for any children we might have. Even they could learn to hate me."

"Oh, Hari." Dela stopped struggling, and pressed her forehead against his chest. "You are such an idiot."

Hari wrapped his arms around her. "You could grow old with any other man. The two of you, aging together."

Dela pummeled his back with her fists, but did not try to leave the circle of his arms. "I thought we already covered this, you numbskull. There will never be another man. You're it. If you leave now, I'll go to a convent, become a nun, and flagellate myself three times daily for the awful sin of remembering you naked."

He laughed, though he had not thought laughter was possible at a time like this. Someone knocked on the door. Dean peered in.

"Are you guys okay? We heard fighting." He gave Hari a suspicious look.

Dela quirked her lips. "Let me ask you something, Dean. If you were madly in love with the woman of your dreams, would you call off the relationship simply because she's immortal?"

"Hell, no. That's every man's fantasy. Ninety years old with a hot chick pushing my wheelchair."

"See?" Dela smacked Hari on the chest. "Except I'll be ninety years old with a gorgeous stud carrying me everywhere I want to go."

"Your feet will never touch the ground," Hari promised, kissing her palm. "Your body will be my temple."

Dean groaned, shaking his head. "Get a better line, man."

"Go away, Dean."

Dean muttered something unflattering, but quickly left. Dela smiled at Hari.

"Finally getting a toehold in the pack, huh?"

"I prefer to think of it as beginning relations with a friendly clan."

"Clan, huh?" She rubbed her cheek against his chest.

"Well, does my fellow clan mate feel like a shower?" Her voice was light, but her eyes were tired, bloodshot. Even, he thought, uncertain.

"Of course," he murmured, as they backed into the bathroom, peeling off each other's clothes. He thought of doing this every day for the rest of Dela's life, and though burdened by sadness, his joy overwhelmed it. Dela was a gift to celebrate, not mourn.

And he celebrated her with his lips and his hands, until she cried out his name, again and again.

And then he held her while she cried for Adam.

CHAPTER TWELVE

ADAM'S suicide continued to weigh heavily upon Dela's mind, and for several days afterward she wavered between melancholy and outright depression. She kept the gallery closed and received several phone calls inquiring into her health, asking if she needed help. Dela always said no, thanking her callers for their concern. "Just undergoing some renovations," she would say. "Things will be back to normal in a couple of weeks."

Maybe.

Dela spent a lot of time in her studio, staring at the cold forge. Her art felt like a memory, distant and unreal. Everything she had created was without meaning or substance. She ignored the unfinished projects on the worktables, shutting her mind away from steel. All she could do was look; she did not touch the sculptures or weapons. She did not listen to their whispers.

When she was not in her studio, she wandered around her home, unable to rest easy. She had trouble sitting in her living room, or eating at the dining table, which overlooked the great expanse of floor where so much blood had poured. No amount of sunshine could wipe away the gloom hanging over that room.

"I want to move," she announced over breakfast, three days after Adam's death. Her friends were still bunking with her, and would continue to do so until they heard some word from the Zhangs. While no one disputed Hari's abilities in a fight, even he agreed there was safety in numbers.

"Thank God," moaned Dean.

Dela glared at him. "Don't hold back, Dean. Tell me what you really think."

"I think you should get the hell out of this place," he said with a straight face. "So many people have died here, I'm afraid heads are going to start spinning."

"I know a good exorcist," Blue remarked, buttering his toast. "But he charges by the hour."

"Oh, stop it." Dela tried not to smile. "I just want a change of scene, that's all."

Someone knocked on the door. Six pairs of eyes swiveled uncertainly at each other.

"Are you expecting anyone?" Hari asked, rising to his feet. His sword lay beside his chair on the floor; he had taken to keeping the blade close at all times. He picked it up when Dela shook her head, and the rest of the men clicked the safeties off their guns. They swiftly took up positions around the living room while Eddie guided Dela into the bedroom. The young man cracked open the door, standing with his shoulder against the wall.

Dela heard the front door open, and then:

"Hey, good morn—holy shit, are those guns?"

Dela raced out of the bedroom and found Kit standing in the entryway, staring openmouthed at the sheepish men trying in vain to cover their shoulder harnesses and weapons. Hari was the only one who did not try to hide; he held his sword braced against his forearm, the nicked steel glinting silver.

"Kit! What are you doing here?"

Kit blinked, tearing her gaze from Hari. "What am I doing here? You haven't called me since you bailed at the concert. I would have tried getting a hold of you, but I had to leave town right away for another gig. I just got back, and what do I find? Not a single message on my answering machine! So I think, I'll just march over and make sure my girl's still alive. And these guys go Hawaii 5-0 all over my ass."

"We apologize, Ms. Bell," Blue said, nervously smoothing back his hair. "We thought you might be someone else."

Her eyebrows rose. "Who? Satan?" When weak laughter was her only response, she turned to Dela. "At the risk of becoming a demanding bitch, I'd really like to know what's going on. And don't tell me it's a family emergency. I haven't seen this much weird shit since the last time I watched a Tarantino movie."

"Um," Dela said, glancing helplessly at the others. They all shrugged, warily noncommittal, but she caught a flicker of amusement in Hari's eyes. For some reason, that made her smile—a quick tight grin—which immediately had everyone but the shape-shifter staring at her like she was a hairsbreadth from hitting a pothole.

"Okay," Dela said. "Let's go to the studio. It's quiet down there."

"I hope so," Kit said, frowning. "If I spend any more time surrounded by all this testosterone, I may just sprout chest hair."

"I'm sure it would look lovely on you," Dean quipped, returning to his breakfast.

"Bite me," she shot back, before following Dela out the door.

Down in the studio they made themselves comfortable on the old green couch stuck in the corner farthest from the forge. Kit put her feet up on the threadbare cushions and wrapped her arms around her knees. Cocking an eyebrow, she stared at Dela and waited. Patient, unmoving.

And utterly terrifying to Dela. Her confidence shattered, Dela opened her mouth to spin lies and half-truths, and found she could not. She had a duty to the agency and her friends—their secrets were not hers to reveal—but she also had a duty to herself, and it was becoming too easy for her to shade the truth. Dela had always understood the necessity and accepted it, but Kit was her friend . . .

You misjudged Adam, and you did not trust him with your most precious secret. How can you be sure Kit will be any different?

"You've never been this nervous around me," Kit remarked quietly. "Come on, Dela. Spill. What is up with you and those guys? No one pulls a gun like that unless they have a good reason. Hell, I've never even seen that many guns in one place. And the way you all left the other night . . . the looks on your faces . . ." She pressed her lips together, grim. "I don't know what you're involved in, but it's serious."

"Yes," Dela said. "Adam's dead. He committed suicide."

Suicide. Such an easy escape. Kit gasped, and Dela grimaced. Her grief tasted bitter, sorrow and hate dancing shadows around her heart. She despised Adam, loathed him with a ferocity matched only by her continuing love. He had been her friend, and she could not forget that—could not set aside those years of camaraderie and kindness. It broke her heart, remembering.

The horror of his betrayal, the blood on his hands,

would never leave her. Adam had made her a part of his pain, dirtied the art she loved. If she ever forged another blade, he would be there in the steel, his memory etched in murder, suicide.

Kit leaned close, dark eyes intense, shadowed with sympathy, questions. Dela sighed, thinking of the men waiting for her upstairs, putting their faith in her discretion. She thought of Hari.

Kit is not Adam, she reminded herself. *But then, maybe that's not the point.*

"I don't know why Adam did it," she lied, making her choice. Kit was her friend, deserved the truth, but that was life; nothing was ever entirely fair, and in this situation, duty had to come before honor.

Kit sucked in her breath, shaking her head. "That's terrible, Dela. I'm so sorry."

"He was a coward," Dela ground out, eliciting a brief look of surprise from her friend. Kit began to speak, stopped, and then sighed.

"Maybe," she said. "I didn't know Adam well. Could be he felt like his life was so far past redemption, the only way back was to wipe the slate clean."

It was a remarkably insightful statement, considering Kit had no idea what Adam had done. But that was Kit; wise beyond her years.

And in her words was an echo. *There are some things worse than mere pain and death. Some acts, which cannot be forgiven.*

But death was still no answer. It was too easy.

"Dela," Kit ventured softly. "What else is going on? Adam's death doesn't explain a room full of armed men."

"There have been some threats on my life," Dela said. Kit recoiled, and Dela hurriedly pushed on. "It's nothing to worry about. The guys upstairs are old friends. They work for the detective agency my family runs. I told you about that, right? They're taking care of the problem for me."

Kit held up her hands. "Nothing to worry about? What kind of shit is that? Have you told the police?"

"The police can't do anything." Dela stirred uneasily; lies were best when simple, and this was venturing into something more complex. "Look, Kit—I'm sorry they scared you, but they didn't know you have a key to the building. I forgot to tell them, so when you knocked . . ."

"It was unexpected," Kit finished. "Yeah, I understand that. Me and . . . me and Adam were—are—the only ones with access to your place. Ah, hell . . . at least I understand now why you didn't call. This isn't something you can just explain over the phone. But Dela, this is ugly. Who's threatening you?"

"Someone crazy."

Kit choked back a snort of laughter. "Yeah, I figured that." She scrunched up her eyes and leaned back against the couch. "Thing is, I don't think you're telling me everything." She shook her head before Dela could speak. "Don't. It's okay. I trust you enough to know you're saying what you can."

Which made Dela feel like crap. Biting the inside of her cheek, she slowly nodded. Kit sighed.

They both needed air, and walked through the studio to the side exit. The garden pressed up against the warehouse; morning glories climbed the trellis, hummingbirds darting between the blooms. Pampas grass swayed to a light breeze, casting shade on the thick herbs sprouting among the bulky decorative stones and antique metal-trimmed benches. Rose petals dotted the ground.

Dela turned her face to the sun. Kit hummed.

"So . . . that guy upstairs. Blue. He single?"

Count on Kit to rope things back to basics. "He is, and he asked the same thing about you."

"Cool. How are you and Hari? I noticed he was carrying a mighty big sword."

"He's a mighty big man."

Kit laughed. "Seriously, Dela."

"Seriously? He's the one, Kit. You remember how we used to talk about whether it was possible to just . . . know? Like, no doubts whatsoever?"

"You didn't think it could happen."

"Yeah, and look at me now."

"I am," Kit said. She touched Dela's arm. "You be careful. Don't make me cry."

"You're too tough for tears."

"Yeah, whatever. I guess I don't have to worry. You've got enough hurly-burlys up there to take down a small army."

"And then some," she agreed, feeling like a fraud. She had never felt so bad about lying.

Dela walked Kit to her car. When she returned to the studio, she found Hari waiting by the forge. His hands traced the stone frame, her resting tools.

"I listened in the stairwell," he confessed. "She seems like a good friend."

"She is. I still deceived her, though."

"You know better than us whether she can come to grips with your secrets."

"Not really. Kit might handle it fine. I just don't know if I can take the risk, especially when it's not only my secret to tell."

"It is a hard decision, but not one I have had much experience with. My only friends have ever been family, and family always comes first."

"Family?" Dela said hesitantly. "Is that . . . is that how you see me?"

Hari blushed. Remarkable, seeing his tawny skin deepen to rose. That such a man could look shy took her breath away.

"I see you in many ways," he finally said. "Family is . . . one of them."

"Oh, Hari." Dela went to him and wrapped her arms around his waist. He touched her hair, her back, enfolding her in his warmth.

After a time, he said, "You still have not shown me your art."

It was true, she realized. The first night home had been awful, the next night worse, and she had spent the past several days absorbed with Adam's suicide. During that time Hari had remained a silent presence, sensitive to her moods. When she needed solitude, he found some reason to leave her; when she needed to talk, to simply *be*, he was there, bearing the weight of her heart. Unselfish, patient, kind.

"I'm sorry," she said, beginning to realize the enormity of his gift.

"You have suffered great losses," he said. "But I would like to see more of your life than just this building."

It was the closest thing to an admonishment Dela had ever heard from Hari, and she felt appropriately chastised.

Dela took him on a tour of the studio, pointing out her tools, her works in progress. He had already seen the weapons, and while those caught his eye, he was equally fascinated by her art, her technique. He asked many questions, and as they talked, a curious itching sensation arose in her fingers, in her heart. A vague desire for the hammer, heat.

In the gallery, Hari pored over her finished work: sculptures, whimsical and fantastic, intricate renderings of famous myths, creatures from legend and fairy tale. Dancing centaurs bore the weight of an engraved tabletop, upon which Puss n' Boots, his namesake gilded gold with platinum tassels, confronted a tarnished, copper-wrinkled ogre. Nymphs, sly and clever, hid in various poses around the gallery, while mermaids lounged on turquoise seashores, silver scales shining seductively.

As Dela watched Hari prowl her gallery, something tight unfurled from her chest; she could suddenly breathe easier, and it occurred to her that she had spent the past three days suffocating.

Maybe things will *get easier,* she thought, and then turned away from such musings. Hari had finally stopped in front of the tree.

"Oh, Delilah," he murmured, gazing up the ten-foot trunk to peer at the intricately detailed branches, flung wide as though to embrace the world—or at the very least, a good portion of the gallery. Birds, snakes, and other small animals nested in the heavy limbs, hidden by veined leaves, many of which had been hammered from copper and silver. Human eyes stared out from beneath the raised foliage; the hint of a mouth, a hand.

No one leaf or branch was alike; like snowflakes, Dela had taken painstaking care to forge individuality, the lifelike essence of something unique and wild. The creatures peering down through the vegetation wore dissimilar expressions of curiosity and merriment, seemingly changing with the light. An eerie effect, some said.

"It took me a year to complete." Dela ran loving fingers over the variegated trunk, the steel rough and raw, cracked like actual bark. The wide thick roots curled around her feet, hiding a fox—and there, a little woman with wings. "It's not for sale, but I couldn't keep it locked up. I have visitors who sit here for hours, just looking."

"A year of staring would not be enough time," Hari said, bending close. He glanced at her for permission, and then stroked the leaves with his fingers. They flexed on their delicate stems, shining.

"The detail is incredible. So delicate. It reminds me of home."

She flushed. "It would have been impossible without my telekinesis. Take the leaves, for example. A molding of an actual plant is what some artists use, especially for mass-produced objects like jewelry. But the detail is superficial. A real leaf is imperfect in its perfection. It has character. I use my mind to picture all those nicks and veins, the rub of the surface, and then just . . . impress the image into the metal. ABANA, the artisan blacksmiths association, has been trying for years to get me to fess up my 'secret technique.' They still think I use molds."

"It is magic," Hari said warmly. "You must not give up your craft, Delilah. You must keep creating."

"I will," she found herself promising. And much to her amazement, she meant it.

They talked more about her work, and then Dela ran upstairs to tell the guys that she and Hari were going for a walk.

"You should take additional protection," Artur said. Dean snickered.

"It's all right," Dela reassured him, with a hard glare at Dean. "Hari is protection enough, and we won't go far."

Artur grunted, barely mollified, but Dela did not give him time to insist. She scampered down the stairs, grabbed Hari's hand, and led him out into sunshine and a sweet breeze.

They ambled up Main Street, looking at window displays, mingling with the late summer tourists. It felt strange to Dela—strange, but good. She rarely wandered just for the fun of it. Usually alone, she always had a destination in mind, a place to go, someone to see.

But now, the only person she wanted to see was Hari. Nothing mattered but him; not time or destination, not even grief. She watched the world through his eyes, and found it exotic and lovely. They talked without stopping, renewing themselves through words, finally resting at a small outdoor café where they ordered tea and warm slices of blueberry pie.

Hari savored each bite, treating every morsel as a luxury. But despite his apparent absorption, the relaxed set of his shoulders, his smile, Dela knew he was on guard. His eyes occasionally flickered to the street, to the people around them, his instincts hunting.

It did not bother her. She suspected Hari would always be like this, the predator waiting. Rather than set her on edge, it made her feel safe. Dela was tired of being alone, of taking care of herself. Until Hari came into her life, she had not realized how ready she was to shrug off solitude, which had always seemed so comfortable.

But then, it takes a good boyfriend to be better than none.

She paid the bill, Hari watching the transaction with a slight frown. When the waitress left, he leaned close and said, "I still do not feel comfortable living off your goodwill, no matter how wealthy you are. I should be able to take care of you. Add to your life in all ways."

"You do that." Dela covered his hand with her own. Hari shook his head.

"In my day, shape-shifters had no use for the material. Our needs were few. A rarity, I have learned. The past two thousand years have taught me much about human society, and what is required to be comfortable." Hari looked at his hands, large and elegant, tight with muscle. "All I know is fighting, Delilah, but that is no longer enough. Not if I wish to provide for you."

"But you don't need to provide for me. Not like that, anyway."

"Yes, I do. It is a matter of honor, Delilah."

His mouth set in a stubborn line. Dela knew this was a fight she would not win. Hari might not mind if she had money, but he wasn't going to use it as an excuse for laziness. She admired him for that, but also found it exasperating.

"Hari," she began, and stopped, tracing a pattern on the tabletop with her fingernail. How could she explain to him?

"You think I am foolish," he said.

"No." Dela vehemently shook her head. "I think you are admirable. It's just . . . I have *a lot* of money, Hari. I have no doubt you could find work, but there are very few jobs that would pay you a salary equal to what I already have . . . and what I have is yours as well."

"I do not want your money."

"As long as we're together you're going to have it," Dela said firmly. "But that's not the point. I need you to take care of me, Hari—but I don't need you to take care of me with money. I need more than that."

"Name it," he said. Just like that. A promise, with no questions asked.

"I need you to be my friend," she said, feeling her courage falter. "I need you to take care of my heart. I need . . . I need your love."

"My love," he echoed, his eyes soft, so soft. "But you have that, Delilah."

"And that is all I need," she breathed, leaning close. She touched his hands and brushed her lips against his mouth. He kissed her, gentle.

"And the rest?" he murmured against her mouth.

"Will work itself out," she promised.

They walked home. Blue was on the phone when they opened the door.

"She's back," he said into the receiver, and glanced at her. "It's Roland. He wants to talk to you."

Dela wordlessly took the phone.

"Not so smart taking a walk without more body-guards, Del."

"I needed some privacy," she said.

Roland grunted. "I've been hearing stories about your new boyfriend. Sounds like a useful guy to have around."

"Don't even think about it."

"Think about what?" he asked, and she heard the sly smile in his voice. "Ah, don't get your thong in a twist, babe. I'm not calling to recruit. I've got an update on that woman, Long Nü."

"Finally."

"Don't give me that. It's only taken this long because the intel I first received didn't make much sense. There *was* someone registered for that particular stall, but under a different name: Lu Xia. Thing is, when my contacts did a full search on this Lu Xia, using her registered government number and address, they were told she'd been dead for the past ten years. Well, they went back to the Dirt Market, found out who the old timers were, and passed off her name. Get this—they all remembered her, and insisted she was the one selling those Tibetan tapestries you mentioned."

"Except she's not."

"Uh-uh. She *is*. But this gal is in her thirties. She has the same name, ID number—the whole nine yards. And the weirdest part is that the government database no longer lists Lu Xia as dead."

"That's . . . very strange."

"No fucking kidding. I don't wanna know how you get yourself into this shit, Del. You know what kind of pull it takes to get into the government database like that? In fucking China?"

A good question. How, exactly, did she get herself into this kind of trouble, especially when her life up until last week had been calm, quiet, and relatively boring?

A build-up of chaos karma, she told herself. *Too much calm requires action. Balance, little cricket.*

"Have you heard anything from Max?"

"Little bastard got his tourists and is in Quito, the capital. There's been a delay with the transport, but he should be back home in the next couple of days."

"Lucky you." Dela hesitated. "I haven't gotten any calls from Mom or Dad. Or Grandma."

"They have no clue what's going on with you," Roland said. "Amazing, I know. But you were right to ask me not to say anything. Your mother will have a nervous breakdown. That, or she'll go commando on my ass."

"Yancy knows. She may let it slip."

"She knows what I'll do to her if she does," Roland said solemnly. Too solemnly.

"What's wrong, Roland? You sound depressed. Gone celibate again?"

Choking sounds, followed by hoarse coughs, filled the air behind her. For once, Roland had no snappy comeback. "I'm worried about you, Del."

His sincerity made her breath catch. "You've got me

surrounded by the best. Don't you worry, Roland. I'll be fine. We all will."

"I know that," he grumbled. "Have you seen anything of that Magi?"

"Not a whisper," she said, uneasy. The Magi was the great unknown, the one threat she dreaded more than any other.

"All right, then. My beeper is going off. You keep safe, babe. Don't do anything stupid."

And he hung up on her.

"Delilah?" Hari tucked a strand of hair behind her ear. She tried to smile, opened her mouth to tell him and everyone else what she had learned, but the phone rang again.

What now?

"Hello?" she answered, stifling a sigh.

Dead air was her first indication that this would not be a good call.

"Ms. Delilah Reese?" The voice was low, feminine.

"Yes." It sounded more like a question than a statement.

"My name is Beth Wong. My employer, Mr. Wen Zhang, is in town and would like to meet with you tonight. If that is convenient."

To Dela's credit, she managed to swallow down the squeak that instantly rose from her throat. "Wen Zhang?" she repeated coolly, barely able to hear her voice over her thundering heart. She glanced at the others, and could feel them mentally loading their guns, sharpening their knives. "I suppose I can make time for Mr. Zhang. Where would he like to meet?"

Dean grinned at the cool tartness in her voice, pointing at his groin and then at her. *You've got balls,* he mouthed.

Brass ones, she thought.

"I believe there is a restaurant near your home called Le Soleil. Have you heard of it?"

If that was the chosen location, then Beth Wong knew damn well she had heard of it. Le Soleil was the most popular place to eat in the city—Dela's favorite, in fact. Several of her sculptures hung from the walls. "I know where it is," she said evenly, hiding her unease that one of her favorite haunts would be the location of any meeting with the Chinese mafia.

"Lovely. Mr. Zhang will be there at eight P.M. You will come alone. If you do not come alone, or if you are late, Mr. Zhang will leave. You will not have another opportunity to speak to him."

"Will Mr. Zhang be under those same constraints? Will *he* be alone? On time?"

"Those are the terms," Beth said, her voice unchanging in its disconcerting serenity. "Good-bye, Ms. Reese."

"Wai—"

The phone clicked. Dead air.

Dela froze, then slammed the receiver against its cradle. Blue winced.

"When you're done punishing your phone, would you mind telling us what just happened?"

"Wen Zhang, whom I presume is the same Zhang who wants me dead, desires a meeting. Tonight. At Le Soleil. Alone."

"That's a bunch of crap," Dean said. "You're not going in there by yourself."

"Agreed." Hari laid his hands on Dela's shoulders. "This is a trap."

"It is a public place," Artur said thoughtfully. "A restaurant where Dela's face is known."

"You're not seriously considering it, are you?" Blue frowned. "You know as well as I do that public places can be just as unsafe as dark alleys. Takes a little more skill, that's all."

"Artur's right," Dela said, frustration and anger merging with fear, creating an even stronger emotion: resolve. "This is going to be my only chance to meet with Zhang. I need to do this, to find out what his intentions are. If he still wants to kill me, fine. Won't be any different from the way I'm living now. But what if he doesn't want to kill me? What if he just needs to look me in the face, tell me I'm scum, then walk away?"

"Delilah, men such as this do not 'walk away' from anything," Hari said. "If his intent tonight is *not* to kill you, he will still want to bargain for your life, and you will not be able to trust any deal you make with him."

"I'm going," she said, stubborn. "And don't you even think about trying to stop m—"

IN THE END, THEY ALL RELUCTANTLY AGREED TO let her go to the meeting—but that was after a prolonged scuffle that began when Hari dumped Dela over his shoulder and locked her in the bedroom, and ended when Dela's screams grew so loud and piercing the men were afraid someone outside the warehouse would hear her and call the police.

"Actually," said Dean, when they released her from the bedroom, "I thought my ears were going to start bleeding."

"Would serve you right," she said, glaring at them all. Hari seemed completely unaffected by her anger—indeed, he appeared every bit as furious, except his ire was completely directed at her.

It was not the first time she had ever felt the brunt of

his anger, but it still brought her up short, made her stare. Hari met her gaze, his lips pressed in a cold hard line.

Without a word, he turned and left the apartment. Dela did not look at the others, although if she had, she would have found them watching Hari's retreating back with identical expressions of sympathy. She ran after Hari and caught up with him at the bottom of the landing.

"Why are you so angry with me?" she asked, breathless. At first Hari refused to look at her, but when he did, his cheeks flushed, his eyes flashing gold.

"When it comes to your safety," he snapped, "you are inconsiderate, and a fool. You have been so from the beginning. I wonder, how many times must you be near death and murder before you listen to a little common sense? Or will you always bare your neck to the blade?"

Dela gaped at him. "Are you blaming *me* for almost getting killed? What would you have me do? Pull the covers over my head? Hide in the closet?"

"I would have you listen to me in this! You are not alone, Delilah, though there are times I think you wish it otherwise. Would it be easier for you? So you can pretend you have no obligations to anyone but yourself? Have you forgotten all the people who love you, who would bleed to see you safe? Do we not mean anything to you?"

"That's unfair," she whispered, stung, "and you know it. You all mean everything to me. That's why I have to do this. The only person who deserves to get harmed is me. My life is my responsibility, Hari. You guys have already been hurt enough in this fiasco. If I can end it tonight, I will."

Hari leaned close, and Dela felt his anger, his fear,

cut through her like a hot knife. "And I say the only way this will end is if you are dead."

"I guess that would solve all our problems, wouldn't it?" she breathed, horrified at herself, but unable to stop the words from tumbling past her lips.

She might have slapped him; the reaction was the same. Hari jerked away, dismay rippling through his face.

"Hari," she said, reaching for him. He shook his head, turning his back on her pleading eyes. He walked down the stairs, silent as a ghost.

No, her mind whispered. *No, please.*

She hurried after him, clattering down the steps, desperation making her clumsy. She tripped, gasping, and tumbled down the final few, landing hard on her back, pain lancing through her body.

"Delilah!" A strong hand swiftly cradled her head, while another fluttered over her body, light as a butterfly, checking for injuries.

"Ow." She grimaced as Hari gently tugged her into a sitting position. He was so close—his arms enveloping her, holding her body—and Dela pressed her face into his chest, taking comfort in his presence, his scent. Her relief was overwhelming—a shocking thing. If he had kept walking . . .

I would have chased him, just like one of those crazy girls in a movie. Screaming his name and acting like an idiot. And it would have been worth it.

"Are you hurt?" When she shook her head, he sighed and ran his hands through her hair, pressing his lips to her temple. "You frighten me so much, Delilah. I wish you could understand how terrified I am of losing you."

"I'm a klutz," she muttered. "And I am inconsiderate. I don't think about how my actions affect other people.

I'm used to my friends caring from a distance, not up close and personal twenty-four hours a day. It's unnerving, and I feel guilty for being the cause of everyone's problems."

"You are not anyone's *problem*."

"Sorry. I can't hear you."

Hari groaned, his breath ruffling her hair, warming her ear. "You are impossible." He leaned back so he could look in her eyes. He cradled her face. "I am sorry I said those things, Delilah. You had a right to be angry with me." He smiled weakly. "We both know how impulsive I can be, as well. It is just . . . I keep forgetting how independent you are, how much courage you possess. The women of my people were like you. Infuriating, intelligent, stubborn. But that was two thousand years ago, and I have had time to become accustomed to . . . duller fare."

Dela raised her eyebrows. "Duller fare? Are you still talking about women, or dinner?"

Hari kissed her hard.

"I don't want to die," she said breathlessly, when they finally came up for air. "I didn't mean it, what I said."

"I know." Hari's eyes dimmed with pain. "But I was ashamed you might think I would consider . . . that I would feel . . ."

"Shhh," she soothed, fingertips tracing his fine cheekbones. "I understand, Hari. I never thought that, not for an instant. But when you walked away from me, I was so scared. I thought you might stop—"

"Never," he promised, standing. He pulled Dela up with him and glanced around her studio, his gaze roving up the stairs. His expression darkened. "I wish we could truly be alone."

"I love your inhibitions," she said, but her smile

faltered when Hari did not relax. He held her against him, painfully quiet.

"It is an old thing," he told her, softly. "Some of my mistresses would command me to pleasure them in front of witnesses—sometimes *with* those selfsame watchers, passing me around like a toy. Several of my masters made me do the same to their wives, or servants. To them it was not rape—they were willing—but it was still shameful. I felt like an animal."

Dela felt Hari tremble, and she wanted to reach back in time to save him from every moment of despair and degradation. *If I could, if I could . . .* she whispered in her mind.

He pressed his lips to her forehead. "I do not want that for us, Delilah."

"Neither do I," she said, holding him close.

Never again, she promised him. *Never again.*

CHAPTER THIRTEEN

L E Soleil was unquestionably one of Dela's favorite restaurants in the downtown area. Nestled between a bookstore and a flower shop, it was the perfect place for lunch or dinner, alone or with friends. Large windows, airy ceilings and a cheerful staff created a pleasant atmosphere enhanced by the heavenly foods sweeping in and out of the kitchen on an aromatic tide of culinary benevolence.

There had been a time, well before Dela's work became famous, when she had gone to Le Soleil almost every day for lunch. The restaurant was only a block from the university where she took her art classes, and she would happily trudge to the little French restaurant for a bite of something warm to eat before heading back for more long hours in the studio.

"Dela!" exclaimed Pierre, as she swept through the glass doors. The small, lithe man smiled, holding out his hands. "You look lovely tonight, my dear. It has been too long since you stopped by."

Pierre LeBlanc was a former member of the French Resistance, a chef who had come to America after the war with his heart firmly set on making a life that would have nothing more to do with the nightmare of the human condition. "There are three things that make me feel safe," he once had told Dela. "Sunlight, a good woman, and excellent food."

And so Le Soleil had been born with the help of a good woman, Marissa, who still ran the flower shop next door.

Dela lightly grasped Pierre's hands, smiling warmly. "I've been busy," she said, "and unfortunately, tonight is more business."

"Always working," he chided her. "Should I buy more of your art, just so you will return and 'talk business' with me?"

Dela shook her head. "No bribes will ever be necessary to bring me back to Le Soleil, Pierre. Your fine food and company is temptation enough."

He quirked his lips, patting his dapper tweed vest with wrinkled hands. "Charming as always." His brow creased, his eyes flickering toward the back of the restaurant. "I know I should not say so, Dela, but this man you are meeting already informed me to expect you. I do not care for him."

"I don't much like him either," Dela said, as several giggling women crowded into the restaurant behind her. "But that's the way things go. Can you take me to him?"

"Of course." He held out his arm.

::Are you on a first-name basis with all the people in this city?:: Blue whispered through the transmitter tucked deep into Dela's ear.

She remained silent, although it made her feel good knowing her friends were with her, even if just electronically. Hari had suggested that some of them enter the restaurant an hour before the meeting—simply eat, blend in with the crowd—but Artur was concerned all of them would be easily recognizable, if not from a description given by the one assassin allowed to escape, then by simple surveillance of Dela's home. It just wasn't safe for any of them to be present.

Luckily—and quite appropriately—Blue was a genius with electronics. Years spent with the Navy Special Operations Group, the SEAL tech unit, had done him good. Tucked within Dela's bra were delicate wires, all for the single purpose of transmitting an instant audio and video playback of Dela's meeting with Wen Zhang. The camera itself was located in a petite antique brooch clasped at the V of Dela's low-cut black silk blouse, a fine line of cleavage darting from the silver toward her throat.

As Pierre led Dela to the center of the restaurant, she had to smile. When Pierre did not like someone, his old instincts kicked in—and in this case, he had given Wen Zhang one of his worst, and most public, tables. Smack dab in the center, squeezed between a portly woman and her even portlier companion, and a large family consisting of squealing children, arguing adults, and the occasional fleck of flying food.

Wen Zhang, a middle-aged man with a receding hairline and narrow eyes, was doing his best to look refined in the midst of Le Soleil's boisterous diners.

Blue started laughing, low in her ear.

"Thank you," Dela murmured to Pierre, as he guided her to Wen's table.

"I am simply an old man who takes pleasure in attending to his guests' every need," Pierre responded, gracing her with a somewhat wicked wink.

::Old fox.:: someone, maybe Dean, said in the background. Old fox, indeed.

Wen rose smoothly from the table as Pierre held out

Dela's chair. They shook hands; his grip was unpleasantly firm, his palm cool and dry. He did not look like a mafia king or a murderer, but even if Dela wasn't already privy to Wen's background, she would have disliked him. Perhaps his broad features did not give the impression of a master criminal, but his gaze was cold. So cold.

"Can I get you anything?" Pierre asked, when they were both seated. Wen and Dela glanced at each other—a quick size-up—and shook their heads. Pierre's smile grew rather fixed, and he tottered off with a deceptive shuffle that Dela knew was for Wen's benefit. Dela didn't know how Pierre did it, but his intuition was on fire.

Maybe he's one of us.

"I hope you are pleased with my choice in restaurants," Wen said, his voice smooth as pearl. "I had my people research you, and we discovered this is a favorite place of yours. I thought it would make our meeting more pleasant."

"How considerate," she said with a cool smile, though her stomach hurt. She hated that Wen could dig up so much information about her, but that was the peril of being somewhat well-known.

"Yes," he agreed, "although I was rather disappointed in the seating. I had hoped for something more . . . private."

"Le Soleil is a popular place," Dela said, switching to Chinese, gambling that the people around her would not understand the language. "But I am sure we can create our own . . . privacy."

"Ah," Wen said, replying in Mandarin. "I was unaware you spoke Chinese."

She heard a scuffling in her ear, and Hari whispered

her name. Hari, she guessed, because he was the only one of the men who could understand Chinese.

"It should make things easier," she said. "But before we go any further, I would like to extend my condolences for your niece's death. And to her parents . . . words will never be enough."

It was blunt, and probably unexpected so soon into the conversation—though Dela was certain she had already surprised Wen with her calm, somewhat casual, demeanor. Nerves of steel, that was what she had. Oh, yeah. And just wait until she got back home and fell apart.

Wen blinked, his cool mask faltering for just one moment. "Thank you. We all miss Lucy very much."

Lucy.

Dela swallowed hard. "I had no idea what would happen when I prepared that particular order for my client."

"Of course," he said smoothly. Too smoothly, in Dela's opinion. She, who had run herself ragged with every possible accusation, who stood ready to take responsibility for her role in the child's murder. Wen's gaze was curiously empty as he said, "Your associate, Adam, absolved you of the crime. He requested we . . . cease hostilities."

"And will you?" Dela asked mildly, unsure how to react to Wen's marked lack of emotion. She reached for her glass of water.

::Do not drink it.:: Hari whispered urgently, and Dela merely fingered the fine crystal, tracing bored lines in the perspiration. *::The water was already at the table when you arrived. He might have poisoned it.::*

Indeed, Wen watched her with a sudden peculiar intensity that was alarming. Dela took advantage of his scrutiny and smiled. Surprise flickered through his dark eyes, quickly suppressed.

Gently, she said, "I feel terrible about what happened, and have said as much. You know I am not directly responsible. Why am I here, Mr. Zhang? Do you and . . . and Lucy's parents still want me dead?"

Wen did not answer. He leaned back in his seat, openly inspecting her face. An odd smirk formed; a curious mix of self-righteousness and disgust. Dela remained impassive, although on the inside she was confused, seething.

"You are a curious woman," he finally said. "On the surface, you seem . . . simple, shallow. You are beautiful, wealthy, an artist for the rich. You have . . . what is it called? A silver spoon in your mouth? And yet, you have managed to survive three encounters with my . . . operators. At first, I thought it was because you surround yourself with trained bodyguards—odd enough, considering my initial impressions of you. But then, a story returned along with your letter. A very curious story, about a bullet, and a man who would not die."

Oh, shit.

::Delilah.:: Hari sounded worried.

Dela raised her eyebrow. "A man who would not die? More than curious, Mr. Zhang. The story must have been fantastic."

"So I said, but the person telling the story was quite persuasive, and I wondered, what if it was true? How remarkable that would be. How . . . advantageous."

It was astonishing that Wen was so ready to believe the incredible, but Dela hid her shock with a dismissive snort. "Beneficial if you believe in fairy tales maybe."

Wen's whole demeanor changed, a disconcerting meltdown from cool suavity to quiet fury. A flush stained his cheeks. The children playing at the next table stopped shoving each other. Their parents stirred uncomfortably.

"I know what you are," he said, deceptively gentle. "I know what your friend is. I have heard of such things. Encountered them, you might say. So no more games, Ms. Reese. No more pretend. I know who you work for, but I don't care—not anymore. My business has been harmed, my niece is dead, and you are the only one who has not yet paid in blood. As far as I am concerned, your luck has run out. If we do not come to some beneficial agreement, you *will* be taken care of, as will your friend, no matter how reluctant he is to meet his maker."

His words sparked transformation. Sweet icy rage poured through Dela; she felt cruelty pool in her eyes, her lips. The mask was slipping, dying, gone. She smiled; a baring of teeth, one animal to another.

"You're right, Mr. Zhang. No more games. If you want to kill me, do it, but your problems won't end there. I'm a well-known woman. I'm even fairly likable. There are many important people who would be mighty pissed off if I disappeared or died, and trust me, my friends know who you are, what you do, and where you live. Kill me, kill some of them—you won't get us all, and once the blood spills, we will come for you. You think you're the baddest badass out there? You don't know shit."

Dela slowly stood, tossing her napkin on the table. "I hope I *never* see you or your people again, but if I do, you better be prepared."

Because it was one thing to threaten her. Menacing her family was something else entirely.

Dela began to walk away. Wen's hand shot out, clamping around her wrist.

"We are not yet finished," he said.

She almost used her powers—she could feel them waiting, breathless for the chance to explode free, to teach this man a lesson for threatening her and Hari. He wore metal, and to Dela—now, more than ever before—all metal could be a weapon.

::*Delilah, be careful.*::

Yes, be careful. There were people watching all around, and her control was fragile at best. She could not risk exposing her family and friends. Dela took a deep breath. Carefully, painstakingly, she calmed herself and tilted her head with a disdainful glare.

"We *are* done," she said, grabbing her glass of water and upending it in Wen's face. His grip did not loosen, but suddenly Pierre was there, as were Marc and Phillip, his two largest busboys.

"I believe the good lady wishes you to let go of her wrist," Pierre said softly, blue eyes glittering. All joviality had left his face, and Dela imagined Pierre as a young man, full of passion and resolve, deadly in a skirmish. Resistance fighter, indeed.

Wen hesitated; Dela could see the calculations running through his head, and she glanced about, spotting at least three other men at a nearby table who immediately stood up, poised, a question in their eyes as they focused their attention on Wen.

"This is over," Dela said in English. "Don't make the mistake of underestimating me or my friends."

Wen's fingers slowly lifted from her wrist; she resisted the urge to rub her throbbing bones. Wen stood and gathered his coat, the mask back in place.

"I wish our circumstances could have been different, Ms. Reese, especially considering all you owe my family."

"I owe you nothing but my apologies," she said, "which have been given, profusely, again and again."

"Of course," he said, his gaze chipping at her face. "Good-bye, then." And with a glance at Pierre, Wen made his way through the restaurant to the door. Dela noted his men did not follow. They sat, their eyes now on her. It seemed to Dela everyone watched her.

"Dela?" Pierre touched her hand. "Come, let me take you to the kitchen and get you something to drink. What an awful man."

"Yes," she said hollowly, wondering what would come next. "He is quite awful."

CHAPTER FOURTEEN

CRAMMED into a windowless van parked half a block down the street, Eddie—off his painkillers and in the driver's seat—saw Wen Zhang leave Le Soleil, shaking water from his hair, rage clouding his face.

"Mad dog alert," he called back to the others.

Blue glanced down at the monitor, watching Pierre guide Dela toward the back of Le Soleil. Three men caught his attention as Dela walked between the crowded tables. Dressed in suits, their meals untouched, they studied Dela with cold and empty eyes.

Blue pointed at the screen. "A hundred bucks says those are Wen's guards."

"They're not following Wen," Dean said.

"No." Hari put his hand on the door handle. "They are waiting for Delilah."

Hari and Artur quickly left the van and walked into the restaurant. At the door, a young woman greeted them with a pleasant smile that faded just a notch when they asked to be directed to Pierre.

"He's with a friend right now," she said, and her voice dropped to a whisper. "There was a minor disturbance with one of our customers."

"Ah." Hari tried to smile, attempting to recollect what it felt like to be charming. Artur glanced at him, raised an eyebrow, and gave a minute shake of his head.

"My dear," said Artur, lowering his deep voice, smoothing out his accent, "we are looking for the friend Pierre is with. Dela Reese? Yes, her brother is not well."

"Oh," she said, eyes wide. Still, she was a cautious girl, and instead of telling them to go ahead, she picked up the phone by her station.

"Monsieur LeBlanc? There are two gentlemen here to see Ms. Reese. They say they are friends. Their names? Um, hold on . . . oh, uh, Artur and Hari. Yes. All right, then."

She smiled up at them. "Thank you for being so patient. If you'll just walk to the back of the restaurant—see where all those waiters are going? Monsieur LeBlanc will meet you at the entrance to the kitchen and take you to Ms. Reese."

"Thank you." Artur bowed his head, as did Hari, although the warrior felt far less noble, manner-wise. While he had been raised to treat others with respect, this seemed more like a potential battleground than a simple, civilized foray into a restaurant for a loved one.

"You should work on your smile," Artur commented, with a casual grin that did not reach his cool darting eyes. Hari followed his gaze, examining the three suited men who had watched Dela. They seemed to recognize Hari and Artur, and shifted uncomfortably.

"I save my smiles for Delilah," Hari responded, suppressing a low growl.

"That is why I like you," Artur replied, inclining his head at Wen's bodyguards. The two groups of men could have touched each other—a finger, outstretched—but Artur and Hari passed them in three steps, entered a sun-yellow corridor, and found Pierre LeBlanc waiting for them in front of the steaming kitchen.

"So you are Dela's friends," the Frenchman said, after a quiet moment of scrutiny. "I suppose there is a reason two strong men allowed Dela to meet with that *bâtard* all by herself? He hurt her wrist."

Hari's jaw ached. "I assure you," he said tightly, "it was not our desire to allow Delilah anywhere near that man."

Pierre grunted. "She speaks highly of you two. I suppose she knows what she is talking about."

Clearly, Pierre LeBlanc did not share her glowing assessment. Hari did not blame him. He himself could not think of a single reason to respect any man who allowed his friends and loved ones to face danger alone. Unfortunately, Dela was very good at convincing him to do things he would normally never consider.

This is the last time, he promised himself. *My heart cannot take any more. I would rather have Delilah angry with me than alone, where she can be hurt.*

Artur and Hari found Dela perched on a stool in a quiet corner of the kitchen, a bag of ice on her wrist and a cup of steaming hot chocolate in her hand. She was trying very hard not to shake, and Hari wrapped his arms around her.

"Dela." Pierre touched her shoulder. "Are you in some sort of trouble?"

Dela reluctantly pulled away from Hari. "No, Pierre. Mr. Zhang is simply a client who has been very difficult to satisfy. His demands are unreasonable; he is rude and inconsiderate. After tonight, I plan on cutting off all contact with him."

"As you say," Pierre murmured, though his eyes were

sharp and canny. He lightly patted her knee. "Try to be more careful the next time you take a project, eh?"

And with a piercing glance at Artur and Hari, he ambled off to check on the rest of his kitchen.

Hari gently lifted the ice off Dela's wrist and sucked in his breath. Slightly swollen, a dark mottled band had already appeared against her pale skin. A murderous rage settled in the pit of Hari's stomach—that, and guilt for not being at Dela's side when she had faced Wen.

"I will never allow you to do something like this again," he said quietly, replacing the ice over her wrist. When her eyes flashed, he held up his hand. "If I am to remain in your life, Delilah, you will have to compromise with me on some things. This is one of them."

She wanted to say no—he could hear the automatic refusal on her lips—and he knew if she were any other person, he would be on his knees by now, brought low by a command, slave to his mistress. But Dela was not like anyone else, and he saw her eyes grow dark with acceptance.

"Okay," she said, and then touched her ear. "Blue said if we want to leave, now would be a good time."

Rather than walk through the restaurant again, they left through the back door, which emptied into a narrow alley that stank with garbage. The alley was poorly lit, but Hari's eyes adjusted instantly, the shadows revealing their secrets to him.

"Come," he said, taking Dela's hand. He led them down the alley, pausing just before the unevenly pitted concrete met the sidewalk. He peered around the wall, and found the windowless white van nearby. No sign of anyone suspicious; men and women strolled down the street, laughing, talking.

Hari signaled Dela and Artur, and they jogged across the sidewalk up the street, Dela murmuring something under her breath. It must have been a warning to the others, because the van door slid open as they approached, and Dean and Blue helped them inside. Eddie pulled away from the curb.

"Well," said Dean. "We've established one thing tonight. Never piss off Dela."

"Ha," she muttered darkly. "I may have just gotten all of us killed."

"Perhaps not," Hari said, tucking her close, sensing the fine tremors still running through her body. "You may have bought us time."

"Time for what? So maybe they don't want me dead, but this is almost worse. You and I working for the mob?"

"I would laugh if it wasn't so scary," Dean said.

Artur frowned. "He said he knew who you work for, but that does not make sense. We have not been compromised."

"How can you be so sure?" Hari asked. Dela stirred in his arms.

"Roland. He's one of the most powerful psi-talents I've ever met. Besides being clairvoyant, he's also a telepath. A very strong telepath. A long time ago he developed this trick, sort of an alarm system. When someone is ready to be recruited into the agency, Roland—with the individual's permission—enters his mind and creates a link, a connection between all the agency's secret information and the emotional center of the brain. Roland is also part of this link, but in a superficial way. If any member of Dirk & Steele discusses the agency to someone who isn't part of the link, Roland knows—but he only hears the emotions behind the discussion. Guilt, greed, anger, hate—those are red flags. Calmer emotions, or no emotion at all, is safer; but Roland investigates every single occurrence."

"He phoned me the afternoon I picked you and Hari up from the airport," Eddie said. "Apparently, I said enough to trigger the link."

"Blabbermouth," Dean said.

Blue began removing Dela's wires. "So what? Does that mean he's just making guesses, or is there some *other* group out there, with people like us?"

"People someone like Wen would know?" Dela frowned. "That's scary."

"Enough," said Artur. "I will inform Roland and let him conduct his own investigation. For now, we have only one concern, and that is Wen Zhang. Men like Wen are driven by profit. His subordinates will be the same— their allegiance is economic. If you disrupt the flow of cash, Wen will lose face. He will become distracted and sloppy. There may be a power struggle."

"You can take the boy out of the mob, but you can't take the mob out of the boy, huh?" Dean smirked.

"Someone is following us," Eddie announced. "A Jeep. The driver pulled out of his parking space the same time we left, and he's been close ever since."

"On it," said Blue, crab-walking through the surveillance equipment to the back of the van. Everyone watched as he carefully peered through the tinted rear window. Moments later, they heard brakes squealing.

"Sent a surge through the battery and spark plugs," Blue said, blowing on his fingers with a sly smile. "Over loaded the car's computer chip, too. Couldn't see much of the driver, though. Too much glare from the headlights."

"Where there is one, there will be others," Artur said calmly, with a Zen-like air that made Dela roll her eyes.

"So what's the plan? It seems like the only way to cut into Wen's profits is to disrupt his human money tree. The typical smuggler earns up to $30,000 a head on illegals, and that's not including prostitution."

"And from what I understand, there's no shortage of takers who want to get out of China," Dean said. "He's got supply and demand, Artur."

"But we can find the transport," Artur countered. "These people are not simply *poofing* into this country. They are taking ships, or overland routes through South America and Mexico. A few carefully placed tips to the U.S. Coastguard or border patrol, and Wen's enterprise will begin to crumble."

"You said *'poofing.'*" Blue grinned. "Are you finally succumbing to American slang, Artur?"

"I am succumbing to many things," he said. "Not the least of which is your wit."

They ate dinner when they got home. Paper plates were passed around the table, filled with sandwiches. When Artur went to find silverware, Dela told him to wait. She looked at the drawer he opened, and a moment later, a fork and knife floated into the air.

Everyone was silent for a moment. Blue reached for some chips.

"We need to have a talk about these new abilities," he said mildly, as Artur plucked the utensils out of the air and returned to the table. "The powers we develop when we're kids are usually the ones we're stuck with, give or take some extra training. You seem to be doing something a little different, Dela."

"No shit," Dean muttered.

"I can't explain it," she said.

Hari examined Dela's troubled face. "This began when you met me, did it not? I am not entirely human, and unusual forces *have* affected my life. Perhaps my appearance, or the act of opening the box, was a trigger point."

"But what we do isn't magic, Hari."

"I don't know about that, ma'am," Eddie said, pushing around his sandwich. "I mean, we all know there's probably some scientific explanation for what we do, but I haven't heard it yet. We tell ourselves the mental ability to start a fire or read the history of an object conforms to some unknown scientific principle, and maybe that's the case. But it seems pretty magical to me—and probably to anyone else who isn't used to it like we are. I mean, look at Hari. We all say he's magic, right? Could be science, though. We just don't know enough to say."

"You've gone and turned deep on me," Dean said. Eddie blushed.

"Eddie is right," Hari agreed. "The Magi himself could do many of the things you are capable of, but he was also able to tap into forces that allowed him to twist reality to suit his desires."

Blue frowned. "His power must have had some limits, or else there would be a history—some record—of his activities. I mean, the way you tell it, this Magi would have tried conquering all of Asia and Europe, otherwise."

Hari shook his head. "The Magi was powerful but alone. You yourselves do not demonstrate your gifts, except to others of your kind. Why? Because you are outnumbered. The Magi came to our land through the mountains, east from China, and he was followed by stories. Uprisings, revolt. We always suspected he had been driven away, though we never knew why or how. Our forests were perfect for him; very few true humans lived there, and the shape-shifters had no qualms with magic. Until he turned on us."

"And yet . . ." Dela mused, tapping the tabletop with her fingernail.

"Merlin," Blue said.

"Morgana."

"Baba Yaga?" Artur shrugged.

The names were unfamiliar to Hari, but he sensed their significance. "Were these people like the Magi?"

"Legendary wizards, magic-makers," Dela explained. "Fairy tales told to children. Supposedly as unreal as the Greek gods or any other myth."

Hari smiled. "Humans were a myth once. A dream, cast to flesh, when animals of different natures wished to mate. They were compelled to find a common body, and so imagined a form that would feel all the pleasures expressed by the heart. The problem, however, was that children born of such unions were human through and through. Sometimes they could change shape, but more often they were locked, confined. Still, they were healthy and strong; they grew and multiplied, and after a time, it became forbidden for shape-shifters to love outside their kind."

"That is a lovely story," Dela said.

"I guess humans aren't off limits." Dean winked at her.

Hari laughed. "Never. The child of a shape-shifter male and human woman will always breed true to the father, while with our females, there is a half chance."

He looked at Dela, and found her staring at her hands, her cheeks flushed bright red. Blue and Dean were trying to hide smiles, while Artur simply appeared grave. Eddie was concentrating very hard on his pizza.

"I am sorry," he said, confused. "What did I say?"

Dean smirked. "You're a male shape-shifter, Hari. Who would you want as the mother of your children?" Hari stared at him, and then Dela. She frowned at Dean.

Hari could not find the words; he had not thought of it when speaking, but of course Dela was the one to whom he passed his desires. Heart-warmth instantly swelled in his throat, tightening his body as he imagined his child growing inside her, a fantasy that had been strong within him for many days.

In their brief discussions of the future, the subject of children had been touched upon, but Hari realized Dela had never stated for certain her feelings on the matter. If she did not want to have a young one with him . . .

His face grew hot. His stomach hurt. "I am sorry, Delilah. I did not mean to embarrass you."

She looked at him then, and her eyes were as warm as her face, dark with promise. "You didn't embarrass me, Hari. The only shocking things at this table are Dean's manners."

"Ow," Dean muttered, rubbing his chest.

THAT NIGHT, CURLED IN HIS ARMS, DELA BRUSHED her lips against Hari's throat. "I know the topic of children has come up before tonight, but I never really thought about what they would be like. Now I understand."

"And does it bother you?"

His concern was palpable. Dela could taste it as she kissed his mouth; slow, deep. She smiled against his lips. "No, Hari. Although we'll have to think about moving someplace isolated if we want to raise a brood of tiger cubs."

Hari's eyes sparked gold, fire flickering in the shadows of her bedroom. "This has all happened so fast.

How long have we known each other? A week, a little more? Even among my people, courtships last much longer. They are full of intrigue, mystery—a dance between man and woman—kept hidden from families until a decision, a moment. Consummation. The man steals his mate away to a home he has built for her, until the birth of a child, and then all families are reunited."

"This is very different from what you're accustomed to," she agreed. "But then, falling in love with a man and planning out my future with him, after little more than a week, is a little off-board for me too. I don't know how to do anything else, though. It's frightening."

"So we can be frightened together," he said, pulling her even closer. "I have told you shape-shifters mate for life, Delilah. If you ever reject me, there will be no other."

"No other," she promised quietly, stroking his face. "I like the sound of that."

"You could be cruel," he laughed, flipping Dela onto her back.

"I could bring you to your knees."

"I think you already did that once tonight."

They breathed in each other's laughter, and it warmed Dela that Hari trusted her enough to smile over something so serious. She was still his summoner, his mistress, and while she would never dream of touching that power, it was there, waiting. She *could* bring him to his knees. Anyone who wielded the box after her could do that.

I can't let that happen. I don't know how to break the curse, but I can't ever let Hari be abused again.

"Hari?" she asked tentatively, as he pressed his lips against her collarbone. "I want you to consider . . . if and when anything ever does happen to me, I need to know . . . oh, Hari. Do you want the box to pass to someone else, someone who can be trusted, like Artur or Blue? Or our . . . our children?"

Such a strange thing, to say "our children" out loud. Extraordinary and breathtaking, a miraculous secret meant for Hari's ears only.

Hari's eyes turned grave. He loomed over her body, his face scant inches from her own. "When you die, Delilah, so will I. I will be dead to the world, and that is the way it should be. I do not want to be summoned again. Let me fall into the earth at your side, and I will be content. An eternity, dreaming of you." He brushed her cheek with the back of his hand, a whisper of flesh.

"Boy," she murmured, kissing him. "You sure can talk."

CHAPTER FIFTEEN

*S*HE *is trapped in the oubliette, embracing darkness,
vomiting obsidian on the cold stone floor. Breathing*
Delilah *breathing—ensnared and no one hears, no one
can, and* Delilah, *she is alone, alone, alone—*

"Delilah!"

Dela gasped, opening her eyes. Sunlight flooded her
bedroom, sweet as nectar on her mind, chasing shadows without words. Hari leaned over her, his skin glowing with the backlit halo of white sun. He cupped her
face in wordless question.

"I'm okay," she lied, wanting to soothe away his
troubled frown. How could she tell him her latest vision, a portent of things to come? Imprisonment, isola-
tion, despair—her own, or his. It did not matter to
whom. Something bad was coming.

"Delilah," he began, but she shook her head.

"Just a dream, Hari. Nothing more." Nothing pre-
ventable, anyway.

*Whatever will be, will be. That is the way of things,
and the future is not set in stone. What I saw is just a
fragment, the dark piece of a puzzle that could be full
of light. I can't let myself forget that.*

Just as she couldn't forget the danger was not yet past.

Hari's eyes were far too sharp, but he respected her word and said nothing. They got out of bed, dressed, and padded into the living room. The television was on, and all four of the house's other occupants were crowded in front of it, rapt.

". . . a body was found late last night in an alley off Monroe Street. Authorities have revealed that the man was the victim of a vicious animal attack, although sources say no one heard any sounds of struggle in what had previously been a peaceful downtown neighborhood. The victim has been identified as a Mr. Wen Zhang, a resident of New York City, and a prominent businessman. Anyone with information pertaining to the attack should contact the police or animal control."

"Shit," Dela said. "Oh, shit."

"Someone had good taste," Dean remarked.

"What the hell happened last night?" Dela stared at them, but everyone shrugged.

"He must have been killed soon after he left Le Soleil," Eddie said.

Blue scrubbed his jaw, which looked like it was three days overdue for a shave. "Do we really think this was done by an animal?"

A furrow appeared between Dean's eyes. "They called it an animal attack, which probably means they found some saliva in the wounds. Something not human."

"Yeah, right." Dela said. Wen's murder—and Dela was sure it was murder—was so unexpected, and so . . . convenient . . . it begged immediate and paranoid suspicion. She didn't think for one second it was an animal, or anyone trying to help. Who in their right mind, except her friends and family, would do that? And if it had been her friends or family, she would know.

"This is too much of a coincidence," Hari said. He looked troubled. "Do you believe one of his own people killed him?"

"Unlikely." Artur cracked his knuckles, an ominous gesture. "If this was murder, then perhaps his death was in retaliation for Dela's murdered client. A face-saving gesture. Eye for an eye."

"With both these leaders dead, the focus should no longer be on Delilah, correct?"

Dela groaned. "Zhang's cronies will think *I* killed him. Me or Hari, depending on how many people knew about our meeting."

"One thing at a time," Dean said. "Eddie, why don't you go downstairs and check out the security system? We may get visitors."

Dela rubbed her arms. "I'll go down with you. I need to walk this news out of my system."

Hari remained with the others. Eddie and Dela went down to her studio. She watched him check the alarm codes; his quick fingers flying over the small pad. His dark eyes were intense.

"I want to thank you," he suddenly said, casting Dela a quick glance. "For saving my life the other night. I haven't had a chance to tell you . . . but no one's ever taken that kind of risk for me."

There was no self-pity in his voice, but Dela still sensed the cautious hunger of a young man who had been kicked too much as a boy and was only just beginning to find his feet. A subtle hope that this, at last, would be the place to call home. *I am surrounded by Lost Boys,* Dela thought, as she touched Eddie's slim shoulder.

She said, "I couldn't have done anything less. Not when you put your own life on the line."

A flush crept up his neck. "I wasn't hurt bad. I think my pride more than anything else. Things should have turned out differently. I should have reacted . . . better."

Dela hesitated. "With your gift, you mean?"

Eddie grimaced. "Since the attack, I've been thinking of all the ways I could have stopped those guys. Heated up their guns, maybe just scorched their hands. Problem is, my control is good but not foolproof. I wasn't thinking clearly. Fire spreads so easily, and I don't . . . I don't want to . . ." His voice trailed off. Dela waited, patient.

"It's difficult," he finally whispered, and his eyes were haunted. "I don't want to hurt people, but I also don't want to lose my friends because I'm weak."

"Oh, Eddie," Dela said. "You did the right thing. Everyone has a line they can't cross, and if hurting people with your gift is what will break you, *don't do it.* Don't take the risk. That's not weak. It's being strong."

Dela's voice sounded hot, fierce to her own ears. She wanted to take Eddie's head in her hands. She wanted him to understand the horrible lesson she had learned from Adam's death.

"Eddie," she said quietly. "Are you with me on this?"

"Yes," he said, swallowing hard. "Yes, ma'am, I am."

She ruffled his hair. He ducked his head, blushing.

When they returned upstairs, Blue met them at the door. He looked at his watch, and crooked a finger at Eddie.

"You have a doctor's appointment in thirty minutes," he said.

"Awww, Dad," joked Dean, as a look of stricken disbelief passed over Eddie's face.

"I forgot," he muttered. Blue grinned.

"It's okay, kid. I'll hold your hand when they come after you with their needles and probes."

Dean glanced at Artur. "Guess we should go take care of that, um, other thing."

"What other thing?" Dela asked, leaning against the kitchen counter.

"Adam," Artur said, grave. "We are going to take his body to be cremated."

"Oh." Dela looked down at her hands. "I kind of figured you guys had already done that."

"Sorry, Dela." Dean shuffled his feet. "We were waiting to see if Wen Zhang wanted him, but now that he's dead . . ."

"I understand. Do I even want to know where Adam's body has been all this time?"

"There are places where people don't ask questions," Artur said. "We make a habit of learning where they are."

Again, *oh*.

No one asked whether she and Hari would be all right by themselves. She almost expected it, some request that they both accompany the departing men. No one said a word, and when Blue winked at her, Dela suspected a conspiracy.

Not that she minded.

When the door shut behind them, absolute silence filled the room.

"We're alone," she said, astonished.

"Yes," Hari said. "But only for a few hours."

"Well, if *you* can wait—"

Hari took two long steps, threw Dela over his shoulder, and carried her into the bedroom. Dela, laughing, hooked her hands around the door and slammed it shut behind them.

THE IRONY WAS NOT LOST ON HARI. TWO THOUSAND years of slavery, countless sexual acts—but here, now, as he gently laid Dela on the bed, he felt untested, clean.

He brushed his lips against Dela's cheek, scenting her desire, hot and sweet. She trembled against him. Not with anticipation, he realized, but with nervousness.

Hari sat on the edge of the bed and held her hands, stroking her palms with his thumbs. "What is wrong?" he asked, sounding far calmer than he felt. Dela did not pretend misunderstanding; she gave him a small, tremulous smile.

"Aren't *you* a little scared?"

He almost laughed; neither magic nor death had made this woman show fear, and yet now her courage faltered. As did his.

"Yes," he said softly. "You are the first woman I will ever make love to."

Dela sighed, and with the passing of that long breath, tension leaked from her muscles until she clung to him, limp. And then her strength returned and she hugged him, tight and fierce. There was nothing shy about her now; nervousness had fled, and in its place was the assurance of a thunderstorm: electric, full of power. Dela kissed him; he felt her essence pour into his body, and the beast howled.

Hari pushed away Dela's sweater, drawing her dress over her head. His hands trailed clumsily over the pale creamy wash of her skin; he lightly squeezed her soft flesh. Dela sighed against his mouth, and then his own shirt came off, his pants pushed aside to the floor.

Dela ran her hand up the side of Hari's stomach, calling blood to the surface of his skin, heating him as powerfully as the desert sun of old. She traced the lines of his muscles, her fingertips trickling down his arms. She kissed his neck, laving the hollow of his throat with her tongue.

Hari picked up her palm and darted his tongue against her skin. Dela's eyes widened, and as he trailed kisses across her wrist, she bent over his chest, soft hair trailing down his flushed body. Dela tasted his scars, careful and deliberate, running her tongue over rough flesh, swirling close and closer until she flicked his nipple, startling a low cry from his throat—and then another as she very gently bit down.

Now *he* trembled. His hands danced against Dela's spine, loving glances of skin to skin, carving a path around her ribs to the curve of her pale breasts, drawn tight and hard, peaked for his touch. Hari tried to watch Dela's face, but she was hidden against his chest, suckling.

Hari ran his knuckles along her breasts, unfolding his hands as Dela drew back, moaning. He pressed his thumbs against her nipples, brushing them with tender care, lightly scraping with his nails. Dela's back arched, and Hari took full advantage, bending her backward over his arm, lowering his mouth to her breast. As she had done for him, he fed on her body, reveling in the miracle of being allowed so intimate a touch. Dela's whimpers electrified him. In all his years, he had never once imagined he could take such aching joy in giving another person pleasure. It was a marvel, a blessing.

Dela's hands fluttered against his shoulders. "You never answered my question," she gasped. "What does it mean to kiss like mates?"

A growl escaped him, and he lowered Dela all the way to the bed, trailing kisses down her body, fingers whispering against her flesh. She shuddered as he spread her legs.

Hari taught her, and when the lesson was done, Dela stared at him with lazy, languid eyes that raked over his aching body with hungry deliberation. He was unprepared for her attack—had only a moment to feel surprise—and then Dela's hair filled his lap and his world became hot and wet. The kiss of a proper mate—except "proper" was not the word to describe the exquisite torture she inflicted upon his body, stringing him out one lick and touch at a time.

Dela suddenly chuckled, and the vibrations inside her mouth, the hot stir of her breath, made him cry out.

"So we're mates, huh?"

"Oh, yes," Hari groaned. Dela licked her entire palm and enclosed him in a loose fist, rotating her hand in a screwing motion that sent his mind reeling past the ceiling into the clouds.

"Oh, yes? Or, oh, *yes?*"

"Both." Hari drew Dela away from him, holding her tight against his body. She gazed at him with liquid eyes, her cheeks flushed, lips parted.

"After this," he whispered, "you are mine and I am yours."

"Forever," she said.

He covered her mouth with his own in the same instant he slid into her body. They caught each other's cries of pleasure, a passionate entwinement of voice and body, spirits merging with each slick, hot, stroke.

Hari felt Dela enter him as surely as he entered her, a bright light set to make him burst. His blood cried for her, his heart spilling over with every murmured breath of her name. He loved her, and his love sang down to the root of his soul.

They sank into each other's eyes, and Hari did not know where he began or ended—everywhere Dela, everywhere—and as she shuddered beneath him, her orgasm bringing on his own climax, he heard a long clear tone inside his head, resonating down to his soul. The heat of that note set his skin on fire, and he cried out Dela's name as his seed poured into her body.

I am complete, he thought, and knew it to be true.

Hari folded his arms under Dela's shoulders and carefully turned them on their sides. Still joined, they ground their bodies tight, writhing with the aftershocks of pleasure. Hari buried his nose in Dela's neck, inhaling jasmine, bathing in the thunder of her heart.

Hari was almost asleep when Dela asked, "When can we do that again?"

Hari smiled against her cheek. For the first time in two thousand years he felt true peace. "As soon as possible," he said. "And as often as you like, for as long as we are alive."

IT WAS THE FUR THAT STIRRED HER TO CON-sciousness—luxurious and warm, caressing her skin as though each individual hair breathed, desired. She felt her body surrounded by that soft heat which was not human, and when she opened her eyes, she found herself embraced by a tiger.

Orange fur, striped with black and cream. A magnificent feline head, pressed against her pillow, pink tongue peeking out from between long white teeth. Dela's breath caught with wonder. Fairy tales sang opera in her mind.

It never occurred to her to be afraid. This was Hari—

miraculous, magical Hari—and he had somehow found his skin.

When the Magi stole my skin, he stole a piece of my heart. A piece of my heart, in the shape of my sister. To find my skin, I have to find my heart . . .

His words trailed fire through her body, an echo of their passion. Could the answer truly be so simple as love? Had their love for each other healed him?

The curse!

Dela began shaking Hari awake. Her shake, however, turned into a stroke, her fingers burying themselves in his chest, trailing low to his stomach. Hari was a huge man—as a tiger, immense. His embrace was heavy, comforting, and—dare she admit it—utterly erotic.

She moved against him, slow, savoring the luxurious richness of fur caressing her skin, the heat of his body. Hari's limbs twitched; massive paws flexed, revealing the hint of claws. When he opened his glowing eyes, Dela saw the man inside the tiger—her Hari, looking down at her with a fevered hunger that stole her breath away.

A sound emerged from the tiger's throat, a low cough. Words, perhaps—unsuited to a feline throat. He tried again, and Dela could not hide her smile. She looped her arm under one of Hari's heavy sprawling limbs, and lifted it up so he could see the striped fur.

Golden eyes sprang wide.

"It's true," she said, laughing in delight, awe. "You *changed!*"

Hari froze, and then muscles began shifting in his face, fur flickering to skin and back again, a shimmering transformation. Dela touched the high bone of his cheek, savoring the sensation of his body changing beneath her fingertips. She pressed close as flesh

replaced lush fur—his torso narrowing while legs
stretched, long and naked—and Hari wound himself
around Dela, tight, full of power, love.

"You are beautiful," she said, heart in her throat.

"Delilah," he whispered, but he did not pull away as
Dela thought he would. Instead he hunched tight around
her body, burying his fingers in her hair, exploring her
face with gentle kisses, light and fine.

"Turn around," he murmured, and she shifted in his
arms until she felt him hard against her back—hard,
then, inside of her—and she pushed deep into his broad
chest, rubbing skin against skin, sliding into a slow
rhythm that was hot and thick.

She cried out as Hari nipped her shoulder. A moment
later he shifted, bracing himself above her, driving her
deep into the groaning mattress with hard sharp thrusts.
Hari's teeth grazed the back of Dela's neck, tangling in
her hair as he held her down with muscle and bone. His
breath burned hot against her scalp—but not as hot as
his long body. Dela squirmed close, raising herself up to
meet him, thrust for grinding thrust.

Hari's fingernails flashed into claws, raking deep
furrows in the sheets; Dela grabbed his wrists, crying
out as she came. Hari growled, but he did not slow his
movements. He pushed harder and Dela glimpsed fur, a
light striped sheen of orange and black rimming his
human hands and arms. Hari grabbed her hips and
waist, hoisting her even higher against his thick heat.
Dela braced herself against the mattress, drowning in
pleasure as Hari rode her hard, his teeth pressed against
her neck.

They climaxed together, Dela bucking against Hari's
hips as he shuddered, a low cry escaping his throat. His
hands flexed, holding her close as he buried himself one

last time into her body. Dela felt his seed trickle down her leg. She wanted to taste it.

"Oh, Hari," she murmured as they collapsed on their sides. For a time, it was enough to feel Hari's body vibrating with contentment, his arms loose around her. Dela listened to her heart slow, and when she could breathe again without gasping she carefully disengaged herself and rolled over to face him. Hari held her close. Dela butted her head against his chin, drawing in his scent. She buried her fingers in his thick hair.

"Delilah," he said, and it seemed to Dela that her name was the only thing he could say. He lifted up his arm and they both watched as fur pierced skin, muscles shifting with bone. He shuddered, a choking sound emerging from deep within his throat.

"Show me," she said. "I want to see it all."

He stared at her, and clarity seemed to return—accompanied by a smile so joyous Dela laughed out loud with delight. Hari kissed her hard and then rolled away, slipping off the bed, shifting as he moved. This time, light shimmered around his body, golden and sheer, sparkling like sun on rippling water until a tiger—a real full-formed tiger—stalked around the room, muscles gliding beneath glorious skin. Hari walked to Dela's side of the bed and set a giant paw in her lap. She sat up, touched his face. Scratched behind his ears. Laughed again, softer this time.

When Hari shifted, it was slow, as though he savored every change within his body, tasting the swing from beast to man, until, finally, he knelt before her, a thin sheen of sweat covering his naked body. His gaze burned.

"You healed me. You healed my heart and gave me back my skin." Laughter burst from his throat, bright. He grabbed Dela's hands, pressing kisses on her palms, and then her face, her throat. He worshipped her with his mouth, tears spilling from his eyes. Dela found herself crying with him, and she clutched his shoulders, tangling her fingers in his hair.

"Does this mean the curse is broken?"

Uncertainty slipped into Hari's gaze. "I do not know. Command me, Delilah. Anything."

Dela hesitated, and Hari kissed her. "It will be all right. I do not mind."

She minded, but thought for a moment and said, "Thou shalt . . . thou shalt stand."

She knew the truth even as the words left her mouth. Power hummed in the air, a devastating thread of cool horror touching her lips, caressing her throat. She felt the power of the box coalesce inside her body, and for one awful moment, she was its mistress—the wellspring of life and pain and death.

The look on Hari's face alone was enough to make her sick. He gave the impression of a tree being strangled by an immense vine. With excruciating sluggishness, he rose to his feet.

Dela began to cry in earnest, but her tears were no longer joyful.

"Delilah," Hari said softly, his face etched with pain. "I cannot come to you until . . . until you release me from your command."

She choked. "Thou shalt do as you please."

Hari instantly relaxed. He crawled onto the bed beside Dela, wrapping his arms around her waist, drawing her unresisting body into his lap. She clasped him, tight. For a long time they silently held each other.

"I thought your skin was the key," Dela finally breathed.

"As did I." Hari looked down at her face, and something soft fluttered in his sorrowful eyes. He kissed her palm, her wrist, achingly gentle.

"You have given me a great gift," he said. "The least of which is my skin. As long as I can live as your mate, it does not matter to me if I am bound by the box."

"I want you to have your freedom, Hari. More than anything else in this world."

"You have already given me freedom." He gently pressed her down upon the bed, caressing her face. "There is so much to celebrate, Delilah. So much to be thankful for. This is a small thing."

It's not a small thing, and you and I both know it. Still, she said nothing. It would only cast a deeper pall, and Hari was trying so hard to forget—to make *her* forget.

Dela kissed him, desperate and clumsy, and he joined her with equal passion. He clutched her, and his hands were kisses, smothering her body with a wide-planed warmth that sheered heat to bone.

Hari smoothed back Dela's hair. "If we were in my own time, I would steal you away to a secret place. A home, built just for you. I would show you all the wonders of the forest and mountains. Every day, my only goal would be to make you happy, safe."

"You can do that here," Dela reminded him.

"And I will." He sighed, passing a hand over his face. "I wish we had more time alone. We have so much to talk about."

"So much to do," she said impishly.

Hari laughed, shadows fleeing his eyes. "I cannot tell you how shocked I was to wake and find that not only had I changed shape, but that you were still looking at me as a man."

Dela blushed. "I expected you to pull away."

"Oh, no." Hari hugged her tight. "That was a cele-
bration in itself. You do not know how rare it is for
shape-shifters to find human mates who do not fear the
beast."

"Why?" Dela asked. "You're still . . . *you*. Just, inside fur."

"I do not know, Delilah. Perhaps, confronted with
the animal, it finally becomes clear we are not human.
That we carry the seed of something strange and dangerous. It can be very frightening."

"Oh, you're still frightening. Just not to me."

Hari's smile was infinitely tender. "You were never
scared of me, Delilah. You saw past two thousand years
of masks wrought from pain, and found the man who
had been lost."

Dela's blush deepened. Hari laughed at her discomfort, and kissed her shoulder. "I was so angry at being
summoned, and there you were, wrapped in the small-
est scrap of cloth I had ever seen, defying and honoring
me at the same time."

"Best disappointment you ever received, huh?"

"A miracle." He kissed her, and she buried her hands
in his hair; then lower, digging her nails into his shoulders. He growled, and she felt fur sprout beneath her
palms, against the length of her body. Thick hard heat
pressed against Dela's thigh, and she reached down and
touched him.

"Do you want me as a tiger or a man?" Hari's voice
rasped low, hungry. His eyes glowed.

"I love you either way," Dela said, stroking him. Hari
trembled, and Dela lay back, watching his body change
above her, savoring the warm glow of golden light bathing her skin. Eerie and exciting and bizarre; muscles
tightened, expanded. His face elongated, cheekbones

spreading outward, lifting—but his eyes, those passionate eyes, stayed the same.

Hari bent his head. When his tongue rasped her breast, she rose off the bed, whimpering. She grabbed great handfuls of fur as he continued his exploration, licking and nuzzling his way down her ribs and stomach, lower still. He paused between her thighs, and the look in his eyes as he watched her panting seemed distinctly amused.

"Just wait until it's *your* turn," she warned him, breathless. His mouth opened in a toothy grin.

Dela lost track of time, all sense of control. Hari was relentless; gentle, yet firm as he played with her body, driving her over the edge again and again. When Dela finally took his thickness into her mouth, resting her cheek on his belly as she sucked and stroked, Hari changed, took her in his arms and made love to her.

Afterwards they lay together, foreheads touching, sharing breath. Dela's thighs felt damp, her body heavy. A thought occurred to her, but it was unpleasant. It must have shown in her eyes because Hari nudged her ribs. "What is it, Delilah?"

She hesitated. "Before . . . when you were forced to have sex with your mistresses . . . do you think any of them became pregnant?"

Hari's lips tightened; his entire body coiled in on itself. Dela reached for him, cold, and he relaxed enough to tuck her deeper into his embrace.

"I try not to think of it," he said. "Many of the women refused my seed. They feared I would give them a child, and that later, their husbands would realize they were not the father."

"Your appearance and abilities are fairly distinctive," Dela agreed. "But the possibility exists?"

"Yes," he said heavily. "But I hope it is not so. It is one of my great fears, that I left a child alone to face the world. A shape-shifter, growing up without guidance, unaware of the changes in his body. That is, if he was allowed to grow at all."

Hari placed his large hand over Dela's belly, holding her gently. "Do you think . . . ?"

She covered his hand. "I hope so. Do you want a boy or a girl?"

He kissed her. "Both."

"Nothing will happen to our children," she promised. Hari nodded, solemn.

A door slammed. Dela heard familiar voices, the approach of feet.

"Yo—Dela, Hari! You guys in there?" It was Dean, sounding as though his ear was pressed to the door.

"Go away!" Dela yelled, Hari growling.

"Just making sure you guys hadn't been kidnapped," he groused, but his footsteps quickly receded.

Hari and Dela looked at each other, and shook their heads.

"We will have a home far from all people," he said. "And I will continuously make love to you."

"You do that already," Dela said, sliding out of bed. "Every time you look at me."

CHAPTER SIXTEEN

THEY held a ceremony over Adam's ashes that evening, driving out to Barrymore Park, a scenic overlook on the edge of the city. The sun threw out arms of crimson and gold, the brilliant light bathing the river and trees, as well as the gathered men and woman, in the hushed, vibrant aura of dusk.

"I'm still going to miss you," Dela said, holding the simple metal box containing Adam's remains. Hari glanced at her friends, who wore conflicting expressions of sorrow—for Dela's sake, he supposed—and hard grimaces.

Hari understood. Though Adam had suffered tremendous loss, he had murdered a child. An unforgivable crime.

Dela leaned against the guardrail and opened the box. She dumped Adam's ashes over the high cliff, and Hari watched them shimmer down and away, lost.

Everyone is lost at death, he reminded himself. *Though it is a sadder thing when you become lost in life.*

Dela did not cry. She fumbled with the box, struggling to shut its lid. Hari took the object from her, drawing her close with his free hand. He kissed her brow. After a moment, she pushed away.

"Do you guys think I could have a moment? I just want to stand here for a bit, and . . ." She shrugged, helpless. "I don't know. Just give me a sec, okay?"

The men walked back to the car. Dela remained behind, a small figure leaning against the wooden rail, her blond hair glowing in the fading light.

Blue leaned against the black Land Cruiser, and glanced at Hari. "How's she handling all this?"

Hari felt the weight of all their stares, and sighed. "Delilah is still saddened by Adam's betrayal, but what you see is her true face. She is not hiding any deeper agony. I think, though, she will no longer put such faith in her instincts."

"That's a shame." Eddie ducked his head, folding his arms against his chest. "I mean, I don't know her as well as any of you, but that has to be one of the things that made her feel safe. Knowing how to read people, knowing she was always right about their motives."

"She was not wrong about Adam," Artur said, surprising them. "His motives toward Dela, anyway, were pure. She will realize that in time."

Hari watched Dela's slender back, hoping that would be the case. If not, he was comforted by the fact that Dela was not alone. She had friends to remind her of her gifts, to renew her faith in trust, loyalty. Love.

In the distance, crows cawed; leaves rustled in the cool breeze. Dela patted the rail, and finally turned to walk back to them. Hari met her eyes, and for a moment felt her love pour into him, strong and pure.

And then the air between them broke apart with the sounds of gunfire. Bullets slammed into the car, the ground, whining and spitting.

"On the hill!" shouted Dean, reaching for his weapon.

Hari was already stripping off his clothes, tearing the cloth like paper. Even as the other men took cover, he ran toward Dela, who was pressed flat against the ground with her hands over her head.

Bullets entered Hari's shoulder; he shook off the pain and flung himself on top of Dela's body. Struggling to kick off his jeans, he pressed his lips to her ear.

"We must move," he said, and she nodded with a sharp jerk of her chin. Shoving off the last of his clothes, Hari changed shape, splitting form with a thought, his vision swimming gold. Beneath him, Dela gasped.

More bullets struck him, burrowing deep, striking bone. Hari growled, and nudged Dela with his nose. She did not hesitate; carefully pushing herself up on all fours, she began crawling toward the car with Hari pressed against her side, protecting her from the bullets with his larger mass. In his human shape, he would not have been able to shield her so thoroughly.

Dean and the others were pinned behind the Land Cruiser. Bullets riddled the metal frame. A metallic roar filled Hari's ears and he watched with alarm as three large cars sped into the parking lot.

Two of the cars' engines suddenly exploded into flames. Men scrambled from the vehicle interiors, shouting. The third car pulled away from the others, driving straight at Hari and Dela. The engine roared.

Dela flung out her hands. The car slowed, swerving, but the driver pulled hard on the wheel and regained control, barreling down upon them. Dela's face contorted with pain, and Hari flung himself around her body.

The car never hit them. Its engine sputtered, dying, and Hari glimpsed Blue peering around the battered fender of the Land Cruiser, his eyes hard, his jaw working.

Men—faces twisted in grimaces of desperation—piled out of the stalled car, some of them shooting the Land Cruiser, others aiming at Dela and Hari.

"Call her off or we'll kill you!" one of them shouted, his eyes bloodshot, wild. "Do it!"

Dela stared, helpless. "Call off who?"

Hari did not care what the men wanted; they smelled crazy, like murder. Shouldering Dela into nearby bushes, he leapt at the speaker, claws extended for the kill. The terrified man got off one shot, but the impact of the bullet did not slow Hari. The blood rage was upon him, hot and sweet. Hari batted aside the weapon and sank his teeth into the man's throat. Blood spilled into his mouth. The beast savored the taste.

Thunder—pain riddled his ribs, but it was nothing—nothing—and he whirled on the men shooting him, claws arcing in the fading light, ripping and tearing into flesh. Distant cries filled his ears, and men dropped weapons that glowed red-hot. Artur, Dean, and Blue rolled out from behind the Land Cruiser, guns trained on the unarmed men. Eddie followed close behind, drenched in sweat, his eyes dark with concentration. The guns continued to glow. Up on the hill the snipers stopped shooting.

"What the fuck is going on?" Dean snarled. Blood streamed down his arm.

Hari changed shape, and everyone but Artur watched the transformation with awed disbelief. A gunman swore something ugly.

"They wanted Delilah." Hari spit out blood, wiping it from his lips. He turned to the bushes where he had pushed her.

Dela was gone.

CHAPTER SEVENTEEN

THE remarkable thing was, Dela had been expecting this. Really. She just didn't think it would happen under the noses of all her friends—although she had to admit, a violent gunfight was one damn fine distraction, even if totally unrelated to her current predicament.

Dela had also held higher expectations for herself; a good struggle, some well-placed bites and punches. At the very least, a scream.

Instead, the Magi had crept up behind her, stuck a needle full of tranquilizers in her arm, then dragged her backward through the bushes. The last thing Dela remembered was Hari's killing charge, raising her hands to try her powers at protecting him from the guns trained on his back.

And then a prick, instant vertigo, a mouth full of leaves, and that sneering cold face, quickly swallowed by darkness.

When she finally opened her eyes, she found herself stretched on a cold hard floor, bound and oh-so-carefully gagged. Her head pounded. The Magi sat cross-legged beside her. His hair was mussed, his cheeks hollow.

"Welcome back," he cooed.

"Grrrr."

"Oh, come now. I haven't hurt you."

No, but Dela knew he would, short of killing her. Until he had the box, until he had Hari. And then, death.

Well, screw that.

She glanced around the room. She appeared to be in an empty basement; handcuffs connected her to one of three wooden support pillars. No windows, and only one light source—a bulb hanging from a flimsy chain in the center of the room. The stairs were behind the Magi. The air smelled damp, moldy.

Dela studied the man, forcing herself to remain calm, to study his face. It was not her imagination; he looked tired, the skin drawn tight around his mouth and eyes. If she had to guess, she would say he was in pain.

The Magi stirred, his fingers uncurling. "You are quite fascinating. "You *and* your friends. In all my years, I have never witnessed such a congregation of talent. And yet, all of you together do not amount to what I was, what I will be again."

A sadist? Dela wondered. *A goatloving son of a—*

The Magi smiled. "I cannot read your thoughts, but I still sense your emotions. Be angry. Rage at me, if you wish." He reached behind him and pulled out a syringe. "I am going to undo your gag, but if you begin screaming, I will dose you again."

Dela thought of biting him, but decided against it. The Magi seemed to be in a talkative mood, and her curiosity was piqued. She might learn something that could help Hari. Or perhaps she just might stall him long enough for someone to find her.

The Magi squirted some water into her mouth after he removed the gag, then sat back, once again watching her.

"Where is the box?" he finally asked, as Dela knew he would.

"I don't know," she said, which was partially true. Blue had taken the box to her local bank and placed it in a security deposit box. Dela did not know the number, nor did she have the key.

The Magi stared, and Dela felt something flutter against her mind. Light as butterfly wings, but infinitely colder.

"You are not telling me the whole truth." Shadows spread beneath his eyes.

"I don't know where the box is," she repeated, concentrating on her ignorance of its exact location.

A breathless moment, and then the Magi leaned backward. "Who does know where it is?"

Ah, the question she would not answer. It was becoming clear to Dela that the Magi possessed the ability to read minds—just not hers. Unsurprising, really. Even Max couldn't read her mind when she shielded, although he was still able to "speak" to her telepathically.

But if the Magi could sense the truth of what she said, it would not be long before he ferreted out fact from fiction, and she refused to put Blue and her friends in danger.

Dela's silence displeased the Magi and he leaned close. "I have been watching your home for several days, following your movements. Watching you with Hari and your friends. What a simple thing, to ask questions of neighbors. I now know your name, Dela Reese."

Dela's tongue thickened, her vision blurring. A strange heaviness coated her thoughts. The hiss of her name leaving the Magi's lips reverberated in her skull, and Dela fought for clarity, struggling to shrug off the strange lassitude flowing through her body.

When you know a person's true name, it opens a crack into her life, into her mind. Your name is not what you are, but it is what you are called, and that is a profound knowledge to have over another.

Hari's warm voice flooded Dela's mind, and she clung to his words.

My name is not what I am. It is what I am called.

"Who knows the location of the box, Dela Reese? Is it one of your friends?"

Dela gritted her teeth against the compulsion to speak, to say anything at all.

My name is not what I am.

I could change my name, throw it away, and I would still be me. Metalsmith, artist, dreamer, lover—

"Tell me his name, Dela Reese."

It is what I am called.

"Tell me."

But Dela is not my real name. It is only one name. And Hari calls me Delilah.

Delilah, never Dela.

My name is not what I am. It is what I am called.

And I am called Delilah.

Dela embraced her full name, silently chanting it, again and again, forming a shield against the Magi's questions. The shadow peeled away from her mind, darkness flaking like ash. Clarity returned; her bones felt light as air.

"You'll have to do better than that," Dela said, raggedly fighting for her breath.

The Magi snarled, slapping her so hard her ears rang. For some reason, his outburst made her grin. She tasted blood, pain, and triumph.

"What happened?" she goaded him. "When you cursed Hari into that box, what was the price *you* paid?"

Too close, too close. The Magi screamed at her, his cheeks sinking into his mouth with each mighty breath, raging in languages Dela did not understand. He asked her again for the box, and she refused him with her silence.

He beat her. With fists and feet, he kicked her again and again, stomping on her stomach, her ribs. He fell to his knees, wrapping his fists in her hair, screeching in her face. His desperation frightened her; it bordered on insanity—it *was* insane.

Dela's only weapon was her mind, but the Magi was relentless, and the pain—perhaps even the drugs still in her system—scrambled her concentration. She instinctively searched for metal—her handcuffs, the light bulb chain, water pipes, wiring—but she could not grasp them, could not do more than rattle weak links. All her new strength, and she was helpless.

When the Magi finally exhausted himself, he backed away from her, stumbling over his own feet. Dela's eyes seemed to be the only part of her body still working correctly; she stared at the Magi, dumbly noting the bright splashes of blood staining his shirt, his pants. His hands were red, wet.

"Your friends are next," he said. "Think on that."

And he turned out the light.

THEY SEARCHED THE UNDERBRUSH, CALLING DELA'S name until Hari stopped them and listened to the sound of his heart, reaching for the compulsion that bound him to his summoner. *East,* whispered the spell. *Go east.*

"She has been taken from this place," Hari said, clutching his ribs. He could not track Dela's scent, no matter how hard he tried. Blood overwhelmed his senses, leaking through his fingers, pooling in the dust. Blood everywhere, with his heart bleeding too, dying for Dela.

Hari slowly straightened, turning on the men who'd attacked them, who now cowered against the ground. He wrapped his hand around the closest available throat, and the transformation rippled, Hari controlling, tempering the split. His arm sprouted fur, claws pushing through his fingernails. His teeth brushed past his lips, his face elongating into something not quite human, not quite tiger.

Someone screamed, and Hari smelled urine; the man in front of him, pissing his pants. He flexed his hand, and claws pierced soft flesh.

"Where is she?"

Atur stepped forward, stripping off his gloves. His eyes were flat, cold. He grabbed the shivering gunman's head. Silence, and then he explained what he saw:

"All of these men are from New York," he said through gritted teeth. "They came with Wen Zhang, an entire entourage. Late last night, after he disappeared, an old woman came to them. Golden eyes. She told them to leave Dela alone. When they laughed at her, she began killing them with her bare hands."

"You sent her!" gasped the gunman, his eyes wild. "You killed Wen Zhang!"

"No," Blue said. "We didn't."

Artur released the gunman. "She was like you, Hari. Except she had scales."

"What of Delilah?" Hari asked, uncaring if another shape-shifter had become involved. He was indifferent to anything but Dela.

"I don't think they kidnapped her," Dean said, interrupting what Artur was about to say. He clutched his head, his eyes squeezed shut. "She's in the trunk of a car. A Jeep. Damn, come on . . . *see* . . . the driver . . . the driver is a man, mixed race, dark hair—"

Hari snarled, releasing the gunman who collapsed, weeping, to his knees. "The Magi has her."

Blue ground his gun into the temple of the man nearest him. "This is the last straw. If you *ever* come near us again, I swear what happened last night, and what happened today, will be *nothing* compared to what we'll do to you. You all thought those warnings we gave were jokes, huh? *No.* Go back to New York, and don't ever leave that shithole you boys call home. The minute you do, we'll know. And you'll be dead."

"Their guns?" Artur asked Eddie.

"Ruined." The young man kicked one of the discarded rifles, the barrel melted.

"Car's going to be a problem." Blue's eyes grew distant. "Bullets ruined the engine."

"Start up their Suburban," Artur ordered, gesturing toward the large vehicle parked beside them. Eddie went to the Land Cruiser and began removing the license plates.

"What is he doing?" Hari asked Dean.

"We don't have time to move the car or wipe it down. Eddie takes off the plates, lights a major fire, and we're good."

"Not quite that easy," Eddie called back at them, "but I know what I'm doing. I burned out all the vehicle identification numbers when I first got the car."

Hari closed his eyes, searching for Dela. The spell allowed him to track his masters; indeed, distance increased the compulsion to find her. She was still heading east, but until he began moving, he would be unable to obtain a more specific location.

The Suburban roared to life. Blue stuck his head out the driver's window, shouting at them to get in.

"What about the dumbasses?" Dean asked Artur.

"No time," Artur said, sharing a meaningful glance with Hari. "Right now, the Magi is the greater threat."

They climbed into the car, leaving behind the gunmen who struggled to their feet. Blue stopped the vehicle less than a hundred yards away, and Eddie leaned out the window, eyeing the Land Cruiser.

"Make her pop," Blue murmured.

The car did not pop—it exploded into a raging fireball, the Suburban rocking with the force of the blow. Hari's ears rang. The gunmen were thrown flat against the ground, covering their heads as burning steel rained down upon them.

"Bitchin'," said Dean, slapping Eddie on the back. "He bakes *and* burns."

"I need a direction," Blue called out.

"East," Hari said, closing his eyes. "Away from the city."

Blue frowned, pulling onto the highway. "Can you get more specific?"

"Not until we're closer to Delilah." Hari clutched the armrest, his claws raking deep grooves into the leather. Blue glanced at him.

"Uh, you might want to change back to full human, Hari. If anyone sees you pulling a Moreau . . ."

Hari did not know what that was, but he settled back into his human skin. He felt the other men watching him, yet he was content not to speak. All he could think of was Dela, trapped, alone with the Magi. His mate. Stolen from him.

I swore I would protect her. I promised I would keep her safe.

The beast howled. Hari fought to keep his human face. The blood rage was still upon him, but this time nothing would stop him until he destroyed the man who had torn apart his life, who threatened to steal away his future.

"You said the Magi needed the box." Eddie leaned forward, his dark eyes agonized. "Dela's safe unless he gets it, right?"

Hari said nothing, and Artur shook his head. "He can't kill Dela. That doesn't mean she's safe."

Eddie paled. Dean slammed his fist into the seat.

"How the hell did this happen?" he raged. "How did that bastard get her, right in the middle of a firefight?"

"Timing," Artur said, staring out the window. "He must have been watching us, waiting for the right moment to grab her."

"I should have sensed him." Hari buried his fists against his thighs. "I should have been more vigilant. I knew he would be coming for us eventually."

"You warned us, Hari. We all knew, and we still couldn't stop him." Blue gestured at the road. "Picking up anything?"

Hari closed his eyes, listening to his heart. "They're moving in a northeasterly direction now."

Blue took the next exit, and they drove for another hour in near silence, broken only when the bullets in Hari's body wiggled free, plunking onto his seat. There were ten in all, each accompanied by a chorus of hisses.

Darkness fell. The city disappeared behind them, suburbia giving way to farmland, farmland to forest, the road growing thick with the shadow of evergreen, hiding the stars.

They were curling around a bend in the road when a stream of vicious invective left Blue's mouth. A moment later, the engine sputtered.

"Shit, no," said Dean.

"Shit, yes."

The car died and they coasted to the side of the road. Hari jumped out while the vehicle was still moving, his eyes sharpening, the world beyond clear as day. He listened, found his direction, and ran into the forest, giving himself over to the tiger.

"Where are you going?" Artur shouted.

Hari spun around; fur rippled through his skin in waves. He was bathed in light. "She is close now. I cannot wait."

He left them before they could say another word, shutting himself off to everything but Dela. Two legs to four—he dropped in an instant, the tiger replacing the man, loping through the forest.

I am coming, he called to her, reaching out with every fiber in his being. *Hold on, Delilah. Hold on.*

HOLDING ON WAS THE ONLY THING DELA COULD DO.

Darkness swallowed her whole; images from her dream licked at the surface of her mind. The oubliette had found her.

After the Magi left, she lay very still, trying to assess her injuries. She thought her ribs might be broken—that, or bruised beyond sensible belief. Each breath was agony, and when she tried to move, she wanted to vomit. She did vomit, but nothing came up. Dry heaves, which almost made her faint from the resulting anguish in her ribs.

Swallowing hard, Dela slowly inched her way up into a sitting position, leaning against the wooden pillar. She could not see anything, and she finally closed her eyes. Trying to see in the darkness was making her dizzy. Perhaps she had a concussion.

The Magi had handcuffed Dela's hands behind her back. She tested the metal with her mind, fighting past the pain to concentrate, focus. The handcuffs had no stories to tell, and the links slipped away from her thoughts, insubstantial as water, until—and Dela held her breath—she felt friction, something tangible. She familiarized herself with the sensation of steel, letting the metal shape itself, her grip firming until she felt strong enough to tug on the links, setting her mental teeth to the steel.

She hurt all over, but again and again she pulled the links, breathless with pain and the smell of blood—her blood—and there were times when it was too much, her concentration faltering until she was forced to rest, and then begin again.

Nothing so miraculous as stopping a bullet. Blue was right. I should have done some experiments, exercises— tested the limits of my power.

Thinking of the men, especially Hari, gave her strength. They would be looking for her, although she could not count on them arriving anytime soon. Dela did not imagine the Magi had left clues.

She heard a series of groans above her; the floor, someone walking. Two great thumps, and then a low feminine cry that sounded suspiciously like a sob. The Magi shouted something, but his voice was too muffled to understand anything more than the raging anger behind his words. Again, Dela heard someone cry out, and her heart ached.

What the hell is this? The floor creaked some more, and the basement door opened. Light flooded the stairs and the Magi appeared, dragging a slight, unwilling figure behind him. A girl, and she was crying—crying, but still fighting every step, wrenching her body with stubborn abandon. The Magi pulled her along by her hair.

The Magi switched on the basement light, revealing a small striking girl who could not have been older than sixteen. Dark wild curls framed a heart-shaped face, almond eyes on fire with both rage and despair. Bruises mottled her right cheek; her blouse was torn, her denim skirt riding high on her legs.

She gasped when she saw Dela, and the two of them stared at each other, their bond instantaneous, forged by a shared hatred for the man standing between them.

"The virgin sacrifice?" Dela asked, alarmed when she had trouble opening her mouth to speak. Her jaw felt wired shut with pain.

A bitter smile appeared on the girl's lips, and the Magi shoved her toward the opposite pillar. He pulled out another pair of handcuffs. There was not a trace of warmth in his actions. Dela felt as though she was watching someone tie up an errant dog.

"This is my daughter, Ms. Reese. It doesn't matter if you won't give up the box. My plan will proceed without it, as long as Hari does everything I say. Which he will. Unless, of course, he *enjoys* watching me torture you."

Dela barely heard him. *His daughter?*

The very notion boggled Dela's mind, as did the Magi's unfathomable motivation for the girl's presence and obvious abuse.

"Hari will kill you first," she said.

The Magi laughed, his eyes glittering. "My dear, he can try, but I am afraid he will find me quite indestructible."

Dela struggled not to vomit. "What do you mean?"

The Magi leaned close, his breath hot against her stinging cheeks. "You were quite right, Ms. Reese. There was a price to pay. Hari is not the only one cursed."

He stood back, watching her digest that bit of information. "Hari will find you. He has no choice in the matter. No doubt he is coming now, with all your friends in tow."

"You don't seem terribly worried."

The Magi's eyes turned distant, and for a moment Dela sensed some great strain upon his body, a terrible twisting in his gut. But all he said was, "I have taken precautions."

He glanced at his daughter, then turned off the light and marched up the stairs. When he shut the door, darkness spilled through the room, filling eyes and mouths, stuffing ears.

Across from Dela, shoes scuffed concrete.

"Hello?" called a soft voice, lightly accented. "Hey. What's your name?"

"Dela Reese. You?"

"Lise Amarro."

Lise Amarro, the daughter of the Magi. Handcuffed in the basement with her.

Shit. This is weird, Dela thought.

She wet her lips. "Are you all right?"

Short, wild laughter filled the darkness. "You're insane, right? I should be asking *you* that question. That man is psycho. He is so completely mental he makes Ted Bundy look sane."

"He's your father."

"Oh," she sobbed, with laughter and rage, "call me Luke. *I am your father.*"

The girl was hysterical, but then, if Dela had the Magi as a father, she herself might be wearing tinfoil hats and hiding from aliens.

Dela tested her bonds. Her mind felt stronger and she used her gift to wrench hard on the links. She felt one give, and triumph roared through her heart.

"How long have you known your father?" She asked, talking to distract her mind from pain. She coughed, reeling against her restraints, and tasted blood. Over the roaring in her ears, Dela heard Lise's voice, calmer now, more in control.

"I met him the first time almost three weeks ago, but he's been paying the bills all my life. My mom died not long after I was born. My dad hired nurses to raise me. I used to dream of meeting him. I didn't have high expectations, but this . . ."

"What has he told you?" Dela pressed her power on the steel. The link stretched.

"Nothing," Lise whispered. "Nothing important, anyway. He tells me to eat, or to be quiet. He tells me to sleep. He tells me I can't escape. He tells me to be a good daughter." A pause then, almost as if Lise was shaking herself. When she spoke again, her voice was stronger. "I don't think he's owned this place long. No furniture, barely any food. I've been locked up since day one, but I've seen out some of the windows. Looks like forest, all around. Mountains, maybe. I'm not sure."

Dela gritted her teeth, wrapping her mind around the handcuff link, pulling hard.

The link snapped.

Dela gasped, and Lise said, "Are you okay?"

"Fine," Dela breathed. "I just freed myself."

"What? How? You're wearing handcuffs!"

Dela found it nearly impossible to straighten out her body. She had to rest, panting, with each small roll of her shoulders.

"Have you ever . . . ah, shit, that hurts . . . been able to do weird things? Lise? You know, stuff you only see in movies? You seen your father do that kind of shit?"

Lise's silence held its own weight, and seemed answer enough. Dela pushed on, even as she gathered her strength to stand. "I don't know why your father brought you here, but—oh, God! Unh!" Dela clutched her ribs as she pushed herself to her knees. She felt broken. Worse, even, like something vital in her body had been smashed, torn into little bits.

"Dela?" Lise sounded panicked; Dela heard the girl's cuffs rattle, and suddenly the basement was filled with light. Glowing orbs danced within the darkness, silver-soft as moonlight.

"Ah," Dela sighed, staring at the girl.

Lise's eyes were wide, startled. "Please don't be afraid," she begged. "Please. They're harmless. I didn't even mean to show you, but when I heard you cry out—"

"Shhh," Dela soothed. "Why did you think I just asked you all those questions? I can do things, too, Lise."

"Is that why he wants you?" The girl leaned forward against her restraints.

The orbs flickered, floating close to Dela. They gave off no heat, but her skin tingled, like static. *Forget science,* Dela thought. *From now on, it's all magic.*

She tried to stand, but couldn't find the strength. Instead, she opened her mind and felt for Lise's handcuffs. Dela kept expecting the Magi to sense her actions, but she heard nothing from above.

"He's using me as bait to attract a man named Hari," she explained. "The two of them are old enemies. Very old. A long time ago, your father hurt Hari in ways that can't even be described. I guess he wants to finish the job."

The handcuff link snapped, and Lise stared at her cuffed wrists and the dangling, separated chains. "That is so cool," she said, clambering to her feet. She rushed to Dela's side. "What can I do to help?"

Good kid. I like her, even if her dad is a psycho.

"Just give me a hand—let me lean on you a bit. I think my ribs are broken."

"He almost killed you." Her voice was low, filled with hate.

"Yeah," Dela muttered, taking in Lise's own bruised face. "But he didn't do you any favors, either."

Lise looked away and gave Dela her hand. With a great deal of effort, they both managed to get Dela on her feet. She swayed, but found standing on her own was not quite the impossible feat she had feared. Still, Lise insisted on being used as a crutch, and Dela was grateful that in Lise's case, the apple appeared to have fallen about half a continent away from the tree.

The orbs continued to light the basement. Dela and Lise shuffled to the stairs, freezing when the first step creaked beneath their feet. They held their breath, but heard nothing from the floor above. The two of them continued up the stairs, Dela struggling to maintain her composure, biting back cries of pain. She bit her lip, hard, and tasted blood.

Lise pushed opened the basement door, a tentative movement that left them both breathless, hearts pounding. Dela expected the Magi to rip the knob out of her hands and shove them down the stairs, but from the room beyond the only sound was the steady drip of water. Lise peered around the door and then stepped back to help Dela through. The orbs blinked out.

The kitchen was battered, the linoleum stained and cracked. Paint peeled in ribbons from the walls, and the stove looked as though generations of spaghetti sauce had lived and burned upon its surface. Dela smelled incense.

The back door was only five feet away, and for the

first time Dela felt truly afraid. The old saying—*so close, and yet so far*—had never held as much meaning for her as it did in that moment. She could taste freedom, but if the Magi caught them . . .

Your life is a movie thriller, Dela told herself, as they crept across the kitchen to the door. *And you're down to the final scenes.*

Like a miracle, the door swung open without mishap, no alarms howling their escape. Night had fallen, but Dela could make out a forest looming just beyond a stretch of overgrown lawn.

"Run," Dela ordered Lise, trying to shove the girl away. "I'll slow you down."

"Hell, no."

"Lise."

"I'm not going to leave you."

"Screw nobility, kid. He brought you here for a reason, and if you're gone, he loses. Now, *run.*"

Lise hesitated, but Dela pushed her again and resolve hardened in the girl's dark gaze. "I'll find help," she promised. Dela knew she meant it.

Lise took off for the forest like a greyhound. Dela hobbled after her as fast as she could, but walking was difficult enough. Lying down on the grass and passing out felt more like her speed.

The hairs prickled on the back of her neck; a warning. Just at the edge of the forest, Lise cried out. A moment later, Dela ran full force into an invisible barrier. The unexpected impact knocked her to the ground, and she screamed in agony, clutching her ribs. Stars danced; Dela thought she might faint. On the periphery of her vision, she glimpsed a shadow running toward her from the house.

A roar split the night, full of wild fury. Dela tried to stand, but a boot slammed hard against her side, knocking her senseless with pain.

"Hari!" bellowed the Magi, his eyes wild and searching. "It's time!"

Dela heard someone crying, and realized it was Lise. She rolled her eyes, trying to see, and found the girl beating her fists against the air.

From the shadows of the forest slipped an immense creature of liquid grace. Lise stopped pounding on the invisible barrier; she backed away as the tiger padded silent as death through the unseen wall, golden eyes burning, burning.

A profound silence settled over the Magi as he stared into the tiger's eyes.

"Your skin," he whispered. He sucked in a mighty breath, and turned on Dela. "You gave him back his skin."

His foot pressed down on her ribs, merciless, and Dela screamed. Hari's own howls melded with her own, and he launched himself at the Magi—

—only to be knocked aside by the invisible wall. Hari found his feet in an instant, swiping at the air with his claws, hurling himself against the barrier, loss and fury and love spilling over into the night.

Golden light bathed the tiger, and a moment later, the man took its place. Sweat covered Hari's body, his eyes glowing like twin suns.

"The spell has not been lifted," said the Magi softly. "I can feel it all around you, despite your skin."

"Release her," Hari ordered, his deep voice filled with death.

"A life for a life, Hari. That is the way it goes."

"My life?" Hari held out his hands. "Take it if you

can. Anything you want, if you will let my mistress go free."

"No," Dela breathed.

"Anything?" asked the Magi. His smile was cruel. "My price then, Hari. My daughter stands behind you. I want you to fuck her."

CHAPTER EIGHTEEN

WHOA.

Even Hari looked stunned. Lise stared at her father like he was the devil.

"You have got to be kidding." The girl held up her hands when Hari turned to look at her. "Stay away from me, man."

An expression of profound disgust settled over Hari's face. "How could you ask such a thing, Magi? What father demands the rape of his own daughter?"

The Magi threw back his head, his lips twisting into a snarl. "A father who has bred his daughter for that exact purpose. Oh, Hari. I have been waiting for this opportunity for over a millennia."

"For what reason?" Hari slammed his fists against the barrier. "Do you wish me to make her pregnant? Are you still, after all these years, lusting after a shape-shifter child of your own blood?"

The Magi's laugh was low, hard. His boot ground into Dela's ribs and she stifled a cry. Hari heard, though. Dela felt his gaze trace every inch of her face, taking in injuries she had no desire to imagine. Bone-deep rage whitened Hari's lips and knuckles. Claws split through his fingernails.

"I once wanted a child of tiger blood," said the Magi, softly. "Someone who would be of both worlds, yet belong to me alone. But I lost that desire a very long time ago. All I care about now is being separated from your life. Your *curse*. Do you know the price *I* paid, Hari? Immortality, yes—but my magic turned against me, turning my power into pain."

The Magi knelt over Dela, pressing his knee into her ribs. He looked up at Hari, and his smile was sickening.

"You've grown close to your mistress, Hari. Intimately so, I suspect. Do you like how I've treated her in your absence? Don't you wonder what else I've done, that you cannot yet see?" The Magi ran his tongue up the side of Dela's face, and she snarled breathlessly at him.

Hari threw himself against the barrier, his face elongating, muscles contorting. His scream was wordless, deep; the air quaked, and Dela wanted him to stop—stop and save his strength.

Don't give him the satisfaction, she pleaded.

The Magi shook his finger at the enraged shape-shifter.

"My daughter, Hari. Or else the only rape performed tonight will be on Ms. Reese."

THE SITUATION WAS UNIMAGINABLE. EVEN IN HARI'S worst nightmares he had never considered such a horrific choice. Rape a girl, or watch his mate suffer the same fate. And even if he did such a thing, the Magi still might kill Dela. Just as he had killed Hari's sister, right before his eyes.

"What are you?" shrieked the girl, staring at her father. "What kind of monster would do this? Why?"

"Hari!" Dela called out his name, and Hari saw what it cost her. Her face was a swollen mass of bruises and blood, her clothes torn, stained red. But her eyes—her eyes were still bright, and they were pleading with him.

Don't do it. Please, don't do it.

If he did, if he succumbed, it would kill them both. He knew this, as did she. Some lines could not be crossed—some rivers were too deep, acid instead of water.

"I love you," he said to her, and it was all he could say, all he could do in that moment to make her understand he had heard her message, that no matter what was to come, he would suffer with her, he would die with her. That in the end, they would both close their eyes and know their hands were clean of everything but love. Untouched, unsullied by dishonor.

Hari stopped fighting. His hands fell to his sides, and he stared at the Magi, who watched him with a sudden trace of uneasiness.

Dela smiled.

The Magi saw and comprehension twisted his face into an inhuman mask of fury. Snarling, he curled his fists and raised them above Dela's head. Hari shouted, throwing himself against the wall.

Dela brought up her own hands. Hari willed her his strength.

Before the Magi could strike, a huge form darted from the sky, knocking aside the Magi. As the man flew through the air, his barrier collapsed. Hari stumbled past, falling on his knees beside Dela.

"Delilah," he breathed, desperate to touch her, unable to find a scrap of skin spared by the Magi's cruelty. Dela reached for his hand, and brought his palm to her lips.

Scales hissed, feathers whispered. Dela gasped, and

for a moment even Hari forgot to breathe. It had been so long.

The dragon's coils writhed against the hard ground, claws piercing stone. Golden eyes spun like watered marbles in a fine, angular head, set atop a delicate neck. The dragon regarded Hari and Dela with a quiet grace, but when it set its gaze upon the Magi, sprawled in frozen disbelief, a rough hiss escaped its thin scaled lips. Golden light shimmered around the dragon's body, and a moment later an elderly naked Chinese woman appeared.

"Long Nü," Dela breathed.

The Magi's stunned expression dissolved, his lips curling into a snarl. "We had a bargain!"

Long Nü's smile was infinitely cold. "I promised not to interfere with Hari. You said *nothing* about the human."

The dragon woman settled her golden gaze upon Hari.

"I believe, brother, you have a man to kill."

HARI KISSED DELA'S PALM, AND SHE WATCHED HIM stand and face the Magi. The Magi, eyes narrowed, began chanting under his breath.

Dela felt something whisper against her neck. It was Lise, kneeling, her eyes wide and dark with fear.

"You should leave," Dela said, but Lise shook her head.

"If Hari is going to kill my father, I have to watch. I have to know he's dead."

Long Nü appeared beside them. Lise jumped away, but the old woman caught the girl's wrist.

"I will not hurt you," she said, then released her. Lise rubbed her wrist, but obeyed the unspoken command. Dela didn't blame her. The merchant from the Dirt

Market was gone; in her place, a creature from fairy tale—only, much more intimidating.

"I would have come sooner." Long Nü's wizened fingers brushed against Dela's ribs. "But I was detained. Helping *you*, I suppose."

"Helping? But—" Dela stopped, and gave the shape-shifter a hard look. "You went after Wen Zhang. His men, too. That's what they meant, when they asked me to 'call her off.' It was you."

Long Nü shrugged. "Wen Zhang was upsetting a particular balance, interrupting a series of events too important to be frustrated by a collection of thugs. You can thank me later."

The Magi and Hari circled each other. Hari began a partial transformation, claws extending from his hands, fur rippling over his thickening arms.

"I thought the Magi's powers had lessened," Dela said, as his hands began to glow.

"He never lost his powers, but after he cursed Hari, his magic turned against him. For the past two thousand years, the use of his gift has caused him pain. How much, I do not know." Long Nü leaned over Dela, her eyes briefly glowing. "There is only one outcome to this battle, Dela, and that is for both Hari and the Magi to die."

"What are you talking about?"

"I have no time to explain. Only, their lives are linked. Each is the other's weakness. They are not immortal to each other, Dela. If Hari kills the Magi, he will die, too."

TWO THOUSAND YEARS FLED PAST HARI'S GAZE, BUT the only thing that made the beast howl was the memory of Dela's face and body, battered almost beyond recognition. The Magi had laid his hands upon Hari's mate—the woman he loved more than life.

No. Dela *was* his life.

"I have waited for this," he said. "Since the day you killed my sister—from the moment I realized you were still alive."

The Magi's laugh was bitter. "And I have thought of nothing but you for the past two thousand years. What a fine mess I wove." His fingers spat fire, blazed with heat. Hari noted a fine tremor race up the Magi's side. "I have had many years to grow accustomed to pain, Hari, and I have held myself down with it. But now—now is the time to remember some of what I lost."

The Magi's hands exploded in a blaze of light and crackling heat, and Hari dodged twin gusts of flame that spewed out into the night. The shape-shifter recovered instantly, sweeping in low with his claws bared, raking at the Magi's throat. The Magi managed to block the blow, glancing fire against Hari's skin.

Steel flashed in the Magi's hand. A dagger, hidden in a sheath beneath his shirt. Hari smiled, flexing his hands, the beast splitting his skin.

Finally. Blood.

"WHAT KIND OF CRAP IS THIS?" DELA STRUGGLED TO sit up, but only succeeded in blasting the breath from her lungs. She collapsed, Lise cushioning her head. Dela glared at Long Nü. "Does Hari know?"

"No, and you cannot tell him. If you do, it might ruin everything."

"You can't get much more ruined than dead!" Dela snapped.

"He does not have to die." Long Nü's eyes blazed with unearthly light. "I would not have invested so much of myself if that was the only outcome."

Dela stared at her, some premonition tugging at her mind; the memory of a dream, a nightmare in a tub in China. Death, sliding in on a sigh. Hari's anguished eyes.

"Explain yourself," she said.

Long Nü skimmed her hands over Dela's face; not touching, but close, close. Dela smelled sandalwood, stone.

"A life for a life. That was the price of the spell, the motivation that cast it. Hari gave his life for his sister. There is no greater gift, but the Magi twisted the power of Hari's sacrifice to create something dark, perverted. He still thinks darkness is the key to ending the spell." Long Nü cast a significant glance at Lise.

Not twenty feet away, Dela saw Hari lash out at the Magi, raking his claws down the man's chest. The Magi screamed, steel and flame flashing in his hands. Hari leapt backward. His movements were a dance; he struck the Magi again, this time in the face. Blood spurted.

"Enough of the story!" Dela cried, sensing imminent death. "How do we break the spell?"

A hint of warmth touched Long Nü's lips. "A good choice," she breathed, soothing back Dela's hair. "*Your* choice, Dela. The only thing that can break the spell, and the bond between Hari and the Magi, is another gift of love. Love to counteract the darkness."

"A life for a life," Dela murmured, sinking down into her mind, feeling her world grow still.

"Do you understand?" Long Nü pressed. "Do you

truly understand the price, Dela? A life for a life. That is what you must pay."

Dela understood, and she nodded.

THE MAGI WAS IN PAIN, HIS EYES WIDE WITH FEAR, rage. Still, he pressed on. Still, he angled his knife at Hari, sweeping down—

Hari laughed, sidestepping the rushed blow, knocking the Magi on his back with one well-timed kick to the back of his knees. Without the use of his greatest powers, the Magi was useless in a fight. The man slammed into the ground, gasping for air.

Hari was on him in an instant, snapping first the wrist holding the knife, and then taking the weapon and slamming the blade, point first, through the Magi's other hand—splitting flesh, cracking bone—pinning the man to the ground.

The Magi howled, his back arching off the ground. Hari straddled him, running his claws across his throat—

"DO IT," DELA SAID, TAKING ONE LAST LOOK AT Hari, poised over the Magi.

Long Nü placed her hands above Dela's heart. The colors of sunset shimmered across Dela's vision, and she thought—she thought—

THE MAGI HAD NO LAST WORDS. THERE WAS A STORY in his black eyes, and Hari wondered—just for one moment—what if? What if the Magi had been a good man?

Hari's sister would have lived, her child born. He would have been spared two thousand years of slavery. So much pain, averted.

But he would not have found Dela.

"Thank you," Hari whispered. "For that, anyway."

The Magi's eyes widened, a question on his lips.

Hari slashed his throat—

—I LOVE YOU, HARI. I LOVE YOU—

—and leaned away from the gushing blood, hearing breath slide through the Magi's lips, his eyes blazing once, then dulling into emptiness.

Feeling rather strange—almost, in an odd way, bereft— Hari staggered to his feet. Blood dripped from his claws.

He stared at the Magi's body until soft sounds of weeping tugged at his attention. Hari turned, and found the Magi's daughter curled in on herself, tears running down her cheeks. At first he thought she was saddened by her father's death, and then he thought her tears were for relief—but as he drew near he saw her gaze was for Dela, stretched still and silent upon the ground.

"Delilah?" Hari called her name. She did not stir, and Long Nü looked at him, her eyes solemn as winter water.

"Your curse is broken, Hari," she said. "A life for life."

He stared at her, at first not understanding, but as he looked down at Dela's pale face, her still chest, comprehension brought him to his knees. He crawled to Dela's side, reaching for her face, pressing his ear to her chest.

Silence.

"No," he breathed. "No, not now. Please, Delilah."

"It was her choice," Long Nü said. "You were linked to the Magi by the spell. If she had not given herself up, you would have died the instant you killed the Magi."

"I would have preferred death!" Hari reached over Dela's body to grab Long Nü around the neck. "You did this, didn't you? You killed her!"

"To save you! To break the cycle. There is a price for everything, Hari. *Everything.*"

"And what price to bring her back?" He dragged Long Nü close. "What price would I pay?"

"A piece of your heart," she whispered. "A piece of your heart, in the shape of your skin."

"Take it, then," he said, throwing out his arms. "Give it to her. She is all the heart I need."

"As you say," Long Nü breathed, after a heart-stopping moment of silence. "Kiss her, Hari. Give Dela back the breath of life. Give her your skin."

Hari covered Dela's mouth, kissing her with every ounce of passion and love he could muster, willing her to live, begging it with every fiber of his being. Tears ran down his face, bathing her cheeks, and he tugged her close into his arms, falling, losing himself to everything but her cool still lips. He breathed for her, wishing dreams into her head, beseeching her with desire, with his soul—because if she left him he would follow.

Light filled him, golden, soft, flooding his vision with unearthly beauty. The shimmering vision passed from his body into Dela's, sinking into her skin. She glowed, and Hari's heart did not feel lessened—he felt so full he might burst, and the beast sidled against the light, wild and content.

Dela's lips moved. Hari choked back a sob and he clutched her tight against his chest, drinking in her sudden warmth, the breath escaping from her sweet mouth. He felt her hands creep into his hair, and he tasted tears.

"I love you," he whispered against her lips. "Oh, Delilah, why? I would have died for you."

"I wanted you to live," she murmured, caressing his throat with her fingers. "I wanted you to live for me. And you did."

CHAPTER NINETEEN

HELP came from an unexpected source.

As Artur and the others later explained, the Suburban quickly proved unfixable, while attempts to flag down cars were met with less than polite responses from passing motorists. The four men were preparing themselves for a long, directionless walk, when a battered minivan pulled up. The driver had a familiar face.

"All you bastards are lucky I'm a curious fellow," Koni said, sitting naked in the driver's seat.

Curious enough to change shape and follow everyone home from the Kosmo Klub, tracking their movements since that night. Sharp enough to see the Magi kidnap Dela, and tail him to his mountain home. Concerned enough to return and find her friends—and just crazy enough to steal a car when he flew over their stalled vehicle.

Long Nü was the first to hear the car's approach, and she warned the others with a sharp word. Scales rippled down her wrist, dancing color against flesh, shaping bone—and then in an instant, gone. Humanity restored. She glided into the shadows, haunting the rim of light coming from the house windows some distance away.

Hari cradled Dela in his lap, his arms warm around her shoulders. He could not stop touching her, his lips pressed against her hair, her cheeks, her brow. Lise sat near them, hugging herself. The handcuffs were gone— Dela had just finished snapping them off.

Dela closed her eyes, feeling a warm glow inside her heart. Like an etching in steel, the imprint of something unnamed and wild slowly turned circles in her chest.

"I was dead," she said to Hari. "What did you do?"

Hari kissed her mouth. "I gave you my skin."

"I can feel it." Sorrow mixed with joy. Hari seemed to see the conflict in Dela's eyes. He held her face between tender hands.

"The transformation is a superficial thing. What matters is the spirit *within* the skin. The tiger is still inside me, Delilah. Just as now, a part of it is inside you. That is the way it should be, and I am not sorry."

"Hari," Dela said, hesitating. "I want you to know . . . the Magi . . . he never . . . he never touched me. Not like that."

Hari briefly closed his eyes, brushing her cheeks with his fingertips.

A minivan drove up the long track; Artur was the first out, hitting the ground at a run. He said nothing when he saw Dela's face, but his eyes were so very grave Dela held out her hands to touch him.

"It's not that bad," she said. "Please, don't look so worried."

It was the truth. Whatever Hari had done, it had healed her ribs and some of her worst contusions. Most of her body still hurt and she was too exhausted to walk, but she would live. She would live.

Blue, Dean, and Eddie fussed worse than a pack of mother hens. Hari stood, cradling Dela in his arms.

Beyond the men, Dela saw Lise tugging her blouse closed. She looked very uneasy and out of place, and she could not stop glancing at the dead Magi, still sprawled some distance away on the ground.

"Lise," Dela called. The girl moved close, ducking her head when the men focused their attention on her. A strange expression passed over Eddie's face. He shrugged off his denim jacket.

"Here," he murmured, holding out the garment, careful not to touch her. Dela hid her smile as the girl took Eddie's jacket, clutching the denim like it was a life vest.

"Lise," she said again. Hari turned slightly so she could better see the girl's face. "Do you have anyone we should contact?"

Lise tore her gaze away from Eddie's face. "No. That man . . . he was all I had."

Hari's chest rumbled, and Dela reached out to touch Lise's cheek. The girl's breath caught, and Dela could see fear and hope fill her dark eyes.

"You're not alone," Dela said. "Don't worry. We'll take care of you."

"Absolutely," Eddie jumped in, blushing furiously when everyone looked at him. Dean bit his lip, fighting a grin.

"Um," he coughed, trying to school his face into something resembling seriousness, "what should we do about El Freako?" He gestured at the Magi.

"I will take care of him," Long Nü said, eliciting gasps as she solidified from the shadows. "I can hide his body in a place where no one will ever find him."

Like your stomach? Dela frowned. "What did the Magi mean when he said you had a bargain?"

Long Nü's smile was cold, tight-lipped. "After I sold

you the box and the Magi failed to waylay you, he came back to my stand. The Magi knew I was a shape-shifter, and was afraid I would try to help Hari out of a sense of loyalty. I promised I would not."

"You're a shape-shifter?" Dean asked, somewhat skeptically. Long Nü's eyes flashed, and she raised a clawed hand. Scales erupted along her flesh.

"Oh," Dean breathed. "Yeah."

"Why did you sell me the box?" Dela asked. "And why were you at that market in the first place? When I tried to find you again, everyone said you were dead. Later, I discovered some woman with an altered ID had taken your place."

"Surely you will let me keep some mystery," Long Nü chided, but she tapped her head. "I had a vision, many years ago, of the person to whom I should sell the box. I am nothing but patient. As for the rest . . ." This time her smile seemed genuine. "There are still some people left in the world who do not mind doing favors for dragons."

Hari narrowed his eyes. "I know your face."

"You know my grandfather's face. Your friend, who came looking for you and found the Magi instead, possessed of an odd little box that smelled like a very familiar tiger. My grandfather, after wringing the tale from the Magi, attempted to kill the man—and found he could not. The Magi was immortal.

"The Magi managed to escape with the box, and though my grandfather searched for him, he never found another trace of the man. Until, almost a thousand years later, the Magi came seeking my father. The Magi wanted our help. He was desperate." Long Nü shook her head. "You did not know it, Hari, but the Magi spent the past two thousand years linked to you. Everything you suffered, he felt. He experienced the deaths of every man you killed. When you slept, he felt the nothingness of the void crowding upon him. Even his own powers turned against him, causing him pain with every use."

Dela glanced at Lise, wondering what the girl made of all this. She was listening carefully, her eyes wide, startled. Behind her, Dela noticed a familiar, very naked figure.

What is Koni doing here? The shape-shifter seemed quite intent on looking anywhere but at Long Nü.

"Where do I come into this?" Lise asked, tugging Eddie's jacket close around her shoulders. "Why did he want Hari to have sex with me?"

"He wanted Hari to have sex with you?" Eddie's brow wrinkled.

"His own daughter," Dela supplied, inviting grimaces and some speculative glances at Lise. Long Nü looked deep into the girl's eyes.

"The Magi finally realized, correctly, that the only way to break the spell—and the connection—would be to exchange a life for the one he had already taken. For some reason, though, he believed the only way to do that would be to sacrifice someone who carried both his blood, and Hari's."

"He was going to kill me," Lise whispered. "He was going to get Hari to have sex with me until I was pregnant, and then kill me. My own father."

"He has been cultivating daughters for the past one thousand years, in the hope that if he found Hari and summoned him, he could force him to impregnate one of his children."

"Does he have more daughters out there?" Dela asked, appalled.

"I do not know," Long Nü admitted. "I also do not know why the Magi was unable to summon Hari in the first place, or how he lost possession of the box after escaping from my grandfather. There are some stories the Magi carried to his grave."

"And how did *you* find me?" Hari asked.

"Good sex." Long Nü smiled. Dean coughed and Artur patted his back. "I was . . . facing the wall, and saw the most curious little box on my lover's nightstand. I recognized it immediately, and in the morning took it with me. That was over a hundred years ago. I was *much* younger."

"Information overload," Lise said, holding her head. "But I think I'll recover."

"Thank you," Dela said to Long Nü. "For everything."

Long Nü inclined her head. "It is you who should be thanked. It was my grandfather's last wish that his family help Hari. We might have spent the past two thousand years searching for him, but you were the one person who could truly set him free."

Blue found two Jeeps parked on the other side of the house, and he and Eddie drove them close to where everyone was still gathered.

"This guy had a thing for Cherokees," Blue commented. "Makes me think he was the one following us that night we left Le Soleil."

"I was nearby," Long Nü said, "but I could not interfere. I, ah, was taking care of your other problem."

"She killed Wen Zhang," Dela said. Dean jumped into the air, crowing, and wrapped the dragon woman up in a tight bear hug. Her golden eyes sprang wide with surprise.

"You're my kind of lady!" Dean grinned, though his

smile turned rather sickly when Long Nü raked a speculative gaze over his body.

"Uh," he said. "You know, it's a long drive back. Maybe we should get going."

As they walked to the cars, Long Nü called out Koni's name. The shape-shifter froze, and then very, very slowly walked back to the dragon woman. She shared several words with him, and he slowly nodded like a whipped dog.

"Wonder what she's got on him?" Blue mused.

"Hell, man. He's probably slept with her." Dean buckled in, reaching back to help Hari settle Dela. Artur climbed into the Jeep.

"Where's Eddie?" Dean asked, peering out the window.

"He is taking the girl back in the other Jeep," Artur said. Dean opened his mouth.

"No jokes!" Dela said. Dean gave her an injured look.

Long Nü and Koni walked up to the car. Hari rolled down the window.

"Good-bye," the dragon woman said.

"Will we see you again?" Hari asked.

"Yes," she promised. "Your family and mine are connected, Hari."

"Thank you," he said. "For all you've done."

She smiled, and stepped away from the car. Koni shrugged, glancing from her to the humans. "I'm, uh, staying behind to help clean up."

"Don't be a stranger," said Blue, grinning.

As they drove away, Dela glanced over her shoulder through the back window. Golden light filled the night, and just as the car rounded a curve in the gravel driveway, she caught sight of a coiled body, rearing up toward the starry sky.

Dela glanced at Hari, and found him watching her. He brushed his lips against her mouth. Warmth spread through her body, chasing away pain and fatigue.

Now this . . . *this* was magic.

EPILOGUE

S IX months later, Le Soleil hosted Dela Reese's return to the art world.

The guests at the private dinner were few in number, but spirits were high, and the walls rang with laughter as mouth-watering dishes were passed around the sizeable circular table.

"I swear," Kit howled, leaning into Blue's shoulder, "Maz Randall nearly died when he saw your new sculptures, *especially* the one of that tiger-man. Dela, honest to God, I saw him touch his *loins*."

Cheers erupted, with quite a few amused glances thrown at Hari. It seemed that everyone knew who had inspired those impressive nether regions—even if the other qualities of the sculpture remained mere fantasy to some.

Hari sighed, trying not to smile.

"Personally," said Pierre, "the dragon woman is my favorite. I might just buy that one for my home, if you do not mind, Dela."

"She's yours," Dela said. "Consider her a gift in return for this lovely party. I haven't had so much fun in ages."

"Are we still going to the Kosmo Klub?" Dean asked. "If we are, I need to pad my ass. Unless *Artuuur* wants to distract Rose for me."

Artur smiled into his glass of wine. "A distraction will be unnecessary. I believe *I* made the better impression."

Which led to an immediate argument over who was the sexier man.

Dela laughed, leaning against Hari. He pulled her close and kissed her cheek, his warm chin rubbing against her skin. Desire thrilled through Dela's body, and she ran her fingers along Hari's thigh, marking the hours until they returned to the hotel.

Dela glanced at Eddie and Lise, their heads bowed together in quiet conversation. Lise was older than Dela had previously thought—on the high end of seventeen—and more than willing to make her own life, away from the memory of her father. Three months previous, Dela had given Lise the keys to the warehouse. In addition to living there, Lise was now Dela's new gallery manager. Dela thought it was a good fit; Lise worked hard, and she had good instincts for business.

It pained Dela, remembering Adam in that job, but time had brought a sense of peace—even, perhaps, true forgiveness. It was no use hating the dead.

If Lise hated her father, she never said so. She never spoke of him, except in the beginning, when she had wanted to learn everything the Magi had done to Hari and Dela.

"My dad was an immortal psychopath," she said, and that was the end of it, even about her psi-abilities, those glowing silver orbs. Dela hoped Lise would relax in time, especially with Eddie helping her. The two of them had become as thick as thieves.

I'm so nosy. Though who could blame me for being curious about the kinds of things she can do? Her father might have been crazy, but he was also powerful.

And if he had more children left in the world . . .

"Would you like to take a walk?" Hari asked.

"That sounds nice." She looped her hand through Hari's arm as he helped her stand. "We'll be back soon," she told the others, who waved their wine glasses at her with merry abandonment.

The air outside was cool, and Hari wrapped Dela up against his side. The night sky bristled with city light, starlight, and the sidewalk was almost empty.

"I can't wait to get home," Dela confided. "I love seeing everyone, but I miss it, just the two of us."

The two of them, alone in their new home set in the forest, nestled in the lee of a mountain.

Hari's laughter was low, soft. "I need to finish the last room."

"Oh, you've got time," she said, leaning into him. "Besides, I really can't see us using it all that much at first."

Hari kissed the top of her head. "I think I like the sound of that."

He froze then, eyes flashing. A shadow slipped free of the alley ahead of them, and Dela smelled the scent of sandalwood, stone.

"Long Nü," she said. The dragon woman glided forward, greeting them with a smile.

"I am glad you are both well," she said. "I thought I would . . . drop in and say hello."

"You could have joined the party," Hari said.

Long Nü shook her head. "I think I would remind everyone of darker days, and this should be a time of joy. Shall we continue walking, though? I am curious to hear of your lives since we last met."

So they walked, telling Long Nü of their new life together; their recent marriage and their home in the mountains, built with Hari's own hands. They told her of Dela's art exhibit, with its shape-shifting theme, and then they told her of the other shape-shifter who had recently joined the ranks of Dirk & Steele.

"How nice for Koni," Long Nü said, though she did not seem very surprised by the news. "The raven has finally found his roost." She looked hard at Dela, and her eyes were sharp, canny. "And what of your powers, Dela? Have they continued to grow?

Dela blinked. "How did you know?"

"I am not just a shape-shifter," Long Nü said. "You should remember; I see with more than my eyes."

"I remember," Dela said, "but no, I haven't grown any stronger. Which is fine with me. I figure stopping bullets and breaking handcuffs is good enough. I don't want to be greedy."

Hari made a low sound in his throat. "It is still a mystery, why Delilah's gifts grew in strength after she met me. We believe it had something to do with opening the box, but even that answers nothing."

Dela thought of the riddle box, locked in a safety deposit box. She and Hari had decided to leave it there. For now.

Long Nü smiled. "I believe the box might be part of the reason, but not in the way you imagine. I suspect you always had great potential, but merely lacked the belief to unlock it. Being near Hari, exposing yourself to true magic, released the block you imposed upon your mind. With Hari, you began to accept anything was possible."

"You haven't been thinking about this much, have you?"

"I am merely wise. The result of advanced age."

Dela shook her head, smiling. "Well, I am neither wise nor old, but something tells me you had another reason for wanting to see us, besides curiosity."

Long Nü sighed. "Am I so transparent? I suppose you are right. Mere curiosity would not have been enough to bring me here, not with all my work left undone."

"Your work?" Hari frowned.

Long Nü stopped walking, and for the first time, Dela thought she could see past the ageless quality of the woman's face to something darker, more weary.

"I told you I helped Hari because of a family promise, and that was true—but I had another reason, one even more important than honor. And that, my dear children, was survival."

"I do not understand," Hari said, but Dela did, and Long Nü nodded at her.

"There are so few of us left, Hari. The world has changed, and we must change with it, or else be lost forever. It is not enough to live alone, stuck in the old ways of clan and territory. We must find each other—help all we can, preserve what is left. Otherwise, where will all the legends go? We are the creatures dreams are made of."

"You want us to help," Dela said.

Long Nü looked up at the stars, scales rippling iridescent against her throat. "I am growing old, Dela, and soon—soon I will be too old to journey the world, in search of my people. It is my one great fear, that I lapse into the shade without this last task complete. Dragons have always been the guardians of our race. It falls upon our hearts to protect the shifting kind. To fail in this, when I am one of the last, does not bear imagining."

She stared hard at Hari, and then Dela, her pupils narrowing into the eyes of the dragon. "Before I met you, I did not think it possible to seek help from a human in a task of this magnitude. But you and your friends have resources, and you are familiar with the unusual. And who knows? Perhaps we can all help each other in the long run."

Dela knew all too well that Long Nü's idea of helping could be quite different from her own, but she had to admit that the dragon woman had taken care of their mafia problem. No one had heard a peep from Wen Zhang's family. Of course, financial problems might have been the cause of that. Dirk & Steele had made good on its plan to expose as many shipments of illegal immigrants as they could. Recent Coast Guard confrontations with ships in the Pacific had been making the news.

They began walking again, until Long Nü stepped into a dismal alley.

"I must go now," she said, "but you will see me again. Take care of yourself, Hari. You are the very last of the tigers."

"No," disagreed Dela, smiling, placing Hari's lean strong hand over the budding swell of her belly. "There will be others."

And the dragon laughed, embracing them with arms of golden light.

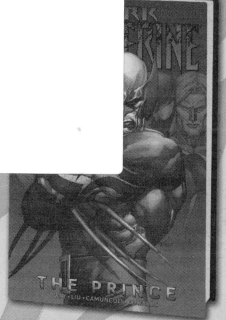

RIE LIU
...h of Wolverine

THE PRINCE
LIU · CAMUNCOLI · EDWARDS